THE FLOOD

Rachel Bennett

avon.

A division of HarperCollins*Publishers*

www.harpercollins.co.uk

Published by AVON
A division of HarperCollins*Publishers* Ltd
1 London Bridge Street
London SE1 9GF

www.harpercollins.co.uk

A Paperback Original 2019
1

First published in Great Britain by HarperCollins*Publishers* 2019

A catalogue copy of this book is available from the British Library.

ISBN: 978-0-00-833328-7

This novel is entirely a work of fiction. The names, characters and incidents portrayed in it are the work of the author's imagination. Any resemblance to actual persons, living or dead, events or localities is entirely coincidental.

Typeset in Birka by Palimpsest Book Production Limited, Falkirk, Stirlingshire
Printed and bound in UK by CPI Group (UK) Ltd, Croydon CR0 4YY

MIX
Paper from
responsible sources
FSC
www.fsc.org **FSC™ C007454**

This book is produced from independently certified FSC™ paper to ensure responsible forest management.

For more information visit: www.harpercollins.co.uk/green

For my sisters, who are actually delightful

1

October 2003

'We need a funeral,' Franklyn said.

She'd been joking about it for a good few days, but now she squared her shoulders, as if prepared for a physical argument. Daniela could tell she was serious.

Stephanie, predictably, was happy to argue. Daniela wondered why Franklyn had bothered telling Stephanie, rather than just going ahead and hoping she wouldn't find out, like usual.

Although, this time, Stephanie did have a point. 'It's weird and morbid,' she said. 'Funerals are for dead people.'

'She might as well be dead, for all we're going to see of her,' Franklyn said. It was only dinner time, but Daniela suspected Franklyn had been drinking already. 'We need some closure. It's for us, not her. Funerals always are. We're closing one part of our lives so we can open another.'

And perhaps, privately, Stephanie agreed, because she took herself off somewhere else in the house while the rest of them made plans.

'How're we actually going to do this?' Auryn asked. She and Daniela had trailed Franklyn into the garage. Franklyn

1

dragged out the cardboard boxes their father had stored away six months earlier, once it'd become obvious that wherever their mother had gone, she wasn't coming back.

'We each take whatever we want,' Franklyn said. 'Two or three items each max.' Franklyn had a way of talking like she'd thought of everything in advance. 'Any more than that and he'll know what we've been up to.' Franklyn rarely referred to their father by name anymore. If he walked into the room, she left.

There was a time – maybe as little as two months ago, maybe as much as six – when they'd each believed their mother was coming home. Franklyn, the eldest of the four sisters, gave up hope first. Stephanie, second oldest but most mature by some distance, had been practical enough to accept the situation quickly. That left Daniela and Auryn. At thirteen and twelve respectively, it'd seemed impossible to them that their mother could've just walked out. For weeks afterwards Daniela would wake with clear certainty: *today she'll come home.*

A month after their mother left, their father went around the house and systematically removed every trace of her. Pictures, trinkets, jewellery; everything went into cardboard boxes to go into storage. When Auryn asked if she could keep the ceramic kittens from the mantelpiece, their dad had snapped at her. Auryn was used to being the favourite, being granted every whim, but apparently that was about to change as well.

Franklyn started taking items out of the boxes and setting them aside. Some she studied for a moment then put back. Others she wouldn't even touch. Her eyes were narrowed, as if she was focusing so hard, she could see nothing except what was right in front of her. Daniela watched her, fascinated and a little worried.

Franklyn glanced into the bin bags of clothes but then shoved them out of the way. She paused over the wooden crucifix that used to hang in the hallway. Daniela had never liked it, with its sad Jesus that watched her every time she left the house. Secretly, she was pleased their father had taken it down. Now, she felt a tinge of regret as Franklyn put it back in the box, tucked securely under a pile of magazines.

At length, Franklyn settled on three objects. A silver-backed hairbrush, a small vanity mirror, and a set of wind chimes, which she had wrapped with newspaper to shut them up.

'All right.' Franklyn sat on her heels. 'That'll do for a start. You guys pick something to add.'

Daniela and Auryn shuffled closer, on their knees like supplicants. It felt almost like a game. Daniela was tempted to smile, but Auryn was chewing her lip and Franklyn looked as serious as Daniela had ever seen her.

'What about Stephanie?' Auryn asked.

'If she wants to join us, she can,' Franklyn said. 'If not, whatever.'

Auryn ran a finger over a string of jade beads. 'Mum will be upset if she comes home and finds her stuff gone.'

If, she said. Not *when*. Not anymore.

'She took everything she wanted to take,' Franklyn said.

Auryn was more rational than Daniela, able to analyse options and make a choice, even when all choices seemed equally bad. Onto the pile she added the jade beads and the ceramic kittens that her father hadn't let her take before.

Franklyn gave her a gentle look. The whole family was gentle with Auryn, as if she was the most likely to break.

Except Stephanie – Stephanie treated Auryn like everyone else, with barely concealed impatience. 'Whatever you pick isn't coming back,' Franklyn said.

'I know that,' Auryn said. She set the cats down next to the jade beads, turning the ornaments so they sat parallel to the hairbrush.

Daniela pulled out a handful of bracelets and laid them on the floor so she could study them. On an intellectual level, Daniela knew the jewellery was pretty, but other than that it held little fascination. She'd never developed an enthusiasm for dressing up like most of the people at school.

Maybe she had her sisters to blame for her rough appearance. Franklyn had no tolerance for posh clothes or nice shoes, which she just wrecked anyway. Stephanie was entirely practical. At sixteen, she was in the midst of another growth spurt, and wore whatever fit her frame. Auryn had been getting their hand-me-downs for years, giving her a mismatched style that she was rapidly losing patience with. Daniela sometimes looked at her sisters, then at the girls from school, and wondered where she fit in.

No, she wouldn't take the bracelets. Daniela couldn't remember her mother wearing them anyway.

She looked for something else. It was a delicate balance, choosing objects that reminded her of her mother, whilst also being something she wanted rid of. Should she take a cheap and nasty item, like the plastic clip-on earrings that even her mother had hated? Or something expensive, like the vintage satchel, to show how angry she was?

But Daniela had spent enough time in the antiques shop, helping their father price up stock, to know how much the small items in the boxes were worth. Her stomach twinged at the idea of destroying anything valuable. So instead she took up the bundle of postcards, sent by her mother's friends from various exotic places, each filled with cramped, excitable writing. Of no value to anyone except her mother.

She took everything she wanted to take.

Franklyn made no comment on the choices. She simply put all the items into an empty box, then stood up.

Their dad was in the sitting room at the front of the house, talking shop with Henry. Henry owned a half-share in the antiques shop, and more than a half-share in their lives. 'Give your Uncle Henry a hug,' he'd often say to Daniela and Auryn. Their mother had always puckered her mouth whenever he spoke like that.

About a year ago, Daniela had realised Henry was an honorary uncle at best. That was a relief – she didn't want him as any kind of uncle let alone a relative. But his son, Leo ... she'd grown up thinking Leo was her cousin. That'd been a blow, to discover he wasn't.

Her dad and Henry used to do their talking in the actual shop, in the centre of Stonecrop, all of half a mile distant. But, since Daniela's mother could no longer object, Henry had started showing up at the home, usually mid-afternoon, to discuss business. Dinner time would come and go while the two men remained sequestered in the sitting room, and the kids foraged whatever they could find to eat from the scant supplies in the kitchen.

Daniela, Franklyn and Auryn carried their contraband through the house. This was the riskiest part of the plan. If their dad caught them, he'd take the items and hide them away somewhere the kids couldn't find them, to moulder with the other memories. Daniela and Auryn would get sent to bed with slapped legs. For Franklyn it might be worse, because she didn't have the sense to shut up when she was in trouble.

Daniela could hear the murmur of voices from the front room as she crept down the hall.

'The problem with all this,' Henry said, with the air of continuing a conversation that'd been going on for hours; days, possibly, 'is it's such piddly stuff. I mean, look at that delivery yesterday. We paid good money, but it's just crap. Who in their right mind wants to buy this?'

Daniela's father grunted, non-committal.

'We need to diversify,' Henry said. 'Furniture like that ... it's had its day. No one wants big, dark, heavy items anymore. It's no wonder our profits are freefalling.'

As Franklyn stepped past the open door of the front room, Henry caught sight of her and called out, 'Frankie, you agree, don't you?'

Franklyn stopped, clocking the conversation. Her body language made it clear she wanted no part in it.

Oblivious, Henry said, 'The shop's gotta move with the times. New stock, new customers. A whole updated look. Get some signage out front so people actually know it's there when they drive past.'

Franklyn tilted her head, then said, 'That'll cost money, right?'

'That's how business works, sweetheart. Spend money to make money.'

'Easily said when it's not your money.' She stepped into the front room so she was out of Daniela's sight.

Daniela, tucked behind the door, listening, could almost hear Henry bristle. 'Now, what's brought that on? We've all put into this business, me and your pa both.'

'Is that so?' Franklyn said. Her tone was light, mocking. It was the same tone that'd got her kicked out of college less than a month ago. 'Funny how it's his name above the door, not yours. Here.' There was a slight scuffle of noise as Franklyn moved the box from one arm to the other.

'What's that?'

'Found it in the garage. It's addressed to you.' It wasn't clear who that comment was aimed at.

Franklyn came out of the sitting room and kept walking, right out of the house.

Henry waited until the front door slammed before he said, 'She should watch that mouth of hers. Get her in trouble someday.'

Daniela's dad chuckled, like maybe he agreed. Daniela dug her fingernails into her palms.

Auryn was drawing back, as if she was having second thoughts about this whole business. Daniela grabbed her hand, briefly, and squeezed. It was as much reassurance as she could muster. Then she pushed forwards, head down, eyes fixed on the floor. She couldn't help a quick glance into the front room. Henry had got up and retrieved a white envelope from the table, which was presumably what Franklyn had left for them. Daniela didn't recall seeing any envelopes in the garage, but there'd been a lot of stuff. She hadn't looked at everything.

While Henry's back was turned, Daniela slipped past the door of the sitting room, holding her breath. No one called out to stop her.

When she reached the front door, Daniela glanced back, assuming she'd have to wave Auryn to join her, but found Auryn right behind her, a silent shadow with both hands clutched to her chest.

Outside, the wind had picked up, rattling the trees and sending loose leaves skirting across the road. It'd rained heavily for most of the day and, although it'd now stopped, every gust of wind brought a flurry of droplets from the branches overhead.

Franklyn hadn't waited. She was already striding away from the house into the woods. The sun was on its way down, leaving the sky dark grey and getting darker by the minute. Daniela had no fear of the woods. Her earliest memories were out here, among the trees that surrounded the house. Either with her sisters, playing, or on her own, walking or running or hiding or crying. When she was in the house, her emotions were tied up tight inside her chest. But the woods saw her as she really was.

Auryn, however, was skittish about being outside once it got dark, although she would happily tag along with her sisters during the day. Recently, Daniela had discovered Auryn's night vision wasn't good, and in the shadows beneath the trees, the poor girl was almost blind. Daniela led the way up the bank that sloped away from the house. At the top she glanced back. The house crouched in the pool of illumination from the windows of the front room and the kitchen. There were no streetlights on the road, and the house sat too far from the village to be included in its ambient glow. The only light was what it created for itself.

The woods were criss-crossed with pathways, lines of trampled mud that wove through the trees and undergrowth. Daniela had walked those paths so often she probably could've found her way blindfolded. She trailed her fingers over the damp ferns at the side of the path.

Franklyn picked a route seemingly at random, heading east.

She didn't bother looking back to make sure the others followed her.

Auryn was struggling to keep up. Loose roots conspired to trip her at every other step. On impulse, Daniela caught hold of Auryn's gloved hand, in a way she hadn't done since they were both much younger. She could just make out Auryn flashing a grateful smile in the gloom. Daniela helped guide her along the path, hand in hand like small children. Their proximity made Daniela realise that a strange distance had grown between them. They'd been close, almost as if they were twins, when they were younger. Was it just their mother's absence that'd pushed them apart?

The rain started again as they walked. Water dripped off the leaves and dimpled the puddles that collected in every footprint along the path. Some of the footprints probably belonged to Daniela and her sisters from days before. The rest had been left by dog-walkers or fishermen or hikers. Even during the worst weather, there were always people out in the woods.

'We should've invited Leo,' Auryn said.

Daniela felt a flash of annoyance. Henry's son Leo was in the year below Daniela at school, but up until recently that hadn't mattered – he'd been best friends with both her and Auryn for as long as Daniela could remember. To all intents and purposes, he was the brother who was missing from their lives. The girls at school thought it weird that he and Daniela were friends but nothing more. They'd ask her, giggling, whether she'd ever kissed him, or thought about kissing him.

No, she'd never thought about it. Why would she?

But that answer marked her out, apparently. Her friends had looked sceptical, side-eyed her and whispered. So next time, Daniela said of course she'd thought about it. Why wouldn't she?

After that, Daniela had started watching Leo. Trying to convince herself she felt something more for him than just normal friendship. As an odd side-effect, she'd become jealous of Auryn, who was in Leo's class and therefore got to spend more time with him.

A magpie in a nearby tree let out a ratcheting cry, close enough to startle Auryn. Daniela said, 'It's just a bird, don't worry,' but the sound had rattled her nerves as well. That was the problem with those woods. They were usually so quiet that the slightest noise could be frightening. She squeezed Auryn's hand again, but the hand-holding felt strange and childish now, so she let go a few moments later.

Inevitably, the path led to the water. To the north of the village, the River Clynebade forked and became the Clyne and the Bade, so if Daniela walked in pretty much any direction from Stonecrop, she would come up against one of the twin rivers that bracketed the village. On quiet nights, Daniela could hear the water muttering as it flowed not far from the house.

This path emerged on the banks of the River Bade, within sight of the bridge and the road that eventually wound its way to Hackett, the next town over. To their right, a fishing platform extended a few feet out over the river. After the recent rains, the waters were almost level with the planks. The structure thrummed with the force of the current.

Franklyn put a foot on the platform to test it. She leaned her weight and bounced twice. Since the boards didn't immediately crack, she decided it was safe.

A wooden rowing boat had been turned turtle on the grass

some distance from the river, where even the yearly flooding wouldn't dislodge it. Daniela sat down on its hull rather than go anywhere near the fishing platform.

'Where do we make the fire?' Daniela asked.

'What fire?' Franklyn asked.

'For the ... y'know.' The word *funeral* still felt melodramatic. 'To get rid of this stuff.'

'Too wet for a bonfire,' Franklyn said. She took a few more paces along the platform, testing its strength with her weight. 'Anyway, not everything will burn. Better to do it this way.' She made an expansive gesture at the water with her free hand. 'The river carries everything away.'

Even though it'd been raining pretty consistently all summer, the river wasn't nearly as high as it sometimes reached. During the winter, it often burst its banks. At least once a year the bridge to Hackett would be closed because it wasn't safe to cross when the water was at its highest. Daniela and her sisters had a healthy regard for the river, drummed into them by their mother.

Not that it was obvious from the way Franklyn was acting. She reached the end of the platform and leaned out over the water. She peered down as if she could see anything at all in the muddy depths.

'Be careful,' Auryn called. She'd stayed well back from the water, about equidistant between the river and the shadowy trees. She looked uncomfortable. Her hands were scrunched in the pockets of her blue waterproof coat. Drizzle beaded her blonde hair.

'It's fine,' Franklyn said. 'Come on out here.'

Auryn shook her head. Daniela didn't particularly want to stand on the rickety platform either, but she wanted to prove she was braver than her younger sister. After all, Franklyn wasn't scared.

As she stepped onto the boards, the platform groaned, and Daniela froze. But it was just the swollen boards acknowledging her presence. Like Franklyn said, the structure was solid. Daniela swallowed the nagging voice that said otherwise.

She glanced at Franklyn, hoping for encouragement or acknowledgement, but Franklyn had already turned back to the water. She'd set down the box. In her hand was a slim bundle of letters, secured with an elastic band. As Daniela watched, Franklyn took the elastic band off, slipped it around her wrist, and started flicking through the envelopes. She selected one and tore it into quarters, then eighths. Then she flung the handful of paper across the water. The white flakes settled onto the surface, turned dark, and were swept away.

'Where'd those letters come from?' Daniela asked. She was certain they hadn't been in the garage among their mother's other possessions.

'Found them.'

'Found them where?'

Franklyn didn't answer. She tore up another envelope and scattered the pieces.

Who are they addressed to? Daniela didn't ask aloud, because she was afraid of the answer. Instead she watched Franklyn methodically tear up each one and consign it to the river.

Daniela took the postcards from the box. Suddenly she wasn't sure she was angry enough to start ripping things. 'This is a weird kind of funeral,' she said.

'It's a weird kind of situation. You want to say a few words? Will that help?'

'You should do it.'

Franklyn blew out her cheeks. 'All right. Let me think.'

While she thought, she finished ripping up the envelopes. Daniela glimpsed the writing on the front. Definitely her mother's. Who were they for?

Are any for us?

In her formal speaking voice, Franklyn said, 'We're here to say goodbye. You're gone, and I guess we miss you. So long.'

She flung the last handful of paper into the air. The wind caught it and sprinkled it like confetti around them.

Daniela threw the postcards out into the water, one at a time, skimming them like stones. Each settled onto the surface and was carried away. The water blurred the writing fast, before the cards were out of sight.

Behind her, Auryn stepped onto the platform. She never made a move until she was completely sure of herself. She walked across the boards until she reached her sisters. Franklyn moved aside to make room.

'Go ahead,' Franklyn said. She put a reassuring hand on Auryn's shoulder.

But Auryn didn't need any encouragement. With quick, jerky movements, she chucked the jade beads into the water. They disappeared with a *plop*. Her other arm shot out and the ceramic kittens followed the beads into the depths, without a single hesitation. They hadn't even disappeared before she was stripping off her coat and flinging it into the river. Next, she pulled off her left shoe. It was only then Daniela realised Auryn was crying.

'Hey,' Franklyn said, 'Auryn—'

'Everything goes,' Auryn said. 'Everything she gave us.' She stumbled taking off her other shoe.

'Stop.' Franklyn caught her arm. Auryn jerked out of her reach and collided with Daniela.

There wasn't room on the platform for pushing and shoving. Daniela's foot slipped off the edge of the boards. She grabbed Auryn to save herself from falling. The platform groaned ominously beneath them.

'Be careful!' Daniela said.

She clung on to Auryn. For a moment they stayed like that, Auryn leaning into her, still crying, both of them listening to the noise of the river beneath them. Daniela felt her own eyes prickle with tears, and she turned her face away so Franklyn wouldn't see.

'Come on,' Daniela said. She kept a hand on Auryn's shoulder as she led her back along the platform onto solid ground. Franklyn stayed where she was.

Daniela wouldn't have admitted how glad she was to get back onto the bank. The thrum of the river beneath the platform had unnerved her. It would've been so easy for someone to slip and fall and be swept away. She told herself that was the reason why her eyes were stinging with suppressed tears. She steered Auryn towards the upturned boat where she figured they could sit down.

Before they got there, Stephanie appeared from out of the woods. She had a scowl stamped on her face. Daniela thought for a second they would get yelled at, for being out on the rickety platform, or for messing around so close to the river. But Stephanie immediately saw Auryn's distress.

'What happened?' Stephanie asked.

Auryn wiped her eyes with the back of her hand. She was

trembling slightly and her bare arms were covered with goose bumps. 'We're saying goodbye,' she mumbled, so quietly Daniela almost didn't hear.

Daniela sneaked a glance at Franklyn, who was still out on the platform. She'd picked up the box containing their mother's possessions and, without ceremony, upended it. The remaining items vanished into the river.

Then Franklyn looked up at Stephanie. 'Hey, glad you could make it,' she called. She put her hands in her pockets and wandered back towards her sisters. 'Come to pay your respects?'

'Dad and Henry had an argument,' Stephanie said, ignoring the question. 'I heard them shouting. Something about a letter? When I got downstairs, Henry had driven off in a temper.'

Franklyn paused at the near end of the platform, looking down into the water. A tiny smile touched her lips. 'Fancy that,' she said.

'What did you do, Frankie?'

'Me? Nothing at all.' But there was satisfaction in her voice. 'All I wanted from today was to get rid of stuff we don't want anymore. Feels good to know we can get on with our lives now, doesn't it?'

2

February 2017

14 Years Later

It took Daniela three hours to wade into Stonecrop, and, by then, her temper was as bleak as the weather. She'd almost turned back when she'd reached the bridge on the Hackett road and found it already awash. Below the bridge, the River Bade was still rising, surging up to the metal arches, muddy brown, swollen, tangled with branches that shot past at worrying speed. Gathering her nerve, Daniela had edged across the bridge. The force of the water made the metal handrail thrum beneath her fingers. Off to her left, a few hundred yards downstream, she could see what was left of the old fishing platform she and her sisters used to play on as kids. Only the necks of its stubby supports remained sticking out of the mud. The ancient, upside-down rowboat was still there, a moss-coloured hillock pulled up away from the bank.

Once past the bridge, the going didn't improve. In places, the road was flooded so deep she had to clamber along the muddy verges, clinging to branches in the hedgerow. Her jacket wasn't nearly as waterproof as she'd been led to believe, and the chill dampness that'd started at her collar and sleeves had seeped through to her skin. Water had overflowed her boots. Her socks squelched with every step. And she still had another two miles of flooded roads to slog through before she reached her home village.

Daniela was sure there must've been dry, sunny days during her childhood, but in her memory, Stonecrop was always wet, always overcast, always unwelcoming. And now it was partially underwater too.

Late winter rains had swelled the rivers on either since of the village to twice their usual sizes, burst their banks, and turned Stonecrop into a giant boating lake. At least now the rain had subsided to a sullen drizzle.

Daniela paused at the top of the high street – the only street, really – to light a cigarette. It took her three attempts to spark her lighter.

Television footage of flooded towns always looked surreal. Water lapping at sandbagged doors. Residents in wellies. Cars submerged to their wheel-arches. Hanging baskets dangling serenely from lamp-posts like botanical lifeboats. It was so unreal to Daniela, to return to a place she knew so well, and find it like this. A kind of jarring nostalgia.

Her eyes sought out the details that'd changed. A plastic sign had replaced the metal one above the Corner Shoppe; the estate agent's had been torn down to leave a gaping hole, and the antiques emporium that her dad had once co-owned was abandoned, its windows filmed with dust. Out of three businesses in the village, only one had survived.

But beneath the surface, the heart of the village was unaltered. Stonecrop maintained that quaint, chocolate-box appearance, like it was illustrating a magazine article about house prices in the rural midlands. The ruddy brickwork exteriors had seen few renovations. It was as if a lid had come down on Stonecrop when Daniela left, sealing everything in stasis. She wondered what she'd hoped to find. An untouched childhood memory? The entire village razed in an unreported hurricane?

Most of the community had been evacuated, but a few stubborn residents remained. Halfway along the street, where a natural dip caused a deep pool, a group of people were shoring up a garden wall. Two men in fishermen's waders judiciously applied sandbags. A middle-aged woman – Margaret McKearney, Daniela recognised with a jolt, who owned the Shoppe and was apparently impervious to ageing – stood with her skirts hiked up to show off her flowery wellies, while she distributed cups of tea from a thermos.

And at the far edge of the pool, supervising the work while eating a chocolate digestive, was Sergeant Stephanie Cain.

She too had changed little in the seven years since Daniela had left. Maybe a touch heavier around the middle and below the eyes, a bit older and more tired, with the weight of the extra years on her shoulders. She'd always been big and broad, like their father. The police vest made her look dumpy. Daniela's eyes flicked to the kit on the vest – handcuffs, incapacitant spray, torch, extendable baton. Prepared for everything.

Stephanie Cain was comfy in her role of village police officer, up to her shins in floodwater, with her police-issue waders and her chocolate biscuit. She'd found her place. Daniela felt a pang of jealousy.

Steeling herself, she waded towards the group.

Stephanie spotted her. Daniela watched the play of emotions across the officer's face: polite alertness until she recognised Daniela, then surprise, disbelief … ah, and anger. That came an instant before the sergeant's expression closed up like a door slamming.

At least now Daniela didn't have to wonder if Stephanie was still upset.

Daniela stopped and waited. She didn't want to interact with anyone other than her sister.

Stephanie took a circuitous route around the flooded dip in the road. Daniela discarded the butt of her cigarette into the water, and the sergeant's eyes flicked to it. Her annoyance gave Daniela a petty satisfaction. In a perverse way, Daniela was looking forward to this fight.

Stephanie halted ten feet away. Like she didn't trust herself to get too close.

'This road's closed,' Stephanie said.

Despite everything, Daniela laughed. 'Is that how you'll greet me? You've got a million things you'd rather say.'

'Why are you here?'

'See, *that's* what I'd expect. Want to maybe say I've got some nerve coming back home?'

Sergeant Cain's mouth drew into a thin, angry line. The tips of her ears reddened.

'Come on,' Daniela said, still smiling. 'Let's sit down and talk, yeah?'

'I'm busy.'

'Too busy for family? That's a shocking state of affairs, Steph.'

Stephanie swore under her breath. She glanced at the other villagers, who'd noticed Daniela's arrival and were peering over.

The two men were whispering. Margaret looked like she'd seen a ghost.

'All right,' Stephanie said. 'We can talk. Quickly. I've got work to do.'

'The water can supervise itself for ten minutes, Steph.' Daniela cast a long look around the flooded village, then smiled at her big sister. 'So, how about the pub? Is it still open, or have the ducks taken over?'

The Crossed Swords stood at the junction between the high street and Winterbridge Farm Road. The land there was slightly higher, leaving the pub currently marooned on a tiny island some hundred yards wide. But it hadn't escaped unscathed. The basement was flooded, and water lapped the back door. A defensive barrier of sandbags blocked the entrance to the car park. The building looked like a castle with an unruly moat.

Daniela stepped over the sandbags ungainly in her wellies and damp jeans. A welcome light burned in the windows of the Crossed Swords. Daniela was more than ready to be inside in the warm.

'Does Chris Roberts still own this place?' Daniela asked.

'Yes.'

That was all the conversation Daniela had coaxed out of Stephanie so far. To be fair, Daniela hadn't said much either. Everything she had to say needed careful wording. Otherwise she could ruin everything. Again.

Above the door, trailing wisteria partially obscured the sign depicting two painted swords on a black background. Fat green leaves dripped water onto the flagstones. Pockets of flood debris dirtied the corners of the doorway.

It felt strange to walk on dry ground after so long wading. Daniela felt lighter, less tired. The door opened with a wash of warm air. Daniela wondered whether to take her boots off, but, judging by the carpet, the other patrons hadn't bothered.

A few things had changed since Daniela's last visit. A partition wall had been knocked through from the main lounge into the gentleman's bar at the back. Plasma screens hung in pride of place. But the décor, a combination of muted browns and vibrant oranges, looked so much like home that a lump formed in Daniela's throat.

A familiar face was behind the bar as well. 'Morning, Sergeant,' Chris Roberts called. 'Not here on business, are you?'

The landlord was a slight man with a receding hairline and square glasses. He looked like he'd wandered behind the bar by accident. But his constant bemusement meant no one could ever dislike him. At present, he was seated near the cash register with a newspaper spread out on the bar.

His head tilted as he peered around Stephanie, blinking to focus. When he recognised Daniela, he put a hand to his chest in over-dramatic surprise.

'Daniela?' he asked. 'Young Daniela Cain? Now, is that really you?'

Daniela waved in acknowledgement. 'Hey, Chris. How's business?'

'All washed up.' Chris cackled. 'You'd think everyone would want to drown their sorrows, but most of them have scarpered. All my precious customers.' He shook his head sadly. 'So, what can I get you, youngster? Bottled lager only, I'm afraid. The pumps are off. The bitter's on a hand-pump though, if you fancy.'

Daniela deferred to Stephanie, but the officer had already sat down by the window, where she resolutely faced forwards. She took off her hat, placed it on the table top, then clasped her hands. Her black hair was pulled back into an austere bun.

'Pint of bitter for me,' Daniela said to Chris. 'Better make it a coffee for the big lady.'

Chris nodded as he rose from his chair. 'You'd think normal rules about drinking at work could be suspended, given the flooding. But she's a stickler.'

Daniela searched her pockets and came up with enough change to cover two drinks, just. She'd brought only limited funds and had to be careful. She eyed the price list while Chris fiddled with the coffee maker at the back of the bar. That was another thing that'd changed.

She glanced at the lights above the bar. 'I see the power's still on.'

'More or less,' Chris said. 'They told us we only needed to shut the electricity off if the building flooded out. Since that's not happened, I figured we'll leave it on for now. Plus, we've got the emergency generator out back if things get desperate. I reckon we can stay open so long as the toilets still flush. That's the important thing, right? So, are you staying, or is this a flying visit?'

'I'm not sure.' Daniela avoided looking at her sister. 'It kinda depends. Might be a day, or a couple of days.'

'Well, if you need somewhere to bunk, we've got rooms. Can even give you mates' rates, since we're not technically open for staying guests.' Chris lowered his voice to a conspiratorial whisper. 'Just don't tell the rozzers, yeah?'

Daniela returned his grin. 'I'll think about it. Thanks, man.'

It felt good to talk to the landlord again. It was as if Daniela had only been gone a few weeks, which was bittersweet. So much had changed for her.

Daniela took the drinks to the table and sat opposite her sister. Stephanie had switched her gaze so she stared out at the flooded streets. She could've been thinking about anything. Beneath her chin was a crescent-shaped scar, where she'd been hit with a golf club, years ago.

Daniela sipped her drink then pulled off her boots and turned them upside down in the vain hope they'd dry out. She considered taking her socks off but thought that might be impolite. She circled her weak left ankle, which always ached when it was damp.

'This place was better before the smoking ban,' Daniela said. She sniffed. 'All you smell now is cheap bleach and old alcohol.'

'That was ten years ago,' Stephanie said. 'You weren't old enough to be in here then.'

'When did that ever stop us?'

At last Stephanie looked at her. 'Get to the point,' she said. 'I'm supposed to be working.'

'We're all supposed to be somewhere. If I had any choice I wouldn't be here. Not right now, anyways.'

'Why *are* you here?'

Daniela hesitated. 'Well now. What explanation would you like? I can—'

'The truth would be a nice change.'

'That goes without saying. But what variant of truth? I can give you a tear-jerking breakdown, or a bald statement of facts, or—'

'You need money.'

Daniela winced. 'Okay, we're going for stark, unvarnished truth.'

'I'm not giving you money, Dani.'

It'd been years since anyone called her *Dani*. Heat flushed her face. 'It's not as bad as you assume,' she said carefully. 'I don't want *your* money.'

'So, why're you wasting my time?'

'I want *my* money, Steph.' Daniela sipped her drink. 'The money Dad left me. That shouldn't be problem, right?'

Stephanie eyed the cup of coffee on the table. Her need for a warm drink was apparently less urgent than her wish to stay angry with her younger sister, and she pushed the cup away.

'You can't have it,' Stephanie said.

'I understand there'll be procedures. Paperwork. It'll take time. What I'm hoping is—'

'You can't have it. There's no money, Dani.'

Daniela's smile slipped. 'What d'you mean?'

'Dad left you a share of the house.' Stephanie clasped her hands on the table again. A police officer's pose; demonstrating calm, concern, patience. 'Once it's been sold, you'll get some of the money.'

'It's not sold yet? Steph, it was two years ago.'

'Three. There didn't seem any hurry to sell.'

Daniela sat back. It was a disappointment, but not unexpected. If the house had been sold and the money released, someone would've told her. 'So, what? It's sitting empty?'

'No.'

'No? C'mon. If I have to drag every answer out of you—'

'Auryn's living there.'

24

Daniela's eyes widened. 'Auryn's here?'

'She was. She left a few days ago, before the floods got bad.'

'God, I thought she'd got out long ago. Isn't she a barrister in London?'

'Solicitor.'

'So, what happened? Why'd she come back?'

Stephanie paused. 'Some kind of breakdown,' she said. 'I said she could come home, since no one was using the house, while she got her head together.'

Daniela's fingers tightened around the glass. Despite everything, she still felt protective of Auryn, the baby of the family, who'd always been quiet and withdrawn, especially compared to the rest of them. Stephanie and Franklyn had looked out for Auryn in their own way, but it'd been Daniela who was closest to her. For a time, anyway.

'Glad the old house is still in the family,' Daniela said, with what she hoped was a sincere smile. 'Lots of memories in that place. I'm surprised you're not living there as well.'

'Why would I go back?'

'Same reason you never left Stonecrop. It's comfortable and reassuring. Are you still living next to the police station in Hackett or have you found somewhere a bit more ... separate from your work?'

Stephanie gave her an unfriendly look. 'Listen, until the house gets sold there's no money for you. So, you can take your sob story elsewhere.'

'That's harsh.' Daniela adopted a thoughtful look. 'But there's *other* money, right? Dad's investments. His savings. You got the pay-out from the insurance company—'

'That's nothing to do with you.'

Daniela leaned forwards. 'I'm asking for a favour, Steph. I know what you're like – you've got that money stashed in an account somewhere, nice and safe. I need—'

'You need a slap. *A favour?*' Stephanie laughed without humour. 'The best favour you could've done would be staying gone. What do you need money for anyway? Drugs? Loan sharks? The old ladies at Payday-Cash-4-U coming to break your legs?'

'I'm not asking for anything that isn't mine.'

'Technically you are.'

'It'd just be a loan, all right?' Daniela resisted the urge to shout. 'A small amount to tide me over. Once the sale of the house goes through, I'll see you right.'

Stephanie sat back and folded her arms. 'How much?' she asked.

Daniela moistened her lips. 'Well, I'm due eighty-five grand once the house is sold ...'

'The house isn't worth that much anymore.'

That sounded like a lie, but Daniela let it pass. 'So how about five thousand? That's not unreasonable, is it?'

Stephanie was already laughing. 'You're hilarious, Dani,' she said. 'Not *unreasonable*.' Again, she shook her head. 'Perhaps if you'd picked up the phone and asked, I might've paid five thousand to avoid seeing your face.'

Ouch.

'I tried calling,' Daniela said. 'You didn't answer.'

'And can you blame me?'

'I've never asked you for anything.'

'You've never given much either.' Stephanie stood and retrieved her hat. 'Well, this has been a barrel of laughs, but I've work to do.'

'Sure. Have fun policing the sandbags. I'm sure it's giving you job satisfaction.'

'I'm surprised you know the meaning of the term.' Stephanie tipped her hat. 'See you in another seven years.'

As Stephanie turned away, Daniela asked, 'Did you ever find her?'

'Who?'

'Mum.' Daniela studied her sister's face. 'I know you and Franklyn were looking for her.'

Stephanie's expression closed up again. 'We stopped looking a long time ago.'

After Stephanie left, Daniela sat by the window for a while. She drank her pint slowly, not wanting to brave the cold outside.

'Can I get you a refill, youngster?' Chris called from the bar.

Daniela shook her head and finished the dregs. As an afterthought, she drank Stephanie's untouched coffee as well. It was cold and bitter. 'I'd better get moving. Thanks anyway.'

'So, have you decided if you're staying or not? I can get the missus to make up a room.'

Daniela felt despondent enough to wade the five miles back to Hackett and catch the first bus she saw. But she hated giving up.

And, of course, there might be another way she could get her money.

She shook her head, smiled. 'It's okay. I think I might go home instead.'

3

In the afternoon the sky darkened again with low-bellied rainclouds, ready to shed their weight at the slightest provocation.

Daniela hadn't anticipated how cut off the flooded village was from the rest of the world. Only a few houses were occupied, and the light from their windows was weak and tremulous, as if aware that the power could die at any second. Looking at the surrounding fields, with the pylons standing in a foot of water, Daniela was surprised the lights were still on, but, according to Chris in the pub, that was usual unless the substation itself was underwater.

A landslip to the west had felled the phone lines. Daniela kept checking the faint signal on her mobile. Amazing that a little rainfall could isolate a whole village.

Daniela ate lunch in the pub – the kitchen was closed, but Chris grilled a fair panini – sent a few text messages, then bundled herself up in her less-than-waterproof clothes. After an hour by the fire in the lounge, her boots were only a little damp inside, her jacket pleasantly toasty.

The warmth didn't survive for long. By the time she'd slogged along the back street to the other end of town she felt the cold again. A light drizzle flattened her hair and chilled her exposed skin. She pulled up her hood and waded on.

The back lane took her around the main street, because she had no desire to chat to the group who were sandbagging the gardens. She'd wanted to get in and out of town without talking to anyone except Stephanie.

Daniela ground her teeth. Stubborn, awkward Steph. It'd been a pleasant daydream, to imagine her sister would hand over a wad of cash without blinking. She might at least have *listened*.

Daniela shook the thought away, set her shoulders, and kept walking.

The old family house was a half-mile outside town, along a narrow lane flanked with high hedgerows. As a child, Daniela had walked that road twice a day, every day, since she was old enough to walk. It held a familiarity like nowhere else in the world. Every footstep felt like a journey home. It wasn't entirely comforting.

The lane rose and fell with the undulations of the land, too slight at normal times to notice, now dotted with tarmac islands that stood proud of the water. In places Daniela was forced to wade. She was careful not to flood her boots again. She also stayed clear of the ditches that edged the road; hidden sinks at least three feet deep.

As she left the village behind, the road wound into the woods. The hedgerows gave way to barbed wire fences. Slender elms and beeches crowded the skyline, their bare branches scratching as they moved with the wind, their roots swamped in mud and water. A rippling breeze scooted fallen leaves across the pools.

At another time, Daniela would've abandoned the road,

ducking under the fence to follow the hidden pathways of the wood. Part of her yearned to rediscover the secret places where she and her sisters had played as children. The hollows where they'd made dens; the winding streams where they'd fished for minnows. Trees for climbing, root-space burrows, hollow deadwoods ...

She paused to light a cigarette. *It's gone. Even if it's still there, it's gone. Those places are muddy grot-holes, or piles of branches, or fallen trees. You are definitely too old to grub around in the dirt looking for your misspent youth.*

The family home stood in a shallow depression, hidden by trees until the road turned and it was suddenly right there. Daniela had to brace herself before taking those last few steps.

She was prepared for the house to look exactly as she'd left it. She was equally prepared for it to have been modernised and updated beyond recognition. What she hadn't expected was it to be derelict.

The house was once elegant, with a wide, many-windowed front and arching gables, but neglect had made it slump, like an old lady giving up on life. Its timbers had slouched and its roof was sloughing tiles. The paintwork had peeled and cracked. A broken window was patched with cardboard. The woodpile under the awning had mouldered into a heap of rotting, moss-covered logs.

It didn't help that rain had flooded the shallow depression, and the house sat in a lake of dirty water.

How did this happen? In Daniela's memory the old place was alive, awake, with washing lines strung across the garden and toys scattering the front lawn. Now there wasn't so much as a light in the window or a trail of smoke from the chimney.

At some point in the intervening years the old house had died.

She'd thought Stephanie had been evasive about how little the house was worth. Now she saw the truth. No wonder they couldn't sell the place.

She made her way down to the front gate. It was wedged open by years of rust.

The water was almost a foot deep around the house. Daniela felt her way along the path. Ripples sent reflected light bouncing across the windows. A half-hearted stack of sandbags guarded the front door.

Halfway up the path, Daniela paused to listen. The only sounds came from the wind in the trees and the occasional hoot of a woodpigeon somewhere among the stripped branches.

Daniela reached the front door. A piece of sticky tape across the inoperative doorbell was so old it'd turned opaque and flaky. She leaned over to peer through the sitting-room window. Floodwater had invaded the house as well. The front room was awash, the furniture pushed back against the walls, a few buoyant items floating sluggishly. Obviously the sandbags hadn't done the trick.

She felt a flush of anger at Auryn. Why hadn't she made sure the place was watertight before she left? And what about Stephanie? She was right here in town but hadn't bothered to keep an eye on the house?

The front door was locked. In a village like Stonecrop, people hardly ever locked their houses, except when they went away. But Daniela had kept her key, or rather she had never got rid of it. It was still strung on her keyring like a bad reminder. So long as Auryn hadn't changed the locks ...

She hadn't. The Yale clicked open. Daniela pushed the door but the water held it closed. She leaned her weight onto the wood and pushed it open a half-inch. It was more than just water behind. More sandbags, possibly. She couldn't open the door enough to get her foot into the gap.

Giving up, Daniela stepped off the path and made her way around the side of the house. Clouds of muddy water swirled around her wellies. Now she risked not just flooded boots but tripping over the uneven ground into the freezing water. She kicked aside debris with every awkward step.

At the side of the house, the small vegetable garden was now an empty lake. A few tripods of discoloured bamboo canes protruded like totems. Against the far wall, the old beehive was a pile of mushy timbers. Dead leaves sailed like abandoned boats. Eddies of twigs had collected below the window frames. Daniela paused by the window of the utility room next to the kitchen, but the net curtains obscured her view.

There was more neglect at the rear. The back porch lay in a crumpled heap of broken wood and corrugated plastic, as if someone had angrily tossed it aside. The apple tree by the porch was dead. A frayed length of knotted rope still hung from a branch – the makeshift swing that Franklyn and Stephanie had put up.

The back door of the house was also sandbagged. When Daniela tried the handle, she found it locked too. Either that or the door was so tightly wedged it wouldn't budge. She didn't have a key. The sash windows on either side were stuck, the wood swollen.

By now she was sick of sploshing around. Despite her best efforts, water had trickled into both boots, and her toes were numb. She was tired and annoyed and already thinking how long it'd take her to get back to the pub.

And, besides all that, a niggle of unease wormed into her stomach. The house felt creepy and abandoned. She felt like an intruder.

She went to the base of the old apple tree that reached up past the roofline. Her eyes automatically traced the route she'd used to climb up and down the trunk a hundred times in her youth. The branches were sturdy and evenly spaced, and it was no more effort to climb than a ladder. Daniela was halfway up before she really stopped to think what she was doing.

The trunk was twisted towards the wall, bringing it close to the window of the old junk room, which Auryn had turned into a separate bedroom for herself when she'd got tired of sharing a space with Daniela. Daniela shimmied along a branch to the window, with only a twinge of vertigo when she glanced down. It'd been a long time since she'd been up a tree. There wasn't a lot of call for it in adult life.

The window to Auryn's room was stiff, but, with a certain amount of effort, Daniela slid the wooden sash up.

'Hello, house,' she whispered.

She clambered in through the window. *Home,* she thought, then shoved the idea away. This place hadn't been *home* in years. Daniela had assumed she'd never come back, especially after Dad died. In fact, until this morning she'd assumed the place had been sold, and she'd never have to lay eyes on it again. Today was not working out at all as she'd hoped.

She paused with one foot on the carpet and one on the sill. It hadn't occurred to her how weird it would feel to step into Auryn's personal space like that. To be honest, the bedroom didn't look much like Auryn's anymore. Auryn had always been tidy to a fault, even as a kid. It was strange to see the bed in disarray and clothes scattered across the floor. On a cluttered table next to the bed was a half-empty bottle of wine and a half-full ashtray. Auryn had never been a big drinker, certainly never a smoker.

Daniela took off her boots and carried them so she wouldn't track mud through the house. On soft feet, she padded across Auryn's room to the door.

Out on the upstairs landing, there were more obvious signs that the house was neglected. The old wallpaper had turned yellow with age. A faint smell emanated from the drains backing up into the kitchen. The whole place was damp and cold. Daniela tried the light switch but the power was off.

She closed her eyes and breathed. The smell of damp and drains couldn't entirely overpower the familiar scent of the house. Daniela was grateful the bedroom doors were closed; she couldn't face seeing Dad's room. Nothing in the house had been updated, aside from a few new items of furniture. A layer of dust and age covered everything.

The door to the attic room squealed as she pulled it open. It released a waft of cold, stale air, loaded with familiarity. It made Daniela nineteen again. She shuddered.

Up in the converted attic, a window in the gable wall was broken, an inexpertly fixed piece of plyboard keeping out the chill wind. All the furniture had been cleared out and the wide expanse of floorboards was patterned with dust. A leak in the roof had spread patches of damp across the plaster walls.

Daniela wondered if Auryn had emptied the other bedrooms or just this one, which they'd shared as kids. Back then, it'd made sense for her and Auryn, the youngest two, to share a room. They'd been so close in age. As time went on and they'd started wanting their own space, their father promised he would fix up the spare room for Auryn, but it remained as a junk room, with a battered futon shoved in one corner, until Auryn lost patience and moved down there anyway, carving out a neat little space among the clutter.

Daniela stepped into the centre of the room like a sleepwalker. Everything seemed unreal, like pictures in a faded book. Her bed had stood against one wall, with Auryn's directly opposite, beneath the skylight. An empty wooden shelf was still fixed to the wall beside the window. Back in the day, it'd been laden with Auryn's paperbacks and emergency supplies – a spare phone charger, AA batteries, and a pen-torch in case of power cuts. Prepared and paranoid, that was Auryn. Even after she'd moved to the spare room, she'd kept a stash of emergency supplies up here.

The floorboards were scratched where the heavy iron frame of Daniela's bed had dragged. Daniela knelt and located a gap between two boards that was slightly larger than it should've been. A short plank that'd been removed and replaced so many times it'd worn smooth at the edges. Daniela used her fingernails to prise up the board.

Below was a musty space. It was a not-so-secret secret; a hidey-hole she and Auryn had used to conceal bits and pieces they considered valuable. As they'd got older, they'd used it less frequently. Daniela doubted anyone had lifted the board since she'd stashed something important there, seven years ago.

So, she was surprised to find a large, rectangular object, the size of a breeze block, wrapped tightly in plastic, taking up most of the room in the hole. Apparently at least one other family member recalled the hiding place.

Daniela reached past the plastic-wrapped object, flinching away when it brushed her arm. Whatever it was, it wasn't hers, and she avoided touching it.

Right at the back of the concealed space, wedged behind a wooden support, so far that Daniela had to lie down flat to reach it, should've been a small bundle wrapped in cloth. At first, she couldn't find it, and panicked. Had someone taken it? But then her fingers closed on the bundle. It was tucked further back than she'd thought.

Daniela drew it out gingerly. The cloth had once been a blue striped tea towel, but long years in damp conditions had turned it into a formless grey mush, coated in dust and rot. It smelled of decay.

Perching on her heels, Daniela unwrapped the old bundle. The last seven years concertinaed and suddenly she was a teenager again, sitting on the edge of her bed, folding the towel around a slim metal object. The memory returned with such clarity it made her flinch. She'd pictured returning here so often it was hard to believe this was real.

She knew it wasn't smart to retrieve the object, but she couldn't stop herself. For years she'd wondered whether it'd remained unfound, awaiting her return. She had to know.

She pulled away the friable cloth to reveal a flick-knife. Rust decorated the once shiny steel, but couldn't obscure the shape of a snake, inlaid in black, along the dark red handle.

Along with the knife, concealed in the folds of the cloth, were four gold rings, tarnished and discoloured, with precious stones that no longer glittered.

The rings were what she'd come to the house for. Daniela

had a rough idea how much they were worth. *Not nearly as much as five thousand, but maybe enough.* By now it should be safe to sell them. In her palm, they were cold enough to make her skin tingle. Here was another chunk of her past. She tucked them in the pocket of her jeans.

She started to rewrap the knife, but her gaze fell on the plastic-wrapped package in the hidey-hole.

What was Auryn hiding?

Curiosity won, and she lifted the package out. It hadn't lain there long enough to collect dust. In the slightly better light, the blue polythene became translucent. Daniela whistled in surprise.

The package contained stacks of twenty-pound notes, bound so tightly they'd become a hard brick. Daniela weighed it in her hand. She couldn't begin to estimate how much money was there.

What the hell was Auryn doing with this?

She hadn't for a moment expected to find money in the house. She'd come back for what was hers, that was all. And yet, here it was, like a gift from God, left hidden for her in an empty house. Just when she needed it most.

How long would it be until Auryn came back to the house? How long before she checked the hidey-hole? It'd be days at least. Possibly longer. She might not discover the money was missing for weeks.

Daniela hesitated a moment more as she struggled with her conscience. Absently she pocketed the knife. Then she replaced the loose floorboard.

Cradling the plastic-wrapped money, Daniela went downstairs. She closed the attic door behind her.

Rather than clamber down the tree, she figured she could

let herself out through the front door if she moved whatever was blocking it. She took her boots and the money and followed the stairs at the far end of the landing down to the flooded ground floor.

Halfway down, she stopped.

The only light came from the round window at the top of the stairs. It wasn't really adequate to illuminate the hallway. But Daniela could see the shape that lay blocking the front door. It wasn't sandbags.

4

Daniela took another step down the stairs. She'd thought Auryn had left the house days ago. If she'd believed otherwise, even for a moment, she would've searched the house properly. She never would've wasted time going up to her old room.

A little more light slipped through the upstairs window behind her. It didn't improve the situation. All it did was let Daniela see her sister's face.

Auryn had slumped against the door, falling sideways so her head rested against the wall. Her nose and mouth were underwater. It appeared that she'd let her hair grow out past her shoulders, normally worn short as a teenager. Loose strands stuck to her forehead and cheek. Her eyes were open. Auryn had always been the odd one out – a blonde-haired, blue-eyed anomaly among her dark-haired sisters.

Daniela dropped what she was holding and came down the stairs fast. She jumped down the last two steps before remembering she wasn't wearing her boots. The shock of the cold water barely slowed her. She grabbed Auryn's shoulders and dragged her upright.

Water flowed from Auryn's slack mouth. Daniela stifled a cry. She shook Auryn by the shoulders as if the woman might suddenly snap out of this. Auryn's head flopped forwards. She was a dead weight.

Daniela pressed a hand to Auryn's neck. She held her breath, willing a pulse to flutter beneath her fingers. There was nothing. The skin was cold and waxy and lifeless. When Daniela moved her hand, the imprint of her fingertips remained indented on Auryn's throat.

Daniela stumbled away and half fell against the doorway that led to the sitting room. Her feet sent waves bouncing off the walls. The reflections from the water gave the illusion of movement on Auryn's face. As if at any moment she might blink and sit up. Auryn's black vest billowed around her stomach. The flesh of her arms and face was the colour of dead fish belly.

Automatically Daniela glanced into the front room, where the phone always sat on the windowsill. It was disconnected, the cable wrapped around the handset.

She managed to get her mobile out of her pocket. With shaking hands, she dialled Stephanie's number.

The line rang four times then went to voicemail.

'Steph, I'm at the old house.' Daniela's voice sounded loud and panicky in the close confines of the waterlogged house. 'Something's happened to Auryn.'

She tried to say more but the words jammed in her throat. Her eyes stung with tears. She shut the phone off and held it gripped tight in her hand.

Turning away, she stared into the front room. It was difficult to tell when the house had flooded. Water lapped the big oak dining table. The table was strewn with papers and magazines, their edges curling. Already the wallpaper was beginning to peel. The threadbare sofa was saturated, and a low coffee table was now an island. Several empty cups sat on the table. Some effort had been made here to move books and magazines to the higher bookcase shelves, and there was a conspicuous empty spot on an entertainment stand where a television and DVD player had been removed. A sodden cushion wallowed in the water like a half-sunk iceberg. The water had an oily sheen.

There was also a lot of rubbish. Cigarette ends and empty beer cans bobbed on the waves. A pair of whisky bottles nestled together in the corner. One was still half-full and rode low in the water.

Auryn … what happened to you?

Looking into the sitting room, Daniela's gaze flitted from one irrelevant object to the next, searching for something solid. The dusty mirror above the fireplace reflected her pale, shocked face, almost unrecognisable. The semi-opaque glass made her look drowned. Daniela stared at the ornaments on the mantel, at scraps of paper and postcards, at the books on the shelves next to framed photographs that'd belonged to Dad. Some of the items were hers. A carved wooden bear brought back from a school trip. The shell casing from a Second World War mortar that she'd dug up in the woods. Small, meaningless things that she'd left behind without a thought, and which had long since vanished from her memory, yet remained here, awaiting her return.

Daniela took a few stumbling steps back to the stairs. Eddies of greasy water followed her. She sat down on the third step before her legs gave out. Her mind sloshed and tilted in her skull. Her jeans and socks were soaked with dirty water. She lifted her wet feet out of the flood.

Again, she tried Stephanie's number. Listened to it ring.

Dad died here as well, Daniela remembered with a jolt. She raised her eyes to the upstairs landing where, three years ago, her father had stumbled, drunk, and tipped headfirst over the banisters. Broke his neck on impact then lay for twelve hours until the postman found him.

Is that what'd happened to Auryn as well? From where Daniela sat, she could see one of the empty bottles that bobbed about in the sitting room. Had Auryn fallen?

Her phone bipped as the call went to voicemail again. Daniela hung up and immediately redialled.

Closer to the water, the bad-drain smell was stronger. Daniela wondered whether the smell and the oily glaze had leaked out of Auryn. The thought made her stomach roil so badly she had to close her eyes.

Voicemail again. Daniela swore. It came out as a sob.

You don't even know if Stephanie's using the same number, Daniela realised. That hadn't occurred to her. Likewise, it hadn't occurred to her to call 999. Despite the years, she'd reached instinctively for Stephanie.

Daniela leant back against the stairs. Her arm brushed something solid and wrapped in plastic. The package of money. She picked it up and let it sit heavy on her lap.

She was about to redial when her phone burst into life, the ringtone loud enough to make her jump. Stephanie's number appeared on the screen, so familiar even after all those years.

5

When the police arrived, Daniela was sat on the wall at the bottom of the front garden, her knees pulled up so her booted feet were clear of the water. She was shivering and red-eyed, not just from the cold.

She heard the police before she saw them. They'd commandeered a tractor – the best way of traversing the flooded roadways – from a local farmer. The steady chug-chug-chug was audible long before the vehicle popped into view.

Daniela didn't recognise the thickset woman driving the tractor. Her wind-burned cheeks and earth-coloured clothes suggested she was either the farmer or the farmer's wife. It stood to reason she wouldn't trust the local bobbies to drive the vehicle themselves. Stephanie stood on the footplate, stony-faced, hanging on with both hands.

The tractor stopped in the flooded turning circle, and Stephanie jumped down with a splash. Daniela took one look at her sister's face then dropped her gaze. She didn't know what she'd hoped for. Sympathy? Forgiveness? Some human emotion, at least. But Stephanie could've been arriving at a train station for all the sentiment she showed. She started up the path with barely a glance at Daniela.

'You'll have to go around the back,' Daniela called after her. 'Front door's blocked. I've opened the kitchen door.'

Daniela didn't follow Stephanie. The idea of going inside again made her stomach churn. Instead, she remained on the wall, lit another cigarette, and watched the tractor perform a six-point turn. The farmer tipped her cap and set off back along the road. Daniela waited.

Within a few minutes, sloshing footsteps indicated Stephanie's return. Daniela studied her cigarette, which had burned down to the filter. She cringed at having to face her sister.

'Dani, what happened?' Stephanie asked. There was a raw edge to her voice that Daniela had never heard before.

Daniela rubbed her eyes with her knuckles. 'I told you on the phone,' she said. 'I found her like that.'

'What were you doing here?'

'I wanted to see the old house.'

'What for?'

Daniela discarded her cigarette into the water, where it bobbed about with the dead leaves and twigs. 'It's still my home,' she said. 'It belongs to me, at least a little.'

'So, you broke in.' Not really a question.

'I couldn't get in the front, and the back door was locked. I climbed through the upstairs window. Look at the state of the place, for God's sake. Of course, I went inside.'

Stephanie let the silence stretch. Daniela felt the police-stare burning the back of her neck, but didn't look up. She was wise to that trick.

'Where did you go when you got inside?' Stephanie asked.

'Through the junk room, down the stairs, into the hall. That's when I saw Auryn.'

'And then?'

'I called you.'

'Did you move her?'

'No. I ... I tried to sit her up. Before I realised.'

'But did you move her? Is she still where you found her?'

'I—' Daniela couldn't shift the memory of Auryn's dead weight under her hands. 'What the hell should I've done? She's dead, isn't she?' Daniela rubbed her eyes again. Her hands were cold. 'I knew I had to call someone.'

'So, you called me.'

'You're the police. I figured it'd be quickest. I mean, if I'd called the control room I would've got put through to Hackett, and God knows how long it'd take them to get here with the bridge closed. Have *you* called anyone?'

Stephanie grunted, which could've meant anything. Daniela noted she wasn't writing this down like she was supposed to. She wondered whether Stephanie was doing any of the things she should've. Shock was hitting her hard as well; Daniela could tell. There was a stricken look on Stephanie's face. She had all the police training to deal with awful, stressful situations, but this had blindsided her.

'I've called a doctor,' Stephanie said. 'They'll be here soon.'

'Is that Abrams?' Doctor Abrams was the local GP and, by Daniela's estimation, had to be a hundred years old.

'Abrams is in Hackett. There's a doctor in town who's coming to examine the body.'

Daniela studied her hands again. *The body.* Already Auryn had ceased to be a person.

'Did you go anywhere else in the house?' Stephanie asked.

'No. Wait, I went into the kitchen on the way out. To unlock the back door. Rather than climbing out through the window, y'know.'

'You didn't go back upstairs?'

'No. Didn't want to track too much mud into the house.' Daniela forced a smile. 'What would Dad have said, eh?'

Stephanie didn't answer.

Daniela took out her cigarettes. She didn't want another yet, but she needed something to do with her hands. Talking with police officers made her uncomfortable. Talking with her sister, doubly so. Daniela focused on the packet and tried not to think about the hidey-hole in the bedroom.

'You said Auryn had left,' Daniela said. 'She left a few days ago, you said. So, why was she here?'

Stephanie didn't answer that either.

'Hello?' someone called. 'Stephanie?'

Daniela looked up. A man had appeared at the top of the road. He was wrapped in a grey duffel coat and shapeless woollen hat, plus obligatory wellies. His young face was stamped with grief. Daniela froze.

'I got here as fast as I could,' the man said as he approached the gate. 'My bloody car got stuck. I figured since it's a four-by-four it should've been fine, but apparently not. Tilly's going to drag it out with her tractor.'

His words spilled out in a rush, as if he had to keep his lips moving or his voice would seize. He went to Stephanie and touched her arm. With anyone else he might've gone in for a hug, but he knew Stephanie better than that.

'Is it true?' he asked. 'What happened?'

Stephanie pulled away. 'You'd better come inside,' she said.

The man rubbed his face with both hands. He had to take

a stabilising breath before he could focus on Daniela. When he did so, his eyes widened. 'Daniela?'

'Hi, Leo,' Daniela said. 'I'm sorry. I didn't know you were still in Stonecrop.'

Leo McKearney tore his gaze away. 'Why is she here?' he asked Stephanie in a fierce whisper. 'Did she—?' He broke off as if afraid to say more while Daniela was in earshot.

'I just got here,' Daniela said. 'I went into the house and found Auryn.'

Leo bit his lip. Then he straightened up and, despite the redness of his eyes, assumed a professional air. 'I'd better see her,' he said.

As he waded up the path, Daniela turned to Stephanie. 'D'you think that's a good idea?' she asked quietly. 'Him and Auryn ...'

'We need a doctor to certify death,' Stephanie said. 'He's the only one in town.'

'He's a doctor?'

'Junior doctor at Dewar's Hospital in Hackett.' Stephanie fixed Daniela with a look. 'Don't move. I'll be right back.'

'Sure,' Daniela said, staring at the water again. The nub of the cigarette she'd dropped had sunk below the surface and hung suspended, turning gently in the currents Leo McKearney made as he waded past.

This was the closest Daniela had been to home in seven years, yet she'd never felt further away.

6

June 2010

'I need money.'

Daniela's father didn't look up from whatever the hell he was reading. An old newspaper, folded and refolded, the printed columns of stocks and shares marked with fingerprints and pencil scribbles. Whenever Daniela came up to the study, her dad was poring over financial papers. It was all he seemed to care about these days.

Absently, her father reached for his wallet. Daniela watched his hands as he thumbed through the notes. The hands and wallet looked like they were made of the same leather. The wallet always contained money. Once a week, her dad went into Hackett and withdrew his pension from the post office, plus anything additional he needed from his savings. Daniela didn't know how much was in the savings, but it had to be substantial, left over from when her dad had co-owned the antiques shop in Stonecrop.

Her father counted off twenty pounds and laid it on the desk. It was far more than Daniela needed but she wasn't complaining. She scooped up the notes.

'Thanks,' she muttered.

Her dad turned over the newspaper and didn't look up.

In the past twelve months, there'd been a scattering, as if a sudden wind had driven everyone from the old house, although in truth it'd started years earlier, when their mum left. When she'd walked out it was like she left the front door open, and let the cold wind in.

Over time, the atmosphere became fragile, friable. Dad refused to let them speak of their mother, until she was nothing but a ghost in their memories.

Franklyn, twenty-six years old and the eldest of the four sisters, was next to move out permanently, but her absence was less jarring, because over the years she'd become an erratic presence. Likewise, it was no surprise when Stephanie started to talk about moving out. She'd completed her probationary period with the constabulary, and was anxious to live closer to the station in Hackett. Plus, Stephanie and their father were too similar. They'd always butted heads.

The real sign of the end was when Auryn announced she was leaving. She was the easy-going one, who rarely reacted to the shouted voices in the house. If the atmosphere became too toxic, she would hide away with her books in the spare room that was now hers. She was due to leave for university at the end of the summer. They'd planned a party and everything. So, it took everyone by surprise when she said – in her quiet, non-confrontational way – that she'd be leaving early, at the end of June, now her exams were finished.

'We wanna get moved in and acclimatise to Newcastle before term starts,' was her excuse.

Stephanie said it was presumptuous, going there before the exam results were in. 'What's your back-up plan if you don't get the grades you need?' she'd asked.

Auryn had shrugged. 'We're still leaving.'

It was understandable. Moving into her own place with her boyfriend had to be better than remaining at home. But the real reason for leaving early was obvious: if the sisters stayed under the same roof much longer, they'd go crazy. There was too much bad feeling in the house.

Now Daniela faced the probability that by autumn she'd be alone with their father.

She was aware of a change; aware of the increased tension when her father was home, conscious of her sisters spending as much time as possible away from the house, but she had her own problems. For years she'd been desperate to leave Stonecrop. The perfect time to do so would've been after her A levels last year. She'd got a conditional offer for Sheffield university, so long as her results were good enough. It turned out they weren't. Then laziness or apathy had stopped her going through clearing. She'd told herself that taking a year out was a smart move. She could work, save up some money, then apply to university the following summer.

And yet, somehow she hadn't got around to that either. Summer was almost there, she'd wasted a year scratching around doing odd jobs, and she still didn't know what she wanted from her life. She only knew she didn't want to live it in Stonecrop.

It was far past time to get out. All her friends had already gone. Auryn would be the last of them. Auryn and Leo, of course.

Those were the thoughts that bounced through Daniela's

brain as she trudged along the footpath away from the old house. She was sick of having no plan. Today her father had been fine, albeit uncommunicative, but Daniela's right shoulder still tingled from the slap she hadn't quite avoided the day before. It'd been aimed at her face, the culmination of some petty argument that'd escalated out of proportion, but she was faster than her old man now, and it'd caught her a glancing blow on the tip of the shoulder instead. It shouldn't have hurt, but still she felt it, like a phantom echo.

Even on a summer day, Stonecrop was grey and sheltered, the clouds close enough to touch. The few shadows below the trees were broad and fuzzy-edged. Headache weather; like a storm that refused to break. It'd been like that for weeks. Daniela walked quickly with hands in pockets. Her leather jacket – a hand-me-down from Franklyn, which was too wide in the shoulders and always smelled like smoke – kept out the intermittent breeze.

She knew every inch of the woodlands. Whenever the atmosphere in the house became too oppressive, she'd take to the outdoors, walking for hours, crossing and recrossing her path, trying to lose herself. Sometimes she'd bring her MP3 player with her; other times she let the white noise of nature fill her head instead.

The woods enfolded the village like protective arms. To the south there was nothing but trees as far as Briarsfield, while to the north, the forest petered out into farmland, bisected by the Clynebade, which diverged around Stonecrop as if around an inconvenient stone. A break in the trees allowed a partial view to the north over low-lying fields and hedgerows. If Daniela had been minded to climb a tree, she could've seen Winterbridge Farm in the distance.

Some people found the trees eerie, especially when the light was poor, and Daniela sort of understood that. The woods were rife with half heard noises and flickering movements. But the trees were the one part of Stonecrop Daniela liked, because, if she put her head down, she could pretend her world wasn't limited to this tiny village, hemmed in by rivers. She could imagine walking in any direction for miles and seeing nothing but trees.

The path led her in a sweeping loop to the banks of the Bade. Flowering garlic perfumed the air. At this time of the year, the woods and the riverbanks were carpeted with wild garlic and fading bluebells, unfurling ferns and bramble tangles. The well-worn paths were trampled streaks of brown through the green.

In a muddy hollow beside the river stood a ruined building. It'd once been the home of a wealthy businessman, back in the early twentieth century, but was now little more than a brick shell, the rotted timbers of its first floor having collapsed, the slates of the roof missing, likely adorning the roof of some other property by now. Above the door a carved stone lintel read, Kirk Cottage.

Daniela went down the bank and circled the building. The area never drained properly and, even months after the last flood, the earth was still sodden, the mud churned by foot-prints from dog-walkers, ramblers or people looking for a fishing spot. Daniela stepped around puddles of stagnant water.

She was annoyed to find someone had replaced the broken board across the side window. She'd smashed the board herself, a few months earlier, to allow access to the interior. Not that anything was inside – more mud, more standing water, a tangle of nettles, corroded and discoloured litter – but that wasn't the point. There was precious little to do in Stonecrop, and kids made their own entertainment.

Now a new sheet of plyboard had been nailed up, along with a notice that the structure was unsafe and trespassing was forbidden.

Daniela glanced around to make sure no one was about. Then she climbed on the windowsill, gripped either side of the stone window for support, and kicked the board.

The hollow boom rolled across the river and back. Daniela drove her foot into the board several more times until the wood split.

She was breathing hard as she climbed down. She worked her fingers into the split and, with some pushing and shoving, loosened the nails on one side. With a final effort and a satisfying splintering, part of the plyboard came loose. It'd been nailed onto a wooden frame fixed inside the window, but not well enough. Daniela tossed the broken piece of wood aside.

The hole she'd made was just wide enough to let a person climb into the building. Daniela wiped her hands on her jacket. She had no interest in going into the ruin today. She just didn't want anybody keeping her out.

She left the ruined house and followed the path until she reached the Hackett road. There she hesitated. Turning left would take her into the centre of Stonecrop, where she could maybe try her luck at the Crossed Swords. The landlord liked her well enough, but his wife really didn't. Daniela had worked there for a few months the previous year, collecting glasses, but there'd been a falling out – a discrepancy in the till one night – which Daniela had got the blame for, and the landlady had never allowed her in the bar since.

If Daniela turned right at the road, she'd eventually reach the town of Hackett. The road wound between fields and crossed the River Bade via the old bridge, which hadn't been designed for anything more strenuous than horse-drawn traffic, and which had been verging on collapse for twenty years.

It was a fair distance to walk, although she'd done it before, and there might be a bus or someone she could thumb a lift off. When she got to Hackett, she could catch a train to the next town, and the next, and the next ...

With an angry shake of her head, Daniela turned left, towards Stonecrop. Who was she fooling? Several times a week she made these long, aimless walks, and fantasised about leaving forever, and every goddamn time she made an excuse not to take the first step. She could circle around and around, and sometimes look wistfully towards other places, but always she was drawn back in, like to a magnet.

The time wasn't right, of course. She was saving up money from her odd jobs, along with the hand-outs from her dad – plus anything else she came across – to raise an escape fund. The savings were squirrelled beneath the loose floor-board in her bedroom. Once she had enough money, she'd be gone.

She heard a car approaching, and crossed to the opposite side of the road so the car would see her when it rounded the corner. Daniela had lost count of how many times some idiot driving too fast along those country roads had almost wiped her out.

When a car appeared, it was indeed driving too fast, and being driven by an idiot.

The car screeched to a halt next to where Daniela had

hastily stepped onto the verge. A woman leaned out of the driver's window.

'Been looking for you all over,' Stephanie said. 'Want a lift?'

Auryn was in the passenger seat, one foot propped on the dashboard, so Daniela climbed in the back, sliding across the leather seat.

'What's going on?' Daniela asked. 'Family outing?'

Auryn flashed a grin. 'We're gonna pick up Franklyn.'

'Frankie's back? She only just left.'

'Apparently she missed us.'

Stephanie made an indelicate noise. 'I can think of a number of reasons why she's back,' she said, 'and precisely none of them are to do with missing us.'

Auryn shrugged. 'Just a suggestion. Anyways.' She twisted in her seat to face Daniela. The round glasses she'd taken to wearing made her look young and owlish. Auryn's fair hair was tidy, worn in a neat, trendy style. *The blonde mistake of the family,* she would joke. 'Apparently Franklyn came in on the bus this morning and wants to meet up. Seriously, I think she misses us.'

Daniela and Franklyn had always been close – perhaps because they were so similar in appearance and temperament – but now Franklyn had moved away from Stonecrop, the times they spent together felt strained and awkward, like they both knew they were growing apart, and neither had the ability or the inclination to prevent it.

'She'll be in trouble,' Stephanie said. 'You mark my words.'

Stephanie drove too fast through the country lanes. Her Subaru was only three years old and the interior was immaculate, but the exhaust had suffered an incident with a cattle-grid and roared like a tank when the car accelerated.

Stephanie had completed an advanced driving course for her job, which she reckoned made her a safe driver, no matter her speed. Daniela disagreed. She fastened her seatbelt and braced against the front seat.

'Where're we meeting Franklyn?' she asked.

'She's having a word with Henry McKearney,' Stephanie said. Her tone indicated her feelings.

Roughly seven years ago, the relationship between their dad and Henry McKearney had gone irreparably sour. Their dad had opted to be bought out of the antiques emporium they'd founded together. Things might've been all right if one family or the other had moved away from Stonecrop and let tempers settle, but everyone involved was way too stubborn. The Cain and McKearney families continued to coexist, relations between them becoming increasingly strained as the years went by.

Stephanie sped into the village, through the square, only slowing as they approached the junction next to the Corner Shoppe. She bumped the car onto the pavement without indicating. Auryn popped open the door.

'Are we picking up Leo as well?' Daniela asked.

Auryn's ears went pink, and she mumbled something. That was another complicating factor – Auryn had been dating Leo McKearney for almost a year. Everyone had realised they were serious when they applied to the same university and made plans to move in together. In idle moments, Daniela wondered what Henry thought about that. She knew her own thoughts well enough.

Daniela followed Auryn out of the car and across the street. The antiques shop was bolted onto the Corner Shoppe, which the McKearney family also owned, and to the house at the back where the McKearney family lived. It was a wide, low-slung shop, a holdover of Seventies' architecture, with broad windows and a constant air of neglect. When Henry took sole ownership, he renovated the façade and commissioned a posh new painted board above the front windows, reading McKearney Antiques. But since then the woodwork had faded and never been repainted. Daniela didn't know how the place ever turned a profit, since she rarely saw any customers. At a cursory glance it looked like it'd shut down months ago. The *Open* sign was dusty.

The Corner Shoppe next door was run by Henry's wife Margaret and was therefore in a much better state. Daniela had heard village gossip that the difficulties between Henry and Margaret didn't just extend to their businesses.

Auryn shouldered the already-open door to the antiques shop wider and stepped inside, Daniela following after her.

The interior smelled of wood polish and air fresheners, intended to disguise the lingering odour of stale tobacco. To Daniela, it was so familiar it always gave her a jolt. As a kid, back when their dad had co-owned the shop, she had spent hours in the overcrowded maze of wardrobes and bookcases, burrowing beneath desks and climbing in and out of cupboards, until either Dad or 'Uncle' Henry got sick of her scuffling presence and sent her outside to play. Now, with so much residual bitterness between the two families, Daniela hated the stink of the place.

Although the stock sometimes changed, the feel of the shop remained the same. Henry had made a big deal of getting rid of the 'ugly, unfashionable' stock and replacing it with 'proper antiques', but it was a cosmetic change at best. Its rotten heart was unaltered. Daniela dragged her fingers over the bubbled veneer of a Georgian dining table. Unpleasant memories over-laid every surface, heavy as the greasy sheen of beeswax. She shoved her hands into her pockets.

Near the front, Leo McKearney was perched on a side table, reading a paperback. He was lucky enough to have inherited his mother's looks, although his hair was the same brick-red as Henry's. A smile brightened his face as he spotted Auryn. He waved at Daniela; a friendly, everyday wave, not nearly so full of meaning as his smile.

Daniela felt a tug at her insides and let herself imagine the smile was for her.

The more time Daniela spent in Leo's company – and it was difficult to do otherwise, since Leo and Auryn were joined at the hip – the more aware she became of him. What had started off as curiosity on Daniela's part had grown over the years to a weird, unrequited longing. She noticed things about him: the way his hair curled around his ears, the dusting of freckles across his nose, the fleck of brown in his green eyes.

She'd long ago convinced herself she was in love with him.

And *that* was why Daniela dropped her gaze. She was certain Auryn must've noticed her infatuation.

Leo put down his book to give Auryn a quick, one-armed hug. He smiled at Daniela over Auryn's shoulder. 'Hey, Daniela.' He sang her name – *Dan-ee-el-laaa* – like he'd done since they were little kids. It gave her a warm feeling every time he did it. No one else bothered with her full name. And it was cute, because Auryn was the one with the pretty, lyrical name, which their mother had insisted on after their dad had named the first three girls after his distant relatives. Daniela liked how Leo made her name pretty too.

'Everything okay?' Auryn asked.

58

Leo's smile scrunched up. 'They're arguing. Can we go? I'd rather not hang around to listen.'

Daniela was already moving off through the furniture maze. A murmur of voices filtered from the back of the shop. Henry's was harsh from years of chain-smoking, edged with a London accent. She recognised the opposing notes of her sister Franklyn's lighter tone, which always sounded like she was mocking you, even when she wasn't.

'Should I get Steph?' Auryn asked.

As if in response, something heavy crashed to the floor at the other end of the shop. Daniela sped up. The layout of the shop meant she could hear Franklyn and Henry but couldn't see them yet.

'It's only money!' she heard Franklyn shout. 'You want to lose everything for this?'

Another crash, which sounded like a chair going over. 'You owe me,' Henry said. 'After everything I've done for your family—'

Daniela at last found her way around a bulky Welsh dresser that blocked the direct route to the cleared area at the back of the shop that doubled as Henry's office. A huge polished rosewood desk the colour of venous blood took up most of the space, with a wicker chair wedged behind it. The desk and two nearby tables were submerged below a sea of paperwork. At the back of the room, the fire exit was propped open with a metal urn, allowing a sluggish breeze to flow in from the walled courtyard behind the building.

Franklyn had been sat in a ladder-backed chair, which she'd knocked over as she stood up too fast. A box of papers had fallen from the desk, but it was unclear who'd done that. Franklyn was thin and wiry like Daniela, with a fringe of black hair that was always in her eyes. Henry was six inches taller and at least five stone heavier. His shirt didn't fit well, the material stretched and strained across his chest. His reddish hair was combed flat.

'Hey ...' Daniela said.

When he saw her, Henry smiled and shook his head. 'How come you invited these guys?' he asked Franklyn. 'I thought you wanted to keep this private.'

Franklyn took a moment to shove her temper back into whatever compartment she usually stored it in. To Daniela she said, 'I'll be done in a minute, Dani. Just wait for me outside, yeah?'

Daniela looked from her to Henry. 'What's going on?'

'Nothing. Nothing.'

'How about you tell her?' Henry suggested with a smile.

'Is that really what you want?' Franklyn asked. 'Seriously, I would've thought you've got more to lose than me right now.'

Henry settled down into a chair and rested his arm on the rosewood desk. He was still smiling, like he was entertained by Franklyn's words. Daniela had learned at a young age that Henry had a pretty good poker face, but all his tells were in his hands. She glanced at his fingers. The table was littered with papers and boxes and trinkets from the shop. Not far from Henry's hand was a stack of post and a knife he'd been using to open the envelopes.

'This isn't a great reflection of your character,' Henry said. 'Coming in here to threaten me. I'm sure your little sister doesn't want to see that.'

Daniela couldn't look away from the knife on the table. It was a flick-knife, a patina of age across the opened blade. On the handle was an inlaid design in the shape of a snake, black on red. It looked like part of the stock from the antiques shop. The handle was less than two inches from Henry's hand.

'Frankie, maybe we should go,' Daniela said, nervous.

'Listen to your sister,' Henry suggested. 'It's good to hear someone in your family talk sense. That's been sorely lacking since your dear mother walked out.'

Franklyn took a couple of steps towards Henry. Wherever she'd put her anger, it hadn't been boxed away securely, because the colour rose back to her face. 'Listen—' she said.

Henry started to his feet. His hand moved over the knife.

Darting forwards, Daniela snatched up a double-handful of papers from the desk and flung them at Henry's face. He flinched in surprise. At the same moment, Franklyn made a grab for him.

Everything happened too fast after that. Daniela lunged for the knife. She succeeded in knocking it off the table, but lost her balance and stumbled. Someone shoved her to get her away – either Henry or Franklyn, she couldn't be sure – and she fell, striking her chin on the table on the way down.

For a second, Daniela lay dazed on the rough carpet. Feet scuffled next to her head. The papers she'd thrown were still fluttering to the ground.

Someone yelled, 'Stop it! What're you doing?'

Leo had run into the shop, with Auryn right behind him, and behind *her*, Stephanie.

Stephanie pushed to the front. She got both hands on Franklyn's shoulders and yanked her away like a dog on a leash.

'All right, what the hell's going on?' Stephanie demanded. 'Franklyn, cut it out.'

Franklyn lifted her hands contritely. 'Sorry, sorry,' she said, with a shrug that implied she wasn't doing anything worth shouting about.

Stephanie shoved Franklyn away, not gently.

Daniela was still on the floor, dazed, unwilling to get up. Her hands shook from the brief confrontation, and there was a dull ache where she'd banged her chin. It took her several moments to work out why her mouth tasted coppery. Her tongue probed a split on the inside of her cheek.

Light glinted off something metal nearby. The flick-knife, which had bounced under the table after Daniela knocked it off the top. Careful to keep her movements hidden, Daniela closed her hand around it.

'It's my fault,' Franklyn told Stephanie. 'We were just having a discussion. Here, let me help you up.' She reached down to grab Daniela's hand.

Stephanie didn't look even slightly convinced. 'What were you discussing?'

'Just passing the time of day. Daniela tripped and fell, right?'

Henry smirked. 'Tripped right over her own feet.'

Daniela felt heat flush her cheeks. She let Franklyn haul her upright. Her head swam. She stayed half-turned away so no one would see she'd picked up the flick-knife. The handle felt warm.

Leo had pushed past so he was between Stephanie and Henry. 'Franklyn started it,' he said. 'You all heard her shouting at my dad.'

'That's not what I heard,' Stephanie said.

Franklyn laughed. But whatever comment she was planning to make, Stephanie silenced her with a glare.

'Go wait in the car, Franklyn,' she said. 'You too, Dani.'

Daniela hesitated. It rankled that no one had bothered to check whether she was hurt, or to get her side of the story. Her fingers tightened around the knife.

'C'mon, kid,' Franklyn said, taking hold of Daniela's elbow. 'Let's give the grown-ups some space.'

Making her expression neutral, Daniela nodded, while she slipped the knife into the sleeve of her jacket, hidden.

7

By the time they reached the car, Franklyn had shrugged off her temper. She kept her head up as she crossed the road.

'You okay?' Daniela asked.

Franklyn gave a tight smile. 'Sure. Why the hell not?' She leaned against the bonnet of Stephanie's car to light a cigarette.

The door of the antiques shop opened and Auryn came out with Leo. She kept wiping her eyes with her fingertips. Leo pushed her away when she tried to touch his arm.

'You don't get it,' Leo was saying. 'Dad's mad at your stupid sister right now, but by tonight he'll take it out on me, or Mum. We're the ones who'll get the fallout.'

'So, come stay at our house,' Auryn suggested.

'That's not going to help Mum, is it?' Leo chewed his lip as he glanced at the open door of the corner shop. 'I better warn her.'

'I'll come with you.'

'It's probably best if you stay away.' Leo softened his words with a sad smile. 'I'll call you later, okay?'

He walked off, leaving Auryn standing helpless in the middle of the road, still blinking back tears.

Daniela loitered by the car. She'd removed the knife from

her sleeve and tucked it into the breast pocket of her jacket, blade folded. It was heavy and warm. Unnerving. Daniela wasn't even sure why she'd taken it, except that she didn't like the idea of Henry having it. He'd definitely been reaching for it during the argument – hadn't he? The whole confrontation had taken less than thirty seconds. It'd left her dizzy and sick, and not just from the bang on her chin.

Auryn rubbed the back of her neck. 'Not that we aren't glad to see you and all, Franklyn,' she said, 'but did you come home just to pick a fight?'

'I'm hurt that you'd suggest that.' Franklyn didn't deny it though.

A minute later Stephanie appeared. Daniela flinched. Stephanie looked so much like their father when she was angry.

'What did you think you were doing, Franklyn?' she asked.

'Nothing.' Franklyn blew out smoke. 'Having a discussion. That's what Henry said too, right?'

'How did you guess?'

'Thought so. Are you planning to be heavy-handed about this?'

'In what way? You mean like reporting you both?'

'Yeah. That.'

Stephanie opened the driver's door. 'Get in the car.'

Franklyn winked at Dani. 'That's what this family's good at,' she said. 'Bending the rules.'

'You don't even know what the rules are.' Stephanie got into the car and slammed the door.

Franklyn climbed into the passenger seat. Stephanie was already revving the engine as Daniela took the back seat.

Auryn hesitated a moment more, unsure whether to go after Leo, then joined them.

Stephanie bumped down from the kerb with more force than necessary. Daniela glanced back. Through the dusty windows of the antiques store, Henry was watching them. He was on the phone.

'Okay,' Auryn said, breaking the tense silence. 'What happened, Frankie?'

Franklyn shrugged. She'd rolled down the window to let her cigarette smoke escape. The breeze tousled her dark hair. 'It was a misunderstanding,' she said.

'Isn't it always?' Stephanie commented.

Franklyn laughed. She sank down in the seat, shoulders low, as if she wanted to hide from the world. She'd always been like that, Daniela realised. Folded inwards so no one would guess what she concealed. Her jacket smelled of smoke and diesel fumes.

'Believe it or not, I had no intention of getting into an argument,' Franklyn said. 'I came home to see my loving family. But I figured you all might have better things to do on a sunny Saturday, so I called on Henry about some business.'

'What kind of business?'

'The private kind.' Franklyn flashed a smile to take the edge off her words. 'Nothing worth getting riled about. Henry takes things so seriously.'

Daniela remembered the partial conversation she'd overheard. It'd sounded like Franklyn owed Henry money ... but why? If Franklyn needed cash, Dad would always put his hand in his pocket.

Daniela asked, 'Where're we going?' Stephanie had spun

the car around the one-way system so they were headed towards Hackett.

'We're taking Franklyn back to the train station,' Stephanie said.

'She just got here.'

'And look how much excitement she's caused already.' Stephanie met Daniela's gaze in the rear-view mirror. 'We'll do the family reunion some other time.'

'Actually,' Franklyn said, 'I quite want to come home. Today's not working out like I'd hoped. It'd be nice to chill for a bit, rather than rushing back to Birmingham.'

Stephanie took her eyes off the road long enough to look at her. 'Is that a good idea?'

'Hey, don't make me pull rank. I'm the oldest; my word is still law.'

Stephanie's voice was tense as she shrugged and said, 'Whatever you say.'

'Cool.' Franklyn went back to staring out of the window. 'Be nice to spend a night in the old house again. No feeling like coming home, huh?'

8

Regardless of circumstances, it felt like a celebration whenever the four sisters were together. Even though their father had retired to his study with the door firmly closed, and nothing could fully dispel the chill absence of their mother, for a short time the house felt full again. It echoed with voices and laughter and movement, and the family could pretend nothing was wrong.

It'd been a while since all four of them had hung out. A longer while since they'd been together without arguing. Franklyn brought a slab of beer in from the garage, placing half the cans in the fridge to cool. Auryn opened a bottle of wine. After some cajoling, they even persuaded Stephanie to have a drink.

Nobody mentioned the altercation between Franklyn and Henry. It wasn't the first time Franklyn had got into trouble, and nobody thought it'd be the last. By nature, she rubbed people the wrong way. Her school record had been a history of near-disasters.

Now she was at ease, sprawled in a chair with one leg thrown over the arm, a can of beer in one hand and an unlit cigarette in the other. Their father didn't mind them drinking or making noise, but drew the line at smoking in the house.

'Hey,' Auryn said, settling on the sofa, 'I meant to ask, Franklyn. Are you really going back to university?'

Franklyn gave a careful shrug. 'News travels fast, doesn't it?'

Guilt needled Daniela. She hadn't been sworn to secrecy, but still ...

'So, is it true?' Auryn pressed. 'Or is *someone* spreading mad rumours?'

'I've not decided,' Franklyn said. Her tone was more serious than Daniela had heard in years. 'But yeah, it's something to think about.'

'Finishing that business course, are you?' Stephanie asked.

'Nah. I'm looking at theology.'

Stephanie raised her eyebrows. 'That's a career departure,' she said. Unlike the others, she'd remained standing, as if even when relaxing she couldn't lose the stiffness her job had hammered into her. A certain tightness marked her eyes. Nothing escaped her notice. It felt like Stephanie was always poised to spring into action at the first sign of anything improper. In a different life she could've been a superhero.

The idea made Daniela snort into her drink.

'Maybe it's time for a career,' Franklyn said. 'A proper career, I mean. No more bouncing from one rubbish job to the next. And let's face it, I was never cut out for the business world. That's for people like him upstairs, isn't it?' She smiled, but the twist to her lips made it ugly. 'I thought you'd approve. Really, I'm just copying. You've got the nice, stable, *legal* career. What's wrong with us wanting the same?'

Stephanie chuckled but said nothing. Daniela looked away, irrationally annoyed that everyone except her was progressing with their lives.

'What would you do with a theology degree?' Auryn asked. 'I mean, what *can* you do? Apart from becoming a lecturer or a vicar.'

It was difficult to imagine Franklyn doing either of those. Difficult enough to picture her knuckling down to complete a university course. Franklyn had always been moody and solitary, without close friends, more content to be off on her own than hanging around at home. She'd also been closest to their mother. Being the eldest meant she'd known their mother the longest, and remembered when there'd been more smiles than silences. Franklyn was the one who'd tried hardest to make her stay. She'd encouraged their mother to make outings, to drive into Briarsfield or take the bus in a long circular journey out along the valleys and back again. Franklyn had kept up the Sunday trips to church with her long after the others lost interest.

And yet nothing Franklyn did was enough to make her stay.

One of Daniela's clearest memories was of a fight she hadn't been meant to witness. Aged twelve, Daniela had watched, through a crack in the door, as her father berated their mother in that whip-tongue voice until she'd pulled off the eternity rings he'd given her and flung them at him. Daniela had barely had time to get clear of the door as her mother strode out. Two days later, their mother had packed her bags, leaving Daniela with a clearer memory of her hands than her face.

She thought of the sort-of funeral they'd held, out on the fishing platform above the swollen river. None of them had spoken of it again. But a few weeks later, Daniela went back to the garage to look through their mother's remaining possessions.

At that time, she'd noticed other items conspicuously missing. Everything of value, like the jewellery, had gone. As had the crucifix from the hallway, the one with the sad Jesus, which was no longer hidden under the pile of magazines.

Franklyn didn't answer Auryn's question straight away. She turned the beer can with her thin fingers. 'It's not something that's come out of nowhere,' she said at last. 'Wanting to change ... wanting something different. It probably feels like I'm springing this on you, but it's always been in my head. I want something different. I want to *do* something. This week was ...' She stopped. 'Anyway, I came home to clear my head. And to get some support.' She flashed a grin. 'That's what we're here for, right? To look out for each other. I bet Auryn hasn't been getting hassled over her academic choices.'

Auryn's ears went pink. She hated to admit how well she'd done at school. Everyone in the family knew she was the bright one – the one with the high-flying career ahead. From a young age she'd known what she wanted to do with her life. Daniela envied that, a lot.

Stephanie was envious as well, Daniela knew, because although Stephanie had her own career – one she insisted she loved – she'd fallen into it more or less by accident, recruited straight from high school. Someone had to keep the peace in the household, and Stephanie was the only one capable. Policing had been the logical, inevitable choice. A concrete way to enforce the rules of the house.

But Auryn was still the smartest, with the best qualifications and the pick of universities.

Daniela had never considered Franklyn might be jealous too.

'I don't blame you for wanting to get away,' Franklyn added

to Auryn. 'Get out, see the world. It'll be good for you. And Leo.'

Auryn nodded. 'I think he's more anxious than me to get away.'

'No surprise. If Henry McKearney was my dad, I wouldn't stick around either.' Franklyn made little dents in the beer can with her fingertips. 'If he's smart, he'll hang on to you.'

Auryn frowned. 'What d'you mean by that?'

'He's not got much to look forward to here, has he? If he can escape Stonecrop and tough it out at university, he's smart enough to go far. But studying medicine is a long hard slog. He'll need support.'

'You mean financially.' A hard edge crept into Auryn's voice. 'You think he's only staying with me because our family's got money.'

'I never said that.'

'You're thinking it pretty loudly.'

Franklyn drained her beer. 'No, I'm not. You and Leo need to support each other. That's all I mean. It's a big, scary, horrid world out there. Even if it *is* better than this fucking place.'

Stephanie raised her eyebrows. 'That's some fine language. Are you sure you're cut out to be a vicar?'

Franklyn laughed and threw the empty can at her, and the tension in the room dissipated for a while.

9

Daniela went to the kitchen for another beer. Although she tried to keep pace with the others, she was still a lightweight, and if she didn't moderate her intake, she'd be asleep in an hour. She was already pleasantly warm around the ears.

The kitchen was a large square that jutted from the rear of the house. Whoever designed the house had included a picture window, even though the kitchen faced nothing more interesting than trees and mud, and didn't get the sun at any time of year. A rustic wooden table with matching chairs took up the centre of the room.

Daniela dropped the empty can into the recycling bin and opened the fridge. Apart from the large quantity of beer on the bottom shelf, the fridge was all but empty. Daniela's stomach rumbled. She'd neglected to eat since lunch. She should've picked something up from the shop, but her mind had been elsewhere.

She still wondered what Franklyn and Henry had been arguing about.

A soft step alerted her to Auryn coming into the kitchen. 'I'm putting the kettle on,' Auryn said, stifling a yawn. 'I need coffee or I'll fall asleep. Is there anything to eat?'

'There might be crisps.'

Together they rifled the cupboards and came up with a few packets of crisps and some chocolate biscuits. It was hardly a fitting meal for the four of them. Auryn tipped the crisps into bowls to take through to the front room.

'Just leave them in the packets,' Daniela said. 'Why make the extra washing-up?'

'You people are savages. Eat food off plates like normal people.'

'Crisps barely count as food.' Daniela stole a salt-and-vinegar crisp. 'Is Leo okay? Has he called?'

'Not yet. I phoned earlier but he said he couldn't talk and he'd call me back.' Auryn arranged biscuits on a plate. Daniela didn't mock her this time. 'I wish he'd speak to me. About his family, I mean. On other stuff I have to fight to shut him up, but as soon as anyone mentions his parents ...'

'Is he still getting grief about going to uni?'

'I think so. His dad's always said he wants Leo to take over the shop from him eventually. But Leo won't talk about it.' Auryn lowered her voice. 'Don't tell him I said anything, obviously, but he's pretty stressed. It's not just being away from home, or what his dad thinks about it. He's worried how we're gonna afford everything.'

'What's he worried for? Our dad will cover it.'

'I know, but ... he doesn't like relying on someone. He knows what people think of him. What Franklyn was saying ... he *knows*, Dani. It bugs the hell out of him. Leo wants to cover his own bills. At least that way he'll know no one's talking behind his back.'

The bitterness in Auryn's tone was so unexpected Daniela dropped the subject.

Auryn asked, 'So, what the heck was going on with Henry?'

Daniela glanced towards the kitchen door. The murmur of voices was audible from the front room. 'Search me,' she said. 'Franklyn and him were arguing when I got there.'

'What was Franklyn saying?'

'I didn't hear.' Daniela shrugged. 'It could've been anything. Those two have always had a personality clash.'

A pause, then Auryn said, 'What did you take from the shop?'

'What?'

'You put something in your sleeve as you were going out.'

Daniela winced. She'd thought Auryn had missed that. 'Yeah,' she admitted.

'What was it?'

Talking to Auryn felt safer than talking to the others. Growing up, she and Auryn had shared everything. There'd been no secrets between them. So, after only a brief hesitation, Daniela said, 'Let me show you.'

She fetched her jacket from where it was hanging in the hallway and brought it into the kitchen. The weight of the knife was a heaviness she'd felt all afternoon as she carried it around. She shook the knife out of the pocket into her hand.

Auryn's eyes went wide. 'Dani, what—?'

'It was on Henry's desk. I thought ... I dunno, I thought maybe he was reaching for it during the argument.' Looking back, Daniela was no longer certain of that.

Auryn blinked several times as if trying to process this. 'You think he would've hurt Franklyn?'

Daniela didn't want to think about that. 'No. No, it was just a dumb argument. He's all mouth, you know that.' She shoved the knife back into its pocket and folded her jacket onto the kitchen table.

'Are you sure?' Auryn didn't look convinced at all. 'There's always been rumours about him. And what happened with Mum ...'

'Mum left,' Daniela said shortly. 'No mystery about it. Anyway, you can't listen to rumours. Literally you can't, if you're planning on being a lawyer. Isn't there a whole bit about not prejudging your clients?'

'Don't take the piss,' Auryn said, without malice. She spooned instant coffee into a cup. 'You know what I mean. There's always been something ... *off* about him. *You* wouldn't mess with him.'

'Me? God, no. But this is Franklyn. She can look after herself, can't she?'

'I don't know.' Auryn watched the kettle come to the boil. 'She's changed since she went away. In a good way, maybe.'

That was true. There'd always been a hardness, a tension about Franklyn, all through childhood, as if at any moment she might fly off the handle. But since she'd left home, the edge had gone from her temper. In every other way she was the same – the quick smile, the easy-going speech – but there was no longer something darker concealed beneath. She seemed ... at peace. No, that was the wrong word. She'd found an internal balance. The fight with Henry seemed suddenly out of character, a relapse to worse times.

It troubled Daniela that things were changing, even though change was what she craved. She felt like someone had nudged a boulder at the top of a steep slope, just enough to start it rolling, but no one was sure how far it might fall or who it would crush.

'Why'd you take the knife?' Auryn asked.

Daniela clucked her tongue. 'Man, you're as bad as Steph sometimes.'

'Thanks a bunch. So, why?'

Daniela thought before answering. 'I just wanted to get it out of Henry's hands. Even if he wasn't planning to use it. I didn't want anyone being tempted to grab it.'

'Why not give it to Steph straight away?'

'Because ... I don't know. The argument wasn't a big deal. Just a scuffle and some shouting. I over-reacted and panicked a bit.' She sighed. 'But if I tell Steph I grabbed a knife in the middle of it—'

'She'll listen if you explain.'

'Maybe. I mean, she'll bend the rules for us, but you never know for sure how she'll react.'

Auryn grunted in agreement. 'It was bad enough when she'd tell Dad on us. Now she can throw us in the cells for the night.'

Daniela chuckled. 'It'd be funny to see her try.'

'Possibly. So, what'll you do with it?'

Daniela hadn't thought that far. 'I'll get rid of it,' she heard herself say. 'I'll get up early and throw it in the river.'

'Good plan.' Auryn relaxed.

In the calm atmosphere of the evening, with the four of them in the same room for what would prove to be the last time, Daniela fully intended to keep her promise and get rid of the knife.

10

February 2017

Daniela hadn't planned to go anywhere, until her sister told her to stay. As soon as Stephanie was out of sight, Daniela pushed herself to her feet. The water compressed her boots like cold hands gripping her ankles. She waded up the road away from the old house.

Seeing Leo again had been an additional kick to the stomach. Daniela hadn't considered he might be in Stonecrop. As far as she was aware, from second-hand reports in Franklyn's letters, Auryn and Leo's relationship had ended shortly after they left for university together. Daniela was glad Leo had become a doctor like he'd intended, and landed a placement at Dewar's Hospital, but she would've liked time to brace herself before seeing him.

What does it matter? Auryn's dead.

In comparison to that inescapable fact, her own complaints were petty and weak.

Halfway back to the village, she passed the farmer in her tractor again, attaching a rope to the rear of a green Land Rover that had two wheels in the ditch. Daniela offered a hand but the farmer waved it away.

'It's all right, lass,' the farmer said. 'I've plenty of experience with this. Really, I should be charging. How much do the RAC cost for a call-out? Sixty quid? Aye, that'll cover it.' She laughed.

Daniela left her to it and walked the rest of the way into Stonecrop.

By then, the overcast sky was darkening towards nightfall. The sun had stayed hidden all day. Daniela suspected the village wouldn't see sunshine until summer. It was a depressing thought.

A tremor ran through her hands. She wasn't aware of it until she took out her cigarettes and fumbled the packet. It plopped into the water.

'Shit!'

Of course, the lid was open enough to let water in, and her cigarettes got soaked even though she snatched them up at once. She cursed several more times. Maybe Chris would let her dry them by the fire at the pub ...

Daniela looked up. She was back in the main street now. A light shone in the cluttered window of the Corner Shoppe. Daniela almost smiled. Margaret McKearney – of course she would've kept the shop open, no matter what the world threw at her.

The sandbags around the door were stacked in a neat, efficient manner, and successfully held the six inches of flood-water on the street at bay. Daniela stepped over the bags and pushed open the door. The bell tinkled.

The smell of the shop produced a much stronger wave of memory than she'd felt in the old house. If anyone had asked her to describe the Shoppe, she wouldn't have recalled anything concrete. But now it came back in a rush. The ordi-nary, everyday rows of newspaper racks, the plastic vegetable crates, the jars of sweets, the cigarettes and rolling papers behind the counter. A hundred stupid, irrelevant memories. The only change was the mostly empty shelves. No fresh produce, no bread, no newspapers. It gave the place a vaguely apocalyptic air.

At the sound of the bell, Margaret came out of the back room, wiping her hands on her blouse hem. It'd always confounded Daniela how Margaret, with her bright smile and sunny demeanour, could've married Henry McKearney. Either she was the most easy-going person in the world, or the smiles and laughter were a front. Daniela had been too self-absorbed to find out.

Margaret looked well. She'd lost the weight she'd always talked about losing, her hair was cut in an attractive bob, and her clothes suited her much better than anything Daniela remembered her wearing. In fact, Daniela realised Margaret wasn't that old. Certainly not as old as memory led her to believe. An unexpected warmth rose to Daniela's cheeks.

'What can I get you, love?' Margaret asked, before she saw who it was. Her expression did something complicated. At last the smile returned, but it was wary and brittle, as if the slightest thing could shatter it. 'Oh. Hello, stranger.'

'Hello, Mrs McKearney,' Daniela said, and she was an awkward teenager again, incapable of explaining her actions or appearance.

Margaret sized her up. 'Look at you,' she said. 'You've done a lot of growing, haven't you?' Some of the brittleness left her smile. 'But don't think just because you're bigger than me I won't be watching you. If I catch you with your hands in the sweetie jars, I'll have your fingers off.'

'Yes, ma'am.' Daniela made a show of looking contrite, with

just the right amount of hurt innocence, like she would never dream of filching sweets. But she couldn't hide her relief. Until she'd walked into the shop, she hadn't properly considered how Margaret might react. After everything that'd happened seven years ago, Margaret had every reason to hate her.

But, although Margaret held herself very stiff, with hands clasped on the counter, chin raised, her gaze contained no malice. 'So, what brings you here?' she asked.

'I—' Daniela realised she didn't want to ask for cigarettes, then immediately felt stupid. She wasn't a kid anymore. She could buy anything she wanted. 'I dropped my fags in the water. Can I get some more please?'

Margaret laughed. She had a gentle laugh, warm and genuine. 'You came all the way home for cigarettes? My, that's dedication.'

Daniela smiled. 'No. No, I came to see Steph. The fags are just, well ...'

'Another senseless victim of this watery disaster.' Margaret *tsk*-ed, then turned to open the tobacco display. 'What's your particular poison, hon?' Then, before Daniela could answer: 'How's your family anyway? I see Steph all the time, big-lass-around-town that she is, but I hardly hear a peep out of Auryn. How's she getting on?'

'She's ...' A lump rose in Daniela's throat, choking her words. Tears blurred her vision.

It hit her all at once. Auryn was dead. Really, forever dead. Not one of their games, not some awful morbid joke, just gone forever. How was that possible? How could her sister just be *gone*? It was like someone had reached into Daniela and torn out a piece of her being.

She put a hand on a magazine rack to steady herself. Her

legs felt like they might buckle. A sob built in her throat and threatened to choke her.

Margaret came around the counter towards her. 'Hey, love, what's wrong? What's happened?'

Wordlessly Daniela pushed away from her. She ran out of the shop. The bell tinkled. She almost tripped over the sandbags.

Out on the street, she sucked in a deep breath. Her heart felt like a solid mass in her chest, suffocating her.

She stumbled away. Behind her, the bell jangled again as Margaret stepped into the doorway. She called after her but Daniela didn't stop or look back.

11

Hunched in front of the fireplace at the Crossed Swords, Daniela stared into the flames. Her mind ached from the stress of the day.

She'd very nearly walked past the pub, out of town, and back along the Hackett road. If she'd done that, maybe she could've got across the bridge and made it back into Hackett not long after nightfall. But the cold that was seeping up from her wet jeans and socks, and the trembling in her arms and legs that wouldn't subside, made her hesitate. She went into the pub and plonked herself by the fire as if that might stop her from shaking.

Chris Roberts saw her expression as soon as she walked in. He left her in peace for ten minutes before coming over to ask if she was okay.

'I'm fine,' Daniela lied, wiping her eyes on her sleeve. 'Is it all right if I ... if I just sit here for a while, please?'

'Go right ahead, kiddo. Can I get you a drink?'

Daniela shook her head. She definitely wanted a drink but she was aware of how little money was left in her pocket. If she started drinking now, she'd never stop.

Chris went back behind the bar, left it another ten minutes, then brought over a cup of coffee.

'This one's a mispour,' he said. 'Still can't figure out all the buttons on that machine. You want it?'

His kindness almost started Daniela crying again. She accepted the coffee gratefully.

She didn't intend to sit there for long. All she wanted was a short while to let the turmoil in her head settle, like ashes drifting to the ground. But once she was sat with her hot coffee and the warmth of the fire on her face, she was unable or unwilling to move. She stared, almost motionless, for a least an hour. Images flickered through her brain. She wasn't thinking, just replaying events, feeling the little jump of shock every time she remembered Auryn was gone.

On the back of her chair she had hung her jacket. Daniela was aware of the object in the inside pocket, resting against her back. The knife she'd taken from beneath the floorboards of the old house. Lying there alongside the package she'd found.

Whose was it? Auryn's? There was no telling how long it had lain hidden. Realistically, anyone with access to the house could've put it there. It seemed unlikely it would've been Stephanie ... and as far as Daniela knew, Franklyn hadn't been back home in years. Could it have even been Dad who'd left it? She kinda hoped that it was.

But, in her heart, she worried it was Auryn's.

Daniela barely knew Auryn now. They hadn't spoken for seven years. But she knew some of Auryn's demons. She knew what haunted her. And Daniela knew Auryn had tried to smother those demons by working too hard and drinking too much, just like their dad.

Initially, Daniela had assumed it must've been illness or

neglect that killed Auryn. Auryn hadn't been taking care of herself; that was obvious. Shutting herself away, drinking, letting the house flood ... it wasn't surprising she could've got sick. A chest infection that, untreated, had blossomed into pneumonia, making her sicker and sicker until she'd been too weak to leave the house. The phone was disconnected. She'd collapsed, and been unable to call for help. People would tut and shake their heads and say how fucking tragic it was – tragic but inevitable. Daniela felt a stirring of anger inside her at the thought of how people in Stonecrop would gossip about this.

But then the package. The questions it raised. Where had the money come from? What was it for? Why was it hidden? And Daniela had started wondering if Auryn's problems were greater than she'd realised. What if, for example, alcoholism had twisted into drug abuse?

For the first time in years, Daniela wished she could talk to her mother. She would've—

Daniela crushed the thought. She couldn't think about her mother just then.

When Daniela was younger, she'd never questioned why their mother left. All too well Daniela understood the need to escape. She'd inherited their mother's dark hair, narrow shoulders, and constant need to know where the exits were. It was only years later that Daniela started to ask the questions she should've asked a long time ago. To wonder if maybe Auryn had been right, and there was more to the story than she'd known.

Daniela glanced up at the clock on the wall. Four o'clock. In another half hour or so it would be dark enough for her to make a move. She intended to head towards Hackett but then double back through the woods to the old house. The cover of night would hopefully hide her movements.

She felt a momentary guilt at leaving Stephanie to deal with Auryn's death alone. But Daniela's natural instinct, whenever anything went wrong, was to run. Put some distance between herself and whatever was broken – usually because she'd done the breaking, but also because she couldn't cope. Other people dealt. Dani Cain ran.

'I thought maybe you'd skipped town already,' Stephanie said from behind her.

Daniela hadn't heard her approach. It was unnerving that Stephanie had appeared at that exact moment, as if summoned by Daniela thinking about her.

Daniela kept her gaze on the fire and pretended she hadn't been about to pick up her boots. 'Chris told you I was here, right?'

'Margaret McKearney. Phoned me to say you were upset and wanted to know why.' Stephanie pulled a chair closer to the fire and sat down. 'Chris is the nearest thing to a soul of discretion around here – you should know that by now. He wouldn't call anyone unless his own feet were on fire.'

Daniela rubbed the side of her face. 'What d'you want, Steph?'

'Honestly? I want to be somewhere else right now. On a beach, maybe. There was this beach in Malta I found on holiday once. I'm sure every local there knows about it, but on that particular day, I was alone for seven hours. Waves and stones and me, that was it.'

Daniela raised her head and looked at her sister properly. Had she ever heard Stephanie speak like that? 'You went abroad? On your own?'

'You reckon I've stayed in Stonecrop for the whole seven

years you've been away? No time off, no recreation, nothing but my job?'

Daniela laughed under her breath. 'Yeah, pretty much. I figured you maybe plugged yourself into a wall socket to recharge every now and again, but that's it.'

Stephanie gazed out of the window at the gathering dark. Daniela sneaked glances at her. For the first time Daniela could remember, Stephanie looked exhausted. Her eyes were red. Daniela felt a pang of sympathy.

'Can we go over what you saw at the house?' Stephanie asked.

'See what I mean?' Daniela smiled. 'Even now, you can't shut down and be off duty.'

'You'll have to make a statement sooner or later. It'll help if you talk things out with me beforehand.' Stephanie leaned forwards, hands held out to the warmth of the flames. 'So, what made you go to the house?'

'I wanted to see it. Seven years is a long time and ... a lot's changed since then. Plus, honestly, I didn't entirely believe what you'd said about the old place.' She laughed quietly and shook her head. 'I thought maybe it'd been sold and you were just feeding me a line to get rid of me.'

'Why did you go inside?'

Daniela stretched her feet and wiggled her toes. Her socks had dried at last, although they'd gone a little crunchy from the muddy water. Lovely.

'Here's a better question,' Daniela said. 'Why haven't *you* been in there? You told me Auryn left town days ago – which we now know is a lie – and at some point in the last two days the place flooded. Why the hell weren't you keeping a better eye on it?'

'Auryn did leave. I drove her to the train station myself.'

So why did she come back?

'Put yourself in my shoes,' Daniela said. 'You tromp all the way back home and find your house is flooded because apparently your big sister is too busy sandbagging the rest of the town to keep tabs on her own family. What do you do? Do you, perhaps, go into said house to find out exactly how much damage has been done already?'

Stephanie rubbed her hands, one then the other. Her expression had closed up again. 'I don't want you to leave Stonecrop until you've given a statement,' she said.

Daniela made an indelicate noise. 'I'm just waiting till my boots are dry then I'm gone.'

'Really? How're you planning to get to Hackett?'

'Same way I got in. Shanks's pony.'

'In the dark, with all the roads shut?'

Daniela resisted the urge to roll her eyes. 'Shut to any vehicle smaller than a hovercraft, sure. They can't close the roads to people on foot.'

'What's the hurry?'

Daniela looked away. 'Even if I wanted to stay, I can't. I don't have anywhere to sleep tonight.'

'Chris has got rooms to hire, right here in the building.'

'That's nice and all, but I can't.'

'Why not?'

Daniela sighed. 'You want me to come right out and say it, don't you? I can't afford it. All right? I have precisely enough money to get me back to Birmingham, with maybe enough left over for a sandwich if I'm lucky. I wasn't kidding when I said I had no money. I literally have no money.'

Stephanie nodded as if confirming something to herself.

'I've already cleared it with Chris. He'll put the room on my tab.'

'You—?' A tightness gathered itself in Daniela's chest. Like a door swinging shut on her freedom. 'You've already spoken to him?'

Stephanie gave her a weary smile. 'Like I say, I don't want you leaving until I've heard the full story.'

'I told you everything,' Daniela said. Annoyance spiked inside her. 'I can go through it again, if it'll help, but seriously there's nothing more than what I told you.'

'No? What about the money?'

Daniela blinked away her surprise. How had Stephanie known about the package in the hidey-hole? But it figured, really. Auryn was good at keeping secrets, but Stephanie was better at finding them out.

'What money?' Daniela asked.

'I'm not in the mood, Dani. I know you searched the house. You found the money and you took it. How much do you want to bet that your fingerprints are all over the house?'

Daniela hesitated. Was Stephanie fishing for info? Throwing out accusations and hoping she'd bite? Even if Daniela's finger-prints *were* found, who's to say they weren't from seven years ago? How long did prints stay on a surface anyway?

She'd been silent too long. 'Listen,' Stephanie said, 'this is an awful situation. Give me the truth, okay?'

'I don't know anything about any money,' Daniela said. It rang false even to her.

Stephanie almost laughed. 'I thought you would've learned to lie by now. Don't they teach that in prison anymore?'

Daniela pushed back in her chair. Her fists were clenched in her lap. 'I don't know about any money,' she repeated.

'Are you sure? A large amount of cash was hidden in the house. It's not there now.'

Be careful. Daniela forced herself to relax; to unfurl her hands. 'Steph, I know this is how you cope when something horrendous happens. You throw yourself into your work. But right now, you shouldn't be the one who deals with this. There're other officers who can do it.'

'Not right now there's not.'

'C'mon. You must be able to hand it off to whoever—'

'There's no one else. The road bridge to Hackett is underwater. And part of the cliff face above the Howstrake road came down so vehicles can't get through that way either. No one can get here.'

Daniela stared at her as that sank in. 'What about … what about Auryn?' Insomuch as she'd thought about it all, she'd assumed Auryn's body would've been whisked away to the facilities in Hackett already.

Stephanie had gone back to watching the flames. 'They were hoping to bring the helicopter in but it's grounded because of the wind. Chances are it won't get here till tomorrow. And that's if the weather doesn't get any worse.'

'So … where's Auryn?'

'Still at the house.'

'Jesus, Steph. You left her—?'

'We moved her out of the water.' Stephanie ran a tired hand over her face. 'Me and Leo carried her upstairs to her room.' The crack in her voice revealed how traumatising it'd been. Daniela felt her eyes start to sting again. 'We shouldn't even have done that. Should've left her where she was.'

Daniela's mind recoiled from the idea. 'What the hell for?'

'SOCO are going to ask why we moved her.'

'So, tell them. Seriously, what does it matter? It's not like she was—'

Daniela stopped in mid-sentence, her tongue stuck to the roof of her mouth.

'Steph?' she asked, her voice a lot quieter. 'What happened to Auryn?'

Stephanie studied her with those red-rimmed eyes. 'It's kind of telling that you've only just thought to ask that.'

Daniela didn't know how to answer.

Her sister leaned forwards so there was very little distance between them. 'She was murdered, Dani. Someone stuck a knife between her ribs.'

It was like she'd sucked the air out of the room. Daniela tried to take a breath and got nothing but the stale taste of ash from the fire. And yet it was like she'd known already. She'd known, as soon as she'd found the package, that something wasn't right in Auryn's world.

But it wasn't drugs, or drink, or neglect. Someone had killed Auryn.

Daniela felt the room wobble. She put her hands on her knees to steady herself.

The worst thing, the absolute worst thing, was the way Stephanie was watching her. Watching to see her reaction. Daniela knew what her sister was thinking. It made her stomach knot.

'It wasn't me,' Daniela said. It was the wrong thing to say.

Stephanie let out a slow, controlled breath. Anyone who didn't know her would've missed the tight anger that hid behind her mask-like expression. She got to her feet, a little too quick.

'Have a think about what else you want to tell me,'

Stephanie suggested. 'Your room is upstairs, at the end of the hall. I'm staying in the one right next door. In case you're considering sneaking off during the night.'

As Stephanie strode away, Daniela felt her chest constrict again. *Trapped.*

12

Daniela awoke early and slipped her trainers on. In this between-time, before the first survivors rolled out of bed, there were a few quiet noises – their father shifting in his sleep, the soft chatter of birds outside – but it was like a blanket had been pulled across the house, kept it sealed it in for the night, with only the swoosh of the windswept trees for company. There were no streetlights along the road to the old house, and therefore no light until dawn, and the attic bedroom windows faced away from the faint glow of Stonecrop.

On the few occasions when Daniela had spent the night at Franklyn's flat in Birmingham, it'd been unnerving to sleep with traffic noise and streetlights. How could anyone cope? The constant movement, constant sound, as if even in the depths of night the streets were alive. It was scary and exhilarating in equal parts. In contrast, Stonecrop felt like it died every night and was resurrected at dawn.

That Sunday was a dull, damp day, the barely risen sun skulking behind thick clouds. Daniela pulled on a fleecy jumper as well as her leather jacket before venturing outside. She was tired and fuzzy-headed from the night before. She'd

93

stayed up later and drunk more than intended, although she hadn't been the last to bed, by any means. Franklyn and Stephanie had stayed up into the early hours, and Daniela had drifted off to the faint murmur of their voices filtering up through the house.

The compulsion to get outside as soon as possible had little to do with the need for fresh air. Daniela tried to make it a habit to be out of the way before her father woke up. There was no guarantee what temper he'd be in.

Sometimes, when the mood took her, Daniela would catch the bus into Hackett and spend the day walking the streets or loitering in shops, looking at items she'd no interest in buying. Other times she stayed in Stonecrop. If Margaret McKearney was in the Shoppe, she'd let Daniela browse the magazines for a half hour, Margaret's tolerant smile tempered by her keen gaze. Daniela already had a reputation – undeserved, she felt, since she'd only been caught twice trying to lift stuff.

Today though, Daniela was restless. She didn't want to cope with public transport or the thin crowds of Hackett. She also didn't feel like making polite, strained conversation with Margaret McKearney, especially after Franklyn's altercation with Henry yesterday. On days like this, Daniela realised with annoyance how pointless her life had become. It was like she was marking time for something more important. Weekdays were wasted, waiting on the clock and the weekend, and then weekends were squandered with nothing to do and nowhere to go.

Daniela took out her phone and scrolled through the short, accumulated list of contacts. No one there could be classed as a close friend. She had no one she could text for a chat. Too many years had been spent staring inwards, turned away from people, until she'd lost the knack of interaction.

She wondered whether Leo was awake yet.

Leo had turned up late last night, tired and washed out from dealing with his family, and hung around awkwardly until going upstairs with Auryn to talk. He'd slept over, sharing the spare room with Auryn, the two of them jammed onto the futon, insisting it was comfortable.

Daniela spent a few pleasant but pointless minutes kicking around the idea of returning home to talk to him. *Hey, Leo, wanna ride the bus into Hackett and poke fun at the trendy kids outside HMV? I'll buy you lunch. We can pretend like we're best friends again.*

But she couldn't think of any sensible way to talk to Leo without waking Auryn. That thought soured her mood. She needed to stop thinking about Leo all the goddamn time. What sort of person fixated on their sister's boyfriend? Daniela knew it was wrong, she knew Leo was utterly uninterested in her, and – above all else – the last thing in the world she wanted to do was sabotage his relationship. Auryn had never been happier, for Chrissakes. But rational arguments had no effect on the reptile-centre of Daniela's brain, which went into a spin-dive whenever Leo was near.

Silently she cursed herself. Why couldn't she be happy being friends with Leo? She remembered the good times they'd shared as kids – her and Auryn and Leo, the three of them charging through the woods together. Her and Leo urging Auryn up trees and down muddy hollows. The time they'd found a clearing so covered with autumn leaves they'd built a leaf-pile six feet high then dared each other to leap into it from a head-high tree branch.

Why couldn't she be content with that?

She almost wished Leo hadn't come over last night. But

Daniela couldn't blame him for not wanting to stay anywhere near Henry McKearney. Daniela's hands shook every time she thought about the argument at the shop. Henry had been reaching for the knife. She knew it.

With a grunt of irritation, Daniela veered from the path and set off cross-country through the woods. The ground was soft, even though there hadn't been a heavy rain for a week, and she picked her way slowly along the easiest route, moving between the trees with an ease born of a lifetime scuffling about in those woods. She still had no direction in mind, but it felt better to be finding her own path.

Inevitably though, she ran out of forest and ended up on the streets of Stonecrop. That summed up her life, didn't it? She didn't know what she was doing, so she did nothing but circle forever, unable to escape.

She wandered aimlessly through the empty market square, which wasn't so much a square as a broad junction with a mini-roundabout. A bakery wagon was delivering to the Corner Shoppe. The warm smell of new bread tugged at her stomach. There'd been nothing in the house for breakfast, so Daniela had gone without.

As she followed the back street away from the square, walking with her head down, she became aware of someone watching her.

Despite the village's small size, there were always a few people on the streets during daylight hours, no matter the time. Dog-walkers mainly, heading for their morning stroll in the woods. But Daniela was immediately aware this wasn't a random passer-by.

The Cain Sense, Franklyn called it. She claimed everyone in the family had it – an awareness of their surroundings, a sensitivity for when something wasn't right. Maybe nothing more than a heightened sense of self-preservation. Daniela was never wholly convinced it was real.

Daniela turned, making the movement casual.

Franklyn was leaning against the corner of a wall, her hand cupped around a cigarette. Her thin face tended to appear drawn and haggard, but today she was particularly pale, her eyes sunken. It looked like she might've fallen over if the wall hadn't been supporting her.

'Didn't think anyone would be up this early,' she said.

Daniela came over. 'You okay?'

'Fine like the sunshine,' Franklyn said with a lopsided smile. 'What brings you out on this beautiful morning?'

She was tucked in behind the corner, too casual to be doing anything other than hiding. A little farther down the road were the back gates to the yard behind the antiques shop. It seemed like too much of a coincidence that Franklyn could be watching any other building. Two cigarette butts lay crushed at her feet. She'd been there a while.

There was a scrape across the bridge of her nose, which Daniela hadn't noticed the day before. Had that happened during the scuffle at the shop?

'I needed some fresh air,' Daniela said. It was as good an excuse as any. 'You?'

'Pah. Fresh air's overrated.' Franklyn blew out smoke. 'There's plenty of air in the house. Mostly hot air, of course. I needed to get away.'

She tilted her pack of cigarettes to Daniela. After a hesitation, Daniela took one, sharing a grin with Franklyn like they were a pair of naughty kids.

'Is Steph awake, then?' Daniela asked.

Franklyn nodded, searching for her lighter. 'And still in a foul temper. Seems to be her default setting these days, doesn't it?'

Daniela had to agree. She watched Franklyn fumble with the stubborn flint of her Zippo. Daniela checked her own pockets. Usually she carried a lighter.

Her searching hands found the flick-knife in the inside pocket of her jacket. A fleeting coldness went down her spine. She'd forgotten the knife was there ... or maybe she'd just put it from her mind.

Finally, Franklyn got a spark and lit Daniela's cigarette.

'I can't stay,' Franklyn said. 'I figured it'd be okay to be in Stonecrop for a day or two, but that doesn't seem sensible now, does it?'

'Because of Henry?'

'Not just him. Steph's less than pleased with me.' Franklyn rubbed the scrape on her nose. 'I'd hoped I could talk to Henry and that'd be the end of it. Stupid, really.'

'What's Henry's problem anyway?'

'He thinks I'm ungrateful, and arrogant, and ... well, a lot of things that're probably true.'

'Ungrateful? For what?'

Franklyn leaned against the wall, twisting so she could watch the yard gates. She looked a lot older than twenty-six. 'You try and get away from things, and they end up following you,' she said. 'I went to the city because ... all right, I didn't know what I wanted, but whatever it was, it wasn't here in Stonecrop. You understand, right?'

Daniela nodded. She understood perfectly.

'You hang on to things that're familiar,' Franklyn said. 'You meet new people, but you feel like you owe something to the people you used to know. The ones who don't question you about your name or your family or anything like that. Henry helped me when I went to Birmingham. He set me up with a place to live, gave me some work, that sort of thing. From the goodness of his heart, of course, and because he was such good friends with Dad.' She studied the glowing end of her cigarette. 'Stupid, naive me. You don't expect people to be bastards. For some reason, it always catches you by surprise.'

Daniela said nothing, because it'd been years since she'd thought of Henry as anything other than a bastard. She only had to look at the way their dad spoke about him.

'Henry asked for a favour in return,' Franklyn said. 'That was the start of it. He asked—' Franklyn pushed her hair out of her face. 'I'm an idiot. I should've run a mile. But they trick you into these things, a little at a time, a small amount of pressure on your back, and you don't realise you're falling until you're already gone.'

'Is that what you and Henry were arguing about? He lent you money and wanted it back?'

Franklyn looked surprised. 'You're kidding. Why would I take money off him? He came to *me* because he needed cash.'

In the yard behind the antiques shop, a car racketed into life. Franklyn lifted her head and gave a tight smile.

'Here we go,' she said.

13

With scraping gravel and squealing hinges, the gates to the yard opened. Henry appeared, scowling at the sky as if the muted sunlight were a personal affront. He opened the gates fully, kicking them into place, then disappeared back into the yard.

Franklyn had retreated behind the wall in a smooth, slow movement to avoid attention. Daniela was clumsier. She ducked too swiftly behind Franklyn, and her foot slipped on the kerb. Franklyn grabbed her elbow to steady her.

Embarrassed, Daniela peered around the corner. A car nosed out of the yard with Henry behind the wheel. It stopped in the middle of the street while Henry got out to shut the gates.

Daniela glanced at Franklyn, who was motionless, her intense gaze fixed on Henry.

'What's going on?' Daniela asked in a hesitant whisper.

Franklyn didn't respond. Her silence and stillness were unnerving. Tension corkscrewed in Daniela's stomach, even though she didn't know why she should be concerned. As far as she could tell, they were watching Henry McKearney going for a drive.

As Henry drove off with a crunch of gears, and the noise

of the engine faded, Franklyn at last unwound. She discarded her half-finished cigarette, then strode to the gates. Daniela followed.

'What're we doing?' Daniela asked.

'I'm getting my money back,' Franklyn said.

She tried the gate but found it locked tight with a bolt and a padlock.

'Dammit,' Franklyn said. 'He doesn't usually lock the place up. Must be feeling paranoid.'

She took a step back to examine the wall. It was seven feet high, made of chunks of local stone, topped with shards of broken glass embedded in concrete. Chinks and defects in the face of the wall provided scant footholds.

Franklyn found a suitable place, set her foot against the wall, gripped a handhold just above her head, and pulled herself up. Daniela watched her sister struggle to find another handhold, then asked, 'Would you like a boost?'

'Um. Yeah, go on then.'

Daniela linked her hands and boosted Franklyn ungracefully over the wall. There was a certain amount of swearing as the broken glass snagged the elbows of her leather jacket. Franklyn swung her legs over and dropped into the yard on the other side.

'How d'you intend to get back?' Daniela asked through the gate.

'One thing at a time, will you? Keep watch for me.'

Franklyn's footsteps crunched on the gravel to the rear door of the antiques shop. Daniela stayed where she was, watching the empty street, but only for a moment. Whatever was going on, the interesting stuff was inside the shop. Daniela made a decision, then climbed the wall, following the same route as

Franklyn. She was smaller, lighter, and more confident at climbing since scaling trees was one of the few things she enjoyed about Stonecrop. She reached the top and slithered over. A shard of glass poked her knee but didn't hurt.

As Daniela dropped into the yard, Franklyn looked up with annoyance. 'You're not big on doing what you're told, are you?'

'Wonder where I get that from.'

Franklyn sprung the fire door of the shop. 'Don't touch anything,' she warned. 'We'll be in and out quickly.'

Daniela nodded. A knot of excitement tightened in her stomach. This was different to the petty trespassing she'd done in the past – like breaking into the abandoned shell of Kirk Cottage – and the thrill was a hundred times greater. In fact, it was so strong, Daniela felt queasy. She was doing something seriously wrong, and wasn't sure how that made her feel. She wondered how Stephanie would react if she found out.

The shop was dark and silent, the hulking shadows of furniture blocking the light from the front windows. Franklyn went to Henry's rosewood desk and started opening drawers.

'Henry thinks he's cleverer than he is,' Franklyn said. 'He figured, since he was travelling the country, buying and selling antiques, getting stuff imported from the continent, he might as well buy and sell a little additional merchandise.'

'Like what?'

Franklyn shoved a stack of papers off the desk, searching for something. The noise of paper fluttering to the ground made Daniela glance at the door. Franklyn grunted with satisfaction as she uncovered a large crate hidden beneath a nearby chair.

She lifted the lid to reveal a porcelain figure nestled in

polythene beads. Underneath the statuette, however, were a dozen rows of neatly packed cigarettes.

'I told him, it's a lot of risk for a slimline profit,' Franklyn said, 'but Henry's done the maths and reckons he's onto a winner. He gets all kinds of counterfeit crap sent to him from Europe. Cigarettes, designer bags, clothes, car parts, all sorts. He acts as a middleman, sells it to people who actually know what they're doing, and takes a tiny profit.' Franklyn shook her head as she put the porcelain figure back and resealed the box. 'The man's crazy. It's bound to backfire.'

The conversation felt surreal. It made Daniela look at Franklyn in a different light. Franklyn had been in trouble throughout her life, but this was new, a world away from petty thievery and pointless vandalism. Despite herself, Daniela thrilled at this glimpse of another world, which Franklyn had chosen to share.

'So, how'd you get mixed up in it?' she asked.

Franklyn grimaced. 'Henry needed money. I had money. I was stupid enough to feel indebted because he'd helped me. He said it was for a completely legit business idea. By the time I figured out what he was up to, I was involved enough that he thought he could blackmail me.' She shook her head. 'I'm such an idiot.'

'Blackmail? What did you do?'

Franklyn ignored that question. She returned to the desk drawers. The lowermost was locked, and resisted all efforts to open it.

'What're you looking for?' Daniela asked.

'My way out.' Franklyn flashed a grin. 'He's not keeping my money, and he's not playing me anymore. I'm getting the hell away from Henry McKearney and his suspect business practices. It's time I did something constructive with my life.'

'That'll be a change.'

Franklyn gave her an irritated look, and Daniela flinched. She hadn't meant to be sarcastic. 'You're as bad as Steph,' Franklyn said. 'If I wanted another lecture, I would've woken her. Or Dad.'

'Sorry.' The tips of Daniela's ears burned. Franklyn had been treating her like an adult, and she'd responded like a child. 'I just mean, you've changed since you've been away.'

Franklyn frowned, either in thought or annoyance. She picked up a metal ruler from the desk and tried to jemmy the drawer.

'I had to,' she said. 'I mean, I don't want to wake up one morning twenty years from now and still be stuck in the same mess. I've always known I needed to change. I can't keep going like this. It'll kill me.'

From anyone else that would've sounded like hyperbole, but Daniela worried Franklyn was speaking literally.

'There has to be more than this.' Franklyn swept her hand to encompass the entirety of Stonecrop. 'Something more important.'

'Yeah, but studying theology? Is that just to piss off Dad?' Since the day their mother walked out, their father had added religion to such topics as politics and sports that were banned from the house.

'A little, yeah,' Franklyn said with a slight smile. 'It's an added bonus, isn't it? Anyway, it's not like any of this is set in stone. It's just a thought. And I know you guys don't approve—'

'I never said that. I mean, I don't completely *understand*, but I'm not about to tell you how to run your life.'

Franklyn chuckled. 'You're the only one, that's for sure.'

A car went past outside. Both Franklyn and Daniela tensed, listening as it came closer, then relaxing as it continued through town.

Franklyn said, 'Something happened last week. It wasn't as dramatic as a bolt of lightning or realising what a godawful person I've been, just ...' She made an imprecise gesture. 'You know when something's staring you in the face for so long, and you feel so stupid because you never even knew it was there?'

'Sure.'

'That's what it was like. I met this person ...' Franklyn noticed the smile on Daniela's face. 'Not like that, c'mon. I was volunteering some hours at a homeless shelter and there was this woman there. She can't have been much older than me. Like, early thirties, tops. But she looked eighty. She'd been a user since she was in her teens, and she'd picked up hepatitis somewhere along the line. It was horrendous. Like she was rotting from the inside. And she'd had such a fucking awful life. She knew she was circling the drain. Been circling it for years. But she had this—' again Franklyn made an imprecise, impatient gesture, as if irritated by her lack of words '—inner peace. That sounds so stupid, doesn't it? There must be a better term.'

Daniela said nothing, because she remembered thinking the same thing about Franklyn. Something internal, calm, but she wouldn't call it peace.

'But, yeah,' Franklyn sighed. 'She knew exactly where she was in the world, and what was coming next, and she was so fucking Zen about it.' It wasn't clear whether she was annoyed at herself or at the woman. 'Anyway. That was it. She had no illusions that anything could save her, not after the life she'd had, but she had comfort. Certainty. And, God help me, I was jealous.'

Franklyn struggled with the drawer but the ruler wasn't enough to open it. All she was doing was scratching the expensive wood. Franklyn stood up, hands on hips in exasperation, then leaned back and drove the heel of her boot into the drawer front. The wooden panel cracked like a gunshot. Daniela instinctively flinched away. Franklyn kicked it twice more.

'Better,' Franklyn said, a little out of breath.

She pulled away the shattered pieces of wood. From the drawer behind, she fished a thick bundle of banknotes and tossed it onto the desk.

'Much better.' Franklyn removed the elastic band from the bundle. There was an assortment of notes, Daniela saw – mostly fifties with a few tens and twenties.

Daniela couldn't stop herself asking, 'So how does this fit with your new improved lifestyle?'

Franklyn paused in the act of counting off notes. 'It doesn't,' she admitted. 'Not at all. That's why I'm doing it.' She removed approximately a third of the bundle, then wrapped the elastic band around the rest and chucked it back into the shattered drawer. 'This'll wipe the slate clean. Once it's done, that's it, the cycle's broken. I can get out.'

The notes she'd counted – thousands of pounds, Daniela estimated – went into her pocket.

'If I could afford to walk away and let that bastard keep the money, I would. But ...' Franklyn hesitated, her hand covering the pocket, her eyes wandering to the broken drawer. Then she shook her head and forced a smile. 'Let's get out of here.'

They closed the fire door behind them and scrambled over the wall. Once they were on the street again, Daniela expected they'd return to the family home, but instead Franklyn headed round the block, towards the front of the Corner Shoppe.

'Where're you going?' Daniela asked. She had to hurry to keep up with Franklyn's long stride.

'Something else I need to do. I've got half an hour before the next bus to Hackett.'

'You're leaving?'

'I should've left last night. Actually, I should've never come back. It wasn't my best plan.'

'You're going back to Birmingham?'

'I doubt it. I need to get properly away and let everything blow over. Too many people know where to find me in Birmingham. Staying there is a bad idea; staying here isn't much smarter. The only thing I'll do is cause more fights.' She rubbed the bridge of her nose. 'It's better if everyone forgets me for a while.'

'So, you're gonna sneak off without saying goodbye?'

Franklyn pocketed her hands and shrugged. 'Seems like the sort of thing I'd do, doesn't it? Anyway, you can say bye for me. Tell them ...' She paused as if struggling for a genuine emotion. 'Aw, crap. Tell them anything they want to hear. You're the only one who'll care.'

'You think so?'

Something clouded Franklyn's eyes, there and gone in an instant. 'I'll catch you later, all right?' she said. She flashed that familiar, reassuring smile. 'Keep out of trouble.'

'Says you.'

'Yep, says me. I make these mistakes so you don't have to, remember?'

Daniela slowed her pace and let Franklyn stride away towards the Corner Shoppe. With her shoulders hunched and her head down, Franklyn looked like a stranger, a thin woman with a sullen, angry face; the sort of person you'd avoid on the street. With mixed emotions, Daniela watched her disappear into the shop. It was always sad to see her go, because out of the whole family, Daniela liked Franklyn best, and now more than ever she had felt a connection.

But on the other hand, Daniela didn't understand Franklyn's world. Whatever she'd done in Birmingham ... it left a sour taste in Daniela's mouth. *Blackmail,* she'd said. What'd Franklyn ever done that anyone could blackmail her for?

Daniela hated herself for thinking it, but maybe it *was* better if Franklyn left, to let everything settle. She brought nothing but trouble when she came home.

14

Daniela slept poorly, as expected. Any hope she'd had of sneaking out of the building in the early hours had been dashed as soon as she saw the hallway that led to the rooms. Stephanie's rented room was directly opposite her own, and all the doors seemed incapable of opening without announcing their intentions to the world. And Stephanie had always been a light sleeper at the best of times.

The room that Daniela found herself in was modern and comfortable, with magnolia walls and hospital corners on the bed. The few touches of life – a jar of budding daffodils, an indifferent watercolour print – couldn't stop it looking like any hotel in the world. Daniela had expected something more homely.

But it had a warm bed, an adequate bathroom, and a window that, with a little encouragement, opened wide enough to prevent the room feeling claustrophobic, albeit not quite wide enough for her to squeeze out through. She hated being shut in.

She'd been too proud to ask Stephanie for money to buy dinner so she'd gone to bed hungry.

Instead of trying to sleep, she'd sat up late, listening to the noise of Chris chatting away to the few remaining regulars in the bar downstairs, clearly audible through the paper-thin walls. For nearly an hour his chatter had been punctuated by the rumble of Stephanie's voice. Daniela wondered what they were talking about. Did Stephanie intend to tell him what had happened to Auryn? Who else had she told?

Daniela used a chunk of her dwindling phone credit to send a few texts. She couldn't bring herself to make a phone call because she knew she'd break down in tears again if she had to talk to anyone about Auryn.

Got here safe, she texted instead. *Gonna have to spend the night, sorry. Will be back tomorrow.*

The reply came back almost immediately. *Stay safe, i heard the weather's bad.*

Daniela almost smiled at that.

Eventually though, Daniela slept, but a patchy and broken night's sleep. Each time she awoke she suffered a moment of panic as she tried to figure out where she was. She'd spent so many nights in a locked room that even the idea terrified her. Outside, the wind continued to howl through the trees. Rain battered the window.

At last dawn found her. Daniela showered, but didn't have any spare clothes to change into. Putting on yesterday's clothes was necessary but made her feel scuzzy. She squeezed toothpaste from the tiny complimentary tube onto her index finger and scrubbed her teeth as best she could. Her reflection in the bathroom mirror was shocking.

When she stumbled out of her room, Stephanie's door was closed. Daniela paused, then put her ear against the door to listen. She thought she heard the hissing of a shower filtering out of the bathroom.

If Daniela wanted a chance to sneak out, this was it. But she was sandy-eyed from lack of sleep, and she could still hear the rain coming down outside. She quailed at the idea of leaving the safety of the pub just yet.

Downstairs, the smell of fresh coffee was so strong it made her heady. Her stomach gurgled. She hadn't eaten anything since yesterday lunchtime.

You shouldn't be hungry. How can you eat after what's happened? But apparently her stomach hadn't got that message.

She padded across the pub carpet on bare feet and leaned on the bar. The coffee machine was percolating quietly to itself. Through the window she could see Stephanie's police car, a fairly posh Subaru covered in luminous facings, sitting conspicuously in the empty car park. Daniela waited a decent amount of time for Chris or his wife to appear. Then she walked behind the bar, located a ceramic mug, and poured herself one of the best cups of coffee she'd ever had.

Sitting at a table near the bar, Daniela checked her phone. She'd received another text a half hour earlier, probably while she'd been in the shower. All it said was, *Thinking of you.*

Daniela let out a breath. She needed to send something good in reply but her head felt scrambled. She tapped out, *Same back at ya*, hesitated, added, *I got the money*, then deleted it again. No sense making an electronic trail that someone could use against her later. Besides, it wasn't entirely true. Not yet. Not until she was home and dry.

She finished her coffee. The bar was still deserted, so she snuck a second mugful. *Might as well – no one's going to yell at you twice.* As she drank it by the window, she watched the

111

rain and thought over the plan she'd put together last night. Judging by the water levels outside, it was unlikely she could get back across Hackett Bridge. But just because a car couldn't get through, didn't mean a really determined person on foot couldn't. She just had to be certain what she was doing.

Once she'd worked up enough courage, she took her half-finished coffee and headed back to her room. She knew now that she wouldn't get away with leaving before she'd spoken to Stephanie. At least she'd had the whole restless night to figure out what to say. Last night, emotions had been running high. They'd both been upset. Today, Daniela felt more confident that if the two of them sat down and talked, like a pair of civilised adults, they could resolve this.

Daniela pushed her bedroom door open, and found Stephanie inside.

Stephanie had pulled all the drawers out of the dresser next to the window. The covers on the bed were yanked back to show the bare mattress. Stephanie was crouched down, checking the underside of the dresser. When she saw Daniela, she sat up. She didn't even have the decency to look guilty.

Daniela stared at her from the doorway. 'Okay, what exactly are you doing?' she asked. 'I didn't even bring a change of underwear with me. What the hell are you looking for?'

Stephanie stood. She looked even rougher and more exhausted than Daniela. 'I know you took the money, Dani,' she said. 'Where is it?'

Daniela came into the room and set her coffee down on the rickety bedside table. She had to fight to keep her anger under control. 'Look, I'm no expert, but this isn't legal. You can't come barging into my room and—'

'You left the door open.'

'That makes no difference and you know it. You shouldn't be here.' Daniela pushed past her and grabbed her jumper from the floor. 'And are you satisfied? There's nothing here. Do you think I've hidden it in the light fittings? Maybe in the toilet cistern, did you check there?'

Stephanie shrugged in a particularly infuriating way. 'I had to be sure.'

Daniela's expression hardened. 'You had to be sure, because you don't trust me. That is fucking wonderful to hear.' She pulled her jumper on, then cast around for her socks. 'On top of that, you're wasting time. Someone killed Auryn. Shouldn't you be on the street, finding out who the hell it is?'

'I needed to—'

'You need to get out of my room. Go downstairs, get some coffee from the unguarded coffee machine, and sort your stupid head out.' Daniela found her socks, which were damp and unpleasant and didn't smell too great. She sat down on the bed to pull them on anyway. 'Are the rest of the police here yet?'

'No. We're still cut off.'

'So, how about instead of coming in here and treating me like a goddamn suspect, you let me help?' Daniela tugged her boots on. 'Someone in this town has to know something. Nothing happens here without curtains twitching.' She stood up. Her jacket lay in a crumpled heap near the door. 'What if the murderer didn't get out before the roads closed? What if they're still here? There's no shortage of places to hide – half the houses are evacuated. We owe it to Auryn to start looking.'

Stephanie shook her head. 'We can't do that.'

'Yeah? Watch us.' Daniela snatched up her jacket. Before

she could put it on, Stephanie grabbed on to one sleeve to hold her back.

'I know you're not telling me everything,' Stephanie said.

Daniela tried to pull the jacket out of her grip, but Stephanie was always strong. Tenacious. 'You keep saying Auryn had money in the house, like that's a big thing,' Daniela said. 'Why? Whose was it? Yours?'

Stephanie didn't answer.

With a final heave, Daniela wrenched the jacket away from her. The effort made her stagger back against the doorframe. Something clattered loose onto the floor but Daniela didn't check to see what it was. 'Looks like I'm not the one who's been keeping secrets,' she said.

Daniela stomped down the stairs, pulling the jacket over her shoulders. Stephanie didn't follow.

15

Daniela started walking. The rain, which had subsided before dawn, was busy starting up again, as if it had specifically waited for her to venture outside. She pulled up her hood with a grimace.

The floodwater had definitely risen during the night. One section of the sandbagging in the pub car park had been breached, with a small waterfall creating a rapidly spreading puddle. Daniela stepped over the sandbags into the flood beyond. Water squeezed her wellies.

She sloshed away from the pub towards the main street. Each stride created little waves, which were pockmarked by rain. She kept to where she thought the pavement was because she was fairly sure if she stepped into the middle of the road the water would be deep enough to overflow her boots.

The Corner Shoppe was already open. Daniela glanced in through the front window and spotted Margaret, cleaning the counter with her back to the door. Daniela felt a familiar scratch in her throat as she looked at the rack of cigarettes at the rear of the shop. But no matter how desperate she was, she couldn't face talking to Margaret again, not right then.

Once she was out of sight of the Crossed Swords, Daniela found a place shallow enough to get across the road. She immediately ducked onto a familiar path that led into the woods. Within a hundred yards the ground rose high enough so that she was no longer walking through water.

With the familiar press of the trees around her, she paused to breathe and collect her thoughts. No matter what she'd told Stephanie, Daniela had no illusions that she could do anything at all to help the police investigation. At best she'd get in the way. And yet, she still had that itch in her brain. She had to know what'd happened to Auryn. She told herself that if she went back to the old house, if she went back inside, maybe she could somehow find something Stephanie had missed.

It was raining heavily by the time Daniela came within sight of the old house. The place had never looked so empty.

She stopped some distance away. There didn't appear to be any police presence, which fit with what Stephanie had said about the rest of the police force being thwarted by the weather. Someone, presumably Stephanie, had strung a line of yellow tape across the doorway.

Auryn was in there. Growing cold and stiff on her bed upstairs.

Daniela's resolve wavered. She'd intended to get into the house the same way as yesterday, up the tree and through the window. The main issue, she'd figured, would be if Stephanie had secured the window before she left. But now, faced with the idea of climbing into Auryn's old bedroom, where her sister was lying dead ...

Daniela couldn't do it. She couldn't see Auryn's empty eyes again.

Angry with herself, Daniela turned away. She set off from an angle away from the house.

Even though she'd only been outside for a short while, she was already tired and cold. She missed her footing far more frequently than she should've, her boots sliding in the mud or snagging on roots. The damp had insinuated its way in under her jacket again. Her fingers ached from the cold. A little water had got into her left boot, numbing her toes. She felt miserable.

She heard a car engine and froze in place. How far away was it? Noise travelled differently in the woods. It sounded like the car might be on an adjacent road.

The noise stopped as the engine was shut off. Someone driving home and parking outside their house. Daniela kept moving, increasing her pace across the sodden ground.

Some distance behind the old house, she slid down a muddy bank into a hollow. Twisted tree roots protruding from the earth were worn smooth by years of children climbing over them. This had been a favourite spot. It'd been a pirate cove, a hobbit hole, a machinegun post; a million other things. Its walls were high, protective. The smell of damp earth was soothing.

She sat while she caught her breath. The air was cold enough to hurt her lungs. How many times had she played here with Auryn and Leo? The memories were so clear she could almost hearing Auryn's shrieking laugh. When they were very little, Auryn never cared who heard her laugh. That was one more thing their mother had taken with her when she left.

At last, Daniela slid to the other side of the hollow. The tree roots overhanging the bank created a natural shelter lined by bare earth and dead leaves.

Bracing herself against the damp and chill, she wriggled into the hole, flinching at the coldness of wet leaves against her neck, then reached up into the tangle of roots beneath the tree.

It took her a moment to work loose the package wedged among the roots.

Daniela crawled back out with the parcel in her arms. She wiped off the mud and felt the crinkle of plastic beneath.

When she'd found Auryn, it was like her mind had shorted out. All Daniela could think of in that moment was to call Stephanie. It was simple, familiar; a throwback to when they were kids. Stephanie will fix this. The package had been in Daniela's hands when she'd phoned Stephanie and told her in broken fragments that their youngest sister was dead. It hadn't occurred to her to mention the money. And after she hung up, with the knowledge that Stephanie was on her way but also that nothing could ever be fixed, Daniela suddenly realised she had a decision to make.

Obviously, she should've told Stephanie about the money. Coming clean, telling her everything, that was always the best option. She should've handed over the package to Stephanie immediately.

But she hadn't.

Daniela needed money. *Badly* needed money. This bundle of cash would solve all her problems. And, as harsh as it was to admit, Auryn had no use of it anymore. If Daniela handed it over to Stephanie, it would end up in a confiscation account somewhere. Daniela had never been a fan of funding the police.

Plus, what if it wasn't Auryn's? Maybe the money really had belonged to their father. In which case, rightfully it could be the inheritance Daniela was owed, couldn't it?

She knew she was justifying her actions. The knowledge didn't make her feel good.

But still she'd quit the house with the money tucked under her arm. She'd hurried into the woods, to this familiar hiding place, and stashed the parcel in the tree roots. Then she'd returned to the house to meet Stephanie.

She'd gambled on no one else knowing the package existed. If she'd known Stephanie was aware of it, and indeed would go looking for the damn thing after Auryn died ...

Too late to think like that. Daniela had made her choice.

And now she had another choice to make. Simple, basic. Stay or leave?

Daniela hugged the package tight. She'd got what she came home for. Now she could go. Just walk away.

That thought made her grimace. Under normal circumstances, leaving the old house behind would be the easiest thing in the world. But right now, she had no idea if she could physically get out of Stonecrop.

She needed to consider her options. Stephanie said the Hackett bridge was impassable, but that could've been an exaggeration. It might be worth walking out there to see for herself. So long as she could afford the time it would take.

What were the alternatives? Aside from the landslide-hit Howstrake road, there was the option of going cross-country, which wasn't much of an option at all, since the fields were waterlogged. At best she'd have to wade; at worst she might have to swim. And eventually she'd come up against the twin tributaries of the River Clynebade, barring the way. That left only the route south, a tractor trail that wound eventually to Briarsfield. It might still be passable.

If she was going to run, heading south seemed like the best choice.

She was still sitting on the cold ground, debating, when she heard a noise from down near the old house.

Splashing footsteps. Someone approaching along the flooded road.

Daniela ducked back down into the hollow, her breath catching. The sploshing came closer. Whoever was down there must've abandoned their car and come in on foot.

Daniela edged around the hollow with the intention of retracing her path through the woods. If it was Stephanie – and she had every reason to suspect it was – then she knew all the hiding spots within a mile of the house. Daniela had no wish at all to be found out here with the stolen parcel of money. She was pretty sure she couldn't talk her way out of that.

What if it's not Stephanie?

God knows what Auryn had been involved with. A concealed package containing such a large amount of money did not come from nowhere. Daniela knew the type of people who dealt in large amounts of cash. People like Henry McKearney, for example.

Someone had killed Auryn. What if they'd returned for their property?

Her hand closed tight around the parcel of money. She peeked up over the lip of the hollow. From that angle, the house blocked her view of whoever had arrived. She could see the ripples leading up to the front gate but not the person themselves. She waited, listening, then made her move.

Unfortunately, she moved too fast. She put her foot down on what she assumed was a solid tree root and it gave way. With the package in her right hand she couldn't catch herself.

She thumped down on her side, then slid backwards down the slope. She made a desperate grab for anything that would stop her. Her left boot caught in a looping tree root and twisted the wrong way. Pain shot through her leg.

She slipped down the bank until the tree root around her left foot halted her progress. Daniela was left hanging half upside down on the steep bank with her head at the bottom of the hollow. She groaned and spat mud. Fire radiated from her ankle. She tried to tug her boot loose and the jolt of pain made her gasp. She jammed her knuckles into her mouth to keep from crying out.

There was a splash from the direction of the house. The person was on the move. Daniela held her breath. She willed them to go away.

How much noise had she made when she fell? Did it carry as far as the house?

It must've, because the distinct sound of someone wading through floodwater was coming closer. The sloshing echoes bounced across the wide depression in the landscape around the old house.

Daniela gritted her teeth and tried again to twist her foot loose. Fire washed her ankle. The pain made her gag. She lifted herself on her arms and tried again. But the angle was wrong. The root had twisted around her boot, holding it in place. She attempted to slip her foot out of the boot but flexing the muscles was agony.

The splashing footsteps got closer, then stopped. The person had reached the drier bank leading into the woods. Daniela heard the dull crackle of twigs beneath boots. The person either didn't know how to move quietly or didn't care if they were heard.

16

June 2010

Trudging home alone, Daniela wondered whether she should tell her family that Franklyn had left. They'd figure it out soon enough. Daniela could feign ignorance and no one would doubt her.

Already Franklyn's absence made Daniela restless and irritated, and more aware of how claustrophobic Stonecrop was. The urge to leave was stronger than ever. Twice she almost turned back to get on the same bus as Franklyn.

She thought of the money Franklyn had taken from Henry's shop. The burglary still sat badly with Daniela, although Henry undoubtedly deserved it – he was a shit person, breaking the law with his petty counterfeit business, and it was Franklyn's money to begin with. Didn't Franklyn have the right to take it back?

Somehow, Daniela didn't think Stephanie would see it the same way. Maybe that's what made Daniela uncomfortable – the idea of being caught. She tried to shove the thought away. She wasn't a goddamn kid anymore. She wouldn't go through life being scared of her big sister.

Why the hell didn't I go with Franklyn?

The weather had turned cooler and the sky was filled with fat, pregnant clouds. The rains that year had been unusually light. Often the River Clynebade broke its banks long before now. But this year they'd been lucky – so far. Daniela looked at the sky and knew it was only a matter of time.

When she reached her house, she circled around to the back and snuck in through the kitchen, intending to grab something to eat before retreating to her bedroom. It was still early and she hoped no one would be about. Stephanie's car was gone from outside. It was unlikely their father would be awake before midday.

Daniela had somehow forgotten Auryn and Leo were at the house. More annoyingly, they were at the kitchen table eating breakfast when she opened the door, and they gave her identical looks of surprise.

'I didn't realise you'd gone out,' Auryn said.

'Didn't know I needed to post a notice.' Daniela kept her eyes away from Leo. She went to the cupboard and rummaged for something edible.

'We left you some bread if you want toast,' Leo said. He started clearing the plates from the table. 'I'm putting the kettle back on.'

Auryn got up and gave Leo a quick, self-conscious kiss. 'I'm gonna take a shower.'

Daniela plonked down in a chair. She wondered if Auryn was avoiding her, but Daniela was too keyed up to worry about it. She still felt the trailing edge of the sick thrill left over from the burglary. If Leo hadn't been there, Daniela might've told Auryn everything.

She watched Leo potter about the kitchen like it was his own. He switched the kettle on and, whilst waiting for it to boil, loaded plates into the dishwasher. Daniela tried to remember her father doing similar things. Or her mother, for that matter. It was easier to picture Leo in that role, growing older alongside Auryn, sharing a kitchen and a life, if not in this house then another similar one. It ignited a spark of jealousy, which Daniela quickly snuffed.

'So, Daniela.' Leo smiled as he drew her name out in his sing-song fashion. 'Where did you go?'

Daniela wished she had a cute nickname for him that she could throw back. 'Just for a walk,' she said. 'I needed some air.'

'It's a shame you didn't go into Stonecrop. You could've got more milk.' Leo shook the half-empty carton. 'Well, there's enough for the three of us. I've half a mind to switch to black tea when I'm here.'

The floorboards creaked as Auryn moved across to the bathroom above them. In that house, it was difficult to go anywhere or do anything quietly.

Leo checked his phone. It was a brand-new model, sleek and shiny, the white cover unblemished. Daniela was sure Auryn had bought it for him. Leo pocketed it.

'I wonder if ...' He trailed off, then glanced at the door and chewed his lip.

Daniela hadn't noticed before, but there was a tension about Leo, not just in his voice, but in how he held his body, his elbows tucked close and his back stiff.

'Hey,' Leo tried again, 'can I talk to you?'

Daniela started to make a flippant remark, but his nervousness stopped her. 'Sure,' she said.

'It's about what happened in the shop.'

For a second, Daniela thought Leo had somehow found

out about the burglary. Then she realised he meant the argument yesterday. 'What about it?'

'Was it serious?'

'Nah, not really. More like handbags-at-dawn, y'know?'

'It looked serious to me.'

'Maybe it depends where you were standing. You guys were all the way at the back. It didn't look so much from where I was. A bit of swearing and a scuffle, that's all.'

'Oh.'

For some reason he sounded disappointed. Daniela wondered if she should've exaggerated her own involvement. *God, what a dumb thought.* Being alone with Leo, aware of his movements and his smell ... it unsettled Daniela. They'd known each other forever – shouldn't Daniela be comfortable in his presence by now? But Leo had an unnerving quality. He wasn't like anyone Daniela knew.

What had started as a harmless if inappropriate infatuation was growing into something worse, and Daniela felt powerless. She stared at the floor because she hated herself for staring at Leo. It was made all the more unbearable because he obviously had no clue how she felt.

He wandered back to the table to get his mug, and Daniela had to shrink back to avoid his arm brushing hers.

'I think Dad sees it as more than a scuffle,' Leo said then. 'He'll take it seriously.'

Daniela shrugged as carelessly as she could manage. 'He can think what he likes. Doesn't matter to me.'

'No? You don't care if he causes trouble for your family?'

'We can deal with anything he does,' Daniela said, but she heard her own uncertainty. How would Henry react when he discovered the break-in?

'It won't just be pushing and shoving next time,' Leo said. 'Sometimes, at home, when he properly loses his temper, it's scary. I know he'd never do anything to hurt me or Mum, but—' He chewed his lip again. 'You don't know what it's like. Franklyn shouldn't antagonise him.'

'Why d'you assume it's Franklyn's fault? No offence, but from where I was standing it looked like your dad started it.'

Leo brushed his fringe away from his face. 'I'm just worried, that's all.'

'About Franklyn? She can look after herself.'

'Can *you?*'

Daniela blinked. 'Me?'

'Dad's never been a fan of your family. He's still bitter about the way your father broke off the business partnership. It was bad enough when me and Auryn started going out, but now …' Leo dropped his gaze. 'You didn't hear the way Dad was talking yesterday, after the fight. I'm scared what he might be planning.'

17

To be honest, Daniela liked the idea of Leo worrying about her. Not because it was fun seeing Leo upset, but because Daniela liked feeling she was worth someone's concern.

She wished she could reassure Leo. But all Daniela could think was, *I'm scared too,* and she could hardly say that out loud. In the silence of the kitchen, with Leo chewing his lip and looking so uncertain, Daniela shared his fear; believed, yeah, maybe Henry was planning something and, yeah, maybe everyone should be worried.

But an hour later, after Daniela left the house on the pretext of going into Stonecrop to buy something proper for lunch, it felt like maybe Leo was being melodramatic. His dad was an occasional nutcase, sure, but if Henry was mad at anyone it'd be Franklyn. He wouldn't care about Daniela.

When she reached the village centre, her feet automatically put her on the road past the antiques shop. The shop was still closed. Daniela peeked through the windows, trying to look casual, but there was little to see inside. Less than three hours had passed since she and Franklyn had broken in. Chances were the damage hadn't been discovered yet.

As she passed the open door to the corner shop, Margaret

McKearney looked up from arranging the magazine rack and gave a cheerful wave. Daniela wondered if Margaret knew what her husband was up to. Did any of the counterfeit cigarettes end up behind the counter?

Daniela couldn't face going into the shop to buy food. Anyway, she wasn't sure she was hungry. Her stomach was still unsettled.

She crossed the main street, passed the Crossed Swords, which wasn't open yet, then ducked into a lane that terminated at a five-bar gate. A path from there took her in a long loop through the woods, wandering almost as far as Winterbridge Farm, then along the back lanes to the north-west of Stonecrop. She had no motive for walking, beyond a desire to be out in the fresh air where she could think. And she hadn't wanted to hang out with Auryn and Leo. Listening to their plans for university made her irritable. So, she walked, knowing each path would inevitably lead her back home.

Even though it was before midday, Daniela felt the sting of another wasted day. Everything she did was just killing time, waiting for something better to happen.

The sun was trying its best to break through the clouds, but it was still chilly in the shadows of the trees. Daniela took a less-worn path that came close enough to the banks of the Clyne for her to hear the water. This section of the woods was deserted. She had the place to herself.

Or so she thought. As she stepped over an outcropping of rock that jutted into the track, she glimpsed another walker, coming towards her.

Daniela disliked meeting anyone else when she was out. It ruined the illusion that those woods belonged exclusively to her. She stepped off the path and cut between the trees in the direction of the river, keeping her head down so she wouldn't have to make eye contact with the person.

She went around a mossy pile of felled branches. The trail was indistinct, used only occasionally by fishermen looking for the perfect spot by the river. The Clyne flowed past a few feet away. The river was high, even with the lack of recent rains, the waters turgid and muddy with runoff from the fields. Unseen currents created patterns on the surface.

When Daniela glanced back, she realised the person had stepped off the main path as well. They were coming towards the river. Annoyed, Daniela shoved her hands in her pockets and walked faster.

Up ahead, she spotted a car park. In the height of summer, it was a popular picnic spot, but at this time of year it was usually abandoned. At the edge of the car park, where tarmac gave way to scrubby grass, a footpath led down to the riverbank. Next to the walkway were two picnic benches on concrete bases. In the sunshine, it might've been a pleasant spot, with trees shading the benches and flowing water cooling the air. Right now, it was dismal.

There was one vehicle in the car park. It looked familiar.

Too late, Daniela realised it was Henry's car. She'd seen him getting into it just that morning.

She turned and saw Henry striding towards her, coming around the other side of the mossy pile of branches to cut her off. He'd covered the distance fast.

Daniela didn't stop to think. She took off at a run along the muddy riverbank.

She should've followed the footpath into the car park, but if Henry wanted to he could've easily intercepted her before she got there. So instead she plunged into the long grass at the side of the river. The weeds swiped at her legs.

Too late she realised her mistake. It'd been several months since she'd last used that route. Last time she'd been there, a narrow trail skirted the edge of the river before widening out and curving back towards the road. But over the winter, heavy rains had washed out a whole chunk of the bank and carried it away. Daniela found herself at a dead end where ten feet of riverbank had been washed away by the river. She could see the path continuing after the gap but it was too far away for her to jump. The bite-shaped chasm between was filled by a sweep of muddy water. To her left was a thick wall of brambles. She could never get through that.

She spun around to find Henry ambling towards her.

'Lost, are we?' Henry said. He stopped some distance away. His expression was bland, but he'd placed himself deliberately so he was blocking Daniela's escape.

Daniela clenched her hands inside her pockets. Why was he here? Had he followed her? Or was it coincidence that he'd spotted her walking and decided to speak to her?

Regardless, Daniela was all too aware that she was alone out there, with no one to help if anything happened.

She swallowed down her fear and went to barge past Henry.

He moved into her way. Daniela stopped short to avoid running into him. She eyed him warily.

'What do you want?' Daniela asked. She hated how her voice wavered.

'A conversation, for starters,' Henry said. 'I'd like to know why you broke into my shop this morning.'

Daniela's stomach contracted. 'I didn't—'

'There were two sets of footprints across my yard. One set belongs to Franklyn, I'm sure. The other? I'm betting it was yours. Correct?'

He took a step forwards and Daniela retreated. 'I don't know what you're on about,' she said.

'No? How about an easier question then? Where's Franklyn?'

Daniela tried to dodge past him on the river side. Henry's arms shot out and pushed her back. Daniela stumbled. Her foot slipped off the bank and she went to one knee. She scrambled backwards, regaining her feet, her heart pumping. The toe of her left foot was wet where it'd dipped into the river.

Henry advanced again. Daniela backed off. She was all too aware of the broken gap behind her, cutting off all escape.

She glanced behind her. The river was six feet deep, and although it looked sluggish, the current was strong. She could picture what it was like to sink, for water to flood her mouth and nose, to be pulled down and down—

'Steady,' Henry said. He was smiling again. 'It'd be easy for someone to slip and fall here.'

'Get away from me.'

'And let you fall in? What kind of friend would I be if I did that?' Henry shook his head. 'Where's Franklyn?'

'I-I don't know.' Daniela heard the edge of fear in her voice. She swallowed and tried again. 'I don't know. I've not seen her all day.'

Henry clucked his tongue. 'Let's skip over that obvious lie. When you *last* saw her, where was she going?'

'Why don't you go find her yourself?'

'That's the trouble. When she doesn't want to be found, she can be difficult.' Henry took another step towards her.

His tone was still conversational. 'She's not here in Stonecrop. I'm guessing she's not anywhere in Birmingham that I'd find her. So, where's she gone?'

Daniela could only shake her head.

Henry had now come forwards so far, he was within arm's reach. There was nowhere else for Daniela to go. Her heels were inches from the broken edge of the bank.

'It'll be easier if you just tell me,' Henry said. 'I don't want to have to trouble Auryn by asking her instead.'

Was that a threat? Daniela tensed. She wished she'd listened to Leo when he'd tried to warn her about his dad. She hadn't taken him seriously. She'd figured Henry was all talk. Their families had known each other for years; she'd grown up thinking he was her uncle. But now, with him right in front of her, she was so scared she could barely breathe.

'I-I can call Frankie,' she heard herself saying. 'I can—'

'You think I haven't tried calling?'

'She won't answer if she knows it's you. She'll answer me.'

Henry held her gaze for another moment. Then he smiled and held out his hand. 'Give me your phone, then.'

If there'd been any space behind her, Daniela would've backed away further. Her eyes darted left and right, looking for a weapon—

Her breath caught in her throat as she remembered the knife in her pocket.

Henry still had his hand out. 'This is very simple,' he said. 'Give me your phone, or I'll go straight home and tell the police that you and your idiot sister broke into my shop this morning. How do you think your dad will feel about that?'

Pretending to look for her phone, Daniela reached into the inside pocket of her jacket. The knife handle was cool against her palm. Her left hand went into her front pocket and got out her phone.

Instead of handing over the phone, she tossed it high over his head. It dropped with a splat into the mud some distance behind him. Annoyance flashed across Henry's face.

'Now let me past,' she said. She managed to keep the tremor from her voice.

The look of annoyance turned into a smirk. Henry held up his hands mockingly and stepped out of her way. To get past, Daniela would have to cross between him and the river. It would be way too easy for him to shove her into the water as she darted past.

'Move,' she said.

Henry stayed where he was, still smirking.

'Move.' Daniela flicked out the blade of the knife.

That got rid of his smile. His eyes moved from the blade to her face and back again.

'Are you still claiming you didn't steal anything from my shop?' he asked with a nod to the distinctive knife.

'Get out of my way.'

With a shrug, Henry stepped backwards. He kept a watchful eye on her face. As he passed where her phone lay in the mud, he bent down to scoop it up, then stepped off the path onto the verge. He pressed back into the edge of the bramble bushes to give Daniela plenty of room to get past.

She considered demanding her phone back. But all she wanted in that moment was to get away. The hand holding the knife was shaking.

'Mind your footing,' Henry said, looking down at the

muddy ground. 'It's a bit cold for swimming at this time of year.'

Daniela edged as close as she dared before darting past him. The knife was gripped tight in her hand, ready to swing at Henry if he so much as moved, but he leaned back well out of her way. His eyes were still cautious.

The moment she was past him, Daniela turned and ran.

She sprinted out through the car park, past Henry's car, across the road and into the trees on the far side. Once she was in the safety of the woods, she glanced back but Henry was already lost to view.

She didn't slow down. The easiest route home was along the road, but it was longer, almost two miles. Daniela could shave a half-mile off the distance by cutting through the trees. Plus, there was less chance of Henry following her. The idea of running down the roads with the constant fear of his car appearing behind her—

Daniela plunged through the trees. She folded the knife and shoved it back into her pocket as she ran. Her feet knew every inch of these woods. They carried her over fallen trunks and around deadwood tangles. But she couldn't stop looking backwards. Even though she knew Henry wasn't following her; even though she was certain—

Her boot slipped in a patch of mud. She went over on her ankle and fell, sprawling on the hard ground. She tried to regain her feet but pain sang in her ankle. Something had snapped as she'd fallen, she was sure of it.

Tears sprang to her eyes, fuelled by frustration and anger and the sick residue of the fear she'd felt at the riverbank. She smashed her fist into the ground. She hated Henry for scaring her like that. Hated herself for being scared.

Why had she let him take her phone? She'd had the knife right there in her hand. She could've demanded the phone back. Or stopped him getting close to her. Why hadn't she done *something*?

She ground her teeth together to stifle her screams.

18

February 2017

Daniela lay flat against the muddy bank, still the wrong way up, feeling the cold press of earth against her shoulders. Rain splattered her face. She reached out on either side, searching for anything that might help. Her fingertips found the plastic covering of the package. Daniela silently cursed. She was going to be caught by the police, yards from a crime scene, with a big lump of incriminating evidence. It wasn't the most stupid situation she'd ever got into, but it was close.

Feeling blindly around, her other hand found a knot of tree roots protruding from the bank. Beneath was a small hollow, hardly bigger than her palm.

The footsteps came closer. The person was casting back and forth like they were searching for the source of the noise they'd heard.

Daniela grabbed the package and shoved it into the hollow beneath the roots. It didn't fit. She wiggled the parcel, ramming it into the space with as much strength as she could muster. Every movement brought a fresh twinge from her trapped ankle. With one final effort, she wedged the package. She couldn't be sure it was hidden from above. There was no time to check.

The unseen person kicked through a pile of sodden leaves near the hollow where Daniela lay trapped. Daniela rolled onto her shoulder, gritting her teeth, and pushed up onto her elbow. It gave her a tiny amount of room to move her foot. She turned her ankle and the sucking grip of the boot relaxed a fractional amount. She twisted and pulled. Her foot came loose from the boot. Daniela tumbled onto her back at the bottom of the depression, gasping.

She managed to sit up just as the person appeared at the lip of the hollow. Daniela held up a hand to shield her face from the rain that blinded her.

'Daniela?' a voice asked.

Relief washed away the shock and adrenaline. She almost laughed, despite everything. It wasn't Stephanie. 'Yes,' Daniela admitted. 'Hi.'

'What the hell are you doing?' Leo McKearney asked.

Daniela looked down at herself. She was soaked through, splattered with mud, with only one boot. She didn't dare risk a glance at the package she'd shoved beneath the roots. But she could see it in her peripheral vision, a smear of blue plastic, shockingly out of place among the mud and dead leaves.

'I fell,' Daniela said sheepishly. 'My boot got stuck.'

Leo glanced down and located the boot wedged like a trophy in the looped root halfway up the bank. 'That was careless,' he said. 'What on earth are you doing out here? Aren't you freezing?'

Daniela attempted a smile. 'A little,' she admitted. 'And I've bust my ankle. It'd be really helpful if someone came by to help me, and that person was by chance a doctor.'

Leo huffed in annoyance. 'Well, that's what you get for running around the woods in the middle of a flood. The falling bit, I mean, not the lucky find.' He picked his way down into the hollow. 'Are you okay?'

'I'm peachy. The ground broke my fall.'

Leo climbed down beside her. The concern in his eyes surprised Daniela. 'No,' Leo said, 'I mean, are you *okay*? What're you doing out here?'

Daniela avoided his gaze. 'I was ... I don't know. What're *you* doing here?'

'I came to make sure the house was locked up,' Leo said. 'Stephanie's a good person, but this has hit her hard. I don't know if she remembered to lock the doors when we left.'

'That's ... thoughtful.'

Leo looked surprised. 'What else am I supposed to do? I owe it to ... to Auryn.' His eyes were wet. He blinked the tears away. 'Anyway. You've hurt your ankle?'

'Yeah.' Daniela attempted to flex her leg, and was surprised to find it didn't hurt as much as expected. It was the same ankle she'd twisted while running from Henry McKearney, all those years ago. It had been weak ever since. 'It felt like I'd broken it. Probably not more than a bruise, right? That'd make me look even sillier.'

She sat up. She was anxious that Leo would turn around. The blue package, clearly visible below the roots, was right behind him.

'Well, I can take a look anyway,' Leo said.

'Can we get out of the mud first?' Daniela asked. 'It's not super-comfy down here.' Before Leo could stop her, Daniela got up, balancing on her good foot, and hobbled towards the far side of the hollow. Away from the package.

Leo followed. 'Seriously, Daniela, what were you doing out here?' he asked in his soft voice.

'Seriously? I don't have a good answer.' Daniela forced a laugh. 'I'm supposed to be staying at the Crossed Swords. But I just ... I don't know. I wanted some fresh air. I only went out for a cigarette. Then I thought I'd walk around a bit. Clear my head.'

'In the rain? With the whole town flooded?'

'I didn't mean to walk far. But I kinda found my way here. Like my feet knew where they were going better than I did.'

It sounded lame. But Leo nodded like he understood. 'This must be hard for you,' he said.

Daniela could only shrug. Anything she said would sound false. And she was uncomfortable with Leo's concern. She remembered the shock in his eyes when he'd seen Daniela at the old house that morning; the way he'd asked Stephanie: 'Why is she here?'

Daniela understood hostility. She was used to it. But this gentle sympathy confused her.

'Come on,' Leo said, all business now. 'Let's get out of the mud. I think we could use a warm drink, don't you?'

'Sure.' Daniela forced the smile again. She looked up at the bank leading from the hollow. 'I think I can climb this side,' she said. 'It's not so bad. Can you give me a hand if I slip?'

Leo followed her. Daniela started climbing, as fast as she dared, using the protruding roots as handholds. She could just about put weight on her injured ankle. Mud squished unpleasantly beneath her sock.

She looked back and realised Leo had turned away. 'Hey!' she said, twisting around.

Her heart froze. Leo was crossing the hollow away from

her. His feet walked perilously close to the concealed package.

Leo stopped right next to it. Before Daniela could open her mouth, Leo reached up and pulled the trapped boot loose from where it was stuck.

'Here we go.' He presented it to Daniela with a flourish. 'You'll probably need this, hmm?'

19

They walked together away from the hollow, Daniela limping. Her ankle pained her more than she liked, but she didn't want to ask Leo for help.

Leo paused to look down at the old house. 'It's so horrible to see the place like that, isn't it?' he said, quietly. 'It looks so ... abandoned.'

'Why d'you think Auryn let it get into such a state?' Daniela asked. It occurred to her that Leo might have some clues as to what'd happened to Auryn.

But Leo just shook his head and turned away. He set off down towards the flooded road. After a moment, Daniela followed.

'You know that hot drink you offered a minute ago?' Daniela asked.

Leo half-laughed. 'Sounds like a good idea, doesn't it? It's the only way to deal with a day like today.'

Daniela had asked because she wanted a chance to talk to Leo, preferably somewhere that wasn't public. She could've suggested they both go back to the Crossed Swords, but she didn't particularly want to run into Stephanie again, not just yet. Daniela was still mad at her for turning over her room.

Of course, Steph was justified, she thought sourly. But what annoyed her more: the fact that Stephanie had suspected her of stealing the money, or the fact that she'd been right to do so?

'Are you still living at home?' Daniela asked Leo.

'Not quite. Mum always said I could move back with her after university if I wanted, to save money, but—' Leo laughed '—I'd only just escaped. It'd feel like such a backwards step to live at home again. Then one of the new-build cottages here in Stonecrop came up for rent. I thought, why not? It lets me be close to Mum without us tripping over each other, and I can commute to Hackett easily enough. Plus, it'll give me a chance to save up the deposit for my own place someday. Perhaps.'

'Why didn't you stay in Newcastle after university?'

'Well. I've got a good start to my career here. I was never cut out to be a doctor in a busy city hospital.' If there was any residual bitterness, Leo hid it well. 'Dewar's is quite frantic enough for me, thank you.'

They stepped down into the water and waded around the perimeter of the old house to the road. Daniela tried not to look up at Auryn's bedroom window.

'Where're the new houses?' Daniela asked. She hadn't seen any new buildings in the village.

'Over that way. Where the ruined mill used to be. They knocked it down three years ago and redeveloped the whole site. Four new houses. There was a bit of fuss with planning permission and all, but they don't look so bad. The trees camouflage them.'

Daniela wasn't listening. Her brain had seized. The ruined mill. *Kirk Cottage.*

How could Leo stand to live there? Even if the area had

been redeveloped, he must think about the old mill every time he opened his front door. Just the thought of that place made Daniela's stomach knot.

Leo noticed she'd slowed as they ascended the road away from the old house. 'Are you sure you're all right?' he asked.

'It's okay. I'm fine.'

'Here, let me help.'

Before Daniela could stop him, Leo hooked an arm under her shoulders. He was six inches taller than Daniela. She was at once aware of the warmth of his body and the smell of his aftershave. She was equally aware of how she herself smelled in her day-old clothes.

'Thanks,' Daniela mumbled.

They walked in silence down the other side of the rise and back into the flooded road. The pressure of the floodwater compressed her welly around her bruised ankle. Daniela moved slowly, favouring her right leg, even though she was anxious to get somewhere warm and safe so she could talk to Leo.

'We're not getting far at this pace,' Daniela said. 'Sorry.'

'I've parked my car down the road,' Leo said. 'It's a bit hairy driving around in six inches of water but it's still possible. We'll go back to mine and get warm.'

Daniela stalled at the connotations of *back to mine*. She nodded. 'Sure. Sounds like a plan.'

The silence stretched as they walked. Even if she'd wanted to talk, Daniela couldn't; her teeth were chattering. Leo didn't seem to mind the silence. Either that or he wasn't sure what to say.

Daniela was aware of Leo's body, his proximity. He was tucked in close, his arm looped around Daniela's back. A stray memory crossed Daniela's mind, of the last time she'd seen Leo before today, and that hurried, stolen kiss. She closed her eyes to banish the memory. For years it'd burned like a brand in her mind. She didn't want to think of it now.

Leo had left the Land Rover blocking the narrow lane where the water got deeper.

'I've already got stuck once today,' Leo said. 'Didn't feel like calling out Tilly and her tractor again. I figured it didn't matter if I blocked the road at this time of day.'

The vehicle wasn't locked. He opened the passenger side door and reached into the back seat, unfolding a blanket. He spread it out across the passenger seat so Daniela wouldn't get mud on the upholstery.

'It's the dog's blanket,' he explained. 'Sorry about the smell.' He picked up a green gym bag from the passenger footwell and threw it onto the back seat.

Daniela slid into the car and pulled the door closed. The rain drummed quiet fingertips on the roof. She huddled down in the front seat, feeling damp and uncomfortable.

Leo reversed the car down the lane until he reached a place where he could turn around. Despite the size of the vehicle and the flooded ditches on either side of the road, he steered with confidence. He also whacked the heater on full blast. Daniela was extremely grateful for the hot air that whooshed from the vents.

She kept her head down as they passed the outskirts of Stonecrop, but no other cars were on the roads. The Land Rover's wheels left a wake in the flooded streets. Leo drove slowly, steering the big vehicle as if it were a ship moving through shallow waters. The wipers swept away stray raindrops.

To reach the new developments, they had to drive the long

way around, even though the location was quite close to Daniela's old home. A footpath through the woods connected them, but Daniela was happy enough to take the car. She was less happy when they approached the former site of Kirk Cottage.

Daniela sank lower in her seat as if that could protect her from memories. She dreaded seeing the place again. Redevelopment wouldn't stop it looking and feeling the same. It was a bad idea to go there.

But when the headlights swept over the white-fronted houses, she got a pleasant shock. The area was so different she wouldn't have recognised it. The ruined building beside the River Bade was gone, bulldozed so cleanly it was like it'd never existed. The whole area had been raised so it overlooked the river. That must've been done to reduce the risk of flooding, and it appeared to have worked, because the four new houses stood clear of the water.

Leo pulled up outside the closest house, a smallish building with a gabled roof and a trellised porch. The new houses were a bit too modern, too smart and slick for the crumbling village. She understood why some residents had objected.

Daniela stayed low in her seat, letting warm air blow directly into her face. She felt an unease about being there but if she was going to figure out what happened to Auryn, she needed to talk to Leo.

Leo helped her out of the car. She sheltered from the rain under the wooden porch as Leo pushed open the front door of the cottage – unlocked, Daniela noted. It would take a while for her to get used to that again. Too much time living in the city had erased her trust in strangers.

Daniela felt the heat as soon as she stepped through the door. She'd begun to feel like she'd never be warm again.

'Make yourself comfy,' Leo said, switching on some lights. 'I'll get the kettle on.'

The cottage was compact but modern, with recessed lighting and the sort of tasteful paint schemes that were found in every rental property in the country. The sitting room and dining room led off from either side of the entrance hallway. A warm bready smell drifted from the kitchen at the end of the hall. Daniela's mouth watered. She hadn't realised how hungry she was. She should've found a way to sneak some breakfast from the Crossed Swords.

She went into the sitting room. A gas heater disguised as a real fire with a guard around it was set to a low heat that made yellow flames dance across imitation coals. A Yorkshire terrier had claimed the warmest spot on the rug. It pricked its ears as Daniela came in but otherwise refused to acknowledge her existence. Daniela stepped around the dog to get close to the fire, turning the heat up to its highest setting. She kicked off her boots, then, after a moment's hesitation, peeled off her socks as well. They didn't smell too good. She tucked the boots up next to the fireguard with her socks draped on top.

Where am I? The house had been built on the site of Kirk Cottage. So she couldn't be more than twenty or thirty feet away from where she would have stood last time she'd been there. Higher up, of course, since the ground had been raised. If she dug down through the soft soil of the back garden, would she find the foundation stones of the original building? Or had everything been erased, scraped away, then buried beneath rubble?

She hoped so.

In the kitchen, Leo filled the kettle. Daniela was torn between wanting to go talk to him and wanting to stay next to the fire. She felt uncomfortable in his house, unable to settle. She wandered the room, looking at the framed pictures on the walls, which were all of landscapes or buildings. No family photos. Daniela was grateful she wasn't confronted by photos of Henry.

She left the warmth of the fire and edged around the door of the hall. From there she had a partial view into the kitchen. Leo was pottering around, choosing mugs from the draining board, humming as he waited for the kettle. While his back was turned, Daniela took the opportunity to twist the latch on the front door. It quietly clicked closed.

She waited until Leo was almost finished in the kitchen, then retreated to the fire. She sat down just as Leo appeared in the doorway with two steaming mugs of tea.

'You look half-frozen,' Leo said as he passed a mug to her. 'Stay put. I'll find a towel for your hair.'

Daniela wrapped her hands around the cup. Slowly thawing, she started to put together the list of questions she wanted to ask Leo. If anyone knew about Auryn's recent past, it would be him.

20

The cottage was well insulated and, once Leo closed the internal doors, the sitting room warmed quickly.

Daniela sat on the threadbare sofa, which was now covered by two bath towels, protecting it from her muddy clothes. She tried to bat away the awareness of how grubby she was. The tea was hot and sweet and milky, with the heat of the mug almost burning her palms. Normally she drank coffee, black and bitter, but she wasn't arguing with a doctor. She'd dried her hair and arms with another towel that Leo had provided. He'd also found a knitted jumper that must've been ten sizes too big for him, which Daniela could wear while her own jumper was drying by the fire. It hung off Daniela's lanky frame like a poncho. But again, it was warm, so she wasn't complaining.

Leo sat on the other end of the sofa. The heat of the fire filled the room. The dog on the rug snored.

'What happened to Auryn?' Daniela asked. The question had been circling her mind, but it wasn't necessarily where she meant to start. 'You examined her, right?'

Leo set his mug down on a side table and clasped his hands, as if organising his thoughts into something Daniela would want to hear.

'Steph told me someone killed her,' Daniela said, to help him out.

'It's too early to say,' Leo said carefully. 'We won't know for sure until the post-mortem.'

Daniela nodded. 'They'll have to take her to Hackett for that, yeah?'

Leo nodded. 'The nearest facilities are at Dewar's. Stephanie's contacted someone to collect the body.'

'How long d'you reckon that'll be?'

'Hard to say. They'll get here as soon as the roads are passable.' Leo's tone was soothing, professional. It was a noticeable difference from the shy young man Daniela remembered.

'I don't like the idea of her lying there all alone.'

Leo looked away. 'It's awful, isn't it? But I don't know what else we can do right now.'

Daniela frowned into her tea. 'So ... I mean, I know you can't say for definite, but ... what d'you think happened?'

'I don't know if I—'

'You don't have to protect me. I found her, remember? I know how she looked.'

Leo paused, sipping his tea, either ordering his thoughts or just stalling. 'What did Stephanie tell you?' he asked.

'She said Auryn was stabbed.'

Leo nodded slowly. 'That's what it looked like, yes.'

'*Looked* like?'

'It's impossible to be sure. There was an injury here.' He touched his flank below the ribs. 'We didn't even notice it until after we lifted her onto the bed. If we'd spotted it straight away, well, we wouldn't have moved her, for a start. We would've had to leave her in situ. But it wasn't an obvious injury. It *looked* like a knife wound. I can't be sure.'

'What else could it be?'

'Anything. She might've cut herself when she fell. It could've happened after death – there was a lot of debris floating around. I told Steph not to jump to any conclusions, because we honestly won't know until the post-mortem.'

'What conclusions?'

Leo shrugged carefully. 'Stephanie was angry and upset. It can make people irrational. She got the idea in her head that someone killed Auryn, and she went off immediately looking for a suspect.'

'Me.' Daniela tried to blink away the idea. 'She came straight to the pub to speak to me. But, I mean, she can't think I'm involved with this, can she?'

Leo paused a little too long before saying, 'Of course she doesn't think that.'

'No, she does. Of course, she does.' Daniela hunched her shoulders. That's why Stephanie was searching her room, why she'd asked those insinuating questions, why she'd stopped Daniela leaving town. 'God, why wouldn't she? I mean, I rock up in town unannounced on the very day Auryn gets murdered. I found the body. Me and Auryn hadn't spoken in seven years.' Their last conversation had ended with Auryn threatening to kill her. Daniela didn't want to remind Leo of that. 'Plus ...' She trailed off. Another unspoken thought: Stephanie knew Daniela's history. She knew what Daniela was capable of.

Leo's smile was sad. 'She's not thinking straight right now. None of us are. But she doesn't believe any of that, not really.'

But Daniela couldn't shake the thought now. It was one thing for Stephanie to suspect her of stealing the money, but did she really think Daniela was involved in Auryn's death? She couldn't honestly think that, could she?

'Who would want to hurt Auryn?' Daniela asked aloud. 'She wasn't the type to make enemies. Was she?'

Leo half-laughed. 'No, not at all. Everyone loved her. She'd go a mile out of her way to do anyone a favour.'

'I know.'

'Remember when we were kids, how we used to send her into the sweet shop in Hackett ahead of us to charm the old folk behind the counter? No one could resist that smile of hers. She'd always come out with a handful of free sweets for us.'

Daniela smiled too, but she was thinking. 'She'd never say no to anyone,' she said. 'What if someone took advantage of that?'

'People often did,' Leo said with a sigh. 'At uni, she was always the one our friends would go to if they were short of cash, or if they needed help with their coursework. I swear she spent more time doing other people's assignments than her own.'

That probably hadn't changed after Auryn moved to London. Daniela could well imagine her, always wanting to help, always willing to go out of her way. Always trusting she wouldn't get hurt in return.

'Daniela?' Leo asked then, breaking her train of thought. 'Can I ask ... where've you been since you got out? Why didn't you come back sooner?'

Daniela snorted. 'What's to come back for? Who'd want to see me?'

Leo didn't answer, and Daniela almost laughed at herself. *What were you expecting? Leo didn't miss you. The best thing you ever did for him was leaving.*

'I've not been anywhere specifically,' Daniela said to cover the moment. 'Just ... building a new life. Getting back on my feet, finding a job, all that stuff.'

'Where're you working?' There was a hesitation behind the question, which made Daniela half laugh.

'It's legit, if that's what you're thinking,' Daniela said. 'Boringly legit. Data entry for a computer company, scanning documents for eight hours a day.' The annoying thing was, there'd been plenty of offers of better paid, more interesting work after she'd left prison. So long as she wasn't fussy who she worked for. 'It's work.' She shrugged. 'I guess Steph's given you any relevant updates about me.'

'I don't speak to Stephanie very often. I see her around town, but we don't socialise.'

'But you've heard. Small towns like this, no one has any secrets.'

Leo nodded. 'I heard some of it. Like you say, people talk.'

Gossip was the bread and butter of a small town, and any scrap, no matter how insubstantial, was circulated and recycled until it lost all flavour. Everyone in Stonecrop knew her life story. Dani Cain was the biggest thing that'd happened to the village. She imagined people whispering. *She's out now, did you hear? It's only a matter of time till she does something else. Her kind don't change ...'*

She still had nightmares about the incident that'd landed her in prison. Seven years hadn't faded those memories. If anything, time and maturity had added a new dimension. She often woke up in the middle of the night shivering with guilt and panic. It sickened her to recall how often she'd told people it wasn't her fault, when they all knew no one was to blame but her. Things might never have got out of hand if she hadn't been carrying the knife that day.

That bloody knife, Daniela thought sourly. Ever since she'd acquired it, it'd caused nothing but grief. Her eyes went to her jacket, hanging over the arm of the chair, with the knife hiding somewhere in an inside pocket. If it was possible to assign malicious intent to an inanimate object ...

'It was stupid of me to come back,' Daniela said. 'If I'd known you were here – I mean, this isn't what I wanted. For you to have to deal with me again.'

Leo tightened his jaw. 'I can't think about that right now. Not with what's happened to Auryn.' He hesitated. 'Why *have* you come back?'

Daniela shrugged. 'It's been a long time. I wanted to see Steph.'

'*Now*, though, with the flooding? You couldn't have picked a more inconvenient time. I'm not even sure how you got here.'

'I walked from Hackett. Waded.' *And now she was stuck.*

'So, it must've been urgent. Couldn't it wait?'

Daniela hesitated, then came to a decision. 'You want the stupid, boring truth?' she asked. 'I'm getting evicted. The place I'm living in is one of those rent-to-buy things, but the land-lord's decided we need to buy *now*. I need a little over four grand by Tuesday to cover the shortfall in the deposit, other-wise I'm out on my ear. I'll lose everything. I came home this weekend to ask Stephanie for money.'

Leo studied the side of Daniela's face. 'Did she give it to you?'

'I never got the chance to ask.' The lie came easy enough. 'After everything that's happened, it hardly seems to matter, does it?'

Because it *didn't* matter, did it? If Daniela lost her home, lost everything she'd worked so goddamn hard to build up over the last year, who would care? Likely it was no more than she deserved.

Daniela rubbed her face. 'Christ, if I'd thought to come last week,' she said, 'Auryn would've still been alive. I could've ... shit, I don't know. I could've talked to her, y'know? Maybe figured out what was wrong.' *Maybe apologised.*

Leo watched her. 'How do you mean?'

'C'mon, you know something was wrong. Look how she was living. She used to be so tidy. Like ridiculously tidy, even as a kid. But when I was there yesterday ... the house was a state, even before it flooded. You saw the empty bottles, right?' Something besides the general state of the house continued to niggle her. 'Steph said Auryn had a breakdown. Quit her job, all that. If I'd just cared enough to visit ...'

Leo squeezed her arm in gentle support. Daniela flinched from the unexpected contact. 'It's okay,' Leo said. 'I mean, it's not; it's awful. But it's nothing we could've predicted. None of us knew. I mean, she was drinking too much, yes. I always told her—' He stopped.

Leo's hand on her arm had distracted Daniela. 'Were you guys still friendly?' she asked.

'Oh, I don't know. Like you say, when you're neighbours you have to stay kinda cordial, don't you?'

'You could've picked anywhere to live,' Daniela said. 'Did you ever think about moving down to London, to be closer to Auryn?' Daniela felt a twinge of a very old envy, which surprised her. She thought she'd drowned those feelings a long time ago.

God, I'm the most inappropriate person in the world. What's wrong with me?

Leo considered his words before he answered. 'It would've never been practical, for me to live in London,' he said. 'But when I heard she was moving back to Stonecrop last year, I did wonder for a time whether she was coming back here for me. I thought maybe she'd change her mind and let me back into her life. Losing her was the worst mistake I ever made.' His voice wavered. 'Actually, no. The worst mistake was when we broke up. I told her I didn't want her to keep the baby.'

21

June 2010

A mile was a long way on a damaged leg. It took Daniela over an hour to reach the old house. Which gave her plenty of time to think.

Now fear and adrenaline had worn off, anger took over. She spent a lot of time planning what she'd do to Henry next time they met.

But she was also angry with herself. How had she got into such a stupid situation? She'd let Henry corner her by the river. She'd let him threaten her and take her phone. Her idiocy made her want to break something.

With every step, Daniela discovered how difficult it was to walk cross-country with a bad ankle. Uneven ground and patches of mud suddenly became insurmountable obstacles. She had to lean heavily on trees for support. Several times she stumbled and once she fell flat onto the grass at the edge of the path. She wondered if she'd be better off staying down.

Keep going. Don't fall. Don't fall.

Even so, she was glad she hadn't walked through town. She was dishevelled, limping, with her eyes red from suppressed

tears. At best she looked crazy. If anyone saw her, they'd immediately call her father.

Daniela definitely didn't want that. She was still trying to
work out how to tell Stephanie about all this.

Her thoughts turned inevitably to Franklyn. Daniela had
screwed up. She'd let Henry take her phone and get
Franklyn's number. If not for her, Henry might never find
Frankie.

He would've asked Auryn instead. Daniela's hands shook at
the idea of Henry, with that insincere smile of his, doing
anything to threaten Auryn. What if it'd been Auryn walking
alone by the river that afternoon when Henry drove past?
What might've happened?

At last, the path led her home. Daniela staggered down the
slope to the old house. The jolting pain in her ankle was now
so familiar she barely noticed it. Her whole body was a map
of discomfort.

It looked like no one was home. No lights showed in the
downstairs windows. Daniela let herself in through the back
door. She paused in the kitchen, listening. The house was
silent.

She went to the freezer to look for ice to put on her ankle.
Among the frozen ready meals that'd been there so long they
were welded together, she located a plastic tray of ice cubes.
They too had been in there for some time, the cubes frozen
tight to the plastic, opaque with age. Daniela whacked the
tray on the counter a few times. When the cubes refused to
come loose, she took a knife out of the kitchen drawer and
started jemmying them out. She grabbed a tea towel to pile
the ice into.

Her hands were still shaking. Angrily, she stabbed at the

ice with more force, sending chips flying across the counter. *Stupid, stupid.*

'What're you doing?'

Daniela spun around. The knife clattered to the tiled floor.

Auryn stood in the doorway. She was barefoot, her blonde hair tangled like she hadn't combed it properly after her shower that morning. She frowned at the knife.

'I-I hurt my ankle,' Daniela said. 'I fell. In the woods. I—'

Auryn came into the kitchen. Her eyes were wide. Gently, almost fearfully, she touched Daniela's shoulder. Daniela flinched away. 'Dani, what happened?' Auryn asked. 'Are you okay?'

Daniela realised she must look awful. Instinctively she wanted to shrug off Auryn's concern and pretend everything was fine. But she felt tears prickling her eyes.

'No,' she said, 'I'm not okay.'

Auryn picked up the kitchen knife and set it on the counter with the blade pointing away. 'What happened?' she asked in a deliberately calm tone.

'I need to sit down. Who else is home?'

'Leo's here, in the spare room. I think he's reading. And I guess Dad's upstairs.' Auryn wrapped the broken ice up into the tea towel then put out a hand to support Daniela as she limped into the front room.

Daniela collapsed on the sofa. She'd never been so grateful to rest.

'Take your shoe off,' Auryn said.

Teeth gritted against the discomfort, Daniela unlaced her trainer and worked it off her foot. Auryn gave her the bundle of ice to hold against her ankle.

Auryn sat down in the armchair. She leaned forwards and

rested her elbows on her knees, lacing her fingers. Daniela wondered where she'd acquired that habit. It did make her look like a lawyer.

'So, tell me,' Auryn said.

Daniela propped her injured leg on the coffee table. The effort made her wince. 'It was Henry,' she admitted.

'Henry did that to you?' Auryn asked, shocked.

It was tempting to say yes. After all, it was his fault she'd fallen. 'He followed me out into the woods,' she said. 'He wanted to know where Franklyn was.'

'Frankie? What for?'

Daniela wasn't sure she wanted to share everything she'd learned about Franklyn. And she really didn't want to tell Auryn about the burglary that morning.

'No idea,' she said. 'He's angry with her for something. He … he threatened to throw me in the river if I didn't tell him.' Daniela tried to say it casually, like the idea of the freezing water didn't still terrify her.

Auryn's expression was appalled. 'Seriously?'

Daniela hesitated. The threat had definitely been there – hadn't it? Maybe Henry hadn't used those exact words, and maybe he hadn't laid a hand on Daniela, but still—

'Seriously, yeah.' Daniela pushed down her damp sock so she could put the icepack against her bare skin. 'I don't know if he really would've done it.'

'Why would he do something like that?'

'Frankie's run off and he wants to find her. He's still mad about the argument yesterday.'

'You said the argument was nothing serious.'

'Yeah, turns out I was wrong.' Daniela couldn't keep the bitterness from her voice. Why the hell was Henry so worked up about a small amount of money? 'Anyways. Nothing came of it. I got away from him and came straight home.'

'But what happened to your ankle?'

If Daniela intended to blame Henry, now was her chance. Auryn would believe whatever story Daniela told. Together, they could tell Stephanie. It might be an opportunity to get Henry put away, which was exactly what he deserved.

Daniela considered it seriously for several seconds. But lying to Stephanie would set off a chain of events. Daniela would have to make a statement. She'd have to tell her story over and over, and keep it consistent and believable each time. Could she do that? And, when the police got involved, there'd be nothing to stop Henry telling them about the break-in at his store, about Franklyn taking the money ... and about Daniela waving a knife at him.

As much as she'd like to see Henry take the hit, she didn't want to get herself and Franklyn into trouble at the same time.

So, she sighed and said, 'I fell, when I was running home. I went over on my stupid ankle. Thought I'd broken it, to be honest, but I guess not.'

'You should go to the hospital and get it x-rayed.'

Daniela shook her head. Her gaze wandered to the liquor cabinet in the corner of the room. She should've gone there first rather than straight to the sofa. 'It's not worth the trouble,' she said. 'I'm fine.'

'You don't look fine.' Auryn watched her. 'Do you want me to call Steph?'

Daniela shook her head. 'I'll tell her when she gets home.' *Once I've figured out how much to say.*

'Definitely?'

'What's that look for? Yes, of course, I'm going to tell her.'

'You're angry.' Auryn studied her from behind those round glasses. 'Can you promise me you'll tell Stephanie, rather than doing something foolish?'

Daniela stared down at her busted ankle. She didn't answer.

22

It was obvious Auryn wasn't happy with the situation. She kept hassling Daniela to go to the hospital, and Daniela kept refusing.

'My foot is obviously not broken,' Daniela said. 'Why should I waste everyone's time getting someone to confirm what we already know?'

Eventually, Auryn threw her hands up in annoyance up and went to find Leo.

Daniela waited until Auryn's creaking footsteps reached the top of the stairs, then she got off the sofa. Putting weight on her ankle was agonising. She sucked in her breath and hopped across the room. On a side table next to the television was the landline phone.

With difficulty, Daniela settled onto the sill of the wide bay window and picked up the phone, dialling Franklyn's number from memory.

As she listened to the dial tone, Daniela rooted in her jacket pocket and brought out the flick-knife. It was a cold, ugly weight. She closed her fingers around it, feeling a dull thrill as if the metal was electrified. Her thumb rested on the push button that would pop the blade. Her mouth was dry.

The phone rang at least ten times, and Daniela was about to hang up, but then Franklyn answered.

'Yeah?'

'Frankie? It's me.'

A heavy exhalation of air. 'Thank God. You all right, Dani?'

'I'm fine, yeah.' *More or less.* 'You?'

'Never mind about me. Henry said he – what happened? What did that bastard do?'

'Nothing. He was just – I don't know. It's all right though. I'm okay.'

'Listen, Dani, I'm sorry. I am so sorry you're involved in this. It's all my stupid fault. I never considered Henry would come after you.' Franklyn loosed a breath. 'I shouldn't have gone into his shop this morning. I definitely shouldn't've taken you with me.'

'I'm not a kid. I can get myself into trouble if I want.'

'This isn't a game, Dani.'

'Yeah, no fooling.' Daniela leaned back so she could prop her bad foot on the corner of the television stand. 'And, if it means anything, I'm sorry too. I—'

'Christ, this isn't your fault.'

'I let it happen. I should've ... should've done *some*thing. I shouldn't have let him take my phone. He wouldn't have been able to find you if it wasn't for me.'

She heard the scratch of a lighter as Franklyn lit a cigarette. 'Right, we can play this game later, when I'm home. For now, we draw a line under it. I'm on my way to meet Henry.'

Despite her ankle, Daniela sat up. 'You are?'

'What else can I do? I've already made the situation worse. I can't risk any of you getting hurt.'

The hard edge in her voice unnerved Daniela. 'I don't know

if it's such a great idea,' Daniela said. 'Henry's pretty angry. I don't know what he's planning.'

Franklyn laughed without humour. 'Don't worry. I can guess. Listen, is Steph working today?'

'Steph? I don't know. Yeah, I assume so.'

'That explains why she's not answering her phone. If you see her, get her to call me.'

Daniela blinked. 'Sure, but—'

'Thanks. I'll see you later, yeah? Take it easy.'

Franklyn hung up. Daniela stared blankly out of the window. The same feeling of helplessness stole over her. She should be doing something. The idea of Franklyn going off to face Henry alone ... anything could happen. Henry was crazy. He'd threatened to drown Daniela over some petty breaking-and-entering. What might he do to Franklyn?

But Franklyn could look after herself, couldn't she? Daniela had to believe that. The alternative didn't bear thinking about.

Daniela awoke on her bed. For a minute she couldn't work out how she'd got there. Eventually she remembered swallowing two paracetamol and filching a bottle of whisky from the drinks cabinet to take upstairs. There'd be hell to pay when her dad realised the alcohol was missing, but Daniela didn't care. Chances were, he'd blame Franklyn anyway.

After that, Daniela must've fallen asleep, although she didn't recall doing so. She was fully dressed, sprawled on her bed with her foot propped on a pillow, the whisky bottle resting at her side. About a fifth of the bottle was gone. She'd left the tea towel full of ice on the hardwood floor, where it'd formed a sodden puddle next to her shoes.

Daniela sat up. She felt dizzy and sick, a combination of

alcohol, painkillers, and sour adrenaline. It was dark in the bedroom, dark outside the window, so she must've been asleep for hours.

Something had woken her but she didn't know what.

Her foot had mercifully gone numb, until Daniela swung her leg out of bed and tried putting weight on it. Then pins and needles raced up her leg and drilled into her knee. She gritted her teeth and waited for the ache to recede. It didn't. Each time it started fading, it returned in a hot wave, fierce enough to bring tears to her eyes. She fished for the whisky bottle and took another burning gulp.

Daniela became aware of voices downstairs, muffled and indistinct. She thought she recognised Stephanie's bass rumble. Daniela's stomach turned. She couldn't put off talking to Stephanie any longer.

The noise of an engine. That's what'd woken her. In her dreams she'd heard the distinctive rattle of Stephanie's car pulling up outside the house.

The other person downstairs raised their voice, and Daniela recognised it. She felt a wave of relief.

Bracing against the jagged pain, Daniela hobbled down the stairs to the landing. Every step was a reminder of what she owed Henry. At some point while she'd slept, Daniela's fear – for herself, for Franklyn – had hardened into anger again. She'd dreamed about getting even.

From the landing, Daniela heard Stephanie's voice in the kitchen. Whatever Stephanie was saying, she was angry. Her voice was low, level – a sure sign. Everyone in the house knew to start running if Stephanie spoke like that.

'She needed to know,' Franklyn answered. Unlike Stephanie, her anger manifested itself conventionally. She was two steps from shouting. 'She has to get away from him. If this is what it takes …'

'Sure. Poor, altruistic Franklyn. Just trying to do the right thing.'

Thank God, Franklyn was home. Ever since they'd spoken that afternoon Daniela had been certain something awful would happen. She padded downstairs, then through the living room to the kitchen. She peeked in.

Stephanie, in her uniform, had her back to the door. One hand rested on the handcuffs at her belt, hopefully just from habit. Franklyn sat on the kitchen table, hands on knees, shoulders hunched.

'I know this whole shitty situation is my fault,' Franklyn said, 'but at least I—' She broke off as she saw Daniela in the doorway.

Daniela's smile died. Franklyn's eyebrow was split, her bottom lip crusted with dried blood. When she raised her head, more bruises peeked out from the neck of her T-shirt. Two fingers on her left hand were inexpertly splinted together.

Daniela opened her mouth but couldn't find her voice.

'It's all right, Dani,' Franklyn said in a quieter tone. 'It's okay now.'

'What happened?' Daniela managed to ask.

Stephanie snorted. 'She got some of the stupid beat out of her. Don't worry, there's plenty left.'

'I went across a road without looking,' Franklyn said, flicking a glare at Stephanie. 'I got clipped by a bus. My own fault.'

Stephanie scoffed.

Franklyn got down from the table. She moved slowly, carefully, as if anything more would break her. Any pain was hidden behind her mask-like expression. 'Anyway, I spoke to Henry,' she said. 'That's the important thing. He got what he wanted from me, so he'll leave us alone.'

'This,' Stephanie said with a gesture, 'looks like more than a conversation.'

'A bus. Like I said.' Franklyn's smile was crooked. From her pocket she produced a mobile phone. It took Daniela a moment to recognise it as her own – the one Henry had taken.

Franklyn held it out. When Daniela reached to take it, Franklyn saw the way she hobbled on her injured leg. Her lips thinned. Daniela saw the assumption in her eyes, but said nothing to correct it.

'I'm sorry,' Franklyn said. 'I can't make up for this. But I swear it's finished now. Henry's got his money back. And, well …' She rubbed the knuckles of her splinted fingers. 'I guess we've reached an understanding. Nothing more will happen.'

It sounded less like reassurance and more like an order. Daniela nodded. Her hand closed tight around her phone.

Franklyn glanced at Stephanie but said nothing more, then walked out of the kitchen. A moment later the front door slammed.

Stephanie was watching Daniela. Daniela met her gaze with difficulty.

'What did you do to your leg?' Stephanie asked.

'Fell.' Even thought it was the truth, it sounded like a lie. 'I was out in the woods and—'

'Got clipped by a bus?'

Daniela glared at her. 'Why're you asking? Shouldn't you be talking to Henry, not me?'

'I'm on my way to see him now. But you're here, so, want to tell me your side of things?'

Daniela took a breath. 'I was out in the woods. Henry started following me. He wanted to know where Franklyn was. He—' Her chest was suddenly too tight to speak. She had to swallow before she could continue. 'He threatened to drown me if I didn't give him my phone.'

Stephanie's jaw went tight. She struggled to keep the anger off her face. 'When was this?' Her voice was quiet, dangerous.

'This afternoon.' Daniela glanced at the clock. It was later than she'd realised. 'I was going to tell you when you got home—'

Stephanie nodded, her jaw still clenched. 'And your leg?'

'I fell. Genuinely. When I ran off.' Daniela's cheeks burned. She relived the shame and frustration at her reaction. Fresh tears prickled her eyes.

Again, Stephanie nodded. 'Stay here,' she said. 'I'll speak to Henry.'

It was only after the front door closed behind Stephanie that Daniela realised she should've told her to be careful.

23

'I don't know how much you heard while you were ... away.' Leo wiped his eyes with his fingertips. 'About me and Auryn, I mean. Things were never the same after ... after you left. She wouldn't talk to me.'

His voice held a thin undercurrent of accusation. Only to be expected. After what Daniela did she was surprised Leo would even talk to her.

'She retreated from me.' Leo's eyes clouded with old pain. 'I thought things might be different when we got to uni. It was supposed to be a clean break, for both of us. We'd talked about it so often ...' He shook his head. 'You can never really escape, can you? It didn't help that I was, well, I was reliant on her.' He lifted his head to face a truth he still tried to avoid. 'I didn't have the money to support myself. We were supposed to be living together, helping each other. I tried to contribute, but it was never significant. And I-I assumed Auryn would always be there if I couldn't keep afloat.' He laughed at himself. 'That's no kind of life-plan – expecting someone else to bail you out. I should've relied on myself.'

He set down his tea and stood up, then went to a bookcase and shifted a couple of paperbacks aside.

'Eventually we broke up,' he said. 'Just after Christmas that year. Well, it was ongoing really, starting before New Year and culminating near the middle of January. A long, drawn-out dying.'

From behind the books he produced a packet of cigarettes and an ashtray. He gave Daniela a sheepish smile as he came back to the sofa.

'I told Mum I'd quit smoking,' Leo said. 'She never tells me when she's coming to visit, so I hide them.'

Daniela had to laugh because it was likely she'd do the exact same thing on Monday when she got home. She'd promised she would quit for good after this weekend.

Her mouth twisted. *After this weekend. If I get home.*

Leo offered a cigarette to Daniela before lighting his own. The simple action made Daniela want to weep. She hadn't realised till then how desperate she'd been for a cigarette.

'When we broke up, I didn't know Auryn was pregnant,' Leo said. 'I only found out a few weeks later. I-I didn't know what to do.' His expression hardened. 'No, I knew exactly what to do. I was convinced it was the right choice, for both of us. We were at university, for God's sake. We were already struggling. The studying was brutal. I was constantly terrified I'd fail and have to retake a year. There's no way I could afford that. So how the hell could we afford a baby? It would've meant Auryn giving up her studies, giving up everything. And Auryn ... we'd broken up. She didn't want me. Why would she want our kid?'

The raw edge to his voice made something crack inside Daniela.

'So that's what I told her,' Leo said. 'I said it was her decision. After that, I didn't ask. I pretended like it hadn't happened.' He hunched his shoulders under the weight of the memory. 'We tried to remain friends, obviously, but with everything else we didn't speak much. Eventually, after she got that job in London, we re-established contact. As friends. A few emails. I would've liked ...' He exhaled smoke. 'Honest truth, I wanted her back. I loved her. I never stopped loving her. I thought we'd have time later, once everything was in the past, and I could make it up to her. We could get back together. Settle down. Start a family.'

His voice broke on the last word. Daniela squeezed her eyes shut against sudden tears.

Leo took a steadying breath. 'Then,' he said, 'she emailed to say she was quitting her job and coming back to Stonecrop. I was living in Hackett, but I'd been looking at moving out.' He gestured around the room. 'This place became available. I took it as a sign.'

'And you and Auryn got back together.'

Leo gave her a sharp look. 'What makes you say that?'

Daniela was thinking of the ashtray on the bedside table at Auryn's house. It'd seemed so out of place. Like someone else had been there.

But that was a dull, prosaic response. Instead Daniela said, 'You loved each other. I never really believed it when I heard you'd broken up. You were always going to end up together.'

Leo's smile was grateful but sad. 'We didn't get back together,' he said. 'Not really. We spent a lot of time with each other, but ... Auryn had a rough time in London. I wanted to be there for her, as a friend.'

He shifted in his seat. The movement brought him a little

171

closer to Daniela. Daniela concentrated on the warmth of the cup resting on her leg.

'When did you last speak to her?' Daniela asked.

'It would be two days ago, I think. No, three. When the rains started, I came by to help sandbag the house. Then she left. As far as I was aware, she was staying with friends in London.'

'You didn't speak to her again?'

Leo shook his head. 'She didn't have a mobile, not recently anyway. She said she lost it, but I think it's more likely she turned it off because she didn't want to talk to anyone.'

Daniela remembered the landline phone in the old house, on the windowsill with the cord wrapped around the handset. She'd assumed Auryn had disconnected it because of the flood. 'Why'd she come back to Stonecrop?'

'I have no idea.' Leo wiped his eyes again. 'She only left on Wednesday. Why would she come back? She must've been determined. Most of the roads were shut.'

Daniela had considered that too.

Leo let out a breath. 'You're right, though,' he said. 'She's been in a mess for a while. Ever since your dad died, really. I think she somehow blamed herself for that.'

'It was an accident. Nothing any of us could've done.'

'I told her that. A hundred times. Auryn reckoned if she'd been there, she could've done something. But that's not how the world works, is it? We can't rely on other people to catch us.' In an angry motion, Leo stubbed out his cigarette. 'Auryn didn't want to talk about your dad either. And I didn't want to pry. That sounds so stupid, with everything that's happened, but Auryn was adamant she could cope. It was just a bad patch. That's what she said, "Just a bad patch".'

'Was she drinking too much all that time? Or did it start recently?'

Leo gave the smallest of shrugs. 'It's hard to say. She hid it at first. Sometimes I'd go around in the evenings and she'd be passed out on the sofa. But it wasn't like she ceased to function. Most of the time, she probably wasn't drinking more than the rest of us.'

'What about ...' Daniela hesitated. 'Was she taking anything else?'

'How do you mean?'

'Anything worse than alcohol.'

Leo frowned. 'Not that I know of, no.'

'If she was depressed, she could've been on medication, right? Did she talk to you about that?'

'She never mentioned it.'

'I only ask because, y'know, you being a doctor and all.'

'I wasn't her GP. If anyone prescribed her anything, it'd be Doctor Abrams.'

Daniela hesitated before saying, 'Listen, I think Auryn was into more than she told you.'

Leo's jaw tightened. 'It's possible. We didn't tell each other everything. Not like the old days.'

The undercurrent of bitterness in his voice refused to go away. 'I'm sorry,' Daniela said. It was hugely, woefully inadequate, but what else did she have? If she could change the past she would. And then she'd make a fortune selling the secret – *How to Erase Past Fuck-ups* by Daniela Cain.

Leo touched Daniela's arm in an absent gesture of acknowledgement. Daniela had to look away again. She hadn't expected to react this strongly to Leo. But a combination of shock and grief, plus the rekindling of so many memories, conspired

173

against her. For the first time in years she thought about the softness of Leo's lips against her own.

Daniela finished her cigarette, took a steadying breath, then said, 'I think Auryn might've been into something bad. Like, really serious bad.'

Leo turned so he could see her properly. His mug of tea sat forgotten. 'What makes you say that?'

'The police found money at Auryn's house.' Daniela watched Leo's face to try and guess whether he already knew this. 'Steph wouldn't give me the details, but it sounded like a lot.'

'Well.' Leo pursed his lips. 'Lots of people keep money at home.'

'I don't mean a few notes under the mattress. This sounded like a substantial amount. And Auryn's not the sort to hide her money beneath the floorboards.'

'No,' Leo agreed. 'Her job in London was basically advising people about investments. She wouldn't be careless with her own money.'

'That's what bothers me. It shouldn't've been there. Where did it come from?'

'Auryn wouldn't get involved with anything illegal. She couldn't.'

Sure, she could. Anyone could get mixed up in something bad, no matter their intentions.

Leo must've been thinking the same, because he said, 'All right, maybe that's naive. I know the stuff people hide behind respectable facades – I see more than enough at the hospital. But Auryn? It makes no sense.'

'Yeah, you're telling me.' Daniela drained her lukewarm tea. 'Except, it *has* to make sense. Somewhere, there's an answer that makes perfect goddamn sense. Just not right now. And sure as hell not to me.' She rolled the empty mug between her palms. 'Someone killed Auryn. I've no idea if the money's got anything to do with it, but I need to find out.'

'Daniela, the police will do that.'

'Auryn came back here, after she told everyone she'd left. Why? Who was she hiding from?'

A frown creased his brow. 'What makes you think she was hiding?'

'I don't know.' In truth, it wasn't something Daniela had properly considered. But it made sense. 'Think about it. If she needed to go someplace no one could find her, where the roads were closed so she couldn't be followed, it makes sense to come home.' Daniela watched Leo's face. 'So, who was she hiding from?'

Leo sagged. 'All right, this will sound bad out of context, but Auryn was still in contact with my dad. I think he went to see Auryn in London recently.'

Daniela stared at him. 'Why would she—?'

'Money.' Leo winced at the word. 'Dad always said your family owed him for the way your father treated him—'

A hammering on the front door made them both jump. Daniela tensed, looking at Leo, but he seemed just as surprised.

Leo recovered first. 'Hang on,' he called. 'I'm coming.'

As he went to the front door, Daniela stood up. She grabbed her boots and socks, and snatched up her jacket. The front room had only one exit, so she had to follow Leo into the hall.

'Who is it?' Leo asked through the door.

No answer. Leo turned the handle, and frowned to discover it locked.

Instinct made Daniela pull her boots on hurriedly. No time for socks.

Leo's fingers released the lock. The door swung open. Stephanie stood outside. She looked past Leo, straight to Daniela.

'Planning to leave?' Stephanie asked.

Daniela had started to relax, but Stephanie's tone stopped her. 'What's wrong? What's happened?' Daniela asked. She realised with a lurch that this looked a lot more like a professional visit than a family one.

'How can you ask that?' Stephanie stepped inside and closed the front door. 'Everything's wrong. But, if we're being specific, there's something I need to ask you.'

'Oh?'

'It's about this.'

Stephanie took a plastic bag out of her pocket. The weight of the object dragged at its confines as she held it up to the light. A metal flick-knife, the handle black on red.

Daniela clutched her jacket, fingers searching for the familiar shape that should've been in there. *No …*

'I found it in the bedroom at the Crossed Swords,' Stephanie said. 'Figured it fell out of your pocket when you stormed out. That correct?'

Leo had backed away, a hand pressed to his mouth. His eyes were wide with disbelief as he looked at Daniela.

'Can you explain?' Stephanie asked. 'Please?'

There was a pleading note in her voice. She genuinely wanted Daniela to explain this away.

Daniela drew a shaky breath. 'It's mine,' she admitted. 'I know I shouldn't have it. But this isn't what you think.'

'No?' Stephanie stepped towards her. 'Then what is it?'

'For God's sake. I didn't hurt Auryn, okay? I know that's what you're thinking.'

Something flickered across Stephanie's face. 'I think we should probably go to the station at Hackett.'

'You're *arresting* me?'

'I don't want to.' Daniela had heard that before, but Stephanie sounded genuine. 'I need you to explain this to me, and it's best if we do that at the station.'

Stephanie reached out as if to catch Daniela's arm. Daniela jerked away. 'Steph—'

'We can do this officially if you want.' She reached for her again. 'Is that what you—?'

Daniela slapped Stephanie's hand away. She used more force that necessary. Incredulity filled Stephanie's expression, washed away a second later by anger.

She lunged for Daniela, who ran.

Daniela fled through the cramped kitchen and threw her shoulder against the back door. The door shuddered but didn't budge. Locked.

Daniela spun to see Stephanie coming into the kitchen. Her bulky frame filled the narrow doorway and made the small room even smaller.

'Wait,' Daniela said. She held up her hands in appeal or surrender.

Stephanie stalked across the room. She'd shoved the incriminating knife back into her pocket. Her right hand now clasped something at her side. Daniela spotted the fluorescent marking on the plastic case. Incapacitant spray.

Daniela backed away until her hip bumped the kitchen counter. She kept her hands up, like she was surrendering, making Stephanie come to her. Her eyes were fixed on the spray. Just the sight of it made her stomach curl. The canister was pointed at the ground. For now.

She won't use it. She won't hurt you.

The look on her sister's face spoke otherwise.

'Hold your hands out in front of you,' Stephanie said.

'No.'

'Don't be stupid about this. You don't—'

Daniela ducked under Stephanie's outstretched arm, and Stephanie threw herself sideways to pin Daniela against the kitchen counter. Their shoulders collided. Daniela bounced off the counter, recovered her balance and sprinted for the door.

Leo was in the hallway. He tried to block her way and Daniela shoulder-barged him, knocking him backwards into the sitting room.

Daniela grabbed the front-door handle. The door stayed closed. Stephanie had locked it behind her.

Stephanie came crashing out of the kitchen like a bull. Daniela took off up the stairs.

On the top landing, she ran for the only open door, which led into the bathroom at the front of the house. The frosted window was partially open. Daniela wasn't entirely sure she could fit through it but—

A weight slammed into her back, jolting Daniela off her feet and knocking all the wind out. She landed hard, her arms taking the brunt of the impact. Stephanie had rugby-tackled her.

Daniela struggled to throw off the bigger woman. A hand grabbed her right wrist and yanked it behind her back. If Stephanie got the handcuffs on her, it'd be over. It was probably over already. Once the police got you on the ground, they didn't let go.

With a grunt of effort, Daniela twisted and managed to flip onto her back. She found her face inches from her sister's. Stephanie's features were contorted. The strength leaked from Daniela's arms in the face of that rage. Stephanie was almost four years older than her, and had always been bigger and stronger. There was no way to fight.

Stephanie got a forearm across Daniela's throat. She leaned her weight on it and Daniela choked. With her free hand, Stephanie raised the canister of incapacitant spray. Daniela really, *really* didn't want to get hit by it at such close range.

She jerked an arm free and rabbit-punched Stephanie in the ribs. The angle was bad, but there was enough force behind it that Stephanie grunted in pain. Her forearm came off Daniela's throat. Daniela gasped for air. Then she punched Stephanie in the face.

There wasn't enough room for a decent swing. But in prison, Daniela had been in three fights, all short and brutal and ending with vicious suddenness. She'd come off worst the first time. After that, she learned to do whatever it took, and do it first.

With anyone else Daniela would've gone for the eyes, a raking swipe to blind and disorientate, or an open-hand strike to the throat that could, hypothetically, crush the windpipe. But even in the madness of the moment, Daniela couldn't do that to her sister.

But the punch was enough. It caught Stephanie on the jaw and snapped her head to the side. Daniela felt the impact all the way to her shoulder. The blow stunned Stephanie and she slumped against the wall. As soon as the weight lifted off her chest, Daniela squirmed out from under Stephanie and scrambled to her feet. She dived for the window.

She'd flung one leg over the sill when Leo grabbed her arm and tried to haul her back. Daniela had forgotten him.

Leo held a small, fluorescent canister.

Daniela jerked her head away as Leo fired the incapacitant spray. If Daniela hadn't turned it would've hit her full in the face. The spray splattered her cheek and neck. She clamped her eyes shut and flailed her arms, striking Leo. Leo cried out, and Daniela heard the clink of the canister bouncing off the linoleum.

Daniela fell backwards. She put out a hand to catch herself. It hit the glass window and shoved it open wide. She lost her balance.

There was a moment of weightlessness, of panic, before gravity snagged her.

Daniela's hip glanced off the sill. Her legs smashed into the frame. She fell headfirst from the window.

The sloped roof of the porch below broke her fall, and very nearly broke her neck. She hit the wooden roof with a bang that must've been heard throughout the village. The impact scattered her senses and blinded her with white light. The roof buckled beneath her weight and spilled her to the unforgiving ground. The second impact hurt more than the first.

Someone yelled something. Daniela heard it as a muddy wash of sound. It felt like something had jarred loose in her head.

Animal instinct got her back to her feet. She stumbled away from the house, holding her breath. Droplets of liquid fire collected on her cheek and in the soft folds around her right ear. She kept her right eye squeezed shut but dared to crack open her left eye. She couldn't run blind. Her vision was blurred and watery but she saw the outline of the garden wall ahead, and, beyond that, the road. Her cheek burned. She swiped at the skin with her jumper sleeve and only succeeded in spreading the spray more.

She started running, a lurching, loping stride. The cold air was a blessing on her streaming eyes. She let out her breath in an explosive gasp. The peppery stink filled her mouth. She gagged, stumbled, kept running.

Even if she'd wanted to, she couldn't look back. Her balance was precarious. At any moment it felt like her legs would spill her to the ground. The fire across her cheek was spreading, eating into her skin, becoming an urgent siren, especially where it'd spattered her ear and nose. She sucked air through her mouth to avoid dragging the fumes into her sinuses. The stink seared her lungs. If any of the substance had got into her eyes she couldn't even have run.

She stumbled onto the road and headed for the woods opposite Leo's house.

24

It wasn't possible for Daniela to move quietly through the woods. She was half-blinded, gasping, winded and, in all honesty, she expected to get caught. Stephanie would come after her. All Daniela was doing was prolonging the inevitable.

She lost her footing on a muddy bank and slid down into one of the many flooded ditches that criss-crossed the woods. Water flowed into both boots.

Daniela dropped to her knees in the ditch, then dunked her face below the water. The cold was an indescribable relief. She scrubbed her cheek with both hands and peeled her eyes open to rinse them. She stayed down as long as she could hold her breath, then came up, gasping and shuddering, sucked in another breath and submerged her face again.

After the fourth repetition, the burning began to subside. She sat up slowly, blinking muddy water from her eyes. Her vision was foggy. Fire itched her face, but it was a throbbing discomfort rather than a stabbing urgency. She sluiced water over her face again, then raised her head. Rain pattered off the leaves around her.

Her desperate flight had taken her less than two hundred yards from the road. If Stephanie – or Leo – had come after her, they would've caught her. She didn't have the strength for a second fight.

Daniela rested against the edge of the ditch, trying to bring her ragged breathing under control, and listened. She heard nothing. That didn't necessarily mean anything. Stephanie wasn't the stealthiest, but she knew the basics of sneaking up on someone.

After a long minute of silence, Daniela pushed to her feet. Water drained from her sodden clothes. She pulled herself up the muddy bank as quietly as was possible. At the top, she paused, listening again.

From the road she heard voices. It was a quiet discussion, not intended to be overheard, but sound travelled easily in the silence.

The logical thing to do was leave. Put as much distance as possible between herself and her sister, give them both time to calm down. But instead, Daniela crept through the trees towards the road.

She got close enough to see Leo's house. The front door was open. Two figures stood just outside.

Stephanie was watching the trees, her expression closed, unreadable. Leo had hold of Stephanie's hand and was talking quietly. It didn't look like he was restraining Stephanie, nor offering reassurance. It took Daniela a moment to figure out he was fixing a support bandage around the officer's wrist. Leo's eyes were red from being too close to the spray when it went off.

'I know you're out there,' Stephanie called.

Daniela flinched, although Stephanie couldn't have spotted her, wedged as she was in the shadows behind a large birch.

'There's nowhere to go,' Stephanie said. Her voice carried

through the woods. 'The roads are closed. You can't get out of town. We'll find you.'

A bubble of laughter surfaced inside Daniela. It was like when they were kids – when Daniela was in trouble and Stephanie was sent to bring her home. Daniela's humour turned sour. They were no longer kids, and this was far from a game.

Leo murmured a quiet reassurance to Stephanie, who didn't seem to hear. Her gaze swept the trees. Daniela shuddered as Stephanie's eyes passed the knot of branches where she hid.

Stephanie must've been more badly hurt than Daniela realised. When Stephanie at last allowed Leo to lead her back to the house, she was limping and her movements were slow, as if the blow to her head had disorientated her. Daniela felt a pang of guilt. She hadn't meant to hurt her. All she'd wanted to do was get away.

She thought of Stephanie holding the incapacitant spray, and the guilt crystallised into something else. She couldn't believe Stephanie had been willing to do that.

Can you blame her? She thinks you killed Auryn.

None of Daniela's actions would have helped convince Stephanie she was innocent. She should've done what Stephanie said and gone with her. But the idea of being arrested, of those handcuffs fastening around her wrists ...

She couldn't go through that again. Not ever.

And now, because she'd panicked rather than acting rationally, her sister thought Daniela was capable of murder. That hurt worse than anything.

Leo helped Stephanie into the house, then paused to look back at the woods. His expression was pained. It twisted Daniela's insides. Somehow Leo had called Stephanie and alerted her that Daniela was at the house. Maybe he'd texted whilst in the kitchen.

Daniela tried to nurture her annoyance; to raise it from a dull glow into a fire. But it was too difficult. She was freezing cold and soaked to the skin again. The few wonderful moments of warmth beside the hearth in Leo's house were already a distant memory. She was too numb, inside and out, to feel anything.

She thought back to the bitterness Leo had tried to hide. Even before today he must've hated Daniela for what she'd done to his family, and for contributing to his break-up with Auryn. And now, he thought Daniela had murdered the woman he still loved. The expression on his face when he'd seen the knife ...

You robbed them of everything. The chance of a happy life. The chance of a family.

As Leo closed the front door, cutting off the heat escaping from his home, Daniela turned away and trudged into the dark forest.

25

June 2010

As she went back upstairs to her bedroom, Daniela flexed her fingers, feeling the ache in her shoulders and arms from her flight through the forest earlier that day. She thought of Franklyn's bruises and broken fingers.

Should Henry get away with that?

Franklyn had given in, handed the money back to Henry, and taken a beating – either from Henry or from one of his friends. Even now, Daniela found it hard to believe Henry would've done it himself. More likely he'd got someone else to do his dirty work.

And Franklyn had accepted it all, to protect her family. To protect Daniela. Henry had used Daniela's weakness against Franklyn, like blackmail, like Daniela was a victim who couldn't fight back.

Daniela's head was so full she couldn't stop thinking, but at the same time there was nothing but static between her ears, preventing her from concentrating. She felt like she was a second away from snapping, from punching someone, from kicking them while they were down.

When she reached the top of the attic stairs, she spotted Auryn stretched out on her old bed beneath the window, reading a hardbound textbook. She hadn't been there when Daniela woke up a short while ago.

'Where were you lurking?' Daniela asked.

Auryn held up her book. 'I was looking for this in Dad's study,' she said. 'I think it belonged to Mum.'

'You've got your own room for reading.'

'It's quieter up here. What was the shouting downstairs?'

'You could've joined in if you were interested.'

Auryn returned her attention to her book. 'I'd rather not. No one can have a civil conversation in this house.'

Daniela sat down on her bed. She wanted to be quiet and think.

Downstairs, she heard the door to their father's study open. His footsteps shuffled down towards the kitchen. If Daniela listened hard, she could follow anyone anywhere in the house, by the echoes that murmured up through the woodwork like a gigantic sounding board.

'What did Franklyn want?' Auryn asked.

'To talk to Steph, I guess.' Belatedly, she realised what was really bothering her – Franklyn had previously confided in Daniela, but now Daniela had let her down, she'd gone to Stephanie instead. Daniela felt the sting of lost trust.

'And she's gone now?'

'Yeah. Why would she stick around?'

Auryn shrugged. 'Why would any of us?'

When she set her mouth into a serious line like that, Auryn resembled their mother so much that Daniela found it hard to look at her. Auryn never cracked a smile unless it was totally warranted. It was like her smiles were rationed. But there was something particular about her seriousness now. She looked older, more worried but more certain.

'Why're you still here, Auryn?' Daniela asked. 'Not that I wanna chase you out, but you said you'd be gone as soon as you could. That was two weeks ago. What's keeping you?'

A flicker of annoyance crossed Auryn's face. 'There's a problem with the flat we're renting in Newcastle. Leo's having difficulties finding his share of the deposit.'

'I thought his dad was going to—'

'Yeah, that won't happen. He won't pay a penny to help him out, not if it means Leo's moving in with me.' Auryn flicked to the next page in her book, although it didn't look like she saw the words. 'I told him not to worry, I can cover for him. But he doesn't want to rely on me.'

'He never bothered about that before.' Daniela said it without thinking.

'I'm getting pretty sick of that attitude,' Auryn said, and only the tension in her voice betrayed her anger. 'You guys think he only stays with me because I buy him stuff.'

'I've never said that.'

'You've implied it often enough. It's bad enough having to deal with his dad without you guys weighing in as well. Stephanie's never liked him.'

'Really?'

Auryn gave her an annoyed look. 'Where've you been, Dani? I know you don't care about anything that doesn't directly impact you, but still ...'

Downstairs, a faint tremor of noise indicated that their dad had switched on the kettle. Daniela swore under her breath.

She didn't want to go back downstairs while he was there. But she also had little enthusiasm for staying to talk to Auryn. She wanted to be alone.

Daniela came to a decision. She grabbed her jacket from the floor.

'Where're you going?' Auryn asked.

'Out. Hey, I had a bottle. Where's it gone?' She'd just noticed its absence.

'Yeah, I didn't think that was yours.'

Daniela held out her hand. When Auryn didn't move, Daniela walked closer, so she was standing over Auryn's bed.

'Give it back,' she said.

For a moment, Auryn held her gaze, but then she sighed and, sitting up, reached under the bed to retrieve the partially empty bottle of whisky. Daniela snatched it off her.

'Where're you going?' Auryn asked again.

'Out. Why's it any of your business?'

'You're not coming back.'

The way she said it made Daniela hesitate. 'What makes you say that?'

'You look like Franklyn always does, right before she takes off.'

Daniela tried to shrug it off. 'Well, who the hell knows? I've missed the last bus into Hackett, so unless I decide to walk ...'

As she said it, she thought about the money she'd stashed in the hidey-hole beneath her bed. A mixed assortment of notes, accumulated over the months. Should she take it with her? If there really was a chance she might not come back ...

Auryn studied her, then asked once more, 'Where are you going?'

'If I tell you—'

'I can't breathe a word to Steph, yeah, yeah. Give me a little credit.'

'Sure.' Daniela managed a tiny smile. She sat down on her bed. 'You're right, I'm not sticking around. If I can leave tonight I will.' It surprised her to find she meant it. 'But I'm not going quietly.'

Auryn raised her eyebrows. 'How d'you mean?'

'I wanna be sure Henry will leave us alone.' Henry's threats still rang in Daniela's ears. *If he hadn't gone after me, it could've been you, Auryn.* 'Frankie says it's finished, but I'm not convinced.'

'You don't trust her?'

'That's not it. I wanna know why he threatened me. That kinda made it personal, y'know?'

Auryn gave a weak smile. 'Yeah, all right. So, what're you planning?'

'I just ... Jesus, don't say it like that. I'm not planning anything. I just want to know what he's up to. That's it.'

'Are you going to turn up at his house and hope he feels like talking politely with you?'

Daniela stared at her pallid, serious face behind the round glasses. Auryn's expression contained no condemnation or judgement. She looked genuinely interested.

'I don't know,' Daniela said. 'I'll figure something out.'

Auryn nodded as if accepting this. She picked up her book again. 'Take care, all right? Don't do anything stupid.'

That's all anyone expects from me, Daniela thought as she limped downstairs. *They still think of me as a stupid kid.*

She snuck through Auryn's room, slid open the window, and climbed down the apple tree that leaned against the side of the house. Once on the ground, she put her hand over the reassuring shape of the knife in her jacket pocket.

I'll show them.

26

The Corner Shoppe and the antiques store were locked up for the night, but a light burned in the room above, peeking through the net curtains to cast a rectangle of yellow on the street below. Those rooms, Daniela knew, were part of the house at the back of the Shoppe, where the McKearney family lived.

Daniela had never been inside the house, but she knew the rough layout. Leo's room was at the rear on the first floor, overlooking the small yard.

Circling round to the back of the corner shop, Daniela passed the yard that led to the house, noting the light that illuminated Leo's room. The flowery curtains were drawn and the window was open a crack. She kept going until she reached the wooden gates behind the antiques emporium. The gate was closed and padlocked. Squinting through the gap beside the lock, Daniela saw Henry's car parked in the yard.

Daniela hugged the shadows while she considered her next move. The night air was cold and made each exhalation steam. The streetlights were slightly too far apart for their pools of light to overlap – poor planning on the council's behalf, which made the lane look shady and disreputable.

This had seemed an easy decision when she'd been at home

with nothing but her anger to dwell on. Sneaking out of the house, walking into Stonecrop, going to the antiques shop, all were automatic actions. The only part she hadn't thought through was what she'd do when she arrived.

Her guilt and anger over letting Henry scare her had intensified until she couldn't rest. It consumed each step, each thought. Because of her, Henry had taken the money back. Because of her, Franklyn had got hurt. Because of her, because of her. Daniela felt sick every time she thought of Franklyn's broken fingers.

She couldn't live with what Henry had done. And she didn't share Franklyn's confidence that Henry would leave their family alone. The bastard would think he was invincible now.

Daniela told herself she was here tonight because she wanted to know exactly what Franklyn was mixed up in. But in truth, she wanted to get back at Henry. To hurt him. To break his fingers and threaten to drown *him*.

And how will you do that? Henry was obviously dangerous. Going up against him directly was a stupid idea.

So, something else was required. Something that would send a clear message.

She had to be as ruthless as Henry. There was no other way.

But now Daniela was standing outside the empty shop, glancing at the lighted windows of the neighbouring house, she wondered what she was capable of.

The alcohol she'd drunk sat sour in her stomach. Whilst walking into town, she'd taken a few more swigs from the bottle, then flung it over a hedge. She hadn't felt like drinking anymore. To be honest, she'd only taken the bottle because Auryn had tried to stop her.

It'd be easy to get over the wall into the rear yard of the antiques shop, even with her bad ankle. She'd managed it yesterday. And she'd watched Franklyn spring the back door. She figured she could do it. The building had no burglar alarm or CCTV.

And what then? Daniela's pulse quickened. She'd have to move fast. Someone might hear her moving around inside the shop. Henry might come to investigate.

Daniela brushed a hand against the front pocket of her jacket, feeling the shape of the flick-knife through the leather. It didn't give her its usual comfort. She felt a little ill.

Just leave. What're you hoping to achieve? Leave, go to Hackett, catch the first train to somewhere better. Franklyn said—

Her fists clenched again. Franklyn had been coerced into saying everything was fine. No, Daniela couldn't leave it like this.

So, what're you waiting for?

Daniela took a deep breath, let it out slow. There was no traffic, no people on the street, no noise apart from the wind in the trees. It was a little after eleven o'clock and fully dark. Daniela was always unnerved by how the village shut down at nightfall, as if the darkness terrified it, but at least she wouldn't bump into anyone on the streets. She glanced left and right, reassuring herself the lane was empty, then scrambled over the wall and dropped soundlessly onto the gravel yard. She rested against the wall until the ache in her ankle subsided.

The fire door at the rear of the antiques shop wasn't designed to open from the outside, but age or misuse had loosened the mechanism. Daniela picked up a bent nail from the gravel, worked it into the gap and sprung the lock. She held her breath as the heavy door swung open. No alarms. Daniela slipped inside.

At night, with the lights off, the interior was even gloomier. The crowded pieces of furniture were solid blocks of darkness. An orange haze filtered through the front windows from a streetlight outside. The darkness had a grainy quality, as if the air itself was dusty. The aroma of aged wood and stale cigarette smoke was like the bottled smell of her childhood.

The first thing Daniela did was search for the box containing the counterfeit cigarettes, but there was no sign of it. Given the mess, the box could've been hidden anywhere. She was hampered by the dark and the need to be silent. It also didn't help that, apart from the statuette box, she didn't know what she was looking for.

Franklyn said Henry was shipping all sorts of stuff. It must be more than one box of crappy cigarettes. What else is he hiding?

The desk drawer Franklyn had smashed was empty, the pieces of broken wood removed to leave just the shell of the drawer.

In a small jewellery box on top of the desk, Daniela found four gold eternity rings, set with diamonds and emeralds. The handwritten price tags made her eyebrows go up. She felt an odd tingle as she picked them up, perhaps because they resembled the rings her mother had once worn, the ones her mother had flung at her father during their last fight.

Daniela hesitated, then slipped the rings into her back pocket. If she was leaving town, it wouldn't hurt to have something she could pawn in the city.

She widened her search, peering into random boxes and pulling open cabinets and dressers. Each cupboard was stuffed with papers, bric-a-brac, and other boxes. A full search would take days. Nothing looked relevant or even interesting.

Irritated, Daniela made her way through the shop, squeezing between furniture. Although she tried to be quiet, she kept banging her knees and elbows. Each time, she froze, certain someone must've heard.

At the far side of the shop were two storerooms. Daniela checked them on the off-chance that Henry was hiding anything incriminating within.

The first door was locked. Daniela shied away from breaking the catch. The noise would definitely be heard. When she tried the second door, it swung inwards, revealing a cramped room with a chair and table wedged in one corner and a washbasin in the other. There was an electric kettle and a stack of old newspapers on the table.

By now, Daniela was losing patience. She didn't know exactly what she'd hoped to find, but she'd expected *something* she could use against Henry.

She eyed the kettle. The plug was frayed, with a section of bare wire exposed. *A real fire hazard.*

She checked her pockets for her cigarette lighter.

Was this an option? She rolled the plastic lighter between her fingers. The frayed wire next to the stack of newspapers was so tempting it could've been set up specifically. With so much furniture crammed into the main showroom, a small blaze could become an inferno. She wondered how long it'd been since Henry last checked the smoke detectors.

Daniela's eyes travelled to the plaster ceiling. Directly above was a portion of the McKearney house. Her resolve faded. If it was just the shop and Henry's possessions, maybe she would've considered a fire. But with the bedrooms above, and Henry and his family asleep ...

An image popped into her head of the building in flames, of Henry trapped upstairs, lungs blackened by smoke, choking, dying. It gave Daniela a weird tingle in the pit of her stomach. Quickly she shook the thought away, disturbed.

No. As bitter as she was, Daniela couldn't justify getting someone killed.

Her eyes fell instead on the washbasin. The tap dripped into the tide-marked sink. Fire was out of the question, but water ...

Daniela turned to survey the shop. She grinned. Yeah, a little flood damage would be perfect.

27

February 2017

One advantage of the mass evacuation of Stonecrop was a surfeit of houses standing empty. Most were locked up, front and back, but it didn't take long for Daniela to find one whose owners had left a window unsecure. She slipped the latch and climbed inside, closing the window behind her. It was a relief to get out of the constant rain.

The house was a detached cottage on the northern outskirts of town, surrounded by extensive gardens. Seven years ago, it'd belonged to the Caronett family, whose daughter was in the year above Daniela at school. Daniela wasn't sure if they still lived here. The house was set far back from the road, but Daniela left the lights off, just in case. Besides, she wasn't certain the power was working. Floodwater had infiltrated the gardens and kitchen, despite the extensive sandbagging.

Daniela made a quick, automatic search of the house, even though she was certain it was empty. She couldn't help but remember how, a few hours earlier, she'd done the same in Auryn's home. This place had that same abandoned feel.

In the bathroom, Daniela stripped off the jumper Leo had given her and dumped it in a sodden heap. Her eyes and nose still ached from the incapacitant spray. It was a constant struggle not to rub her eyes. She removed the rest of her clothes and gratefully dried herself with a fluffy towel from the airing cupboard. She tried the hot tap and was delighted to find it working. She hesitated, then filled the bathtub.

It felt wrong to do all this in someone else's house. Invading a property brought back uncomfortable memories of breaking into the antiques shop, seven years ago.

But this, right now, was necessary. Daniela had lost her jacket during the scuffle in the house, and everything else she wore was soaked, right down to her underwear. She was chilled to the bone and couldn't feel her toes. The constant shivers racking her body made every movement a chore. If she didn't get warm soon, she'd shake to pieces. Running a bath felt less invasive than wrapping herself in every blanket in the house.

She filled the bath as deep and hot as she could stand. As she sank into the water, she swore she would never venture outdoors again without appropriately warm clothing. It always surprised her how unpleasant it was to get cold and wet. She thought she would've remembered.

She fingered the back of her head and found the large tender area where she'd crash-landed coming out of the window. Daniela winced. There could be a concussion underneath. She was amazed she'd been able to keep moving. She definitely felt dizzy, but wasn't sure how much was due to her head injury, exhaustion, adrenaline, or the cold.

Daniela stayed in the bath for a long time. With the lights off and the warm water cocooning her, she dozed, allowing the horrors of the day to seep out through her skin. For a brief time, she pretended none of it was real. She held her breath and slid beneath the surface. Heat prickled her scorched cheek.

All too soon the water cooled. Daniela reluctantly clambered out of the bath and wrapped the towel around herself. Despite not wanting to invade the house more than necessary, she went into the master bedroom and rifled the cupboards until she found a sweater and some jogging pants that were only a bit too big. She balked at the idea of wearing someone else's underwear, so she opted, reluctantly, to go without.

She was pulling the clothes on when her phone rang.

Daniela went back to the bathroom, holding up the waistband of the jogging pants. Her phone was vibrating in the back pocket of the jeans she'd dumped on the floor. It was a shock to see it still working. Daniela had assumed the damp would've killed the electrics.

She fished the phone out and her heart dropped into her stomach. Stephanie's number.

Daniela padded back to the bedroom and sat on the bed. The phone kept ringing: ten rings, fifteen, twenty. She wondered how long Stephanie would keep trying. The jaunty ringtone was loud in the silent house.

Finally, Daniela answered the call.

'Yeah, I'm here,' she said.

'You're where, exactly?' Stephanie asked. Her voice sounded close, as if she was calling from the next room.

'Steph,' Daniela said, 'I know how all this looks. But I didn't do anything. I swear.'

She could almost feel Stephanie's anger radiating through the phone. The officer was keeping her emotions reined in behind that chill tone, but Daniela knew her well enough.

Daniela swapped the phone to her left ear; the touch of the screen against her face aggravated the rash from the incapacitant spray.

'You hear?' Daniela asked. 'It wasn't me.'

'What wasn't you? What *didn't* you do? Spell it out for me.'

'For Chrissakes. Do you seriously think I'd have done anything – *anything* – to hurt Auryn?'

'Convince me. Because right now you look pretty guilty.'

Daniela smoothed her wet hair back from her face. 'You didn't give me much chance to explain.'

'I gave you every chance. I asked you to come with me and tell me everything.'

'You tried to arrest me.' Daniela heard the petulance in her own voice. She took a steadying breath. 'Steph, I had *nothing* to do with what happened to Auryn. For God's sake, I only arrived yesterday.'

'So you say. For all I know you've been here for days. You could've gone straight to the old house.'

'Yeah? And then what? I decide to hang around in Stonecrop, for old times' sake? Do you think I would've sought you out, come and talked to you, and then fucking *phoned* you from Auryn's house after I found her? C'mon. I know they're getting complacent in police school but—'

'I've seen people do worse. People acting normal, like they've done nothing wrong—'

'I *have* done nothing wrong.'

'—to make it seem like they've just come into town. Laying a false trail and hoping we'll fall for it.'

'You think I'd do that?' Daniela laughed. 'Seriously, you credit me with too many smarts.'

'This isn't a game, Dani.'

'I was thinking that myself.' Daniela lay down on the bed, staring at the ceiling. Rain drummed against the windows.

Stephanie was silent for a moment, then asked, 'Why were you carrying a knife, Dani?'

Daniela closed her eyes. *That fucking knife.* 'Look, I know this is what you're trained to do. Put little bits together and come up with a fitting answer. But you're wrong. I'd never do something like—'

'That's a lie and we all know it. Otherwise you wouldn't have spent five years in jail for knifing Henry McKearney and leaving him for dead.'

Daniela took the phone away from her ear. A vehicle went past on the distant road, and the reflection of its headlights slid across the bedroom ceiling from one end to the other. On the phone, Stephanie waited.

It was unfair, of course. The police made a big deal of not judging people on past mistakes. But that was on paper. It never translated to real life.

Daniela was trying to escape the past; trying harder than she'd ever tried anything before. But the past was never forgotten. Especially in Stonecrop, where time had stood still for so long that nothing was ever considered history.

It'd been a mistake to come back. Stupid to think she deserved a happy ending.

She should've stayed at home.

The thought twisted her mouth. For years, the old house had been *home.* No matter where she went or what she did, it was a touchstone in her heart. Even though she'd never wanted to come back, she'd liked knowing the house was here if she needed to return.

Now Daniela knew the truth. She hadn't come home. She'd

returned to a place where floods had washed out half the residents, and those who remained hated her, the way only family and childhood friends could. For all they cared, she could've stayed in prison forever.

At last, Daniela put the phone to her ear and said, 'I never killed anyone.'

'It's hard to believe you,' Stephanie said. She sounded tired. 'It feels like I've been waiting for something to happen, ever since you got out. It felt inevitable. After what you did to Dad—'

'Hey, you can't blame me for Dad. I wasn't even there.'

'Exactly. You were the last straw. After you went to prison ... you don't understand what that did to him.'

'Oh, come on. He barely cared about me.'

'You think so? He blamed himself for the way you turned out. He blamed Franklyn for being the worst possible influence, and he blamed me for not helping you when I had a chance.' Bitterness was a harsh tang beneath each word. 'But he never blamed you. In his eyes, you were the victim. It was the last thing he said to me before he killed himself.'

Daniela went cold. 'What the hell, Steph? He didn't kill himself. It was—'

'An accident. Yeah, I know. He went over the top banister while drunk. An accident waiting to happen, given the state of the house and how much he was drinking. Except the certifying doctor never knew about the other times he tried. The times I saw him with bruises from chucking himself down the stairs. Or when he called me because he'd jumped off the roof and broken his hip. "Accidents," he said. Just a clumsy old man tripping on the stairs or slipping while mending a loose tile.'

'Jesus Christ, Steph, what're you saying?'

'He wanted it to look like an accident,' Stephanie said, her voice heavy. 'To spare us.'

'Jesus Christ,' Daniela said again. She pressed her fingertips into her eye sockets until sparks appeared. 'Why didn't you tell me?'

'Would you have cared?' Stephanie asked.

Daniela thought of the letter she'd received in prison from Stephanie, the one that'd told her in stark terms that their father was dead, and Daniela was not welcome at the funeral. 'That's harsh. Yes, I care. You know I do.'

'Yeah? What day did Dad die? What date?'

Daniela was quiet for too long.

'See, there's the issue,' Stephanie said. 'You don't have the slightest clue what it's like, trying to hold this family together. I did everything I could to help Dad. And Auryn. But you ... all you ever wanted to do was break things.'

Daniela pressed the button to end the call. She let out a shaky breath. There was a deeply unpleasant feeling in her chest, as if someone had punched her solar plexus, leaving her winded and on the verge of tears.

She touched the back of her neck. Between the sixth and seventh cervical vertebrae – that was where Dad had broken his spine when he fell. Daniela moved her hand to her flank, just below the ribs on the left side. That was where Auryn had been stabbed. The area was soft, vulnerable. Angling upwards, a knife blade could easily find the heart.

Seven years ago, Daniela had seen how easy it was to seriously hurt someone. In a way she'd been lucky – although not as lucky as Henry – because the knife had gone in at an awkward angle, glanced off his ribs and perforated the bowel instead of the heart. Daniela ended up doing four and a half years of a seven-year sentence for wounding with intent. Her lawyer had argued it down from attempted murder. Daniela couldn't contest it. Eight stab wounds were difficult to mitigate.

It could so easily have been murder.

It made her sick every time she thought about it.

But the past was the past, wasn't it? She wasn't the same person. She couldn't be, otherwise what was the point of her time in prison? The authorities had devoted so many hours to her rehabilitation. All those probation officers, therapists, psychiatrists … they believed it'd work, didn't they? Or was it just a cynical game? Both sides pretending to make an effort, upholding justice and curbing reoffending, whilst exchanging knowing winks because they all knew none of it would change a thing. She'd always be an almost-murderer.

Daniela pushed off the bed. Enough. Everyone else could hang on to the past. She didn't have to.

In a drawer she found warm socks and, in another cupboard, a fleece jacket that looked like it hadn't been worn in a long time. Daniela pulled them on, then tidied up as much as she could. She straightened the bedcovers and shut the cupboard doors. In the bathroom, she drained the bathtub, folded the damp towel into the airing cupboard, and picked up her clothes. She removed any sign she'd been in the house. The idea of traumatising the owners made her uneasy.

Daniela transferred the contents of her pockets to the fleece jacket. Her entire worldly possessions amounted to a mobile phone and the four eternity rings she'd taken from Henry McKearney's antique shop a lifetime ago. Her wallet, along with the last of her cash and her house keys, was in the jacket she'd lost at Leo's house.

She came downstairs with an armful of damp clothes. Her boots were still wet inside, and she shuddered at their chill grip around her dry socks. In the kitchen, Daniela paused to drink from the tap, and to search the cupboards. She hadn't eaten all day. She snacked on crisps and biscuits, shoving the empty wrappers into her pockets.

She carried her clothes outside, then closed the window behind her.

There would be traces, she knew. A muddy tidemark on the bathtub. Footprints on the hall carpet. Something small she'd forgotten. But Daniela hoped the owners wouldn't notice, or would shrug it off as something they'd done themselves. There'd be more important things to worry about, after all, like the flood damage to the garden.

Outside, although it was still raining, the air felt warmer, but Daniela attributed that to her dry clothes. The wind snatched at her hair as she hurried through the garden and climbed the rear fence. The gardens backed directly onto the woods. Daniela walked some distance through the trees before finding a suitable hollow beneath some roots, where she stashed her wet, muddy clothes, including the jumper Leo had given her.

Whilst lying on the bed, her mind had grasped for a solution to her problems. She needed to get out of town. She needed to retrieve the money she'd hidden in the woods. She needed to do both without being caught.

But, more urgently, she wanted to know who'd killed Auryn. And she wanted Stephanie to believe she was innocent. Those two thoughts filled her mind.

Henry McKearney. Leo said Henry had been in contact with Auryn. Why?

Daniela had deliberately avoided thinking about Henry since she'd arrived in Stonecrop the day before. Her plan had always been to get in and out of town fast, so she'd assumed she could avoid Henry, if he was even still here. No one had mentioned him. She'd hoped he'd packed up and left long ago. But maybe not. Maybe Margaret had stuck with him, despite everything.

Maybe he was in Stonecrop right now.

Maybe he knew something about Auryn's death.

Rationally, she knew she should leave it to Stephanie and her colleagues. That's what they were for. But at the moment, Stephanie was the only officer in Stonecrop, and she was wasting time chasing Daniela.

By now, Stephanie must've contacted the station at Hackett and told them about Daniela. People would be looking for her. As soon as the weather broke for long enough for a helicopter to take off, they'd come.

They would definitely bring dogs. Attack dogs – or *general-purpose* dogs, whatever the hell they were called now. The idea of being chased through the muddy woods made her stomach churn.

So, she needed to be gone.

She *wanted* to find out if Henry McKearney was in town. But she had to consider her own self-preservation. She couldn't help the police investigation if she was busy hiding from the police.

Daniela put her hands in her pockets and started walking. It might take her all day just to figure a way past the closed roads and swollen rivers. And she still needed to get her money.

28

She circled around the back of the old house, trying to ignore the empty, abandoned look of the property. Trying not to think about Auryn lying alone in the upstairs bedroom.

Daniela had turned off her phone, in case Stephanie tried contacting her again, and so couldn't check the time, but it felt late. The sky had darkened to murky twilight, grey and horrid. It was still raining. The noise of the rising wind was like a battle or a riot, which easily masked any sound she made. A tree had come down across the path and she had to detour around it. The ground was littered with broken branches. She tucked her hands into her sleeves and wished she'd thought to steal some gloves.

At last she reached the hollow where she'd stashed the plastic-wrapped package. Exhaustion dragged at her. Exhaustion and residual anger. She didn't like being chased out of town like this. But she made herself focus on the path ahead: this one last task, then the long walk south to Briarsfield. If she could get home, if she could hide the money, if she was given just a few quiet hours to get her story straight before she called Stephanie and explained everything ...

Daniela closed her eyes. If she started thinking about it, she would have to admit how bad her situation was. The only solution was not to think.

She clambered down the bank into the hollow, crouched in the mud, and reached under the tangle of roots where she'd hidden the package.

It wasn't there.

She searched the rest of the hollow, frantically at first, then forcing herself to be slow, methodical. The package wasn't there. It hadn't slipped loose, otherwise it would be lying in the mud at her feet. Daniela walked a circle from one side of the hollow to the other.

The money wasn't there.

Tears prickled her eyes. No, this couldn't be right. She was in the wrong place, the wrong mud-hole. She must have got herself turned around and was looking beneath the wrong tree.

But she knew that wasn't true. This was exactly where she'd left the package. And now it was gone.

Frustration made her fists curl. Someone had come here in the last couple of hours and taken it. *Stephanie?* Leo might've told Stephanie about finding Daniela out here in the woods; might even have led her back to this spot. Daniela knuckled tears from her eyes. Yeah, that's how it would've happened. Stephanie had the parcel, and it'd be one last nail in Daniela's coffin. No way would Stephanie believe Daniela was innocent now.

Daniela put her hand to the pocket of her jogging pants, where she felt the clink of the four eternity rings she'd stolen from Henry's shop, all those years ago. They were each worth a few hundred pounds – at least, that's what the price tags had said. That would have to be enough. She'd lost all chance of taking anything else home.

Time to cut your losses and get out.

The wind bustled and roared in the trees overhead like a living creature. Daniela crouched, listening to the noise, her eyes tracking over the rain-splattered mud. There was the slide-mark where she'd tumbled down the bank. There were Leo's prints where he'd come to help. Her eyes roamed further. There, by the far side of the hollow, was a trail of prints, coming down the bank then back up. Wellies, definitely, but that meant nothing because everyone wore wellies in a flood. Someone moving fast, judging by the way the prints slid and blurred on the steep part of the slope.

But the trail didn't lead back towards the flooded road. Daniela got up to study them properly. She pulled herself up the bank. At the top, she followed the prints until they reached a well-trodden path that wound through the woods towards Stonecrop.

That made her pause. Stephanie wouldn't cut through the woods like that. She'd wade along the road and come at the hollow from the direction of the old house. And she wouldn't be hurrying. She always walked with deliberate care, especially in these woods.

Someone else had been here and taken Daniela's money.

She followed the path for a quarter mile until it reached the main road through Stonecrop. As she'd known it would, the end of the trail came out almost directly opposite Henry McKearney's old antique shop.

Once out on the flooded streets around the village centre, Daniela moved cautiously. At anything faster than a steady pace, her splashing boots sent echoes bouncing up and down the length of the street, audible even over the wind. She already looked suspicious, since the last few residents had retreated into their houses, pulling the curtains and shutting the doors against the approaching night.

The main streetlights were off. It left the village darker than usual in the twilight. The unlit houses added to the eeriness. Normally, cracks of light would sneak around curtains and under doors. Each house would have a warm glow of life. Now the buildings were hollow. The few that remained lit looked like huddled survivors engaged in a last desperate defence against the grim dark.

With every step, Daniela became more convinced she shouldn't be here. It was a stupid risk.

Yet she kept going, and eventually reached the back of the McKearney house.

There was no point going to the front, because Margaret McKearney never left her shop unsecured at night. Years ago she'd told Daniela – in her usual charmingly direct manner – that if she left the front door unlocked, she'd come down in the morning to an empty shop and a village of sugar-filled children.

Daniela lifted the latch on the back gate and slipped into the garden. On occasion, when she was a kid, her father would send her for a packet of tobacco after hours. Margaret had always given Daniela a shrewd look and a lecture about how it wasn't right to be buying tobacco at such a young age. On the way home, Daniela would peel back the seal on the packet and filch a pinch for herself.

It was odd how that memory had lain dormant but to then resurface at this precise moment, drawn by the rasp of the latch and the way Daniela automatically slipped through the gate without opening it more than a few inches, because the hinges would creak.

She remembered the last time she'd been here. She'd walked past the house and scaled the wall into the yard behind the antiques shop. The reminder was painful and distracting, and she pushed it away.

There was a gap between the downstairs curtains. A light was on in the back room, which, if memory served her right, was the main sitting room. From the angle of the light, it looked like it came from a lamp on a side table.

The yard, like everything else, was under several inches of water, and she moved slowly. Apart from the light seeping from the back room, the yard was in gloom. Daniela used one hand to feel her way along the wall.

Her foot hit a submerged flowerpot and she almost over-balanced. Gingerly, she nudged it away with her boot. Little ripples danced across the small walled yard and reflected flickers of light.

Daniela edged towards the window. The back door into the unlit kitchen was to her left, heavily buttressed with sandbags.

Through the gap in the sitting-room curtains she saw a sliver of the room beyond. The light she'd seen came not from a lamp but from a trio of candles on top of a sideboard. The rose-quartz chandelier hanging from the ceiling was unlit, either because the power had at last gone off or because someone preferred mood-lighting. Daniela peered left and right but couldn't see more than a thin section of room. The edge of an armchair and the corner of a Welsh dresser. The room looked empty.

She risked shuffling closer. An acquaintance in prison had

told her that, when lights were on within a dwelling and it was relatively dark outside, the people inside couldn't see out of the window. Even if someone happened to look, all they'd see was their reflection. Daniela had never tested it.

There was more debris beneath the window. Daniela nudged aside what felt like an earthenware planter. She steadied herself against the wall and leaned in as close to the glass as she dared. Angling her head, she could see the rest of the armchair and a bit of sofa. The room was only slightly changed from the house she remembered. Even the unpleasant wallpaper with the green leaf pattern remained.

Daniela stepped back, considering her next move. She didn't know if Henry McKearney was still living here with Margaret. But if he *was* …

Daniela pictured him watching the old house from the woods yesterday when she'd left with the money. She imagined him waiting until the next day when no one was around before returning for it.

The only reason he would've been there was if he knew something about Auryn's murder.

Daniela put her hands on the sash window to see if it was unlocked.

An upstairs window opened and a torch beam flashed down. Daniela looked up at the wrong instant and the light blinded her.

'Hello, down there,' Margaret McKearney called. 'Something I can help you with?'

29

Daniela lifted a hand to shield her eyes and gave a sheepish smile. 'Good evening, Mrs McKearney.'

'Well, *crap*. Dani Cain. I don't see you for years and suddenly you're all over the place.' Margaret shifted the torch so the light was no longer in Daniela's eyes. 'What on earth are you doing here? Do you know what time it is?'

'I'm sorry, I know it's late. I was, well—'

'You're looking for Henry.'

The accusation in her voice made Daniela flinch. 'I-I need to speak to him. Is he here?'

A pause. The main light in the upstairs room was switched off, and Daniela couldn't see Margaret's face. 'Stay there,' Margaret said. 'I'll come down.' The torch withdrew and the window closed.

Daniela stood in the shadowy yard with water rippling around her boots. It was getting cold again.

A minute passed before Margaret came into the kitchen. She opened the back door – unlocked, as it turned out – pulling a dressing gown around her slim frame with her other hand. Underneath she wore polka-dot pyjamas. She stayed behind the protective barrier of sandbags and planted a hand on her hip, waiting.

'Auryn's dead,' Daniela said.

Margaret's expression softened. 'Steph told me. I'm sorry. Although I'm not sure that justifies you turning up on my doorstep.'

'I know. I shouldn't've disturbed you.' Daniela couldn't keep still. Her eyes darted to the darkened windows. Was Henry inside? Maybe staring down at her right now?

'No, you probably shouldn't have.' Margaret sighed. She stepped back, holding the door. 'Come inside. There's no point standing around in the rain.'

Daniela withdrew. 'I don't know if—'

'Oh, don't be daft. I'm sure as hell not coming out in this state of undress. If you wanna talk, you can come in.'

Daniela hesitated a moment more before nodding. She stepped carefully over the sandbags.

'Leave your boots outside, please,' Margaret said. 'I've enough damp in here already.'

It would be nice to take the boots off, but Daniela was wary of leaving them. What if she needed to exit in a hurry again? What if Stephanie caught up with her here, like at Leo's house? Daniela didn't fancy her chances on the flooded streets without footwear.

With a feeling of deep misgiving, Daniela placed her boots by the back door.

The galley kitchen was narrow, and Daniela had to brush past Margaret before she could shut the door. She caught a whiff of Margaret's flowery shampoo. Daniela shoved down an inappropriate feeling, embarrassed.

'Through to the sitting room, if you would,' Margaret said, flapping a hand. 'D'you fancy a cuppa?'

'No, I-I can't really stop.' She peered down the darkened hallway. Was the house empty?

Despite her intentions, Daniela was herded into the sitting room at the back of the house. Her first impressions of the place had been wrong. The garish wallpaper remained, yes, but the rest of the room had been updated and modernised. Tasteful throws covered the sofa. A substantial Victorian bookcase was loaded with books and DVDs. The threadbare carpet had been removed and the original wooden boards polished to a dark shine.

'It's been a long time, hasn't it?' Margaret said. 'Here, sit down, you're making the place untidy. Must be strange, coming back here after a good few years. Does everything feel different?'

'Henry's not here. Is he?'

'I wouldn't have let you in if he was. Some of us are forgiving and, well, some of us aren't.'

Daniela looked away. Her hands, hidden inside her sleeves, were still bunched. She forced herself to open her fists. *So, where is he?*

'He's not been here for a while, right?' Daniela guessed. Framed photographs took up space on shelves and tables, of Margaret and Leo, but none of Henry.

'Oh, a couple of years, I suppose.' Margaret curled into the armchair, her legs drawn up. 'I've not kept track of dates, but yes, must be about two years. Of course, I could've had him out a lot sooner if I'd drummed up the courage. Everyone told me I should've. But that's how it goes, isn't it?' She gave a sad smile. 'We make ourselves so afraid of breaking the cycle, and when we actually get around to it, we find it's been a lot of fuss over nothing. Then all you can do is look back and regret all the hurt you caused.'

Daniela sat down on the lumpy sofa cushions. 'You didn't cause anything,' she said carefully.

'I allowed it to happen, and that's nearly as bad.' Margaret waved a dismissive hand. 'Oh, he never laid a finger on me, of course. I wouldn't have tolerated that. But things weren't easy. Especially for Leo. I should've never let him witness so many arguments.' Her face brightened. 'He's doing well for himself. He's a doctor, did you know?'

'I saw him today, yeah.'

Margaret picked up a framed photo from the crowded dresser and handed it to Daniela. It showed Leo looking stiff and awkward in his graduation robe. 'I'm so proud,' Margaret said. 'Look how well he turned out, despite everything. If only I'd got him out from his dad's influence sooner ... Well, you can't spend your life regretting everything.'

Daniela gave the photo back. Her eyes kept darting to the doorway, as if Henry might at any moment appear. 'Where'd Henry go?'

'Off to Sheffield, as far as I know. That's where his other woman lives, anyway.'

'So, he's not in Stonecrop anymore?'

'He doesn't *live* here, no.' Margaret wrinkled her lip. 'But he doesn't seem in any hurry to pack up and leave for good. He's got a long-standing rental with Eric Winters over at Winterbridge Farm for a holiday cabin. He can use it any time out of season. So, yes, he'll come back, like a bad smell, four or five times a year. There's no obvious rhyme or reason to it.' Margaret held up her hands. 'Who can understand the shallow machinations of the male mind? He comes and goes when he feels like it, for no evident reason, other than to remind me I'm not rid of him.'

She leaned forwards in a conspiratorial manner. 'He's being awkward about the divorce, of course. He's never made anything easy for anyone in his life. Now and again, I'll wander into the pub and there he'll be, propping up the bar like he's never left. Like he has every right to be there.'

She got up and went to close the crack between the curtains, as if talking about her ex-husband made her uneasy.

'When did you last see him?' Daniela asked.

Margaret made an indelicate noise. 'Just last week.' She settled into her chair. 'The bastard popped into town with the excuse that he wanted to make sure his cabin was secure before the floods. I suppose that proves he does listen to *someone*, even if it's just the weatherman.'

'That's all he was here for?'

'Well, who knows?' Margaret gave her a smile tinged with sadness. 'It wasn't to see Leo, if that's what you mean. Those two don't speak anymore. I don't think Leo even knows that his dad stays at Winterbridge Farm when he's in town. Honestly, I don't know what brings Henry back here. He doesn't have the antiques business anymore. That closed years ago, after ... well.'

Daniela dropped her gaze.

'You know,' Margaret said with a sigh, 'I never figured out whether I was supposed to hate you. I can't understand what you did. You think you had your reasons, I'm sure, but ...' She absently massaged the spot on her left finger where a wedding ring had sat for so long. 'You only ever saw the bad side of Henry. But he loved us. He would've done anything to protect us. I know what you thought of him – what everyone thought of him – and by extension what everyone thought of *me* for standing by him. And I did stand by him. After he was injured, I helped him through the physio, through the trial, and before that, when his business was falling apart and your father cheated him out of all that money ...'

Daniela blinked. 'My dad did what?'

Margaret pursed her lips. 'It's not something you'll want to hear, but when they fell out, Henry and your dad, and they split the antiques shop, your father didn't behave very well. He made Henry buy him out, and pay twice what the business was worth. He knew Henry couldn't afford it but he did it anyway.'

'So, why did Henry agree?'

'Oh, pride and stubbornness, the usual. Either Henry paid up, or he lost the business. He wasn't fond of losing.'

'Yeah. Neither was Dad.'

'Each as bad as the other.' Margaret half-smiled. 'Anyway, it's stupid to defend Henry now. I know he wasn't blameless. But everything he did, every penny he earned, every fight he felt he had to start, it was for us. He genuinely thought he was doing the right thing. Probably still does.' She stirred restlessly in her seat. 'After they shut down his shoddy counterfeiting business and put him away, it gave me a chance to think. Those twenty months made me realise I didn't want Henry back.' She gave a tremulous smile. 'I sometimes think you would've done me more of a favour if you'd killed him outright.'

Daniela studied the floor. She was aware of time ticking past. If Henry wasn't home, then Daniela needed to go. There was always a chance Stephanie might think to look for her here.

'His heart was in the right place,' Margaret said, almost to herself. 'But that wasn't enough. It doesn't excuse his behaviour, or mine. Both of us acted poorly. I just hope I didn't get out too late. For Leo's sake, not mine.' She sighed again. 'I'd love to say me and Leo were still close, but that's simply not true. I have no idea how he feels about any of this.' Margaret sat up straighter. 'But I'll tell you this, I've forgiven Henry. For every hurtful word, for every threat, for every time he came *this* close to breaking his word – the word he gave on our wedding day that he'd never lay a hand on me – I forgive him all that. Because you can't carry these things around forever. And I forgive you too. You thought you were protecting me, or Leo, or your sisters, or your father ... who knows what you were really thinking? I assume you've had plenty of time to consider it.'

It was more statement than question, so Daniela didn't answer. She glanced at the door again, ready to make some excuse to leave.

Margaret laughed, with a mixture of regret and bitterness. 'Anyway, none of it's my concern now. I'm purely selfish in my old age. The only people I care about are me and Leo. I don't know where Henry is, or what he's doing, and I'll be happy if I never lay eyes on him again. Just because I've forgiven him doesn't change anything. Ultimately, everything was his fault. I wish I'd realised that then, instead of blaming Franklyn.'

'Franklyn? Why her?'

Margaret looked surprised. 'Well, mainly because she was sleeping with Henry. You must've known. Everyone knew.'

30

Daniela set it up to look like an accident. Atop the cabinet above the sink was a pile of paper towels. It was easy to arrange a small avalanche, as if the pile had slipped into the sink, where a tap had unfortunately been left running. She was quite proud as she poked the paper into the plughole and watched the swirling water fill the basin.

She stepped out of the storeroom and pulled the door almost closed. Already the water had reached the top of the sink. In a few moments it would patter onto the carpet. By morning – assuming no one discovered it before then – the shop would be awash. Daniela smiled as she thought of the papers and boxes littering the floor. In a few hours they'd be wrecked.

You're being petty. Daniela brushed the thought aside. Sure, on the surface this was nothing more than mindless vandalism, but taken in a wider context—

'Who's there?' someone called out.

Daniela startled and only just bit back a curse. The voice had come from the back door. Hurriedly, Daniela moved away, into the deeper shadows.

'I know you're in here,' the voice hissed, and this time Daniela recognised it.

Leo. He must've heard a noise or seen Daniela scrambling over the wall.

Daniela hesitated, torn. Should she reveal herself? Or could she sneak out without being seen? Her stomach twisted at the thought having to explaining why she'd broken into the shop.

As quietly as she could, Daniela crept away. If she could force the front door, maybe she could escape. Otherwise she'd have to go past Leo.

With scuffle of noise, Leo advanced into the shop. 'Daniela?' he said. 'I know it's you. Where are you?'

Daniela squeezed past an upturned bedframe and reached the front door. She'd hoped the door was secured with a bolt, but instead she found a Yale lock, with no sign of the key. She shoved the door in frustration. It rattled in its frame.

The sound alerted Leo. Daniela heard him moving through the shop with the confidence of too much time spent within the maze of furniture.

It occurred to her that Leo had kept his voice low, and hadn't switched on the lights. He didn't want to wake his dad.

But if he'd seen Daniela sneaking in, might Henry have seen too? Daniela put her hand on the breast pocket of her jacket to feel the knife hidden inside. Sick adrenaline churned her stomach. She had to get out without being caught.

It was brighter near the front of the shop, with the illumination of the streetlights falling through the windows, which gave Daniela fewer places to hide. She slipped between the close-packed furniture towards the rear of the shop. Her heart was hammering and her palms were slick.

She made a mistake as she ducked into a narrow space between two wardrobes. The streetlight was directly behind her and cast her shadow huge across the shop floor. Leo spotted it and changed course.

'Daniela, just stop, will you? Let me talk to you.'

Trying to run was making Daniela look daft. So, she stopped.

Leo appeared around a corner. 'What're you doing?' he demanded in an angry whisper. 'What're you after?'

Daniela tried a smile, but Leo's expression withered it. 'Nothing,' she said.

'Are you kidding me? What the hell were you thinking?' Leo grabbed her arm to lead her away. 'Get out of here before you wake my dad.'

Daniela dug in her heels. 'Leo, you don't understand. Your dad—'

'I know.'

'You—?'

'I know what happened to Franklyn. That's why you're here, right?'

The hitch in his voice made Daniela hesitate. 'How d'you know what he did?'

'I heard him talking on the phone. Organising someone to go find her.' Leo bit his lip. 'I know what it meant.'

'You don't know the half of it.' Daniela pulled loose from his grip. 'If you'd seen what he'd done you wouldn't defend him.'

'I'm not. But things can't go on like this. You—'

'He broke Frankie's fingers.' Without meaning to, Daniela took a step towards him. 'Am I supposed to just ignore that?'

Leo's eyes cut away. 'I wish you would,' he said, his voice

harsh. 'What do you think it's like for me and Mum? This *feud* has pushed him to the edge. I'm genuinely worried what it might make him do. Please, forget about this.'

'Are you serious?'

'Of course I am.' Leo lost his temper. 'It's wrecking our family. If Franklyn could've just left us alone—'

Daniela laughed incredulously. 'You're blaming Franklyn? Did she break her own fingers?'

Leo's expression hardened. 'Do you even realise what she's done? Stealing the money was the last straw, but it's been everything else. She—' His voice cracked. He shook his head angrily. 'If Dad finds out you're here it'll make things worse. For everyone. Don't you understand that?'

Daniela thought of the overflowing sink in the storeroom. If she strained her ears, she could hear splattering water. 'Leo,' she said, 'he threatened to kill me today. If we let him get away with this—'

'Please keep your voice down.'

'Who knows what he'll do next? I'm not going to wait till he goes after Auryn.'

Leo turned his face away. 'If you want to help people,' he said, 'the best thing you could do is get lost.'

The way he said it was heart-breaking. Daniela realised at that moment how much she wanted Leo. The idea of anything bad happening to him—

The rear door of the shop banged open, and the roar of Henry's voice filled the room.

'What's going on? Who's in here?'

31

February 2017

It's not true.

Daniela swallowed. Blinked. Her heart felt too big for her chest.

Franklyn would never do that.

Aloud, Daniela said, 'They hated each other.'

'Funny how it works out like that.' Margaret shifted in her seat. 'Are you sure I can't get you a drink?'

'No, I—'

'Doesn't have to be tea. I'm sure I've got something else.' Margaret unfolded her legs and went to a walnut drinks cabinet. From inside she produced a bottle of whisky. 'Here we go. That'll take the edge off the cold.'

'I don't—'

'Hush, no excuses now. I was planning a snifter before bed anyways. And a lady shouldn't drink alone.' Margaret snorted laughter. 'Although, when you get to shuffling around in your pyjamas at this time of day, letting strangers into your house, I think you've eluded the definition of *lady*.'

Margaret poured generous measures into a pair of crystal tumblers. The label on the bottle looked expensive.

'One of the few good things Henry left behind,' Margaret said as she held out a glass to Daniela. 'In all the kerfuffle he overlooked two cases down in the cellar. D'you want ice?'

'I – no.'

'Good girl.' Margaret pushed the tumbler into Daniela's unresisting hands. 'Drink up. It'll make you feel better.'

Daniela was shaking. 'When did it happen?'

'Franklyn and Henry? It started when she went off to Birmingham. They were working together, then ...' Margaret sighed. 'Sorry, love. I thought you knew. Everyone else did.'

'They did?'

Margaret sat down with her drink cupped in both hands. 'I don't know how long it went on. Honestly, I never wanted the details. But it was a while. More than one occasion, certainly.'

Why?

'*You feel like you owe something to the people you used to know.*'

'*He thought he could blackmail me.*'

She wouldn't have done it willingly. But Daniela couldn't bring herself to say that aloud.

'How did you find out?' Daniela asked.

'Franklyn told me.' Margaret swirled her drink. 'She came to me ... well, it would've been that weekend. The day Henry got hurt. She came into the shop early that morning, flipped the sign to closed, made me sit down, and told me everything. About her and him and – well, let's just say it wasn't the first time he'd strayed, according to her. She told me everything. And I—' Margaret forced a laugh '—I chased her out. Threatened her with all sorts.'

Daniela couldn't imagine Margaret threatening anything.

226

But then, she also couldn't picture Franklyn and Henry together.

'If I hadn't yelled so much, maybe Leo wouldn't have overheard.' Margaret's lips pulled into a tight line. 'Maybe he wouldn't have confronted his dad about it. Maybe ... well, maybe a lot of things.'

Daniela gulped her drink. It burned.

'That was the last time I spoke to Franklyn,' Margaret said. 'I thought she was trying to hurt Henry, driving me and Leo away, ruining his business – because I held the purse-strings to the antiques shop, of course. If I'd walked, he'd have been left with nothing. And that's almost what happened.'

That was why Henry had cornered Daniela out by the river, and why Franklyn came home with broken fingers. Not because of the money they'd stolen. Because Frankie had taken so much more.

Margaret's grip tightened around her glass. 'It wasn't till later – years later – I realised she'd been trying to help me. In her own stupid, backwards way, she wanted to give me a reason to kick Henry out forever. Something I could never forgive him for. Wish I'd listened.' Margaret shook her hair out of her eyes. 'Henry's like a harbinger of bad news. Every time he shows his face, disaster is right behind. Or maybe I just see it that way.'

Daniela nodded. She tried to focus. 'But you're sure he's not in town at the moment?'

'Who's ever sure about anything? You think you've got a little stability, then *pfft*, off it goes like a fart in the wind. I think Eric's stayed at Winterbridge Farm – he couldn't leave the cows – but the cabins are locked up. I doubt Henry's there now.' Margaret cocked her head. 'Why're you asking?'

'I ... I don't want to run into him.'

'No. On top of everything else, you don't need that.' Margaret looked sympathetic. 'It must be terrible for you. You and Auryn were always so close.'

Daniela had to laugh. 'You think so?'

'Oh, you had your falling-outs, I know. Who on this planet doesn't, especially with family? But there were always the four of you, the Cain sisters, and everyone could see how much you meant to each other.'

Daniela shrugged, embarrassed. 'I guess things change.'

'Everything changes,' Margaret agreed. 'It's such a shame. The way you kids scattered to the winds after your mother left ...'

'We didn't scatter, so much. I mean, Steph's still here.'

Margaret waved away the distinction. 'I always knew you weren't for staying. There's too much wildness in all of you.'

Margaret was sipping her whisky – only little sips, but she'd already drunk half the substantial glass. Daniela kept pace. She still felt the same urgency, the need to leave the house as soon as possible, but for the moment all she could do was sit there, numb. The alcohol made her warm around the ears.

'I probably shouldn't tell you this,' Margaret said in her conspiratorial tone, the one she used for gossiping over the counter, 'but years ago, my granny came to stay, and she happened to see all four of you in the street. She said, "You know how it goes with large families?"' Margaret held up the fingers of one hand, thumb tucked in. She counted them off. '"The first child goes to the priesthood, the second to the police, the third to jail, and the fourth to the devil."'

Daniela felt a tingle up her back. Margaret was smiling in

that soft, guileless way, and somehow it didn't sound like an insult.

'She must've known us well,' Daniela said carefully.

'Oh, she didn't know you at all. That was just her way – an off-the-cuff judgement based on nothing but the things folks say back home. She didn't mean a thing by it, and I forgot about it, until years and years later, when Franklyn up and took her vows.'

For the first time, Daniela realised what Franklyn had really wanted to atone for.

Margaret smiled over the rim of her glass. The way her eyes twinkled made her look years younger. 'I always thought my granny got it a little wrong,' she said then. 'You were always the one with something of the devil about her, Dani Cain.'

'I'm ... not sure how to take that.'

'You'll take it for what it is. A passing comment from a woman who's known you since before you could walk. So, have you heard from Franklyn these past few years?'

She asked too casually, her eyes avoiding Daniela's. 'Not really,' Daniela said. 'She wrote to me a few times while I was inside. Just keeping me up to speed on the family. She came to visit me once, after Dad died, but I-I didn't want to talk to her, not right then.'

'That's a shame,' Margaret said softly. 'Still, if you do get to speak to her, tell her she was right. About pretty much everything. And I'm sorry for how it turned out.'

Margaret knocked back the last of her drink. Daniela examined the quarter-inch in her own glass, then followed suit. The raw burn of expensive alcohol made her cough.

'So, do you believe what your gran said?' Daniela asked.

'I'm the third-born, so I've been written off from the start? Because, I have to say, that's not greatly comforting.'

'Then change.' Margaret shrugged, her movements softened by alcohol. 'Look at me – I used to be a tired old woman with an arsehole husband, working in a tiny shop in a village in the middle of nowhere. Now I'm a single lady in her prime who runs her own business.'

Daniela couldn't help but return her smile. 'Sounds like you made a good swap.'

'Didn't I just?' She beamed. 'Henry keeps playing these games, coming back to town, wanting me to know he's still around, but I'm not playing anymore.'

'Do you know if he's still in touch with my family?'

'Oh, I doubt it. He didn't have many kind words for Stephanie, but—' She paused, frowning. 'Mind, when I saw Henry last week at the Crossed Swords ... I went to meet some friends, and there was Henry, sitting by the window. He had his back to me so I could've snuck out without him spotting me, but I thought, why should I be on eggshells all the time? This is my home village, and I'm damned if he's going to scare me away. So, I went to the bar, and I was keeping a weather eye on him, just in case, and I realised he was talking to Auryn.'

Daniela stood up and took Margaret's glass. She refilled them both from the bottle on the cabinet. 'What were they talking about?'

'I wasn't close enough to find out. But it didn't look like a friendly chat, if you know what I mean. Auryn wasn't happy. And Henry was in close—' She leaned forwards to demonstrate. The loose neck of her pyjamas gaped. 'Like he didn't want to be overheard.'

Leo had said Henry and Auryn were still in contact. Daniela hadn't realised he'd meant as recently as last week. 'And this was last week?'

'A bit less than a week. Perhaps five days.'

So, before Auryn left Stonecrop – or said she'd left. Sometime between then and now, she'd returned to hide away in the old house. Had Henry found out she was there? That she was alone in the house? Her family thought she'd left. There was no one there to protect her.

Daniela felt anger curling in her stomach again.

'Did they talk for long?' Daniela asked.

'About ten or fifteen minutes that I saw.' Margaret sipped her new drink. 'I met up with my friends and got distracted, and when I looked back, the pair of them were gone.'

'I wouldn't think they'd have much to talk about,' Daniela said.

'Well, I couldn't hear, but I can hazard an astute guess.'

'You can?'

Margaret hesitated before saying, 'You have to understand, Henry's still bitter. Specifically, about the way your father treated him. They were in business together for a lot of years. I know it was Henry's idea to start bringing those awful shoddy goods into the country, but if your dad felt so strongly about it, he should've said something at the start, rather than—'

'Wait.' Daniela frowned. 'How long was Henry doing the counterfeit thing? I thought it was only for a short while.'

'Oh, God no. It started long before your father sold his half of the business.'

'And you knew about it?'

Margaret gave her a look. 'Yes. I handled the finances for

my shop and the antiques business, so of course I found out eventually, despite the best efforts of my estranged husband. He's good at disguising his tracks – there's a nebulous element to buying and selling antiques, since mostly it's done in cash – but not enough to fool me. I'd thank you not to judge me, by the way. I saw what he was doing and turned a blind eye. I'm aware of that.'

Daniela shut her mouth.

Margaret's gaze became reflective. 'The problem was, your mother figured it out at about the same time that I did. She didn't find out from me, but secrets have a way of disclosing themselves, don't they?' She took a long swallow of her drink. 'She left your father not long afterwards. And I always felt terrible about that. Whether I contributed directly or not, the last thing I wanted was for you kids to grow up without a mother.'

Daniela shifted in her seat. The topic made her uncomfortable. 'I doubt that's why she left,' she said, recalling years of arguments and silences and worse. 'It definitely wasn't your fault.'

'Some of it might've been. I told her a few things I should've kept to myself. I told her about her jewellery – those rings your father bought for her, one for each of you kids? The truth is, they weren't his to give. They belonged to my grand-mother. I thought they'd been lost in a house move, until I saw them on your mother's hands. Henry sold them to your dad and assumed, even if I noticed, I'd say nothing rather than cause a scene. Perhaps that would've been best.' Margaret sighed. 'Little, awful things like that. Nothing bad enough to keep her away from you all these years, I would've thought, but who knows. Mind you, there was a few things she could've told me in return, but didn't.'

232

Daniela said nothing.

'Some of us can put up with more than others,' Margaret said with a soft shrug. 'After your mother left, when things got rocky between Henry and your father, and the business folded, Henry got it into his head that your father cheated him. Stole from him, effectively. And now your father's passed on, God love him, the money must be somewhere. I'm only guessing, but if Henry was talking to Auryn, it'd be because he wants what he thinks he's owed. Auryn was in charge of your dad's finances. Her professional experience, and all that.'

Daniela's head ached. Was this what it was about? Dad's money? She thought of the package below the floorboards. Had Auryn hidden it there to avoid Henry getting hold of it?

'How much did Henry reckon he was owed?' she asked.

'A lot. He used to say your dad robbed us of half a million, but that was probably hyperbole.'

Daniela shook her head. There'd been a substantial amount of money under the floor, but not half a million. Did that make her feel better or worse? Her heart ached with every beat.

Henry McKearney had been in Stonecrop recently. He'd talked to Auryn, he wanted money, and he hated Daniela's family.

Was that enough reason for him to kill Auryn?

Margaret was staring into her glass. 'Auryn was a great kid. She never had a bad word to say about anybody. I always hoped she and Leo would sort things out. They were wonderful. And now she's gone.' She tipped her head back and drained her glass. 'He's distraught, of course. Leo. I phoned

233

him earlier but he could barely even talk. He kept asking if I knew where his dad was. Like a little kid. It's heart-breaking. This sort of thing, it never makes sense, does it? Auryn should've looked after her health. She shouldn't have lived alone. Or she should've gone somewhere warm to ride out the floods—'

'Stephanie said she *did* go, a few days ago.'

'Really? Why on earth did she come back?' Margaret frowned. '*How* did she come back? She doesn't drive, and there've been no buses for a week. I wonder if Leo knows ...' She shook her head sadly. 'None of it seems fair. Why couldn't the good Lord have stolen Henry instead? It's not right that a young girl should take ill and die like that.'

'Take ill?'

Margaret tilted her head. The alcohol had smoothed the creases of her face. 'That's what Leo told me,' she said. 'They couldn't say for certain, but it looked like she'd neglected herself and took ill. Probably pneumonia, and no surprise in this weather.'

She doesn't know. 'It wasn't pneumonia,' Daniela said. 'Someone killed her.'

A number of emotions crossed Margaret's face. Finally she settled on simple denial. 'Well, that's not possible,' she said. 'They wouldn't know yet. They'd have to do an – an autopsy, and other investigations, wouldn't they?'

'Steph seems pretty sure it was murder.'

Margaret's hand went to her mouth. 'Oh God. That ... God, that makes even less sense. Why didn't Leo tell me?'

'He probably didn't want to say anything until it was definite.'

'God,' Margaret said again. 'Who would do something like

234

that? There's not a soul in the world who'd wish harm on Auryn.'

'Apart from Henry?' Daniela said it without thinking.

Margaret's expression froze. 'Is that why you're here?' she asked. There was no trace of drunken laughter in her voice now. 'You think Henry did this?'

'It's a possibility, isn't it?'

Margaret shook her head firmly. 'No. No, he'd never do something like that.'

Are you sure? Daniela remembered bruises and broken fingers; the twinge in her ankle that'd never fully healed; the soul-deep fear she'd never lost whenever she thought of that day by the riverbank; Henry's smile. *'It'd be easy for someone to slip and fall here.'*

'He hates our family,' Daniela said.

Margaret's lips thinned. 'Can't dispute that, can I? You gave him more than enough reason. But if he wanted to take it out on you kids, don't you think he would've done something before now? He's never lifted one finger against Auryn or Stephanie, not in seven years. Why now?'

Daniela didn't have an answer to that. 'But he *does* hate us,' she said.

'Maybe once. But the day you got put away, he said, "That's it, it's over." He's never spoken of it since. And any bad feeling was towards *you*— Well, to you and Franklyn. And Steph, I suppose. But he *liked* Auryn.'

'Even when Auryn was dating Leo?'

Margaret sat back and folded her arms. Her eyes shone. 'All right, perhaps there was some bad feeling there as well. But that was years ago. Henry wouldn't still hold a grudge. He certainly wouldn't kill someone. God.' Margaret pushed

235

her hands through her tangled hair. 'You know what I should do? I'll call Stephanie.' She reached for her phone, on the table beside her. 'I can—'

'No!' Daniela was out of her chair in an instant. She swiped the phone from Margaret's hand.

Margaret stared at her in shock. Then she drew herself up and gathered her dressing gown, closing the gap at the top of her pyjamas as neatly as she'd closed the curtains. 'You're no better than you used to be,' she said. 'And you're lucky Henry *isn't* here. What were you planning to do to him this time?'

Shame took away Daniela's breath. *I'm not that person anymore.* But if that was true, why was she here? Why had she tracked across the village to confront Henry when the sensible thing to do was to just leave?

The urge was for her to turn on her heel and walk out. Take her anger. Let it fester forever inside. But for once in her life she made herself stop.

She held out the phone to Margaret. 'I'm sorry,' she said. 'For coming here. For coming back. I never meant to dredge everything up again. I should've stayed away. I've hurt you all so much already.'

'Well.' Margaret sniffed. 'That's as may be. But you're here now. I don't want to know why you're hiding from Stephanie, but I'd advise you to stop doing that. You need all the family you can get right now.' She took the phone. 'And you need to quit holding on to the past like this. It's doing you no good at all.'

Margaret took Daniela's glass and put it back on the cabinet. As Daniela watched her, she thought about the gold rings in her back pocket. One more thing from the past she was clinging on to. One more thing to which she had no claim.

Without Margaret seeing, Daniela slipped the rings down the side of the sofa. Next time Margaret lifted the cushions she'd find them. God knows what she'd think, but Daniela would be long gone by then, one way or another.

When Margaret turned back, she was all business. 'You've got somewhere to stay tonight, I assume,' Margaret said.

'There's some rooms at the Crossed Swords,' Daniela said. 'I'm sure Chris will let me stay if I need to.' Not that she intended to stay, of course, but the answer seemed to satisfy Margaret.

Margaret sighed. She reached to straighten Daniela's collar. 'Honest to God, you and your folks drive me to distraction. You realise that in another life we could've been family, don't you? If Leo and Auryn had stayed together, I mean. I might've liked some daughters.'

She ushered Daniela to the back door. As Daniela brushed past, Margaret caught her arm and pulled her close to plant a kiss on her cheek. The gesture caught Daniela so much by surprise that she didn't know how to react.

'I'm sorry for what I said,' Margaret said. 'I know you're a different person now. Otherwise you wouldn't be here – you would've stayed away forever.'

Daniela mumbled a reply.

'Take care of yourself,' Margaret said seriously. 'The police will figure out what happened to Auryn, but until then, you stay safe, okay?'

'I will.'

Margaret rubbed away the spot of lipstick she'd left on Daniela's cheek. 'You get yourself home,' she said. 'Back to – where is it you're living now?'

'Birmingham. We've got a flat in King's Heath.' *Although not for much longer if I come home empty-handed.*

'Oh, "we", is it?'

Daniela bit her tongue. 'Yeah. Me and – and the person I'm living with.'

Margaret gave a knowing little smile. 'Serious, is it?'

'Yeah.' *About as serious as it gets. I hope.*

'I'm glad. You deserve a new start, Daniela.'

'Thank you,' Daniela said, and meant it.

Margaret flashed that smile again, then shut the door. Daniela heard the key in the lock.

32

A straight line from Margaret McKearney's house to the Briarsfield tractor trail would take her back through the woods, along the path she'd used most frequently as a child. Daniela wondered if she should take a different route, in case Stephanie was out looking for her. But she didn't want to go near the site of the old Kirk Cottage, or the Crossed Swords, or ...

She was running out of safe places in this village.

Then, without consciously making a decision, she turned north instead of south. Towards Winterbridge Farm, where, according to his ex-wife, Henry McKearney rented a cabin when he was in town.

The back of her mind itched with the need to know what'd happened to Auryn. It was more urgent than retrieving her money; more urgent than getting out of Stonecrop. She had to know if Henry was involved.

As she walked, she clutched her mobile phone in her pocket. Should she call Stephanie and tell her Henry had been in town recently, talking to Auryn? Daniela would've liked to let the police take over. She had no particular dislike of the police beyond her own unpleasant interactions with them. But they were no more infallible than anyone else. They made mistakes and assumptions, they misinterpreted words or actions, they held opinions.

Stephanie, despite her myriad faults, was an honest person. A good officer. Unfortunately, she'd weighed up the evidence and found it pointing at Daniela. And, like the good and unbiased officer she was, Stephanie acted on what she believed was the truth. Even if it meant taking down her sister.

Daniela knew what would happen if she got arrested. She was still on licence from prison. Never mind if the truth eventually came out – she couldn't afford to spend another night in police detention. There was too much at stake. Much more than just her liberty.

Winterbridge Farm wasn't far outside Stonecrop, situated in a scenic but exposed position next to the River Bade. Daniela remembered it as a run-down homestead with a few cowsheds. From what Margaret had said, Eric Winters had done some renovations. Daniela struggled to remember Eric. A middle-aged farmer with a much younger wife and a notoriously short temper. Daniela recalled being chased off his land at least once.

She stuck to the roads. If any cars came along, she'd hear them and dive over the hedge long before they got close. It was a risk worth taking. She'd left the woods behind, and had no urge to go cross-country through the muddy fields.

Behind the thick clouds, the sun had long ago sunk below the horizon. The wind and rain came in little bursts and flurries, sometimes dropping off to nearly nothing. Daniela wondered how long it'd be until the police could get here.

The floodwater deadened all sound. Apart from the wind rustling the hedgerows, the evening was silent, the fields empty. Most of the farm animals had been moved elsewhere to escape the floods. It occurred to Daniela there would've been no such escape for the wild animals – rabbits and foxes and badgers, all drowned or driven out of their burrows. Daniela had never considered the cost to the land and the wildlife.

That's because you never consider anyone but yourself.

She drew her stolen jacket tighter. The stress and the cold conspired to send her thoughts in random directions. The day felt like one endless bad dream.

She wondered if this was Hell; a deserted, flooded town, where she would wander forever without escape, always pursued, never allowed to rest.

She thought about her dad, at the banister on the landing, planning how to make a dive look like a fall.

She thought about Auryn, growing cold and stiff on the bed in the junk room of the old house.

She wished she had a home she could long for.

She kept walking.

Winterbridge Farm, when it finally came into view, looked deserted. The farmhouse was a large, blocky structure, visible only as a smudge in the darkness because it'd been repainted brilliant white. The three cowsheds were blobs of shadow. The air was tinged with the thick smell of manure. Most people would've been put off by the smell, but to Daniela it was a pungent reminder of home.

Closer to the road were a number of smaller structures, the size and shape of shipping containers – the holiday cottages Margaret had mentioned. On the road beside the gate, a blue estate car wallowed with floodwater up to its wheel arches, its nose pointed towards Stonecrop.

The lane sloped down to the farmhouse and the river

241

beyond. The gradient was so slight it was only noticeable when the river flooded. The low-lying fields around Winterbridge suffered the brunt of the damage, with half the land fully waterlogged. It was a wonder the family hadn't given up and moved long ago ... except who would buy the place? The holiday cottages looked like an effort to mitigate the income lost to the river each year. A few tenants during the summer months would cost less in terms of space, food, and general hassle than a herd of cows.

Daniela paused. The place was so quiet. The river was too swollen and turgid to make any noise.

As she descended towards the farm the water became deeper by imperceptible increments, until it lapped the top of her wellies. She was glad when she reached the gate to the holiday cottages and pulled herself up onto a raised pathway that, although also flooded, was easier to traverse.

The holiday cottages, on closer inspection, were little more than wooden cabins with rough-hewn edges and a coat of paint to make them more enticing. They were set on concrete mounts out of the floodwater. Each had a small area of decking, a redbrick barbeque pit, and a pleasant view of the river and the fields. Behind them, partially sheltered by a hedgerow, was a square building that housed communal toilets and showers.

All five cabins looked empty, their doors locked and their windows shuttered. Daniela didn't know which one Henry rented. She stopped in front of Cabin 4 because its shutters were open.

Daniela stood on the deck debating how difficult it would be to break in. The windows were single pane, easy to smash. On impulse she tried the handle of the door.

33

The door was unlocked, but Daniela paused with the door half an inch open. No one locked their doors in Stonecrop, but this was different. A holiday cottage, next to the road, away from the farmhouse ... No matter how trusting or complacent Eric Winters had become, he wouldn't leave this place unsecured.

'Hello?' Daniela called quietly. 'Anyone here?'

No reply. The air that breathed out through the crack smelled of wood sealant. Daniela eased the door open.

As expected, the cabin was compact but well designed. A small kitchen was wedged into one corner. A fold-out table formed a barrier between the kitchen and a tiny seating area, with two chairs and a broom in the corner. The other half of the room had a double bed covered with a rumpled duvet. A small TV was mounted on the wall.

There was nowhere for anyone to hide, but Daniela checked under the bed and table, just in case. The place was empty. Dark, too. Daniela stood in the middle of the room, unsure what to do next. There was a light switch next to the door, but even if the power was still working, turning on the overhead light would make the cabin visible from a mile away.

She switched on her phone as token illumination. As soon

as she did so, an incoming text message beeped loud enough to make her jump. She swore under her breath.

Ignoring the unopened message, Daniela used the screen as a makeshift torch and searched the cabin. She pulled her sleeve down over her hand to avoid leaving fingerprints. She lifted the mattress but there was nothing beneath.

Under the table she found a bin bag containing some twists of used Sellotape and a ripped piece of blue plastic. It looked identical to the plastic that'd covered the bundle of notes Daniela had found at Auryn's house. Her heart leapt. But there was no sign of the money.

She checked the floor under the table. The dim light from her phone wasn't an effective torch. Every so often it went dark and she had to unlock the screen again to re-illuminate it. She wasn't even sure what she was looking for.

In the gap where the table folded into the wall, she spotted a scrap of paper, no bigger than a sweet wrapper, crumpled and ragged as if it had got damp. Really, it could've been wedged in the hinge for months. But Daniela flattened it out anyway.

A mobile phone number was scrawled in hurried, spidery writing. The ink had faded with age or exposure to water.

Daniela stood up. She didn't know what else she might be looking for.

She moved the chair to check the floor underneath and nearly knocked over the broom leaning against the wall. Except it wasn't a broom. It was a twelve-gauge shotgun.

Someone had left it propped with the barrel pointing at the ceiling. Daniela's blood ran cold. There could be a perfectly reasonable explanation for its presence – Eric Winters probably owned shotguns for vermin, and it was entirely likely he might stash it away from the main house if, say, he didn't have a licence. But, coupled with the blue wrapper in the bin bag, Daniela felt it was more than that.

Who would leave all this evidence lying around in an unlocked cabin?

It was too careless; the actions of someone who wanted to get caught. If Henry *had* been here, why would he leave these things behind? Why wouldn't he lock the door?

Unless he hadn't left. There were no obvious signs that the cabin was in use – no clothes or personal items or cooking utensils left on the counter – but that wasn't necessarily proof.

On impulse, Daniela opened the slimline fridge. The light came on; she wished she'd thought to do that while she'd searched the cabin. Inside was a packet of bacon, two cans of beer, and an open pint of milk, all in date.

In the better light, she found a cupboard set into the wall beside the bed, containing a holdall of clothes.

Okay, so someone had used the cabin recently. They must've left in a hurry, Daniela reasoned, because otherwise they would've locked the door—

She turned, realising what was missing from the small space. When she'd walked past the other cabins, she'd seen but hadn't fully registered the communal shower block outside.

If the occupant needed to piss during the night—

Daniela shoved her phone and the scrap of paper into her pocket and ran for the door. Before she could reach it, a torch beam swept across the decking outside.

She retreated fast to the far side of the cabin. There was no back door, not even a window other than the two on either side of the front door. She was trapped.

Outside, she heard the steady sloshing of someone wading through ankle-deep water. The noise stopped as the person stepped up onto the decking, accompanied by a bobbing circle of light from the torch.

The cabin door opened and Henry McKearney stepped inside.

He reached out automatically and flipped the overhead light on before he clocked that someone was in the room with him.

There was a frozen moment when they both blinked in the harsh of wash of electric light. It'd been a long time since they'd seen each other. Henry hadn't aged gracefully. His eyes were pouchy and the skin of his cheeks slack, as if gravity was twice as heavy for him. His red hair was thin and greying. The collar of his bulky black jacket was turned up against the cold, and he carried a roll of toilet paper tucked under his arm.

Instantly Daniela was taken back to that night seven years ago. The smell of water, and blood, and metal. She felt cold fear squat in her belly.

If Henry hadn't been entirely blocking the door with his bulk, Daniela would've barged past him to freedom while he stood gawking at her. Instead, she spun around and snatched up the shotgun.

Henry didn't move, even when she levelled the shotgun at him.

'This,' he said in his familiar, smoke-gravelled voice, 'is a surprise.'

Daniela's hands shook. The shotgun felt heavy and unnatural in her hands. It was unnerving how easily her finger slipped inside the trigger guard. The metal chilled her palms.

Without taking his eyes off her face, Henry slid away from the door to stand by the bed, allowing room for her to bolt for the exit. When she didn't move, he said, 'Why're you here?'

Daniela kept the weapon trained on him while she grabbed the blue plastic wrapper and threw it onto the table. 'That,' she said. 'Explain that.'

Henry lowered himself to the bed. Every move was slow, cautious. Daniela tried to steady the shotgun at waist height. Now Henry was sitting down, it put her aim on his head rather than his stomach.

'Your sister came to see me last week,' he said.

'Which one?'

A smile ghosted across his face. 'Auryn.' He savoured her name. 'She was finally willing to see sense and give me the money I'm owed.' He gestured at the plastic wrapper. 'Almost all of it, anyway. It took a bit of convincing for her to hand over the rest.'

Daniela almost pulled the trigger on him there and then. 'You killed her for that? For money?'

Henry's face underwent a transformation. 'She's dead?'

Daniela steadied her aim. 'Stand up.'

'Wait.' Henry's brows creased in a deep frown. He rubbed his mouth with shaky fingers. 'That can't be right. She can't be dead.'

'Stand up!' Even though Daniela was the one holding the gun, she'd never been so scared. She couldn't think.

Call Steph. Get her here.

Daniela took one hand off the shotgun to awkwardly fumble her phone out of her pocket. Henry watched her. He was thinking.

'There's something you haven't asked that you probably should,' he said. 'You wanna know why that shotgun is here?'

Daniela didn't answer. She was trying to find Stephanie's number without taking her eyes off Henry. The shotgun was heavy and kept dipping.

'I'm doing a favour for Eric Winters,' Henry said. 'He lent me the shotgun so I can keep the vermin levels down while I'm here. The flood's pushed all the rats out of their holes. They're popping up everywhere.' He reached towards the cupboard next to the bed.

'Sit still,' Daniela barked.

Henry ignored her. He opened the cupboard and put his hand inside. 'See, even I'm not irresponsible enough to leave a loaded weapon lying around my bedroom.' His hand withdrew, holding a small cardboard carton. He rattled the contents. 'First rule of firearms. Ammunition is kept separate.'

He stood up.

Daniela stuffed her phone back in her pocket so she could hold the shotgun with both hands. For all the good it'd do now. She broke the weapon open and saw the two empty barrels.

'Were you calling the police just now?' Henry asked. 'Or someone else?'

Daniela flung the shotgun at his head. Henry got his arms up in time to stop it from beaning him in the face. Daniela dived under the collapsible table and scrambled for the door.

She tripped on the doorsill and went sprawling. Winded, she twisted round and saw Henry standing over her. The shotgun was cracked open across his arm. Deliberately, making sure she was watching, Henry took two cartridges out of the carton and loaded the weapon, then closed it with a snap.

Daniela leapt off the decking into the flood. Water soaked her legs as she ran, stumbling, half falling, away from the cabin. At any second, she expected to hear thunder and feel the punch of buckshot between her shoulders.

But nothing followed her except Henry's laughter.

34

She backtracked half a mile down the road, until the sodden fields on either side gave way to trees again, before she clambered over a gate and took refuge in the woods. The trees protruded from the mirror-like water, which was cold and still and could've been six inches or six feet deep.

'Some of us are forgiving … some of us aren't.'

Daniela followed what might've been a path until she was out of sight of the road. Then she pulled out her phone again.

Her hands tremored as she dialled Stephanie's number. Her jogging pants were wet from the knees down and she was exhausted from running through shin-high water. The space between her shoulder blades still itched.

The line rang three times before Stephanie answered.

'Don't hang up,' Daniela said before Stephanie could speak. 'I've got some stuff you need to hear.'

'Come to the station with me,' Stephanie suggested. 'Tell us in person.'

Daniela almost laughed. 'Yeah, no. Listen, Henry McKearney is here.'

A pause, then: 'So?'

'He's in Stonecrop. Right now.'

'He never really left. What's your point?'

'He's renting a cabin at Winterbridge Farm. You know that as well, right?'

Stephanie said nothing. It was a police officer's trick – keep quiet and let you talk yourself into a hole. At that moment, it suited Daniela fine.

'Cabin Four,' Daniela said. 'There's a bunch of stuff that shouldn't be there.'

'Like what?'

'Like Henry McKearney, for a start. Margaret told me he'd left town and only comes back when he wants to harass her, but he's here now.'

'When did you speak to Margaret?'

'Yesterday, in the shop.' Which was true, as far as it went. 'Pay attention, will you? Why is Henry here when everyone else has been evacuated?'

'Are you there now?'

'No.'

'Then where are you?'

'Don't be thick, I'm not telling you.'

Stephanie let out a long breath. 'Daniela, I don't know what you're doing, but the best thing for everyone is if you tell me where you are. We can talk about this properly.'

'Yeah, with me in handcuffs, I get it. Will you helicopter in a lawyer for me?'

'If necessary.'

Daniela kicked a submerged root in frustration. 'I didn't kill Auryn, Steph. I can't believe you'd think that. But someone *did* do it. And Henry's right here in Stonecrop. He has to be on your list of suspects, doesn't he?'

'What are you basing that on?'

'Oh, seriously. He's got a good enough reason.'

'If he'd killed *you*, sure, he'd have good reason.'

Daniela leaned against a tree and stared down into the water. 'I went to the cabins to talk to Henry, okay? There was—'

'You went to find him?'

'Why do you always assume the goddamn worst about me? There were things in his cabin. A blue plastic wrapper. And a shotgun.'

'What do plastic wrappers prove?'

Shit. Daniela had as good as admitted she knew about the money in the old house. She closed her eyes. 'I spoke to him, Steph. Auryn went there, to his cabin, a few days ago. She gave him a load of Dad's money. But I don't think it was enough. I think he went looking for the rest.'

Stephanie covered the mouthpiece for a moment while she spoke to someone. Who was there with her? Had the rest of the police finally turned up?

'Look,' Daniela said, 'I'm telling you I didn't kill Auryn, and I'm further telling you I know who probably did. It's like you're not even listening. You've already made up your mind.'

A pause. 'You've done very little to convince me,' Stephanie said in a careful tone. 'If you're so innocent, why're you running?'

Daniela rubbed her forehead. 'I can't go back, Steph.'

'Back where? To prison? If you haven't done anything—'

'I'm serious. You've no idea what's at stake. I understand what you're saying, but I'm not gonna hand myself in when I've done nothing wrong.' Daniela sighed deeply. 'We can't let Henry get away with this.'

'We?'

'Auryn's my sister too. I want you to catch the fucker who

252

killed her. You have to call for reinforcements to go get him. An armed response unit. I don't care if they have to swim to get here. I literally saw Henry loading a shotgun. And—' Daniela rubbed her forehead again. 'And tell them to be careful, all right? Make sure they—'

'Come to the house, Dani. We'll talk. The forecast says the weather should break during the night, and when it does, I won't be the only person looking for you. They'll bring tracker dogs. Once that happens, I can't protect you.'

Daniela tried to reply but the lump in her throat choked her. She hung up. Her eyes were burning.

For several long minutes she remained slumped against the tree, until the ache in her chest subsided. She wiped her eyes with her sleeve. Exhaustion was piling up, dragging at her nerves. She was in no state to deal with this.

As Daniela put her phone away, her fingers touched the twist of paper she'd found in Henry's cabin. She brought the paper out and smoothed it flat again. Whose number was it? Did it have any connection with Henry? It could've lain undisturbed and irrelevant in that cabin for months.

One way to find out.

It took Daniela two attempts to dial the number. The numbers on the paper were difficult to read. On her first try, she got the tone that indicated the number wasn't recognised. On the second attempt it rang.

Daniela peered around the tree, towards the road, watching for headlights. The dial tone burred in her ear. Chances were no one would answer. It was late in the evening. Whoever the number belonged to was likely busy—

'Hello?' a woman answered, voice fuzzed with sleep. The line clicked like a long-distance call.

'Hey. Who's this?'

A moment of silence. '*You* called *me*, so who the hell are you, and why are you calling at—? Christ, the actual middle of the night.'

Daniela's insides had frozen.

'Franklyn?' she asked.

35

June 2010

Both Daniela and Leo froze at the sound of Henry's voice. Daniela came to life first. She broke away and scurried for the front door of the antiques shop.

Leo called to his dad, 'It's all right, it's just me!'

'Leo? What're you—?'

A table blocked Daniela's path. She scrambled over it and ran for the front door, colliding with furniture, bruising her legs and arms in her haste.

Henry heard her and started shouting.

At the door, Daniela raised her foot and kicked the lock twice, no longer caring about stealth. The metal frame bent and the glass of the top panel cracked diagonally. Two more kicks burst the door open and spilled Daniela out onto the street.

Henry shoved through the maze of furniture. Above, lights flared in the upstairs windows of the McKearney house.

Daniela sprinted away. Before she'd covered a dozen yards, she heard a squeal of tyres from somewhere behind. The headlights of a car slashed across her, flinging her shadow up the nearest wall.

Who the hell was that? Could Henry have got his car out so quickly?

The car sounded loud as a tank as it came after her.

The main street was long and straight, with terraced houses on either side. The nearest junction was a hundred feet away. There weren't even any gardens Daniela could duck into. She swore as she ran. There was nowhere to go.

The car overtook her, then veered across her path. It mounted the kerb ten feet in front of her. Daniela skidded to a halt. Before she could spin around, the driver yelled through the open window.

'Dani!'

Daniela stopped. She took a step backwards. She knew she should keep running, but her heart was pounding so hard it felt like her chest would burst.

The car door was kicked open and Stephanie stepped out.

Daniela backed away, hands raised in surrender or innocence. Her mind raced for a plausible explanation for why the hell she'd been in the shop.

'Steph—' she started to say.

Stephanie grabbed her and threw her against the wall of the nearest house. The force knocked out what little breath Daniela had left.

'You idiot,' Stephanie hissed.

'I didn't—'

Stephanie slammed her into the wall again. Daniela's head smacked the brickwork. Dazed, with blood in her mouth, Daniela could only feel amazement, because Stephanie had never raised her hand against any of them, not once.

'Tell me what you think you were doing,' Stephanie said.

Daniela couldn't think of anything that would help, so she kept silent.

Stephanie made a quick, efficient frisk of Daniela's pockets. She found the phone, the cigarette lighter, and the wallet. Somehow, she missed the gold rings tucked in the back pocket of Daniela's jeans. Daniela tried not to tense. Stephanie would find the knife. It was too much to hope that she'd overlook it. Daniela couldn't meet Stephanie's eyes. Her sister's anger radiated like a heat haze.

The door to the antiques shop was swinging slowly closed. There was no sign of Henry yet. Daniela hoped Leo was trying to stall him.

Stephanie's hand paused over the breast pocket of Daniela's jacket. Daniela felt the shape of the folded knife pressing against her through the fabric. She closed her eyes as Stephanie reached into the pocket.

Stephanie let go of her. Daniela opened her eyes and looked up, then at the object Stephanie held. It was a slim pen-torch.

'Want to tell me what you were doing?' Stephanie asked.

Daniela couldn't answer because she was staring at the torch. It was roughly the same size, shape and weight as the flick-knife, and looked a lot like the torch Auryn kept on the shelf above her old bed ... Through the thickness of the jacket, she hadn't noticed the difference. But someone had swapped it, someone—

'Well?' Stephanie asked.

'I – how'd you know I was there?'

Stephanie pushed her against the wall, at arm's length, as if debating whether to slap her. Daniela flinched but didn't raise a defence. She couldn't believe Stephanie would hit her. Besides, Daniela was too busy trying to catch her breath.

It wasn't just the sprint that'd winded her. Residual adrenaline made her hands shake, and acid burned in her stomach. Nothing she could say would get her out of this. But if the knife had been in her pocket, she couldn't imagine what Stephanie would've done.

'Who told you I was here?' Daniela asked.

Stephanie let go of her and shoved the phone and other possessions into Daniela's hands. 'Get in the car.'

'Who was it?'

Before Stephanie could answer, the door to the shop banged open. Henry McKearney strode out. In his right hand, he carried a golf club.

'Shit,' Stephanie said under her breath. 'Get in the car, Dani.'

Henry hoisted the golf club to his shoulder like he was striding up to the ninth tee. He pointed a finger at the broken door. 'What the fuck is that about?' he asked.

Stephanie moved to intercept him. Deliberately or not, it put Daniela behind her, protected by her bulk. 'Calm down, Henry.'

'Don't tell me to calm down. Look what that girl's done to my shop.'

He was still advancing. Stephanie held out one hand. The other rested on the extendable baton at her belt. 'Stay there, please. Don't come any closer.'

Henry stopped a few yards away. He lowered the club so it hung loose at his side. He narrowed his gaze at Daniela. 'What were you doing in my shop?' he asked. 'What did you take this time?'

Behind him, Leo came out through the broken front door, leaning against the shattered frame. Stephanie caught his eye and tried to indicate that he should keep out of this. But Henry caught the glance and turned.

'Get back in the house,' Henry shouted at his son. 'I told you.'

Stephanie used the moment to step closer. She drew the baton and extended it with a sharp wrist-flick. 'You need to calm down and get rid of the golf club,' she told Henry. 'You hear me? Put it down.'

'All I'm doing is protecting what's mine,' Henry said. His face darkened. 'My life is falling apart because of your family.'

'Put down the club, Henry. Now, please.'

Henry pointed at Daniela. 'You're all the same. Every single one of your family. A bunch of thieving, immoral bitches.'

'Hey!' Daniela couldn't keep quiet. She clenched her fists.

Stephanie blocked her way. 'Will you get in the car, Dani? You're not—'

Faster than anyone anticipated, Henry swung the club. It was a wide, sweeping arc, starting low and driving up to head height, like a weight on a string. Stephanie was half-turned, her attention on Daniela, and only saw it coming a fraction too late. She'd just started to raise her arm in defence when the club struck the underside of her jaw.

The force snapped her head back. Stephanie spun as she fell, hitting the ground face first, out cold before she landed.

36

There was a moment of stillness after Stephanie fell. To Daniela it felt like an age. She'd never seen anyone laid out like that. It seemed impossible. She expected Stephanie to get up immediately. In a moment Steph would stand up and shake it off and ...

Stephanie didn't get up. She lay on her front with eyes and mouth half-open. Blood drooled onto the tarmac from the corner of her mouth.

Daniela let out a hoarse, inarticulate cry, and threw herself at Henry. In that instant she didn't care about the club. She tackled Henry, knocking him back against Stephanie's car, then threw a hasty punch. Henry twisted aside and the blow missed. Daniela was left off-balance and exposed. Before she could recover, a left-handed punch pistoned into her ribs, winding her. A second punch caught the side of her head.

Somehow, she stayed on her feet, in time to see the golf club coming at her face. She jerked out of the way. The club head whistled past her nose.

'Stop it!' Leo yelled. He grabbed his dad's arm and tried to drag him away.

Henry shoved him aside. He pointed that warning finger at Leo again. 'Why can't you stay out of this?'

'Leave her alone,' Leo said. His eyes were wide with shock at seeing his dad like this. 'She's done nothing.'

'You know exactly what she's done. What her whole lying family's done. I won't let them take you from me.'

Leo had his phone in his hand and, with eyes still fixed on his father, he thumbed three numbers into the keypad.

'What're you doing?' Henry demanded. 'Cut that out!'

Leo held the phone to his ear and said in a clear, calm voice, 'Police, please.'

Henry slapped the phone from his hand. It clattered to the ground and Henry caught it under his boot. He ground his heel until the screen splintered.

Daniela's head was spinning. She was dizzy and sick, and couldn't stand upright. Fire ran up from her jaw. Her mouth tasted coppery. She pushed away from the car and tried to grab Henry.

Henry swung the club two-handed at Daniela, who stumbled out of the way.

'Liars,' Henry yelled. 'Thieves.' The club sliced the air like punctuation. 'You won't be happy till you've taken everything.'

Daniela danced backwards. She was aware of Leo snatching up his shattered phone, and Stephanie still unmoving on the ground. Lights were snapping on in houses up and down the street, but she didn't dare take her eyes off Henry. The man looked insane. His hands were tight around the club's handle. Right then his attention was focused on Daniela but at any second, he might go for Leo or Stephanie again.

Get him away from them.

'You deserve to lose everything,' Daniela said. 'Look what you've done to us.'

Henry advanced on Daniela, no longer swinging the club

wildly but instead holding it at shoulder height. Daniela retreated. *Watch his hands, not his face.*

'So, yeah, I broke the door of your shop,' Daniela said. 'If you'd given me another ten minutes, I would've had the place on fire.'

She heard Leo gasp.

Henry's eyes bulged. 'You—'

Daniela spun and ran off. Behind her came the smack of feet on tarmac as Henry gave chase.

Instinct steered Daniela onto the lane to her own house. But within fifty yards she jinked left onto a narrow path. She glanced back to ensure Henry was following.

Twelve minutes. That's how long it takes the police to get here from Hackett. Someone would've called the police. And an ambulance. Daniela's stomach contracted as she thought of Stephanie. *Need to keep Henry away for twelve minutes.*

The path led into the woods that crowded the eastern edge of Stonecrop. Within a few yards, Daniela was beneath the protective spread of branches. Shadows enfolded her. Daniela had lost her night vision and ran blind, afterimages careening across her vision.

Henry was at a disadvantage. He hadn't grown up in Stonecrop and therefore didn't know the woods. Daniela heard his shoes pounding the hard-packed mud of the path.

Years of heavy rains had worn away the earth, and the ground was a constant trip-hazard of exposed roots and fallen branches poking up from the mud. Daniela had a good sense of direction and knew the woods well, but in the dark, with someone chasing her, it was easy to panic. She knew what would happen if she mistimed a step. Cold fear joined the adrenaline that burned her arms and legs. Her left ankle sang with pain.

Don't fall, don't fall, don't fall …

She had no real plan beyond leading Henry away, losing him in the woods, then looping around back to Stonecrop.

The police will be waiting for you. But that didn't matter now. The petty vandalism to the antiques shop, the stolen rings in Daniela's pocket – none of that mattered. So long as Stephanie was all right.

The memory of Stephanie hitting the ground made Daniela gasp with physical pain. Tears burned her eyes. *Please let her be okay.*

Henry was close behind. Closer than expected. For an old, out-of-shape guy, he was keeping pace with Daniela.

A dark shape loomed up on the left. The ruins of Kirk Cottage. Daniela hadn't deliberately aimed for that location, but she veered towards it now. Her night vision still hadn't recovered, but she could see enough to make out the huge, solid shape of the exterior walls.

'Come back here!' Henry yelled.

Daniela slid down the slope to the building. She angled towards the window at the front of the building. It seemed a lot longer ago than yesterday morning when she'd last been there, kicking a hole in the boards covering the window, out of an undirected desire for destruction.

The ground around the old mill was slick with mud and fallen leaves. The dark and silent River Bade flowed by just feet away. Given its position adjacent to the river, it was inevitable the area would flood every spring; after years of neglect and inadequate drainage, the ground was always sodden.

This was an ideal place to lose Henry. Daniela could sneak around the exterior of the building, get back onto the path, and retrace her steps without Henry knowing where she'd gone. More than twelve minutes had elapsed. In the distance, Daniela was certain she heard the swoop and wail of sirens arriving in Stonecrop.

She tried to swallow the fear that pulsed through her. When Henry knocked Stephanie down, it'd shocked all the bravado out of Daniela. Although she'd known he was capable of snapping, she'd never seen it first-hand. And now he was chasing her and she didn't know what would happen if he caught her. She was alone out there with him. Could she really make it back into the village without him catching her?

Daniela felt her way along the stone wall and located the broken board on the window. The moon behind its veil of clouds cast a little light, not really enough to see by. The hole at the base of the window was just large enough for Daniela to squeeze through. Inside was pitch black.

She heard Henry slithering down the slope behind her. Quickly, she pushed through the hole in the window. Her shoulders scraped the jagged plyboard edges.

The interior of the house smelled of stagnant water and mud and rot. The dead smell of a long-abandoned space. Jumping down from the window, Daniela splashed into an inch of freezing water. She swore in surprise and annoyance. The rains hadn't been particularly heavy that year, so this water must be left over from the last flood. The earth beneath the house was too sodden to drain.

The last time Daniela was there, aside from the brief visit the previous day, the floor had been a spread of mud and mulch, with a few deep, oily puddles. In the corners were discarded cans and bottles – some left by Daniela – along with patches of scraggy nettles and, against the far wall, a set of stone steps that led to where the first floor used to be. But she could see none of it now. Outside it was dark; inside it was a tomb.

She moved forwards, aware the darkness could be hiding anything. Above her head a shelf of rotted boards jutted out into space. Most had collapsed. In a few years the rest would follow. The roof was a latticework of exposed wooden beams that opened onto the sky. The thin moonlight was too faint to penetrate the interior of the gutted building.

Outside, Henry cursed as he lost his footing on the slope. Daniela slipped into the darkness at the side of the window. The gap she'd squeezed through was an irregular patch of grey.

In the water at her feet she located a loose chunk of brick. She weighed it in her hand. The drip of water was louder than her breathing.

37

She heard scuffling as Henry found the window. A shadow covered the gap in the board. Daniela gripped the brick tighter and prayed Henry wouldn't see the hole. She wanted him to think she'd run back into the trees. As soon as he set foot back in Stonecrop the police would have him and this would be over.

Henry stopped. His shadow retreated, allowing the patch of light to reappear, and Daniela knew he'd spotted the hole. Daniela held her breath. Would he come in, or wait for her to come out? The thought of staying here all night to out-wait him made her shiver.

'Got you,' Henry said in a triumphant whisper.

He tried to get through the gap in the window quickly, one arm in front, waving the golf club to ward off attack, but his shoulders were too wide and they jammed against the plyboard. Daniela was less than two feet away. Her fingers were sweaty around the weight of the brick. She watched Henry force his way through the window with his unprotected back turned.

Daniela let him get clear of the window. He staggered upright, turning one way then the other, feet splashing through the shallow water.

'Where are you?' Henry shouted. 'I know you're here!' His voice bounced off the damp walls.

In that instant, Daniela could've run. But all she could think of was Stephanie, unmoving on the ground.

Daniela took two steps so she was behind Henry. With a swift, vicious kick, she sent the toe of her boot into the back of his knee.

He cried out as his leg buckled. Daniela kicked him again, in the small of the back. He dropped to his knees in the water.

Daniela grabbed his collar. Henry flailed his arms. He'd lost the golf club. She raised the chunk of brick and smashed it down on his skull.

Henry yelped. He tried to strike out with his right arm, and she hit him again, bringing the brick down behind his ear.

That took the fight out of him. He dropped onto his front, barely conscious enough to keep his face clear of the water.

Daniela knelt to straddle his back, one hand gripping his shirt, ignoring the chill of freezing water through the knees of her jeans. The tight knot of hurt inside her chest was at last released. She was conscious of the most inconsequential details – the rough texture of the brick in her hand, the decaying sweetness of the air in her lungs, the copper tang of blood dripping into oily water. It'd be so easy to bring down the brick again, or to shift her weight and force Henry's face below the surface. More than just easy: instinctive, natural.

'Wait,' Henry gasped. 'Don't.'

Daniela almost laughed. She liked this reversal, with Henry the one who was terrified. His voice sounded thick, like he was hurt bad. She realised she might've already done something irreversible. The thought both horrified and excited her.

'Give me one good reason why I shouldn't drown you,' Daniela said.

'I didn't start this,' Henry said, the menace gone from his voice, replaced by a tinge of panic. 'Franklyn—'

'Yeah, I saw what you did to her.'

'And you think she didn't deserve it?'

Daniela tightened her grip on Henry's collar, forcing his head closer to the water. 'Whatever you think she's done, it wasn't worth breaking her fingers.'

'No?' Henry let out a huff of laughter that rippled the water. 'You've no idea. I bet you haven't heard half the stuff she's done these last few years.'

'You can't convince me she's worse than you.'

'You think? I've never killed anyone.'

Daniela stared down at him. In the darkness she saw the outline of Henry's head and the pale ghosts of his hands braced in the mud beneath the water. Faint starlight glittered off the disturbed surface.

'Yeah, I'm sure she didn't tell you that, did she?' Henry laughed again. His voice was stronger. 'She likes to pretend she's never put a foot wrong, especially now, making a big deal about her crisis of conscience. You fell for it, didn't you? She's persuasive, I'll give her that.'

Daniela shook her head as if she could fling Henry's words away. 'Franklyn would never—'

'Ten months ago, she cut the brakes on my van. I skidded out, flipped the van, ditched into a canal. She meant to kill me. *That's* the sort of person your sister is.'

'You're lying.' Daniela shifted her weight so Henry was an inch closer to the water. 'Whatever you say she did—'

'There's more. A lot more. And now she's tried to turn my

own family against me. So, yeah, you bet I got my friends to deal with her. It's what she deserved. Be thankful she's still breathing.'

Daniela's arms and fingers were cramping from keeping the brick raised. The cold made her shake. She focused on the back of Henry's head, on the darker patch of bloodied skin just visible in the faint light, and wondered how much force it'd take to shatter the skull. Her stomach rolled.

'Yeah, you don't like me saying that, do you?' Henry chuckled. He was becoming braver, certain Daniela's threats were empty. 'But it's the truth, and it'd be what she deserves. She's her father's daughter all right. I never should've trusted her.'

'You took her money easily enough.'

'And what did it get me, apart from trouble? She was happy enough to pay me when she wanted to be part of my business, but then she gets cold feet, tries to run out on me, just like your old man did, and when I say no, she goes and tells Margaret everything.' Henry's shoulders bunched. 'She wants to take Margaret and Leo from me. That's why her fingers are broken. One for my wife, one for my son. Because they're the people she'll hurt most.' He turned his head a little so he could almost see her. 'And now here's you, breaking into my shop, threatening to burn down my house. And you assume you'll get away with it. You think you're protected, by your dad, by your sisters.'

Stephanie. A sob lodged in Daniela's throat. She raised her arm.

A slight noise caught Daniela's attention. She been distracted, otherwise she would've realised sooner that someone was behind her.

Daniela twisted around. The person was between Daniela and the boarded window. A thin woman who wore shirt sleeves regardless of the cold, and whose straggly blond hair was almost luminous in the darkness.

'Auryn,' Daniela said in surprise. 'What—?'

'Dani?' Auryn felt her way through the water. Her night vision had never been good. 'Leo saw you run off. He said you went—'

'Get out of here. Go!'

Auryn stumbled over a piece of debris. 'Dani? What—?'

Daniela suddenly saw herself, hunched like an animal over Henry. Daniela let go of him and shoved herself upright, leaving the man gasping in the mud. She flung the brick away. It clonked off the wall and splashed into the water.

'Nothing,' Daniela said to Auryn. She felt breathless. 'Nothing. Why're you here?'

'I-I followed you. I thought—'

'Why didn't you stay with Steph?'

'She's okay. The ambulance is with her.' Auryn peered past her with wide eyes. 'Dani, what—?'

'You should never have told Steph where I was going. She went to the antiques shop because you told her I was there, and look what happened to her.'

Auryn blinked at her. 'I didn't—'

'You should've minded your own business.' Daniela glanced back at Henry, who was struggling upright. She gave Auryn a push. 'C'mon. Let's get out of here.'

Henry staggered a little but stayed on his feet. He shook water from his fingers.

'All of you girls should've minded your own business,' he

said. 'That's the whole problem with your family. Your mother was just the same.'

'Don't talk about her,' Auryn snapped with a rare flash of anger.

Despite the blood on his scalp, Henry smiled as he looked at her. 'You could've taken a lesson from her, if you'd been smart,' he said. 'She knew when to cut her losses and get out.'

Auryn's fists clenched. 'It's *your* fault she's gone. *You* did it.'

Henry shrugged. The momentary fear he'd shown when Daniela knocked him down was long gone now. 'Who knows why she left? But I can tell you it's not my fault she never came back. Have you ever considered that? What could it take to keep a mother away from her kids for so many years?'

'Shut up,' Daniela said. She took a step back towards the window. Her hand moved to her pocket before she remembered the knife wasn't there. Auryn had swapped it out for that stupid pen-torch, back at the house.

Auryn held her ground. She was trembling with a rage Daniela had never seen before.

'You must've figured out the truth,' Henry said. 'I know Frankie did. Your mother stayed gone because of you. Because she couldn't stand the sight of you.'

Auryn made a lunge for him. Daniela only just managed to get in front of Auryn and hold her back.

'Don't,' Daniela tried to say, before Auryn shoved her aside.

Daniela's foot came down on a hidden piece of debris and she fell, sitting down hard in the freezing water. Unhindered, Auryn went for Henry again, who laughed as he fended her off.

He stopped laughing when Auryn took the flick-knife out of her pocket. The black and red snake glittered in the faint light. Her finger found the release button and the blade popped out with an audible click.

'C'mon, sweetheart—' Henry started.

Auryn lunged for him again. Henry shoved her back, the flat of his hand catching her across the face. But she was too close to him.

It all happened so fast that by the time Daniela was back on her feet, Auryn was stumbling back, her lip bleeding from where Henry's hand had caught her. More blood dripped from the blade in her hand. It made bright ribbons in the muddy water at her feet.

Henry sat down; a slow, gentle movement, like an arthritic man lowering himself into a chair. When he passed the halfway point, he fell backwards and sat down hard. The front of his shirt was soaked.

Daniela's brain was running at half-speed – no, her brain was fine, it was screaming at her, but her body was too slow. The wet stain spread across Henry's shirt, and it was far darker than water, darker than the shadows.

Daniela felt her legs go out from under her. She fell heavily against the nearest wall. It was like something important had been severed inside her. Although she felt her legs trembling, she couldn't make them work.

Henry made another weak attempt to rise but fell back again. Each breath was a gasping wheeze. The knife had struck him in the left side of the chest, below the lowermost ribs. It might've punctured a lung or torn open an artery. He could be bleeding to death internally. The horror of what Auryn had done made Daniela reel.

'You're dead ... bitch ...' Henry's eyes were as wide as Daniela's, as if he too couldn't believe what'd happened. 'You

272

'... and your family ... the lot of you, you're dead ... I'll burn your fucking house to the ground ... I'll kill you. All of you.' He looked at Daniela as he said it.

Daniela's chest hitched. She clenched her teeth to stop from throwing up. 'We have to go,' she said. Her voice was a shocked whisper. 'Now. We've got to—'

But her brain was stuck. All she could think was *get out, get out,* as if this was something she could run away from.

Henry spat blood into the water. 'You,' he said at Auryn. 'You're finished. You and Leo ... you'll never be with him again. You think I'll let him run off with you? After what you've done? You're not going anywhere, and neither is he.'

Auryn paced towards him. Daniela made a grab for her arm but missed. Auryn's face, the set of her expression, scared Daniela more than anything else.

Henry was dragging himself away on hands and knees through the shallow water. There was nowhere to go. Blood leaked down his stomach, stained his shirt, dripped from the waistband of his jeans. He reached the bottom of the stairs and clung to the lowermost step like a life raft. He tried to rise but dropped, gasping, with his cheek pressed against the stair. He must've been hurt worse than Daniela had realised.

'All I ever wanted was for you to leave us alone,' Auryn said in her quiet voice. It was unlikely Henry even heard her.

Right then, the moon emerged from the clouds, to shine a faint illumination into the old house. It stained the water silver. Painted everything else the colour of bone. Henry slowed his breathing as he gathered his strength and smothered his pain. Like somehow, he could still fight.

Daniela was paralysed; like a hand was pressing down on her shoulders to hold her in place. She still leaned against the wall for support, legs numb, staring at her sister but barely recognising her. Even though she saw what would happen, she couldn't prevent it, like it was a drama on TV; distant and unalterable, the outcome inevitable.

Auryn turned the knife in her fingers, running her thumb across the inlaid snake on its handle.

'This is for your family,' she said to Henry.

38

February 2017

'Congratulations,' Franklyn said on the phone, 'that's me. What d'you want?'

Daniela felt like she'd been punched in the chest. 'Franklyn, it's me. Daniela.'

There was a rumple of noise as the woman sat up in bed. 'Dani? What the hell are—? Are you all right?'

'I'm fine, yeah. Fine.'

Her sister laughed. The sound was so familiar it sent chills up Daniela's back. '*Fine,* she says. Like it's been five minutes and not five years. Hey, how'd you get this number?'

'Am I not supposed to have it?'

'Nah, it's just ... it's a new phone. I've not given the number to many people.' Franklyn coughed, the sustained hacking cough of a life-long smoker roused from a deep sleep. 'So, what's up? What's the big emergency?'

On the road behind Daniela, headlights appeared from the darkness and swept in the direction of Winterbridge Farm. Daniela wasn't close enough to see the vehicle. Who was it? The police? There hadn't been nearly enough time for

275

Stephanie to find an armed responder. They wouldn't be stupid enough to go after Henry unarmed, would they?

The engine was cut off as the car pulled up near the cabins.

'Franklyn, have you spoken to Steph?' Daniela asked.

'Steph? Not for a week or so. Why?'

Daniela closed her eyes and leaned her forehead against the damp bark of the tree. 'It's Auryn,' she heard herself say. 'She's dead.'

There was silence on the line apart from the hiss of long-distance static.

'Say something, Franklyn, for Chrissakes.'

When Franklyn spoke, her voice was soft and faraway. 'What happened?'

'I – they don't know yet. She's dead. That's all I know.'

Another moment, where all Daniela could hear was her sister breathing. At last Franklyn asked, 'Where did it happen?'

'At the old house.'

'Okay. Okay. I can't get there till tomorrow evening. I'll need to ... it'll take me a while to get home. Okay? Where are you? Are you in Birmingham?'

'No, I-I'm in Stonecrop. Hey, Frankie? You've not spoken to Henry McKearney, have you?'

Franklyn's voice became careful. 'Henry? Why?'

'Just tell me if you have.'

'No. God, no, of course not. If I can avoid talking to him for the rest of my life, I'll die happy. I swear.'

Daniela let out a breath. It'd completely thrown her to hear Franklyn's voice, and her thoughts were a mess. But Franklyn's number had been in Henry's cabin. Why had Henry—?

From somewhere in the distance came a muffled *bam*, like a car backfiring. Daniela's head came up fast. No, not a car ...

'Dani?' Franklyn asked. 'You there?'

'I gotta go. I'll call you in the morning, yeah?' Daniela hung up quickly before Franklyn could say anything else.

From where Daniela stood the cabins were hidden behind a hedgerow. She hurried through the wood to where the trees gave way to fields. She could see the flat top of the cabins and part of the road. A police car was tucked in behind the blue estate that was parked outside the cabins. It had to be Stephanie's; there were no others in town.

No, she wouldn't, she wouldn't be so stupid ...

Daniela held her breath, heart pounding. Maybe she'd misheard. Sound was tricky at night. It could've been anything; it hadn't necessarily come from the cabins ...

Following the hedge, Daniela hurried towards the road. A car door slammed, the sound echoing, and a moment later the engine restarted. Daniela pulled back behind the nearest tree as the headlights swung along the road. The vehicle was a shadow. Stephanie's car? Or the other?

Was it Stephanie or Henry returning to Stonecrop?

The chill sickness that'd been growing inside swelled until it choked her. All she could think about was that goddamn shotgun in Henry's hands, and the look on his face as he'd loaded it.

Daniela ran to the road. By the time she got there, winded and out of breath, the car was long gone. She hesitated, then went in the direction of the cabins.

She slowed as she approached. Floodwater dragged at her feet. A stitch needled her side. She was gasping for breath and felt like she might be sick. Rain began to fall again, pock-marking the water, stinging her face.

The police car was still parked near the gate. There was no sign of the blue estate.

No. No, no, no, no …

Daniela sprinted up the path. Cabin Four was in darkness. It looked no different from before. Daniela stepped onto the decking. Her breath was ragged in her chest. She wiped rainwater from her face.

She tried the handle and found the door locked.

A moan rose in her throat. It was too dark inside to see through the window. Hands shaking, Daniela unlocked her phone and held the screen up to the glass. The weak glow illuminated the interior.

The table had collapsed or been folded away. It made the kitchen slightly more spacious. She angled the light towards the rear, and saw the blood.

It was splashed up the wall and across the cabinets in a wide swipe. The fire-engine red looked unnaturally bright, mottled with darker specks and congealing lumps. A few droplets created trails as they wound their way down to drip onto the sprawled body on the floor.

39

Daniela's stomach contracted so sharply she doubled over. Gasping, clutching the phone so hard her knuckles turned white, she clenched her teeth until the wave of nausea receded. Her knees were trembling to the point of collapse.

After what seemed like an eternity, she straightened up and shone the weak light through the window again. She had to be sure.

The body lay with feet towards the door. One bloodied hand was flung out. The person wore dark trousers and a bulky jacket that looked a lot like Stephanie's police vest. The side of the head she could see was a mess of red and white, pulped flesh and chipped bone, a concave divot that'd obliterated the left eye and ear, as well as most of the jaw.

Daniela leaned close to the window. She held her breath so the glass didn't fog. Blood pounded in her ears and made her feel like she would pass out.

Was it Stephanie? She couldn't tell. She had to get inside, even if—

Someone grabbed the back of her head and slammed it into the window. The glass shattered. Before Daniela could do more than gasp, fingers clutched a handful of hair and yanked her head back, then bounced it off the window frame. Pain lanced through her cheekbone. Her vision went black.

A kick to the back of her knee buckled her leg. The only thing that stopped her falling was the hand gripping her hair. Daniela drove an elbow into what she hoped was the attacker's ribs, but the blow glanced off. The attacker shoved her against the wall. Again, Daniela's head cracked off the wooden boards. She bit her tongue and tasted blood.

Another kick to her leg dropped her. The hand let go of her hair. Daniela fell, unable to catch herself, her wits scrambled. She was blind. It took her a moment to realise this was because she'd dropped the phone and the light had gone off.

The attacker kicked her hard in the stomach. All Daniela's breath went out in a single gasp. She curled over, hands clutching her abdomen, her lungs clawing for breath, all thoughts of defending herself gone. She could focus on nothing but trying to breathe around the hurt.

She heard the rush of air as another kick angled towards her ribs. Daniela rolled away. The boot caught her elbow and set a jolt of fire up her arm. Daniela grabbed her attacker's leg and heaved. The move brought the person down on top of her. Daniela rolled, attempting to get out from underneath. She didn't realise how close she was to the edge of the decking until they both tipped off the side and dropped into six inches of water.

Daniela panicked as water closed over her face. The freezing cold attacked her nose and mouth as if relishing entry to her airways. The dark shape of her attacker was above her, their weight keeping her below water. The person fought to get untangled from Daniela.

In desperation, Daniela punched them in the ribs, but the

angle was weak and the blow had no effect. Daniela struck out again and again, kicking and punching in a blind effort to get free. Her attacker put an elbow on her chest to get upright. It crushed the air from her lungs. Through the watery blur Daniela saw her attacker as a hazy shadow. Her vision was fading. Her chest hitched from lack of oxygen.

Then the weight came off her chest and hands grabbed her, dragging her above the surface, and she could breathe again.

She was so grateful for air that she didn't resist as fingers strong enough to crush bone dragged her hands together in front of her. The pain was a pale shade of the agony that echoed through her chest and ribs with every breath. It was only when cold metal closed around her wrists that she started paying attention.

Daniela blinked several times to clear her vision. It was too dark to see properly. But she saw her outstretched arms, with the hands stacked one above the other, and the handcuffs around her wrists.

She raised her head. Her attacker stood over her, breathing hard from exertion or sheer anger. Despite everything, the first thing Daniela felt was relief.

'Steph,' she gasped. She would've laughed except it hurt too much.

40

Stephanie dragged Daniela to her feet. The action wasn't gentle. Daniela staggered, unable to keep her balance, and would've fallen if Stephanie hadn't yanked the handcuffs. The sharp pain cut into Daniela's wrists. She stayed upright even though her left leg was very reluctant to take her weight.

Daniela sucked in a deep breath and winced. 'I thought you were dead,' she said. Her voice sounded as weak as she felt.

Stephanie didn't reply. She dragged Daniela up onto the decking. Daniela swayed, focusing all her attention on not falling over. Stephanie peered into the cabin through the window. Her expression was lost in the shadows. She stooped to pick up Daniela's phone from the decking and pocketed it, then yanked the cuffs again, pulling Daniela into a stumbling walk. Daniela had no choice but to follow.

'I thought he'd killed you,' Daniela said. 'Seriously, when I looked in there ... What the hell happened, Steph?'

Still no response. Daniela's relief was wearing off, replaced by something chillier.

'Steph?' she asked. 'C'mon, talk to me. Please. What happened?'

She tried to resist, but had no strength. When Stephanie

pulled her arms, Daniela had to comply. Her chest hurt. Her boots were full of water and sloshed with every step. She could still feel the chill of being below the surface, unable to breathe.

Stephanie dragged her along the submerged path and onto the road. When Daniela saw the police car she balked again; an instinctive reaction. She hated being locked in.

'Seriously, Steph, just talk to me, will you?' Daniela dug in her heels as best she could. 'Tell me what happened.'

Stephanie pulled open the rear door. 'Get in,' she said.

Daniela looked back at the cabin. Her mind was working at half-speed, numbed by pain and shock, but she knew things were badly wrong. Someone was dead in the cabin, and if it wasn't Stephanie it had to be Henry. Henry McKearney was dead. And if Stephanie had been the only one there ...

'Listen,' Daniela said, 'whatever happened, I'm not going to say anything. Whatever you've done—'

Stephanie hit her, a solid punch to the gut that doubled Daniela over and dropped her to one knee. With a snarl, Stephanie shoved her into the car. Daniela fell onto the back seat. Stephanie slammed the door closed.

Daniela lay gasping on the upholstery. Rain drummed on the roof. The overhead light in the car made stars dance before her eyes. Her lungs hadn't recovered from being kicked, bruised, and almost drowned. No matter how hard she tried she couldn't draw enough air.

Stephanie stayed outside for a minute while she spoke on her radio. Daniela could only guess what she might be telling the police.

Just lie still. It's over. Daniela squeezed her eyes shut. She didn't want to believe Stephanie had killed Henry. But things were going so badly wrong. Every kick and punch had only emphasised that. This wasn't Stephanie. Stephanie was a cool, calm professional who'd never struck out with her fists towards her family, not once. She'd been the rational voice in the chaos of their home. Franklyn was the troublemaker, and Auryn's placid exterior had masked a cold hostility that none of them had ever suspected, but Stephanie was the peacemaker, the biggest and most self-assured of the four. It'd been her voice that kept them in line.

The car's suspension shifted as Stephanie climbed into the driver's seat. She had to search around for her keys, which were on the passenger seat. Stephanie switched on the engine, then stared straight ahead for several moments before putting the car in gear.

Carefully, Daniela sat up. She slid over so she could see her sister's face, lit by the backwash from the headlights. If Daniela had wanted to, she could've lunged forwards and taken a swing at Stephanie. It wasn't just the handcuffs that stopped her. She slumped into the seat as Stephanie turned the car around.

'Where'd Henry's car go?' Daniela asked. 'The blue car that was here. Did you move it?' Then: 'Did someone else? Was someone with you?'

No answer. Stephanie stared at the road as if Daniela wasn't there. The car's tyres hissed through the floodwater.

The car keys had been on the passenger seat. That wasn't the sort of thing Stephanie would do, even in a security-blind town like Stonecrop. Daniela glanced at her sister's legs; they were streaked with fresh mud, not all of which had been washed off by getting dunked in the water by the cabins. The pattern was like Stephanie had run here along the flooded lanes from the centre of town.

'So, who took your car?' Daniela asked. 'I take it you didn't lend it to them. You must've been pretty pissed, having to chase them all the way out here, then discovering they've already been and gone.'

Daniela rotated her hands in the cuffs, experimenting to see how much movement they gave. The answer, as always, was not much. The old-style handcuffs at least provided some wiggle room. These plastic-coated beasts with the spacer in the middle were more secure, obviously, which was why the police used them, but Daniela wasn't a fan.

With a certain amount of contortion, Daniela touched her jacket pocket, at which point she remembered Stephanie had taken her phone. She found something else in her pocket though. A twisted scrap of paper that was now soaked.

'I spoke to Franklyn,' Daniela said. 'I told her about Auryn.'

Stephanie's hands tightened on the wheel.

'She was kinda surprised to hear from me,' Daniela said. 'It's been a while since we spoke. And she was surprised I had her number, since she hasn't given it to many people.' She studied her sister's face. 'But she gave it to Auryn, didn't she? It makes sense they'd stay in contact. She gave Auryn her number, and she wrote it down.' She switched her gaze so she was staring out of the window. 'And Auryn dropped the piece of paper in Henry's cabin when she was there last week.'

'Auryn didn't even know Henry was in town,' Stephanie said. 'They weren't in contact anymore.'

Daniela gave a hollow laugh. 'See, you police officers get all the training in how to spot a lie, but no one teaches you how to *tell* a lie, do they? Auryn knew Henry was here. And, I'm guessing, so did you. Did Auryn tell you she intended to

285

give all of Dad's savings to Henry? Or is this a fun surprise for you too?'

Stephanie went back to saying nothing.

'Is Franklyn involved in this?' Daniela asked, and steeled herself for the answer. *Someone* had driven the blue car away.

'Don't try to shift the blame. Franklyn's not here to take the fall for you.'

Daniela let out a breath. 'Y'know what? I'm glad. Despite everything she did, all the mistakes she made – no, *because* of those things – I'm glad. She changed, and she put the past behind her, and she got out of this godawful town. But you – you're still here, doing the same as always, hanging on to the past, and now it's got Auryn killed.'

Stephanie tapped her fingers on the steering wheel, then said, 'You think being in prison has made you smart. It hasn't.'

'No. If I was smart, I never would've let you get me into this car. Because I'm right, aren't I? There's a lot you're not telling me.'

Stephanie set her mouth into a grim line. 'We'll have plenty of time to talk about everything.'

'Yeah.' Daniela rubbed her face with her cuffed hands. 'That's what I thought.'

41

June 2010

Auryn stood at the bank of the river, staring into the water. Her arms were at her sides, and she shivered, her thin shirt no protection against the night air.

Daniela climbed out through the broken window and stepped into the mud. Her clothes were soaked, her jacket streaked with mud, and freezing water had ruined her shoes. She couldn't remember ever being so cold in her life. And yet, heat burned in her veins, the residue of adrenaline and shock, a fire inside. The cold pressed in from the outside; she felt it but it couldn't touch her.

The stiff paralysis hadn't let go of her until Auryn had stepped away from Henry's body and walked to the window without so much as a glance at Daniela. Then, at last, Daniela had got to her feet. She should've checked Henry. But he was lying face down on the stairs, his legs in the water and his face turned to the bare stone wall, and even in the darkness the blood had glistened as it dripped from his fingers. Henry was dead. Daniela was certain. She'd watched Auryn stab him an additional seven times, each one a payment, and Henry had stopped moving after the fourth.

As she walked away from the building, Daniela wiped her hands on her jeans. She had the unpleasant feeling that some of the dampness on her cuff was blood.

The preceding minutes had already taken on an air of nightmare. As soon as Daniela was outside it was like she'd stepped into another world – or more accurately, stepped back into the rational world after losing it for a time. When she glanced at the broken board covering the window, she saw nothing but the familiar ruined mill where she'd played as a kid.

Daniela walked to the riverbank. Part of her was aware she was leaving footprints in the soft mud, which the police would eventually find. Although, with so many old prints around the house, from dog-walkers and bored teenagers, how would they separate out hers and Auryn's? She knew she should think about these things, but her head couldn't cope. She felt lost.

Auryn didn't look up as Daniela approached. She appeared lost as well; her gaze unfocused, her shoulders slumped. The knife was still in her hand, but held loose, forgotten. Or so Daniela thought. A tremor ran through Auryn's body. Moving as if in a dream, she lifted the knife and pressed the blade against the inside of her forearm.

'Hey!' Daniela yanked the hand aside. She twisted the knife out of Auryn's fingers.

Auryn blinked as if shocked to see her. She made a weak grab for the knife but Daniela held it out of reach.

'What the hell are you doing?' she asked. The blade had left an indentation on Auryn's forearm, right across the vein.

Auryn moistened her lips. 'I didn't think this through,' she said in a low voice. 'I thought this would make life better. But

I've ruined everything, haven't I? Leo will never forgive me. Neither will Steph.'

The thought of Stephanie made Daniela's stomach twinge. Had the ambulance taken Stephanie to Hackett yet? How badly was she hurt?

But there was too much else to think of. Daniela folded the blade and put it in her pocket. Auryn's gaze slipped away again, back to the river. Perhaps unconsciously she swayed closer to the edge.

Daniela put a hand on Auryn's arm. 'You realise if you fall, I'll have to go in after you, right?'

'Perhaps that's for the best.'

Despite everything, Daniela grimaced in annoyance. They were in a bad situation but that was no reason to fall to pieces. She cast a glance in the direction of Stonecrop, but the trees were too thick to see the glow of streetlamps or the strident blue-flicker light of police cars. Likewise, the woods were silent, empty of shouts, footfalls or the crashing sounds of pursuit. Inevitably the police would find their way to Kirk Cottage, but not soon.

'We should go,' she said.

Another fine tremor shook Auryn's body, like she was a piece of wire wound too tight. Daniela could offer no comfort. Maybe she should've put an arm around Auryn's shoulders ... but they'd never been physically close; hugs and reassurance were not something their family did. Daniela felt the distance, not just from Auryn but from everyone, as if she'd taken a step away from the world.

'C'mon,' Daniela said. 'Let's get back to the house. We can talk then.'

It seemed like Auryn hadn't heard. Daniela put a hand on

her cold elbow to guide Auryn away from the river. Auryn wiped a hand across her mouth. Her lip still oozed blood where Henry had struck her in the face.

As Daniela turned, her gaze tried to slip back to the ruined building. She avoided looking at it, because if she did, something would crumble inside her and she'd panic. She couldn't suppress a shudder at the thought of Henry lying in the mud, his blood already cooling.

Together, Daniela and Auryn clambered up the slope and started back along the path. The enormity of what they'd done was rising like a tide, starting in the pit of Daniela's stomach and working its way upwards until it drowned her heart and strangled every breath in her lungs.

I didn't do anything – it was all Auryn.

Self-loathing rolled in her gut. Who was she fooling? She'd intended this. She'd lured Henry out here, and she'd passed up the opportunity to escape. Even before Auryn arrived, Daniela had wanted to hurt Henry. She'd picked up the brick. Hit him when his back was turned. She could've killed Henry with that first strike.

And worse, Auryn had only got involved because of Daniela. It was stupid to pretend otherwise. Without Daniela, Auryn never would've come into the woods; she wouldn't have brought the knife. She could've steered clear of this whole mess.

Already Auryn was sagging beneath the weight of guilt. It dragged her down and slowed her pace. Daniela had to keep hurrying her along.

It should've been me who killed Henry. Maybe it was shock that pushed the idea into Daniela's head. *That's what I was there for.* In some inexplicable way, she felt cheated.

The path wound through the woods towards the old house. Heading home bothered Daniela. She didn't want to return. But she needed to get Auryn somewhere safe.

She looked back, even though Kirk Cottage had disappeared among the trees. The silence seemed odd and incongruous. There should've been light and noise, police sirens and blue splashes, but instead the woods were still, empty, as always. Like nothing had happened.

Daniela kept walking because she couldn't think what else to do. Her jeans clung to her legs. The clammy dampness inside the cuff of her jacket chafed her wrist.

As she walked, Daniela took out her phone and dialled Franklyn's number. There was no answer. She tried several times then gave up in disgust.

'Are you calling Steph?' Auryn asked.

Daniela startled in surprise. The thought hadn't occurred to her. 'No.'

'We should call her.' Auryn checked the pockets of her jeans. Every movement was sluggish, as if she'd been drugged. 'I don't have my phone ... you should call her.'

'She'll be at the hospital by now.'

'We should still—'

'We're not calling anyone. Let's just get home.'

Auryn fell silent, but kept walking.

Daniela glanced at the sky, the fat clouds pregnant with rain, and felt a stab of clarity. 'Listen,' she said. 'This is what we're gonna do. We'll say nothing. Understand?'

'But—'

'I mean it. You'll keep quiet and not say a goddamn word. You know nothing about any of this.'

Auryn was shaking her head. 'They'll find out.'

291

'Yes. But there's nothing to tie it to you. We're the only ones who know what happened.' Apart from Henry, who was silently bleeding out in a flooded house, far from help. 'If you keep quiet, no one will ever know you were involved. You'll tell them you went into the woods but couldn't find me.'

Auryn stopped walking. Her face was a pale oval in the darkness. 'What about you?' she asked. Her voice was subdued. 'They'll know you were there.'

'I'll leave. I'll get the hell out of here and they'll never find me.' Daniela willed herself to believe it. 'It doesn't matter if they figure out what I did.'

'But you didn't—'

'Listen to me.' Daniela caught Auryn's arm. 'You didn't do a damn thing, you weren't here, and if anyone asks, that's what you'll tell them. We need to be smart, Auryn.'

'The smart thing is to call Steph.'

'We're not calling the police,' Daniela said through clenched teeth. 'We're going back to the house, and when we get there, if you make one move towards the phone, I'll break your fingers. Understand?'

Auryn made a noise in her throat. Daniela didn't think she was hurting her, but Auryn shied away as if expecting a punch.

She's scared of me, Daniela realised. *Even after what she's just done, I'm the one she's scared of.* Sickened, she shoved Auryn away. But the damage was done. The look in Auryn's eyes would haunt her for a long time.

42

For what would turn out to be the second-to-last time in her life, Daniela stepped into the old house. She came through the back door and stood in the kitchen for a moment, listening to the familiar ambient noises. A tap dripped. Outside, the shushing of branches was a constant murmur.

If she'd listened harder, if she'd crept up the stairs, she might've heard her dad snoring. Daniela didn't do so. Already she felt removed from this house. It was no longer hers, and she hesitated, like an intruder, ready to flee at the slightest noise.

Once she was sure no one was around, Daniela pushed Auryn into a chair at the kitchen table. Auryn was freezing, shivering, her skin clammy. A numb kind of shock prevented her doing anything but sitting with arms crossed tight over her chest.

Daniela filled the kettle, then went into the utility room and pulled clothes from the dryer. She swapped her muddy clothes for a pair of jeans and a hooded top, and put on the old pair of trainers she kept by the door. Her muddy clothes and shoes she shoved into a backpack. It would've been good to change her jacket as well, but she didn't have a spare. She surface-washed the leather in the kitchen sink to get rid of the worst stains. Likewise, she washed her hands and arms. The knuckles of her right hand were scraped. She remembered the jolt of impact when she'd brought the brick down on Henry, and her stomach rolled again.

Turning, she cast a critical eye over her sister, trying to overlook the puffiness of her lower lip. Auryn had somehow avoided getting blood on her, but her trainers and the cuffs of her jeans were soaked.

'You need to get changed,' Daniela said. 'Throw everything in the wash. Shoes too.'

Auryn stared at the floor and said nothing.

'Hey!' Daniela barely resisted the urge to slap her hand on the table. 'Pay attention, will you? I'm trying to help. The least you can do is listen.'

Slowly, Auryn raised her eyes, and nodded like she understood.

The kettle boiled. Daniela made a quick cup of tea, dumped several spoons of sugar into it, then pressed it into Auryn's unresisting hands. Whilst doing so she kept one eye on the clock. How much time had elapsed since they'd left Kirk Cottage? Every minute Daniela wasted could potentially doom her. She needed to be gone. Fast.

Apart from the change of clothes, she wanted nothing else. Except money. Anything she needed she could buy later.

Daniela left Auryn and snuck through the house to the foot of the stairs. Pausing, she listened, but heard no sound from her father's room. She ascended the stairs quickly, crept past her father's closed door, then up the second flight to the attic room.

Again, the sense of unreality washed over her. This morning

the room had been hers; now it belonged to a stranger. All her books, CDs, clothes, shoes ... so many things that meant so little. Daniela felt the urge to touch and memorise each object, to seal them forever in her mind. She shook the thought away. This must be a kind of shock, she reasoned.

She crouched next to her bed and levered up the loose floorboard. Daniela lay down flat to reach the back of the hole, where a bit of wood concealed the box she'd hidden. Since Auryn and possibly Stephanie knew about the hidey-hole, she'd taken to hiding her money at the very back, tucked behind a floor-support.

She removed the box, which was mottled with dust and bits of spiderweb. Inside was the money she'd set aside. Almost five hundred pounds in total, composed of money she'd earned, hand-outs from her father, the loose notes Daniela had skimmed whenever she was sent to the shops, and a certain amount she'd lifted from around the house. It'd seemed like a lot. Now she wondered whether it was enough to buy a new life.

It's a start. You'll get more once you find your feet.

Before she stood up, Daniela hesitated. The knife and the stolen jewellery were still in her pocket. She knew she should get rid of them – what point was there in concealing her tracks if she was carrying around the weapon she'd used, and property from the victim's shop? She took out the knife. On the floor by her bed was the tea towel she'd used to hold ice for her damaged ankle. It was still wet. She wrung it out onto the floor, then wiped the blood from the blade and handle of the knife.

Then she wrapped the knife and the rings in the towel, lay down, and shoved the bundle back into the hollow beneath the floorboards. She made sure it was tucked out of sight. No one would find it unless they knew it was there.

She was straightening up when her phone rang.

The jangling ringtone was too loud in the silent house. Daniela fumbled the phone from her pocket and answered without looking at the screen.

'Hello?'

'Dani?' It was Franklyn. 'That you?'

Daniela glanced towards the stairs, hoping her dad hadn't heard. 'Yeah. It's me.'

'What's wrong? I've got half a dozen missed calls.'

'Oh. Right. Yeah.' Daniela tucked the phone under her ear and put the floorboard into place. 'Sorry about that.'

'What the hell happened? Are you okay?'

'I'm all right, yeah.'

'Dani ...' Franklyn's voice was hesitant. 'I told you not to be stupid. You weren't, were you?'

Daniela padded to the far end of the room. 'No,' she said, although she was no longer certain. 'I wasn't stupid. I didn't do anything I regret.'

Something in her tone put Franklyn on guard. 'What *did* you do?'

'I made sure Henry McKearney is out of business.'

Franklyn swore, so softly Daniela almost missed it. 'What did you do *exactly*?'

'Look, I know you said it was finished, but how d'you know he wouldn't change his mind? I had to stop him before someone else got hurt.'

The line went silent. When Franklyn's voice returned, it held an edge Daniela had never heard before. 'You're an idiot, Dani.'

'Hey, I didn't start this—'

'Whatever you did, you need to tell Steph.'

'I— *What?*'

'I'm serious, Dani. I don't want to know what you've done. But you have to tell Steph. Right now.'

Daniela couldn't believe what she was hearing. 'You want me to hand myself in to the police?'

'To Steph. If you don't call her, I will.'

'You—' Daniela shook her head in disbelief. 'But I-I did it for you. Because you—'

'Let me make this perfectly clear: whatever you did, you did it because you're an idiot and you don't listen.' Franklyn let out a breath. When she spoke again, her voice was softer. 'I'm sorry, Dani. I can't help you right now. You need to call Steph. She'll—'

Daniela hung up. It took a real effort to put the phone back in her pocket instead of flinging it across the room.

The house was still silent. The only noise was her own ragged breathing. Daniela had tensed up from head to toe, her shoulders hunched and her hands forming tight, painful fists. The urge to punch the walls was overwhelming.

Instead, she snuck downstairs. She was on the first-floor landing when the front door opened.

Stephanie, Daniela thought with freezing panic.

'Hello?' Leo's voice wafted up the stairs. 'Auryn?'

Daniela's relief was tempered as she heard her dad stirring. Quickly, she ran downstairs. Leo froze in the act of closing the front door.

'Where's Auryn?' he demanded. 'Where's my dad?'

Daniela held up a hand to hush him. 'Auryn's in the kitchen. I-I don't know where your dad is. I lost him in the woods.

Auryn found me and we came back here.' The lie sounded all right. 'Is Steph okay?'

Leo kept his distance, backing into the front room. Daniela followed and shut the internal door so her dad wouldn't hear them. 'I don't know,' Leo said. 'She wouldn't go in the ambulance. She's telling everyone she's fine. And there're police all over the antiques shop. I heard someone calling for tracker dogs to be brought from Hackett so they can look for my dad.'

Fear twinged in Daniela. She hadn't considered they might bring dogs. Why hadn't she left sooner? 'Listen,' she said, 'I need you to look after Auryn. She – she's had a scare.'

'What d'you mean?' Leo's eyes narrowed. 'What did you do to her?'

Everyone always assumed Daniela was to blame. The conversation with Franklyn had already stretched her temper gossamer thin. She took a step towards Leo. She thought Leo would back away but instead he glared at Daniela with chin up and face set.

'What did you do?' Leo asked. 'If you've hurt her, I'll—'

Daniela grabbed his shoulder, harder than intended. 'Listen to me,' she hissed, 'I never wanted to hurt anyone. I wanted to stop this before it got out of hand. Why would I hurt my own family?' Abruptly her eyes prickled with tears. 'Why would I hurt *you*?'

Leo hadn't pulled away. His face was inches from Daniela's. With a cry of frustration, Daniela closed the distance and kissed him. It was a fierce, impulsive action, and it caught her as much by surprise as it did Leo.

This is what I want, Daniela realised. *Someone who cares what happens to me.*

Leo made a strangled noise then shoved Daniela hard in her ribs. Daniela yelped and let go.

Leo's face was livid. 'Daniela, what the *hell*?' he spat.

'I love you, idiot,' she blurted. 'How could you never see that?'

Disgust flickered across his face. He backed away.

Daniela's anger flared back to life. She shot out a hand and grabbed hold of his shirt. Leo struck out with both hands, trying to shove her way. Daniela never did figure out what she intended to do. Kiss Leo again, or hit him, or—

With a rush of footsteps Auryn was in the room. She must've heard everything. She charged at Daniela, who couldn't raise her arms in defence quick enough. Auryn threw her hard against the wall.

Gasping, winded, Daniela pushed herself upright. Auryn stood over her, fists half-raised. The look on her bruised face was frightening.

'Touch him again and you're dead,' Auryn said, her voice harsh.

Daniela moved away from the wall and Auryn retreated to keep distance between them. Her eyes flicked to Daniela's hands.

She thinks I've still got the knife.

Daniela wanted to tell her not to be stupid, that she would never hurt her or Leo, that she never meant to hurt anyone. She wanted to say anything that would erase the way Auryn looked at her.

'I'm sorry,' Daniela tried. 'I didn't—'

Leo's mouth twisted up. 'She's crazy,' he told Auryn. 'She was going to set Dad's shop on fire. She could've killed us.'

The blood drained from Auryn's face. She stared at her sister like she'd never seen her before.

'No,' Daniela said with a weak shake of her head. 'No, of course, I-I wouldn't do that. I would never—'

'Get out,' Auryn said, her voice low and hollow. 'Get out before I tell him what else you've done.'

For a heartbeat Daniela stared at her. She opened her mouth but her voice had seized.

Leo's eyes were wild. 'What did she do?' he asked Auryn. *'What did she do?'*

Daniela backed away. Maybe if she'd denied everything, or told Leo what'd really happened; if she'd pleaded with them to understand, or even just pleaded, maybe she could've changed her fate, but Leo's voice was rising, and the expression on Auryn's face was brutal and broken, and upstairs their dad's bedroom door slammed open, and Daniela couldn't breathe. She ran.

Outside, in the cold night air, she drew a shaky breath. She set off at a jog towards the path through the woods with her backpack bouncing on her shoulder.

She had two choices. Either turn herself in or run like hell.

Once it was set out like that, in black and white, it took her less than a second to decide.

She disappeared into the trees, following the pathways she'd trodden throughout her life. She didn't need to see where she was going. Her feet knew the way out.

She didn't look back at the house. If she'd known it was the last time she'd see Auryn alive, she might've changed her mind.

43

'So, can you tell me who was with you when I called?' Daniela asked. 'Or should I keep guessing until I hit the truth?'

'If you want to be helpful,' Stephanie said, 'you could tell me where the money is.'

Daniela made an indelicate noise. 'Why're you stressing over *that*? I thought this was about Auryn.'

'You came here because you needed money. Did you know Auryn had it before you came, or did you go to the house on the off-chance she'd have something you could steal?'

'I didn't know Auryn was there.' Daniela watched the headlights sweep the flooded streets. The windscreen wipers squeaked as they valiantly fought the rain. '*You* told me the house was empty. So, was the money Auryn's? Or yours, perhaps? Because, y'know, you seem pretty fixated on it.'

'Where's the money now?'

'I hid it in the woods.' *But it's not there now.*

'What, all of it?'

'Yeah.'

301

'How did you carry it all? Did you make more than one trip?'

Daniela studied the side of Stephanie's face. 'How d'you mean? I just put it under my arm. It wasn't heavy.'

Stephanie raised her eyes and, briefly, met Daniela's gaze in the rear-view mirror. 'You couldn't carry all those packages in one trip,' she said.

Daniela frowned. 'I only found one package. About this big.' She demonstrated with her cuffed hands. 'Under the floor in my old bedroom.' Her frown deepened. 'Was there more?'

She remembered Margaret saying, *Half a million.* Were more packages hidden around the house? It'd make sense that Auryn wouldn't hide so much money all in one place. Although it still didn't make sense that she had it at all.

'Was it Dad's money?' Daniela asked. 'Why wasn't it in the bank?' Something else occurred to her. 'Margaret said Dad was involved with Henry's counterfeiting business. Is that where the cash came from? Please stop doing the silent thing, it's making life very difficult.'

'What do you want me to say?'

Daniela sat forwards. 'Henry wanted that money back,' she said. 'As far as he was concerned, Dad stole it from him. He's been trying to convince Auryn she should—'

'Henry didn't do this.'

'He killed Auryn to get the money he thought he was owed. Steph, you have to—'

Stephanie banged the steering wheel with the palm of her hand. 'Goddammit, Dani! I know you took the money. You came home because you needed cash. So, you found this convenient stash and helped yourself.'

302

That, essentially, was the truth. Except ... 'I didn't kill her. Why can't you believe me?'

Stephanie lost her temper. She stomped on the brakes and, at the same time, reached into the back seat to grab hold of Daniela, who couldn't defend herself. 'Two people are dead,' Stephanie grated. 'Stop lying to me.'

'I'm not! I didn't kill her. I didn't kill Henry.' Daniela flinched away. 'Why would I do something so stupid? You know I'd never get away with it. I'm not smart. I can't plan. If I make another stupid mistake, I'll go back to prison.' Her voice wavered. 'Listen, I've got too much to lose. You don't under-stand ... I've got a kid on the way.'

Stephanie froze. Her eyes went to Daniela's midriff.

'Not me, idiot.' Daniela yanked free of Stephanie's grip. 'My girlfriend.'

Stephanie's gaze narrowed. 'Your—?'

'Yeah, see, this is why I didn't tell you.' Daniela squared her shoulders. 'We've been together six months, me and Annetta. She was pregnant when we met. It was – it doesn't matter. We ... we're keeping the baby. It's going to be ours. Our son.'

Stephanie recovered from her surprise. 'D'you want congrat-ulations?'

'No. I wanted money.' Daniela looked away. 'I didn't tell you about Annetta because I knew you'd either dismiss it or you'd think I was playing some cheap sympathy card. I didn't want to use her as an excuse. This is important. *She's* impor-tant.'

'It doesn't explain why you need money so badly.'

'Because.' Daniela stared at her hands. 'You don't get how difficult it is, all right? She's the first person I've been close to since I got out of prison. The first person who *gets* me. I couldn't tell her what I'd done, not at first. When I did tell her ...' Daniela shook her head against the memory. 'I promised it was all in the past. I'd never do anything like that again.'

She'd told Annetta she was going back to Stonecrop for the weekend to get the money they needed. There was no reason for them both to go. More than anything, Daniela wanted to keep Annetta safe and separate from the past. And Annetta had just smiled that understanding smile and told her to stay safe.

With a jolt, she realised she hadn't phoned Annetta that evening like she'd promised she would. And now it was too late.

'I can't lose her,' Daniela said. 'She's all I've got.'

Stephanie gave a cynical laugh.

'Just hear me out, okay?' Daniela's irritation rose. 'We moved in together, but we've no hope of scraping together the deposit to buy the flat we're in, not without help. I need the money so we can keep our house.' She swallowed. 'Our home. I can't lose it all. Not now.'

'So, get a bank loan.'

'Gee, I hadn't thought of trying literally everything possible to avoid coming back to this goddamn village, thank you.' Daniela flexed her hands against the cuffs. 'I didn't want to have to ask you. But I need this. If we lose our home, everything starts to slide. I'm scared we'll end up eking out an existence for the next twenty years on some sink estate. I want to give our kid a chance. I don't want him falling into the cycle where he can never make a life for himself. I've seen it happen. Guys in their thirties with teenage kids who're following so closely in their footsteps they wind up sharing the same prison cell. And those kids have toddlers of their own who'll be in juvenile court in ten years.'

'And now your life will fall apart because of me. That what you're saying?'

Daniela sighed. 'I was asking you for a chance. Our flat's in a good part of town. Decent schools. Nice community. I'd like a proper start for my kid.'

'You had a good start.' Stephanie waved a hand at the outskirts of the village. 'Money, security, a nice house. Family. Didn't do much good, did it?' She put the car in gear and started moving again through the flooded streets.

'There's no excuse for me,' Daniela said quietly. 'I'm a fuck-up. Always have been. Doesn't mean I can't change things. Even if it's too late for me, our kid doesn't deserve to suffer just because I'm an idiot.'

'Your high-mindedness is kinda undermined by the fact you stole the money. Those packages contained a lot more than five thousand.'

'Apparently so.'

'So, what was your plan? You figured on taking it home to stash under the bed? Pay it into an account in the Cayman Islands? When the police come knocking – and they will, you know that – what's your plan? They'll find the money and lock you up. How does that fit with you being there for your kid?'

Daniela couldn't answer.

They were heading east, out of town along the Hackett road. Daniela half expected Stephanie to turn off onto one of the smaller lanes, but the car kept going, ploughing through the floodwater, until Daniela accepted they couldn't be headed anywhere but the Hackett bridge.

'Where're you taking me?' she asked.

'To the station.'

'In Hackett? The bridge is closed. Isn't it?' If it wasn't, why weren't the police here already?

'We'll get across,' Stephanie said.

At last they slowed to a halt. In the headlight glare, Daniela saw the dark shadows of trees on either side, like bars in a cage. She leaned forwards to peer through the rain-streaked windscreen.

The bridge was under water. Not just a thin skin of water, but at least two feet's worth, surging halfway up the handrail on either side of the bridge. The river had risen steadily throughout the afternoon, turning the roadway into a wide stretch of churning mud-coloured water. If not for the sawhorses left behind by some officious workman, Daniela wouldn't have known where the bridge started and ended.

'What're we doing?' Daniela asked. 'We can't get across here.'

'We'll make it.'

Stephanie popped open the driver's door, and Daniela caught hold of her shoulder with both hands. 'Wait, what're you doing? We can't—'

Stephanie shook her off. 'I'm moving the obstructions.' She nodded to the sawhorses blocking the road. 'Then we're driving to the station in Hackett.'

'You want us to get swept away? I know your car's pretty heavy, but—'

'We'll make it. Tilly went across and back a few hours ago. It can be done.'

'Tilly? The farmer? A tractor's significantly different to a police car.' With the door open, the noise of the river was so loud Daniela had to raise her voice. 'Why would she do something so daft anyway?'

'I asked her to. She went to fetch the coroner's officer and bring them to the old house.'

'She—?'

'You think I'd leave Auryn lying on that bed until the floods cleared? They're at the old house right now.'

Daniela reached for her again, hesitated. 'The bridge isn't safe, Steph. Look at it.'

Stephanie had one foot outside the car, the door held open, rain dripping on her arm, but even she seemed unsure. The water on the roadway eddied around the car wheels under the force of the river pounding past.

'We'll think of something else,' Daniela said, softer. 'You've caught me. I'm not going anywhere.'

Stephanie paused, then reached to open the glove compartment. She took out a bulky square object and placed it on the dashboard. There were fluorescent markings and a ton of warnings on the plastic casing. It looked a lot like a taser.

'What the *hell*?' Daniela asked aloud. 'Where'd you get that? Are you even trained to have it?'

Stephanie didn't answer. She was getting a second item out of the glovebox. Even before Stephanie held up the clear plastic bag, Daniela knew what it was. A metal flick-knife with an inlay on the handle in the shape of a snake.

'You still haven't explained this,' Stephanie said.

Daniela slumped against the seat. 'I didn't kill Auryn. Please stop thinking that.'

Holding the bag by a corner, Stephanie turned it so the knife caught the light. 'There's blood on it,' she noted.

Daniela leaned closer. There were indeed a few brown flakes

caught in the hinge of the blade. 'That would be Henry's,' she said. 'From seven years ago. Ever wonder why no one found the knife I used on him? The one he described in his statement? It's because it was hidden under the floorboards of the old house.'

'So, why'd you have it today?'

Daniela rubbed her face with shackled hands. 'Because I'm stupid,' she said truthfully. 'I should've got rid of it while I had the chance. But—' She groped for the correct words. 'I always knew it was there, hidden. If it hadn't been found by now, chances are it never would. But *I* knew it was there. It was a bit of my past I couldn't delete. I wanted to get rid of it now so I could stop thinking about it. You've got to close one part of your life before you can start a new one.'

'You told me you didn't go anywhere else in the house when you found Auryn.'

'Yeah, that was a lie. I went up to my old room.'

'And you told me you didn't take the money.'

'Also, a lie. There was a package of cash stuffed under the floorboards in the bedroom. That was the only one I saw. The only one I took.'

Stephanie left it a moment before she said, 'You also keep telling me you didn't kill Auryn.'

Daniela stared at her in the half-light. 'I didn't kill her,' she said. The words tasted sour. Daniela knew Stephanie still didn't believe her.

Stephanie didn't reply. She pocketed the bagged knife, then pushed open the car door and stepped out. She held on to the car roof to brace against the swirling water. Before she shut the door, she picked up the taser from the dashboard.

She won't use it. It's just for dramatic effect.

But Daniela wasn't certain of that. Not nearly certain enough.

As Stephanie waded to the sawhorses, the water surged higher, up past her knees. Daniela gripped the edge of the seat. If Stephanie fell—

It'd be a good time to run.

The thought caught her by surprise – not so much the idea of running, but that it hadn't occurred to her until that moment. Normally it was her default option. Things got bad; she ran. But for the second time in her life she was caught with no obvious means of escape, and her flight reflex had shut down, like her brain knew she was trapped so there was no point fighting.

Daniela tried the rear doors of the car but, as expected, the security locks were in place. If she clambered into the front seat, she could get out through the driver's door ...

She glanced at the trees on either side of the flooded road. If she could get into the woods, onto drier ground away from the river; if she could outrun Stephanie ...

If, if, if.

Outside, Stephanie lifted the first sawhorse and began dragging it out of the way. The rain hampered Daniela's view, but she knew Stephanie was keeping one eye on the car. If Daniela was going to do something, it'd have to be fast. She couldn't let Stephanie catch up to her. Stephanie and that taser.

Daniela shuddered. *Concentrate on getting into the woods.* She couldn't think beyond that; couldn't think how far she'd get on foot, along flooded roads, handcuffed, soaking wet. Her entire focus was on the next few seconds.

At the side of the road, tucked into a lay-by about fifty yards behind them, with the overgrown hedgerow shrouding its roof, was an abandoned car. It only caught Daniela's attention because she was sure it hadn't been there that morning.

A blue estate car.

Daniela scrambled over into the front seat and shoved open the driver's door. 'Steph!' she hissed.

Stephanie spun round. The taser appeared in her hand. 'Get back in the car!'

'That's Henry's car, Steph.' Daniela put one foot outside, into the deep water. Rain soaked her hair. 'It was parked outside his cabin. Someone—'

'Get in the car, Dani.'

'Someone drove it here! Whoever killed him drove it here.'

Stephanie advanced on her and Daniela put up her hands.

'All right, stop, wait,' Daniela said. 'I'm getting back in the car. Just – look, for God's sake, that's Henry's car right there. I swear to you.'

Daniela pulled her foot back inside then reversed awkwardly through the gap between the seats. Stephanie waded to the car and yanked open the rear door.

'Please don't hurt me,' Daniela said. She hated herself for begging but couldn't stop. If Stephanie chose to fire the taser into the close confines of the car, there wasn't anything Daniela could do. She drew up her knees to her chest like that would protect her. 'Please, Steph.'

'Stay here,' Stephanie said. 'You make any move to get out—'

'I won't. I won't do anything.'

Stephanie slammed the door then backed away towards the blue estate car. Daniela stayed pressed against the seat. Her chest ached. Outside, the river thundered and the rain drummed fingernails on the roof. She watched Stephanie click on her torch and sweep the light through the windows of the blue car.

Whatever Stephanie saw inside made her pause. She leaned close to the windows. Daniela held her breath. Then Stephanie circled round the car, her torch beam picking out bits of the hedgerow. Directly behind the car was a gap in the branches that led through to the wood beyond.

Stephanie hesitated in front of the branches, as if she might have seen something. The moment hung before she pushed through the gap and disappeared.

Daniela stayed in her seat for several heartbeats. She expected Stephanie to return straight away. But she didn't. The road remained empty, the ripples on the water quickly swallowed, until it was like Stephanie had never been there.

Go.

Without consciously making a decision to move, Daniela climbed over the seats again and opened the driver's door. The roar of the river filled her ears. The floodwater was a heavy grip around her wellies. Rain flattened her hair and ran down her face. She grasped the doorframe to steady herself.

No sign of Stephanie.

Daniela breathed. This was her only chance, she knew. She could head north, into the trees, vanish. If she moved fast enough Stephanie would never catch her.

She only hesitated because a new, chill fear had seeped into her stomach. Someone had shot Henry, then driven his car here and abandoned it. Where had they gone? Across the bridge on foot? That seemed unlikely. But where else? Why would they stop here?

How far would they have gone in the few minutes since they'd arrived?

And that was what froze her in place. The possibility that the killer was here, in the woods, maybe close enough to hear everything she'd said. Maybe close enough to see her.

Did the killer leave the shotgun in the cabin? Or did they keep it?

Daniela had just let her sister walk into the woods where an armed killer might be hiding.

Run. Get out of here.

Daniela swallowed. She stepped away from the car and shut the door. The water pushed against her legs like the river was anxious to take her.

You're no use to her anyway. Just go.

Daniela waded awkwardly along the flooded road until she reached the blue car, and went through the gap in the hedgerow beyond.

44

A narrow track wound its way into the woods. Daniela could only see its route by the scraggly bushes on either side. The ground itself was underwater. But within a few paces, the earth rose so Daniela was stepping through just a few inches of water.

She immediately saw what'd caught Stephanie's eye. A streamer of torn blue plastic that had snagged on a low branch and twisted like a banner in the wind.

Daniela shuffled along the path with her bound hands held blindly in front of her. She paused to tip some of the water out of her wellies but her feet still squished. The fleecy jacket was a hindrance now it was sodden. The wind dug chill blades into her body. Her teeth chattered. She couldn't even wrap her arms around her chest because of the goddamn cuffs.

'Steph?' she whispered. 'Steph?'

Like all the woods around Stonecrop, this one was achingly familiar, but in the darkness, the trees were rendered alien and threatening. An inch of water lined the ground, puddled deeper in places. Buds of garlic plants, just beginning to sprout, delineated the path.

Daniela kept her eyes on the ground to avoid tripping. *Don't fall,* she told herself. *Don't fall.*

The path took her through a clearing then split, one branch going east towards Stonecrop, the other dropping down to the riverbank. Daniela didn't know where Stephanie had gone. Over the noise of the rain and the river she could hear nothing. She shivered.

Check the river, then go back to the car. You're no use to anyone out here.

Daniela shuffled to the edge of the trees. The grassy bank that led down to the water was much shorter than she remembered, much of it having been swallowed by the river. Three hundred yards upriver was the bridge, just visible in the gloom. Directly across from her was the Hackett road, sloping up, away from the flood, to safety, as unreachable as the moon. Downriver, to her right, were the remains of the old fishing platform where they'd held a funeral fourteen years ago. Its last soggy timbers were all but submerged. On the grass next to it was the rowboat. That morning it had been upside down, but someone had very recently hauled it right-side up.

There was something in the bottom of the boat. At first Daniela thought it was just accumulated rainwater. She went closer, careful of her footing on the wet grass. The boat contained a certain amount of water, true, but also a number of packages, each the size of a house brick, each bound tight in blue plastic wrap.

With the thunder of the river and the rain, and her thoughts in turmoil, Daniela shouldn't have heard the slight noise behind her. But she did.

She turned.

The man stood at the edge of the trees, one shadow among many, framed by slanting rain. Leo McKearney, now Doctor Leo McKearney. Formerly the shy young boy who'd shared the school bus with Daniela and Auryn, who'd always sung Daniela's name, and from whom she'd stolen her first kiss.

He looked different now. The redness of his eyes and the hard line of his mouth were new. Also new was the shotgun he carried.

'Leo—' Daniela moved towards him, stopped.

Leo stepped out of the trees. Light glinted off the wet barrel of the shotgun. He held the weapon comfortably against his shoulder, aimed at Daniela, like he'd been handling guns all his life.

'Why did you do it?' Leo asked.

Daniela couldn't tear her gaze away from the shotgun. It was the same shotgun from the holiday cabins at Winterbridge Farm; double-barrelled, twelve-gauge, holding two shells – which was one more than Leo needed at this range – unless he hadn't reloaded it after – after—

Daniela fought to raise her gaze. 'What happened to your dad?' she asked.

Leo took two steps down the slippery bank. The natural urge was to back away, but Daniela was suddenly totally aware of the river behind her, the torrent of water mere feet behind. She had nowhere to go.

Leo was with Stephanie when I made the phone call. Daniela should've guessed. *He heard me saying where Henry was.* Leo had been trying to find his dad earlier that day, according to Margaret. It must've been pretty urgent, for Leo to steal Stephanie's car and race out to the cabins.

And then what? Daniela tried to picture the confrontation in the cabin. An argument, accusations, Henry losing his temper and snatching up the shotgun. Leo struggling with him ... Was that what'd happened? An accident? No matter

315

what Henry had done, she couldn't imagine Leo hurting his dad, not ever. And it must've been fast, because Daniela had only been on the phone for minutes ...

Those thoughts skidded through her mind, there and gone, impossible to analyse. All she could focus on was Leo and the shotgun.

Where's Stephanie?

The thought punched Daniela in the heart. Stephanie had been in front of her. What if she'd blundered right into Leo? What if—?

'Why did you do it?' Leo asked again, with a crack in his voice.

There was so much he could've been referring to. Daniela held up her shackled hands in futile protection. 'I didn't do anything. What're you talking about?'

'Auryn.'

'Oh, God. I didn't do anything.' Why would no one believe her? 'I swear I didn't kill her, Leo.'

'I know that.'

Daniela blinked. 'You—?'

'But it's still your fault she died.' Leo held the shotgun steady. 'She never got over what you did.'

Daniela couldn't focus. 'Your dad killed Auryn,' she said, 'right?'

Leo shook his head. Angry tears stood in his eyes.

'C'mon.' Daniela edged towards him, hands outstretched. 'Your dad held a grudge over the money he thought we owed him.'

'You *did* owe him. Your dad siphoned funds from the antiques shop for years. He made Auryn hide it.'

The resentment in his voice shouldn't have surprised

Daniela. 'Okay, but how did Henry react when he found out Auryn had that cash lying around the house?'

'You don't understand,' Leo said. 'When your family cheated Dad, you cheated us too – me and Mum. The money should've been ours. If we'd had it, everything would've been different. Me and Auryn could've stayed together. We could've kept our child.'

The rain was heavier now, flattening Daniela's hair, creating pockmarked puddles in the mud. It amplified the roar of the river. Daniela's hands shook. She couldn't breathe. 'Leo, what happened to Auryn?'

Leo let out a strained laugh. 'She didn't listen. I wanted what was best for us. When the floods came, I convinced her to move in with me for a few days ... I wanted a chance. A proper chance. I knew she'd been talking to my dad and I wanted to know why.'

'You killed her,' Daniela said. Even as she spoke, she couldn't believe it. Not Leo. Never Leo.

'It was an accident,' Leo spat.

Auryn hadn't been hiding from Henry at the old house. She was hiding from Leo. 'She told everyone she was going back to London just so you wouldn't go looking for her.'

Leo's fingers tightened, and for an instant Daniela was certain she'd made her last stupid mistake.

'I saw the lights on in the old house,' Leo said, his voice brittle. 'When I got inside, I found Auryn. She was drunk. Must've been drinking steadily since she left my house. She'd got hold of a kitchen knife and kept saying she wanted to die.'

Daniela went cold.

'She said she deserved it,' Leo said with tears in his eyes.

'That it was her fate, because of what she'd done.' His voice cracked. 'Because of what she did to my dad, seven years ago.'

Shit. Daniela hung her head. *Auryn, why did you have to tell him?*

'She told me everything,' Leo said. 'She begged me to forgive her.'

'It wasn't her fault.' Even now, the words came instinctively. 'It was me who—'

'I *know* it was your fault. She never would've done it without you. She always followed your lead. And then you let her carry that guilt all those years and she couldn't even talk to me about it. *Me.* I was supposed to be with her forever. But you destroyed that.'

'I—'

'I never meant to hurt her. I got the knife off her but she still wouldn't shut up. I didn't mean for anything to happen.' He took a wavering breath. 'You know the worst thing? She begged me to forgive her, to phone for an ambulance ... but I couldn't. How could I help her, after what she did?'

Daniela stared. 'You—?'

'I knew I'd hurt her when I ... when I lashed out, but I thought she'd be fine.' Leo's lips twisted. 'She was too drunk to even stand. I left her sitting there in the water. Alive. I left her alive.'

But the water had still been rising. 'You let her drown?' Without thinking, Daniela took a step towards him.

The shotgun barrel had started to dip, but Leo raised it again, although his hands shook. Rain ran down his face. His jacket and hair shone with water.

A movement behind him caught Daniela's attention. A shadow edged out past the treeline onto the grassy bank. In the meagre light, Daniela could just see the outline of the person, and a lighter blur held out in front – the fluorescent markers along the side and top of a taser.

Stephanie.

Daniela stopped. Her jaw worked. 'You left Auryn to drown,' she said, louder. 'And you let Stephanie think I'd done it.'

'Stephanie came to that conclusion all by herself,' Leo said. 'I never said anything.'

'You didn't correct her either.' Daniela's chest hitched. 'Why didn't you say something? Stephanie wants to lock me away.'

'And what a big shame that would be.' Leo gestured with the shotgun. 'Step back.'

'What?'

'Go on. Two or three steps should do it.'

Daniela risked a glance behind her. Two or three steps would take her right to the edge of the river.

Leo intended to kill her and let the river sweep her body away. It wouldn't matter if his aim was bad – the water would do most of the work.

I was always going to end up here.

For as many years as she could remember, she'd had nightmares about the river; dreams where she was drowning, flailing, pulled down by weighted feet and bound hands. The idea paralysed Daniela.

Her eyes flicked to Stephanie, motionless in the shadows behind Leo. *What the hell are you waiting for?*

But if Stephanie hit Leo with the taser, there was every chance Leo's finger would spasm around the trigger. Maybe that was why Stephanie hung back.

Or maybe she wanted to see what Leo would do.

Daniela dropped her gaze. She found herself staring at the

plastic-wrapped packages in the boat. *Half a million.* It didn't look like so much. Not enough to kill three people over. Did Leo have any plan beyond loading it all into the rowboat and letting the river drag him off down past Briarsfield?

'What about your dad?' Daniela asked. 'Why'd you shoot him?'

A tremor ran through Leo's whole body. 'Auryn gave him the money. Almost everything she had. But not for me. Not because of anything I said, even though I'd spent years trying to convince her it was the right thing to do.' His mouth went thin again. 'My dad told Auryn a bunch of lies. Filled her head with them, to guilt her into giving him the money. He showed her a letter – I don't know where it came from or how he got it but she said it was from your mother, from years ago—' Leo took a breath to steady his voice. 'He told Auryn she was my sister. He was her dad too.'

In the moment that followed, Daniela looked straight at Stephanie. Stephanie's face was hard as stone, but there was no surprise in her eyes.

'Leo,' Daniela started.

Leo shook his head. The shotgun shook too. 'It doesn't matter if it's true or not,' he said. 'He made Auryn believe it. He wanted to make sure she'd never take me back. Then he went into hiding. He intended to run off with the money, never mind that half of it should've been Mum's. I promised myself I'd find him.'

'I'm sorry,' Daniela said, unsure who the apology was for. 'Please.'

Leo gestured again for her to step back, but Daniela had no intention of moving. The roar of the river was like thunder. She'd rather die here on the bank than beneath the water.

'Leo,' Stephanie said; a police officer's bark that made Leo wheel around. 'Drop—'

Leo swung the shotgun and fired at Stephanie.

Daniela lunged at Leo, tackling him to the ground, but the noise was echoing from the trees, and she knew she'd moved too slow, too late, because in the frozen muzzle flash she'd seen Stephanie thrown back by the blast.

Daniela scrambled up and over Leo, catching him in the face with a careless elbow. Stephanie was trying to sit up. Her jacket and the stab vest had taken some of the impact but not enough. Dark fluid welled up in a palm-sized hole on the upper left side of her chest, and from smaller pellet holes in her neck and shoulder.

Daniela tried to grab her, to keep her upright. She forgot her hands were still restrained. She could do no more than hold the front of Stephanie's vest. Stephanie looked at her with a slight frown, as if she couldn't work out what'd happened. Already her eyes were glazed. Her left hand was pulled up against her chest with the taser clutched tight.

'Steph—'

Behind her, Leo was struggling to his knees. He lifted the shotgun.

Daniela grabbed the taser from Stephanie's unresisting fingers, spun and fired at Leo.

There was no time to aim. In the bad light she could barely see anyway. But Leo wasn't expecting the attack and made no effort to get out of the way.

The metal prongs hit him in the flank and upper leg. He cried out and his body went rigid. Sparks and flashes arched from the barbs. It was sheer luck his finger wasn't on the trigger.

Leo collapsed like a ragdoll as the charge dissipated. He tumbled down the grassy bank until he came to rest with his lower half in the river. The water grabbed his feet and tried to drag him away.

On shaking legs, Daniela started towards him.

'Dani,' Stephanie said. She'd pushed herself up on one elbow. Her breathing was laboured; her eyes unfocused. She looked so pale Daniela was startled she was still conscious.

Leo slid another few inches down the wet grass. Any further and the river would take him.

Daniela stumbled towards the water. The shotgun had fallen on the bank. Daniela threw the weapon behind her, out of reach, in case Leo was faking. She grabbed Leo's shoulder. Her fingers slipped on the wet fabric of his jacket.

Leo gasped. He was conscious, but only barely, his body half-paralysed by the effects of the taser. The river swirled around his legs and dragged him further down the bank.

Daniela heaved but her grip was insecure. She tried to hook her shackled hands under Leo's arm. His body was a dead weight. Daniela's feet slipped on the grass.

'C'mon,' Daniela gasped. 'C'mon!'

A surge of water closed around Leo's waist like a fist and pulled him off the bank. Daniela fought back, digging in her heels, straining all her weight to keep hold of Leo. But her fingers weren't strong enough. The current lifted Leo into the river. His unseeing eyes blinked. His arms moved, slow, weak, as if he were coming back to himself but not nearly fast enough. Daniela slipped down the bank, leaned out over the water, and made a grab for him. She missed.

Leo's jacket spread out like wings. The water rolled him over.

Daniela stumbled into the shallows. The river sucked at her boots as if anxious to swallow her too. She could only watch as the current found Leo, pulled him under, and made him vanish.

Daniela ran back up the bank. Stephanie had half sat up, dazed. Blood soaked the front of her vest.

'Keys!' Daniela hissed. Frantically she patted down Stephanie's pockets. 'I need the keys. I can't go after him without my hands free.'

Stephanie stopped her by closing her hand around the spacer of the cuffs. 'Dani,' she said.

'Steph, I need the keys!' Already Leo had disappeared. Every second swept him further away. 'Where the hell are they?'

'Don't.' There was little strength behind Stephanie's voice. 'Don't go after him.'

'Steph, he—'

'I won't let you kill yourself for him.' Stephanie's grip tightened. 'I won't let you drown.'

Daniela tried to pull away but Stephanie held on to her, as if every last bit of strength was channelled into this. Daniela glanced over her shoulder.

Behind her, the river had swallowed Leo without a trace.

45

Daniela started to cry, the tears flowing unchecked down her cheeks. She dropped her cuffed hands onto Stephanie's shoulder.

How had she ended up here? Irrationally she thought of her childhood: the four sisters, together, looking out for one another. Daniela and Auryn, close enough to be twins. Franklyn with her quick grin, suggesting mischief. And Stephanie, always determined to protect them from the outside world.

She wished with all her heart their paths could've led them someplace else.

Moving as if every action might make her pass out, Stephanie reached into her pocket for her phone. The keypad lit up as she dialled a number.

'I need an ambulance,' Stephanie said when the call was answered. 'This is Sergeant Cain, collar number ...'

Shit, I should be doing that, Daniela thought. She was kneeling there like a stump while Stephanie sorted out her own emergency care. Belatedly she pressed her hands down over the bleeding wound in Stephanie's shoulder. Stephanie grunted in pain, but kept talking, giving the operator her location and status.

'No, I'm on my own,' Stephanie said. 'Yes, I'll stay on the line. But I think my battery's low.' With that, she hung up, then thumbed the button to turn off the phone.

'Steph?'

With another effort, Stephanie dug out the keys for the cuffs. 'Here,' she said.

Numbly, Daniela took the cold metal keys. 'Why'd you tell them you were on your own?'

'Unlock your damn hands.' Stephanie took a couple of deep breaths, as if steeling herself. 'I need your help to get back to my car.'

The journey back to the road lasted a lifetime, but later Daniela couldn't remember a single step. Her mind was numb, her body shuddering so hard it felt like she would shake to pieces. She was soaking wet – again – and freezing cold. Whenever she closed her eyes, she saw Leo disappearing beneath the surface, the current turning his body like a drowned log.

She thought of Margaret McKearney and grief overwhelmed her. *Margaret.* In the morning, Margaret would wake to the news that her son and ex-husband were both dead.

'I lied to you too,' Stephanie said suddenly.

'What?'

'About our mother. We didn't stop looking for her.' She set her jaw. 'We just didn't find anything.'

Daniela wasn't sure she could process that right then. 'Auryn always thought she was dead. You think she was right?'

'Maybe.' It was an effort for Stephanie to get the words out. 'Auryn was talking to Henry a lot recently. Maybe he told her more than he ever told us.'

At last they staggered out to the flooded road. It felt like an age since they'd left the police car. Daniela got the driver's door open and manoeuvred Stephanie into the seat. Stephanie was deathly pale but still somehow conscious. When the overhead light in the car came on, Daniela recoiled from the ragged gash in Stephanie's shoulder. The harsh light turned the blood cherry-red.

'They'll send a helicopter for you,' Daniela said. 'First-class treatment, all the way. I'll stay with you till it gets here. All right?'

'No,' Stephanie said. 'You need to go home.'

'Home?'

Stephanie went through the laborious process of getting something else out of her pocket. Daniela searched the skies. The police helicopter must be able to fly now the wind had dropped. How long would it take to get here? Absently she massaged her wrists. It'd felt so good to take those damn cuffs off. And even better to fling them into the river.

When Daniela looked down, Stephanie had produced a phone, and something in a plastic bag. *My phone,* Daniela realised. *And that goddamn knife.*

Stephanie pressed them into Daniela's hands. Daniela was so cold she fumbled the knife into the water at her feet. For a moment she considered leaving it there, but then stooped to retrieve it, flinching at the feel of the plastic.

Stephanie settled into her seat and closed her eyes. 'It'll be easier if you're not here,' she said.

'Easier for who?'

Stephanie opened one eye. 'I'm serious. You should get yourself clear of this mess while you can.'

Daniela winced. 'That won't work.' She thought about the trail of evidence she'd left – her jacket at the pub, her muddied

326

clothes under a bush, the conversation she'd had with Margaret – and what she'd tell the police when they inevitably came to speak with her.

'Tell them whatever you want,' Stephanie said, as if reading her thoughts. 'About the rest of it anyway. But this here?' Her baleful eyes searched the river. 'You weren't even here. I'll tell them what happened. The flood will wash everything else away.'

Daniela narrowed her eyes. 'You don't want me contradicting your story. Is it because you've got a taser you're not authorised to use?'

'Go home,' Stephanie said again.

'Aside from anything else, I can't. I'm not going to leave you.'

'Quit arguing, Dani. Just take your money and go.'

Daniela stopped. 'What money?'

Stephanie jerked her head towards the blue car parked at the side of the road. She switched her own phone back on and almost immediately it rang.

'That'll be the cavalry, calling back,' Stephanie said. 'Go on. Get lost.'

Daniela stood up. Above the noise of the river, she thought she heard a low, regular thumping. The rescue helicopter. She moved a few steps away from the car, and paused by the sawhorses blocking the road. Rain dripped off her nose.

She still held the knife. She shook it free of the plastic bag, feeling its weight in her hand one last time. Then, without hesitation, she threw it as hard as she could out over the water. She made sure the river swallowed it before she turned away.

She almost fell as she stumbled back to Stephanie's car. Her legs and arms felt like they were made of wood. Stephanie was talking on the phone, her voice a dull echo of her usual authoritative tone. She broke off long enough to nod to Daniela.

It was as close to a goodbye as Daniela would get.

She waded across the road to the blue estate car she'd first seen parked outside Henry's cabin. She pulled her sleeve down over her hand to avoid leaving fingerprints, then tried the passenger side door. It was unlocked. The overhead light came on. On the front seat was a green gym bag Daniela last recalled seeing in Leo's car.

In the footwell behind the front seats a dark blanket covered something lumpy. Daniela leaned over and twitched aside the blanket.

Beneath were a number of bundles wrapped in blue plastic.

Daniela counted eleven in all. The ghostly outline of bank-notes was just visible through the plastic wrapping. If each contained, say, twenty thousand pounds ... Daniela was too tired to do the maths. She couldn't remember how many had been in the rowboat. Leo must've taken as many as he could carry from the car to the boat, and was coming back for a second load when Daniela blundered in.

Her attention went to the gym bag on the passenger seat. Still careful not to leave fingerprints, she tugged open the zip.

A dull sheen of translucent blue plastic, wrapped around another stack of banknotes. It had to be the package Daniela had hidden in the woods. Leo had cleaned some of the mud off it.

She wondered what Leo's next move would've been. Where was he planning to go? The river would've carried the boat for miles, if it hadn't wrecked and swallowed the vessel, but where would he have landed? Maybe Leo had a plan, but Daniela was too exhausted to figure it out. It could remain lost for all she cared.

She stood with her hand poised over the bag. Here was the money she'd wanted – more than she'd wanted, as much as she'd need for the considerable future. More than enough to make sure they kept their flat, and for Annetta's unborn child to get the start he deserved.

The money in that package was a fractional amount, in the grand scheme of things, given how much the police would recover from the car and the boat. Stephanie knew no one would care if a relatively small amount went astray.

Daniela thought of the people who'd died because of that money. Still she hesitated.

46

June 2010

The metal door of the police cell was far heavier than necessary. A simple locked door would've stopped her escaping. But its sheer weight was a statement. Every slam was the sound of her future closing off.

Daniela sat staring at her hands. The Formica table was pitted and scarred with cigarette burns. She wondered how many others had sat there, staring at nothing, listening to doors slam.

She hadn't got nearly as far as she'd hoped.

Her mistake had been following the main road to Hackett. She'd figured it was best to get out of Stonecrop quickly. But a police car had caught up with her just after the bridge. She could've run, but ... but.

Unreality kept stinging her. Half the time she couldn't believe any of this was happening. The other half she was a mess, sometimes shaking with anger, sometimes so scared it felt like her insides had frozen into a solid block.

She tried not to think about Stonecrop. Faces swirled before her eyes – Auryn, Stephanie, Franklyn, Henry, Leo. Irrationally, she thought of Leo more than anyone. The memory of that kiss burned in her mind. What the hell had she been thinking? That one stupid, thoughtless action made her angrier than anything else she'd done. Had she really thought she could kiss Leo and he would *welcome* it?

A succession of police officers had spoken to her. From them, Daniela learned what'd happened since she'd started running.

She hadn't thought to check whether Henry had a mobile phone. It seemed obvious in hindsight, but even if Daniela had thought of it, she would've assumed the water had wrecked it, and Henry was in no state to call for help. She'd been wrong on both counts.

The police had been looking for her even before she left the old house. It sounded like dozens of officers had streamed into Stonecrop that night on an ongoing operation centred around the antiques shop. Daniela didn't know the full picture. But at least one car had been dispatched specifically to track her down.

Meanwhile, an ambulance had taken Henry first to the hospital at Hackett, then to a specialised unit in Birmingham. Daniela hadn't considered what might happen if Henry survived long enough to give a full statement. From what the police were saying, it was still touch and go whether Daniela would end up charged with murder.

She'd greeted this with numb acceptance, and when they asked if she wanted to contact a family member, she'd said, 'No.'

At one point, a policewoman looked across the table at her and said with disgust, 'Nineteen. You're nineteen. What the hell were you doing?' but Daniela couldn't remember anything else from that conversation and now didn't know if she'd imagined it.

Daniela's clothes and jacket had been taken for forensics. She wondered if the police would find the knife hidden below the floorboards of the old house. She wondered how much Henry had said. Would he spill everything about the counterfeit imports? Would he implicate Franklyn? Daniela didn't know. And what would he say about the attack? What if he woke up and told the police it was Auryn who'd stabbed him, not Daniela? Was Daniela sitting here for nothing?

She didn't know what to hope for.

The heavy door swung open and another officer stepped into the room. This one wasn't in uniform, instead wearing jeans and a black jacket. Daniela raised her eyes, then looked away.

'Tell me what happened,' Stephanie said.

She looked rough. Externally she was composed, professional, but dark circles shadowed her eyes, and new creases marked the corners of her mouth. A line of Steri-Strips covered the nasty bruised cut beneath her chin where Henry had clubbed her.

'I'm surprised you didn't get here earlier,' Daniela said.

'I'm not supposed to be here at all. You don't realise how much of a protocol breach it is for me to talk to you, before you've been charged, before you've even been interviewed. I could get suspended for this, even before they start looking at who I bribed to let me in.'

'You shouldn't have bothered.'

Stephanie sat down and folded her hands on the table. The plastic chair squeaked under her weight. Despite the civilian clothes, she couldn't disguise she was a police officer. Everything underlined it, from the hardness in her eyes to the deliberateness of her speech.

'Why didn't you call me?' she asked.

Daniela regarded her. The distance between the two of them, in that tiny airless room in the Hackett police station, felt like a million miles. It was difficult to believe they'd ever been close. Impossible to think they were blood relations.

'Why the hell would I do that?' Daniela asked. 'What, did you want the fun of arresting me yourself?'

Stephanie didn't blink. 'I could've helped you.'

'Really? Helped me how?' Daniela indicated the interview room. 'I got here just fine by myself, didn't I?'

'Perhaps I could've kept you out.'

Daniela's smile faded as she realised Stephanie was serious. 'No,' she said. 'You couldn't.'

'You don't know that. I could've helped. Like I helped Franklyn.'

'Franklyn?'

Stephanie leaned back and studied the room. There wasn't much to look at. 'She was in way over her head,' Stephanie said. 'Thinking she could jump into a business like that, helping Henry bring counterfeited crap into the country.'

'You knew about that?'

'It's a small village. This was a big deal.' Stephanie scratched the cut on her jaw, winced. 'I wish I could've stopped her.'

'Why didn't you?'

Stephanie was silent for a span of time. 'What should I have done?' she asked. 'You reckon I should've arrested her? Arrested Henry?'

'That's your job, isn't it?'

Stephanie nodded in blunt agreement. 'You're right. It's what I *should've* done. I got into this line of work because I thought it'd make my choices easier. But when I found out what Franklyn was doing, I talked to her, and she persuaded me that she was getting out, and there was nothing to worry about. I believed her. When it transpired she couldn't get out, I stepped in to help.'

'You did?'

'We've got officers at the antiques shop right now, pulling it apart, getting all the evidence. Evidence that'll point to Henry, not Franklyn. That's what took the time. I had to make sure nothing would implicate Franklyn. We could've done without your interference. Half the goddamn shop is flooded, do you know that?'

Daniela glanced at the security camera in the corner of the room. Was it recording? Somehow, she doubted Stephanie would speak so freely if they were being overheard.

Daniela said, 'So you reckon I should've ignored Henry threatening me – threatening us all—'

'That's exactly what you should've done. Going after Henry was stupid.'

Daniela sat back and folded her arms. She wanted to match Stephanie's cool indifference, but the simmering anger wouldn't let her. She was aware of the sour alcohol smell of her own body from the whisky she'd drunk earlier. With a start, she realised she smelled like her father.

Daniela said, 'It sounds like you're more interested in protecting Henry than me.'

'I don't give a damn about Henry McKearney. At least, not more than I'm professionally obligated to. It's his family I'm concerned about.' Stephanie drummed her fingers on the table top. 'Leo called me earlier today to tell me everything.'

'He did?'

'Yes. He was scared you'd come after his dad. While he

was on the phone, he spotted you breaking into the antiques shop.'

That gave Daniela a pang of guilt. She'd blamed Auryn for telling Stephanie her plans. 'Henry deserved it,' she muttered.

Stephanie drew her chair closer to the table. 'Right now, we don't even know if Henry will make it through the night. You should maybe think about that before you make stupid statements.' She held Daniela's gaze. 'As for Leo ... we need him.'

'For what?'

'He has to testify in your defence when this whole mess comes to trial.'

Daniela dropped her eyes. 'There won't be any trial. I did it. I've admitted it. As soon as they give me something to sign, I'll sign. Anyway, it seems kinda optimistic to think Leo would help me, after what I've done.'

For the first time, Stephanie looked down, and her voice became soft. '*Did* you do it?'

Daniela tried for a sarcastic answer, for a way to throw her anger in Stephanie's face, but the softness in Stephanie's voice made something break inside. Her sister didn't want to believe this.

'Yes,' Daniela said, and had to fight to stop her voice cracking.

Suddenly irritated, Stephanie sat back again. 'There has to be a way out,' she said. 'We'll get the mental health team to assess you—'

'I'm not insane, Steph. I knew exactly what I was doing.'

Stephanie wasn't listening. 'We can claim self-defence. He'd already assaulted me. Half a dozen witnesses saw him chase you into the woods with that golf club. It'll be tough, but with no independent witnesses to the attack it'll come down to your evidence against his ...'

No independent witnesses. 'What's Henry said?'

'Very little. He's in no condition to give a statement yet. All he's given us so far is your name.'

At that time, Daniela couldn't fathom why Henry would choose to protect Auryn.

Everything he ever did was to protect his own blood.

Daniela ran a finger over a nobbled burn on the table. 'Have you spoken to Auryn?'

'Briefly. I called round to make sure she was okay.' Stephanie set her mouth into a thin line. 'Who punched her?'

Daniela said nothing.

Stephanie let the silence hang for a moment, then said, 'Leo's looking after her. Apparently she followed you through the woods. Tried to stop you. That true?'

Daniela realised Stephanie had misinterpreted the scrapes on her knuckles. 'I didn't hit her,' Daniela muttered. But she couldn't tell Stephanie what'd actually happened without admitting Auryn had been in Kirk Cottage with her.

She wondered what Auryn had told Leo. Whether she intended to tell him the truth. Or whether the hurt and betrayal were too much, and Auryn was happy for everyone to think what the hell they liked about Daniela.

Stephanie watched her. 'An officer's on his way to the house now. He'll take a statement from them both. Then I suspect Leo will go to the hospital for his dad.' She let out a long breath, like she was deflating. 'Dani, if you'd just called me ... There has to be something we can do.'

Was there anything anyone could've done? The situation

felt inevitable, as if Daniela had been sliding to this point for her entire life.

'I don't want your help,' Daniela said quietly. 'I never have and I never will. It doesn't suit you to come here and be such a goddamn hypocrite, after you've spent your life lecturing me, just because you're feeling guilty.' She breathed the silence for a moment, then added, 'Is that everything you came to say?'

'Will you tell me what happened? All of it, from beginning to end, with no lies?'

'I think I should wait till a lawyer gets here.'

'Then I'm done.' Stephanie was already getting up. Her expression showed no more emotion than if they were having the conversation in the kitchen at home. 'This is the last time I break the rules for you. Understand me?'

'Go home, Steph.'

At the door, Stephanie paused. 'Tell them the truth,' she said. 'It'll work out best in the long run.'

Would it? Daniela wasn't so sure. From where she was sitting, she couldn't see any kind of happy ending. She said nothing, and let her sister walk away.

47

Halfway around the field, when mud had caked her boots so thickly she was questioning the wisdom of her escape route, Daniela heard an engine. She'd been dimly aware of it for a while, but tractors were such a feature of the landscape that she'd paid no more attention than to the continued noise of the wind in the trees.

Her instinct was to hide. But she wasn't making substantial progress on foot. It was fully dark by now, and she'd covered maybe half a dozen fields. Each field was flooded out, with vast lakes at the centres and only thin, muddy strips standing clear of the water alongside the hedgerows. The rain had subsided to a sad drizzle. It might take her another five hours to reach Briarsfield. By then she'd probably be dead from exhaustion.

At first, she'd spent all her time looking behind her. The trees obscured the field where the helicopter had found a dry space to touch down, but for a long time she'd still heard the choppy sound of its rotors and caught glimpses of its searchlights.

They'll look after Stephanie. There's nothing more you can do for her.

Her conscience insisted otherwise.

Daniela angled away from the hedgerow and cut the corner of the field, hopping over flooded furrows, to reach a nearby gate. Just before she got there, a tractor hove into view, its big lights on its roof casting circles on the ground. The driver was a bulky outline in the fogged cabin. Daniela waved. She wasn't sure the driver had seen her until the tractor lurched to a halt near the gate.

'You lost, youngster?' the driver yelled from the cab.

Tilly. The farmer who'd towed Leo's car out of the water. She was also the one Stephanie had convinced to go across the flooded bridge to Hackett and pick up the scenes-of-crime officers.

An immediate and hopeful smile came to Daniela's face. 'Any chance of a lift?' she called.

Tilly turned the engine down to an idle, then waved her over. Daniela awkwardly climbed the gate and splodged towards the vehicle. The fields were saturated, with several inches of standing water in the furrows, and each step was an effort. The tractor was following a raised track that was muddy but not impassable. When Daniela got close enough, Tilly leaned out to drag her up onto the footplate.

'Seems like I've spent all weekend doing favours for you kids,' Tilly said with mock annoyance. 'Don't you know I've got a farm to run? When am I supposed to get my tea?'

'I'm sorry.' Daniela leaned into the scant warmth of the cab. The smell of wet dog was quite strong in there. 'Don't suppose I could trouble you for a lift, could I? I've got to get to Briarsfield.'

Tilly puffed out her cheeks. 'I've already been out to Hackett and back. What do I look like, a taxi?'

'I know, it's an awful imposition.' Daniela put on her best smile. 'Please?'

Tilly sighed greatly, but her expression softened. 'Aye, I suppose you've been through a lot, haven't you? It's a terrible situation with Auryn. The policemen at Hackett were kinda surprised when I rocked up there with my trailer, I can tell you. But—' she wrestled the tractor into gear '—they got here safe and sound. That's the main thing.'

Daniela hung on as the tractor lurched forwards. There was no room for her in the cab with Tilly, so she remained on the footstep, clinging to the handrail.

'Decided not to stick around in Stonecrop then?' Tilly said. She had to yell to make herself heard. 'Can't say I blame you. It might be days before they reopen the Hackett bridge. Did you decide not to wait?'

'Pretty much, yeah. When it's time to leave ...'

Tilly laughed. 'Oh, I hear ya. Why d'you think I spend so much time out in the fields? I'd go spare if I had to stay home all day. You look like you've been in the wars,' she noted.

Daniela glanced at her clothes. The tracksuit bottoms and fleece were a uniform muddy brown. 'I fell,' she admitted. 'A few times.'

'Didn't think to bring a change of clothes, huh?' Tilly asked, looking at Daniela's bag.

Daniela tucked the green gym bag more securely under her arm. 'I remembered spare socks and the bus fare,' she said. 'Didn't think I'd need anything else. That'll teach me, right?'

Tilly swung the tractor to follow the raised track south along the hedgerow. The chill morning air made Daniela shiver. But it smelled clean and fresh, and she was happy to be away from Stonecrop. She didn't look back. It seemed unlikely she would ever return. What did she have there now? Auryn was dead, although really, she'd been lost years before, through solitude and guilt and internal darkness. Franklyn had escaped, but in doing so had fractured her family, whether she'd intended to or not. Stephanie ... well, maybe one day those bridges could be mended. Just not any time soon.

And Daniela ...

Fourth to the devil, Margaret had said. That sounded more apt for herself than for Auryn.

'You grew up here, didn't you?' Tilly said, breaking her train of thought. 'I only moved back to Stonecrop a few years ago so I don't remember you kids. Oh, apart from Steph and Auryn, everyone knows them.'

On impulse, Daniela asked, 'Do you remember my mum and dad?'

'I don't know if I met your old man more than a few times. He died not long after I came home. Sorry, I don't think I knew your ma at all.'

'Me neither.'

The engine noise changed. No, a second noise had cut into it. Daniela leaned out of the cab and looked back towards Stonecrop, in time to see a black shape veer up out the trees, its lights glaringly bright in the darkness. The helicopter hung, pinned to the sky for a moment as if getting its bearings, then nosed away, off to the east, in the direction of Hackett. The thump of its rotors faded until Daniela could no longer hear it over the tractor. Still she felt the rhythm internally, like a counterpoint to her own heartbeat.

Holding on to the tractor with one hand, Daniela fumbled her phone out of her pocket to see if she could get reception. Somehow the mobile had survived the traumas of the weekend. Daniela intended to send the manufacturers a delighted email when she got home.

An icon flashed on the screen to inform her she had an unread message. Daniela couldn't remember when it'd arrived. She opened the message and a slow smile spread across her face as Annetta's number popped up.

Can't sleep, junior's given me indigestion, lol. Hope all is going well. We miss you! xx

The noise of the tractor was too loud to let Daniela make a phone call. But once they stopped, as soon as she had a signal, she would call and tell Annetta that everything was okay, that she loved her, and that she was coming home.

Acknowledgements

It's difficult to know where to start, because so many people have helped me in so many ways to bring this book into the world.

Thank you to my agent Leslie Gardner, my editor Rachel Faulkner-Willcocks, and all the wonderful team at Avon. I'm still amazed and delighted that I can refer to 'my agent', 'my editor' and 'my publishing team' in everyday conversation.

Thank you to various health care professionals and members of the police force who answered a string of increasingly ridiculous questions from me (like 'what would happen if someone got tasered whilst standing in a puddle?' and 'pepper spray – is it really that bad?'). All mistakes are my own and I apologise.

Thank you to the team at Manx Litfest, who gave me the courage to put my work out into the world in the first place. Equally, mega-thanks to my various writing groups, to Helen and Roz, to my NaNoWriMo friends, to the Happy People, to CT Phipps who read a shockingly early draft, and to everyone who has helped and encouraged me over the years. I owe you all a pint.

Thank you as always to the voices in my head, who do the real work here.

And, of course, to my family, who are really very lovely and supportive and nothing like any of the characters in this book. And first-last-always, thank you to John, Jacob, and Elliott for always looking after me. I couldn't do any of this without you.